Dead Air

Mike Brogan

PUBLISH AMERICA

PublishAmerica
Baltimore

© 2005 by Michael J. Brogan.

This novel is a work of fiction. Names, characters, places and incidents either are the product of the author's imagination, or are used fictitiously. Any resemblance to actual persons, living or dead, events, government entities, corporations, or locales, is entirely coincidental.

First printing

ISBN: 1-4137-4700-0
PUBLISHED BY PUBLISHAMERICA, LLLP
www.publishamerica.com
Baltimore

Printed in the United States of America

For Marcie, Brendan, Chloé and Jay

Acknowledgments

This novel would not exist without the helpful advice of the following people. My warmest thanks go to:

Leslie Kellas Payne, for her editing insights and encouragement.

Elmore Leonard, for his encouragement a while back.

Dr. Sam Brooks, Dr. Homeria McDonald, and Dr. John Brooks, for their comprehensive expertise on biochemistry, medical subjects and medical-legal autopsies.

Dr. Barbara Schiff, for her insights into the behavior of psychopaths.

Dr. Roger Walpole, for his vast knowledge of toxicology.

Mr. James Allingham of the US Military's Aberdeen Proving Ground, for his patient and masterful counsel on weapons of mass destruction, terrorism and related subjects, and the suggestions of his colleagues and scientists at the Edgewood Area in Maryland.

Detective Doug Manigold and fellow officers at the Birmingham, Michigan Police Department, for their guidance on police procedural matters.

Marge Kelly, for her artistic gifts that led to the cover of this novel.

Brendan Brogan, for his editing skills and help with five languages and all things international.

And to all the rest of you who helped along the way, my heartfelt thanks.

One

Sunday

Reed Kincaid rearranged his living room furniture for the fourth time, looked around and slumped down onto the sofa, a defeated man.

Even worse, he realized.

The ivory leather sofas and mauve chairs worked together, but not sprawled across the reddish Persian carpet. The striped draperies were stylish, but clashed with the leopard footstool. And the expensive antique mahogany desk was distinctive, but seemed defiled by the pink lava lamp glowing on the corner.

The room needed help.

In fact, he knew, all the rooms in his new home located in the affluent suburb of Birmingham, north of Detroit, needed a great deal of help. Since moving in a week ago, he'd managed to prove only one thing: he had the decorating flair of a yak. Fortunately, Hallie, the woman who could rescue him, would be walking through the front door any minute.

He picked up a *Runners World* and started quickly thumbing through it when the phone rang. He grabbed it.

"It's me, Kyle." His brother sounded very excited and faint, like he was on a cell phone deep in the mountains.

"Hey, Kyle, what's up?"

"I need to talk to the police fast."

"So why call me?"

"My detective pal in Grand Blanc is out." Kyle coughed. "What's Norm's number?"

"I don't know. Norm retired to Florida."

"Damn. He's the only other cop who'd believe me."

"Believe what?" Reed asked. Kyle, who never worried, sounded very worried.

Kyle coughed again. "A man I met Friday and this morning. I'll explain at your house. I'm five minutes away. But I have to talk to the police *fast*!"

7

Another cough, then the connection crackled and died.

Reed stared at the phone. Why did Kyle need the police? He tried to remember the last time his brother had sounded this frightened and realized it was many years ago, the day of their parents' accident. He started thinking back to that horrific day, when he heard a car turn into his driveway.

He stood and watched Hallie Mara walk toward the house. Her thick dark brown hair, wind-tossed over her eyes, could not conceal her beautiful face any more than the bulky green sweater and slacks could conceal her stunning figure. He loved her creamy complexion, leggy stride and every other genetic gift her Irish mother and Japanese father bequeathed her. The fact that Hallie was an M.D. in molecular genetics, trilingual, and a fun person with no obvious psychological zits, were also nice touches. He'd never known anyone like her, and had felt that way about twenty seconds after he walked in her office two months ago.

Opening the front door, he was once again lured into her large emerald eyes. He had to force himself to look down at a plastic container in her hand.

"Sorry, miss, I have enough Tupperware." He started to close the door.

"With warm chocolate chip cookies?"

He opened the door. "*Mi casa es su casa.*"

Smiling, she stepped inside and looked around at the rooms and furniture. "Hummmm ... very nice. Great potential."

"I feel the same about you."

Another smile. "You mentioned a sick room?"

"Rooms." He led her to the den and gestured toward the two older leather chairs, one with a faint red wine spot, a coffee table, VCR and his brand-new large-screen television that occupied most of a nine-foot section of wall.

"Wow—a drive-in theater!" she said. "Where do you park cars?"

"Hey, I *need* a big screen. See my commercials better. Check details up close."

"Like nasal hair?"

"That, gingivitis, and the infernal horror of hemorrhoids."

She laughed a nice laugh. "By the way, how are your new Mason Industries commercials doing?"

"Great. Mason's currently setting new sales records. But the account director, as usual, wants to *fix* the commercials."

"Which aren't broke?"

He nodded. "Not at all."

She walked over to his computer screen, which displayed a television commercial script he'd been working on, and looked at his stacks of work papers, bulging green file folders and a tower of TV commercial cassettes.

"Work, work, work!" she said.

"Guilty as sin," he said, knowing she thought he worked too hard at times.

She turned, studied the furniture and high-tech equipment and ran her finger along her lower lip, focusing like an urban refuse planner at the city dump.

"Maybe," she said, "a nice entertainment center could enclose all this stereo and audio stuff."

"Sound advice."

She ignored his pun. "And maybe a nice sofa opposite your drive-in theater."

"I like nice sofas." He pictured them getting real comfortable on one.

"And maybe you could put that cutesy butter churn with the Daffy Duck sticker somewhere. Perhaps with your Nehru jacket."

He heard the loud ding of metal—a car bottoming out in his driveway. Looking up, he saw Kyle's dark blue Chevy Tahoe pull in behind Hallie's car.

Reed walked to the door, opened it, and couldn't believe his eyes. Kyle looked like he'd gone a few rounds with Mike Tyson. Kyle's ears had no tooth marks, but his face was flushed and damp with perspiration. Clumps of dark red hair hung over his bloodshot eyes and his clothes had more wrinkles than a corrugated roof.

"Nice pajamas," Reed said.

"I belong in pajamas and in bed," Kyle whispered, coughing and attempting a smile. He stepped inside and glanced around. "Terrific house."

"Hi, Kyle," Hallie said, walking from the den.

"Hey, Hallie...." he said, coughing harshly. "Sorry, guys. I've been feeling *awful* the last two days."

You look awful too, Reed thought, wondering what the hell was wrong with his older brother, the healthiest person he knew.

"How about some water?" Hallie asked.

"Please." He cleared his throat again and swallowed with obvious pain.

As Hallie went to get water, Reed led him into the living room.

"Call the police quick," Kyle whispered, rubbing his throat.

"Sure. But what's this all—"

"This man I met...." His brother suddenly stopped, stared ahead as though watching a train wreck, then clutched his chest. Terrified, he looked at Reed, stumbled backward and collapsed onto the sofa.

"*Hallie!*" Reed shouted, moving to his brother's side.

Kyle's eyes, pink and wild, locked on Reed's. His brother's face turned scarlet as he gasped for air. Reed held his trembling shoulders as Hallie ran in and unbuttoned his collar.

Kyle opened his mouth, attempted to form words. Reed leaned in to listen.

"Poisoned ... me...."

"Who?"

"K-kill many Friday.... S-stop him...."

"Someone poisoned you?"

Kyle blinked a yes.

"Who?"

Kyle's lips opened to speak, then froze.

"Quick, lay him on his back," Hallie said.

Reed eased him onto the floor and watched pain twist his brother's face. His eyes darted wildly, then seemed to go blank as he fell unconscious. Frothy saliva slid from the corner of his mouth.

Quickly, Hallie tilted his head back and placed her fingers beside his Adam's apple to check for a pulse. "Phone 911!" She breathed hard into his mouth, placed her palms over his heart, pushed down, and began CPR.

Dazed, Reed hurried to the phone and dialed 911. Two rings ... three ... four.... *Answer the damn phone!* he shouted silently.

Finally, someone picked up. He described Kyle's condition to a woman who calmly told him to continue CPR until MedExpress arrived in minutes. The ambulance was not far, she promised.

Reed's pulse pounded in his ears as he knelt beside Hallie and helped with CPR. He felt semi-present, as though someone else's hands were pushing down on Kyle's chest. Each minute his brother did not respond, Reed's panic grew.

Minutes later, the ambulance screamed into his driveway. Doors opened and slammed. He continued CPR as Hallie let in two paramedics. She explained she was a doctor, mumbled medical jargon and rushed them over to Kyle.

Reed backed away, searching their eyes for hope, seeing none. Quickly, they opened a blue defibrillator unit beside Kyle. From white bags they took two paddles, stripped off the coverings, pressed the paddles on Kyle's chest and connected the electrical cables. The blond paramedic pushed a panel button, and the console screen displayed a flat green line.

The paramedics looked at Hallie. She nodded and leaned back.

"Two hundred," the blond said. "Stand clear!" He checked that no one was touching Kyle's body, then said, "Hit it!"

The other paramedic pushed a panel button. Two hundred joules of electricity jolted Kyle's body, whipsawing his arms up and down. His eyelids twitched.

"Yes!" Reed said, then looked at the green line.

Flat.

Reed swallowed a dry throat.

"Three hundred," the blond said. "Clear! Hit it!"

The jolt of electricity arched, then dropped Kyle back down. His body remained still, the green line stayed flat. Reed looked at Hallie for some hint of hope, but her eyes were on Kyle.

"Three sixty," the paramedic said, staring at Hallie. She nodded.

"Clear. Hit it!"

Kyle's body jerked up and down hard, but his face remained as rigid as the green line.

Reed felt cold perspiration cover him as they tried again and again. Each time electricity jolted Kyle's body, Reed felt the jolt. Each time his brother's back arched, Reed's back arched. Each time the green line remained flat, Reed's heart stopped. He slumped against the wall.

Silently, he screamed at his brother to live. *Don't leave Anne and the girls. Don't leave me!*

"Hit it!"

The words ripped into him like spears. He closed his eyes and prayed, smelling the medical equipment, electricity, fear.

Minutes later, the blond paramedic, his face dotted with sweat, looked at Hallie. She rubbed her temples, then stared at the man for several moments and nodded. Quietly, he lifted the paddles from Kyle's chest, placed them back in the defibrillator unit and closed the lid.

Reed stared at Hallie.

Slowly, she looked up at him, her moist eyes shouting what he already knew.

Two

Hallie stared out the windshield as Reed drove his Chevy TrailBlazer past a gray, weathered farm house with broken shutters swinging in the wind. Nearby stood a rickety barn with a faded Mail Pouch tobacco sign and a rusty tractor sunk halfway into a pond slick with oily scum. In the middle of the pond, a large yellow fish floated belly-up. Poisoned.

Like Kyle.

Tall evergreens swept past, then a large billboard for the Great Lakes Crossing Mall, touting "1.4 Million Square Feet of Eye-Popping, Jaw-Dropping Shopping." She noticed sprawling new homes nestled among the pastels of an autumn forest. The birch trees had shed chunks of white bark and some sugar maples flashed yellow leaves, a sign their sap would soon flow.

Normally, these forests calmed her. Today, their serenity couldn't begin to penetrate her growing concern for Reed.

He looked numb, drained of feeling. Even the cold air spilling through the window onto his face didn't register. Reality seemed to have branded his soul with the hard, brutal fact that his brother Kyle was forever gone.

She noticed a billboard with Tiger Woods leaning on a Buick, and remembered that nearby Flint was the home of Buick Motors. Tiger's smile, as usual, was dazzling.

Reed's smile had vanished with Kyle's death.

They were driving back from Kyle's home near Grand Blanc, a pleasant town of thirty thousand. She'd been with Reed since Sunday night, when they'd driven up to tell Kyle's wife, Anne, the horrific news. They'd remained there, helping her and her two young daughters cope, making funeral arrangements, phoning family members, trying to ease the pain that could not be eased.

Anne's disbelief when Reed told her, the anguish, the raw cry of despair that arose from deep within her, the excruciating torment as she told her daughters were forever carved into Hallie's mind.

To spare Anne further pain, Reed had not told her that Kyle said he was poisoned. Later, when he knew the poison, he'd tell her.

Hallie studied Reed. His handsome face was drained of its natural warmth and color. Tiny razor nicks dotted his chin. The wind had tossed his thick chestnut hair down over cobalt blue eyes sapped of their energy. His tall, powerful body slumped in the seat.

"You okay over there?" she asked.

"Been better."

"Memories of Kyle?"

He nodded. "Kyle decking the bully picking on me in third grade; Kyle sprinting past the Seaholm High defensive back for the winning touchdown; Kyle stuffing my inebriated buns through the college dorm window at three in the morning; Kyle collapsing in my arms...."

She laced her fingers through his, knowing that memories were part of his healing.

"The funeral home was kind of overwhelming," he said.

"So were the large number of mourners. Your brother was loved by so many."

"Always was."

She closed her file and pictured the mourners. "I liked Kyle's friend, the medical director of Dunne Chemical."

"Dr. Katcavage. He and Kyle were close. They started at Dunne the same week. I asked him if Kyle had enemies at Dunne."

"And...?"

"He laughed. Said Kyle was genetically engineered to only make friends."

She smiled. "But Dr. Katcavage gave me cause for concern."

"About what?"

"Those two other young people he mentioned."

"Because they died so young, like Kyle?" Reed asked.

"Yes. And so recently."

"And both lived in Grand Blanc."

"Statistically, all that seems rather high for that small population." She circled a large 2 on her notepad.

"Maybe their deaths are connected to Kyle's?" he said.

Exactly what she was wondering. "Maybe."

She glanced in the side mirror and noticed a dark blue Lincoln cruising about two hundred feet back. *Is that the same Lincoln I saw near the funeral home?* she wondered. As the big car drew a little closer, she realized it was. The same two large men stared ahead like statues.

13

Reed adjusted his air vent. "Dr. Katcavage and another friend of Kyle's, Phil something, told me they'll ask medical colleagues if they've heard of similar deaths in the recent past."

"I'll ask, too," Hallie said. "But right now, let's see if the pathologist identified the poison." She grabbed the cell phone and dialed.

"Thanks," he said, gently touching her hand.

"For what?"

"For everything. Being here ... and just being ... you."

She liked that answer a lot.

"And for helping me through some of the darkest days of my life."

I wouldn't have been anywhere else, Reed, she thought as she lifted his hand to her lips. The phone rang in her ear.

She hoped that the pathologist, Dr. McDonald, had some news. With the poison identified, Detective Woody Beachum could greenlight an investigation. Beachum, who'd arrived at Reed's home minutes after Kyle died, had found no visible evidence of murder and was waiting for the autopsy findings.

"Homer McDonald...."

"Dr. McDonald, this is Hallie Mara. I'm calling about Kyle Kincaid."

"Yes, Hallie. Hang on, let me get the autopsy."

She waited, knowing how anxious Reed was to hear the results. Dr. McDonald returned and began taking her through the specific toxicology tests and findings. She jotted notes, but the more he revealed, the more concerned she grew. When he told her the cause of death, her pen froze on the paper.

"You're certain?" she asked, her heart racing.

"Yes," Dr. McDonald said.

Reed drove past an old VW van driven by a man with a gray ponytail who flashed her the peace sign. She flashed it back, but she knew that what Dr. McDonald had just told her would *not* bring Reed peace.

"I understand," Hallie said softly, leaning forward, listening to more details. "Yes, Doctor. And thank you." She hung up, reviewed her notes, then stared out the window, trying to think of how best to tell Reed.

Reed was staring at her. "Well?"

"They completed all the tests, Reed," she whispered, swallowing a scratchy throat.

"And...?"

"The autopsy found no poison. Absolutely no trace."

Reed fell back as though struck by lightning.

"Kyle died from natural causes," she said.

14

Reed stared ahead at the empty road. "But that's not possible. There has to be a mistake, switched autopsies, a missed test, a lab screw-up, *something*."

"The autopsy was quite comprehensive," she said, feeling equally stunned. "Extensive toxicological testing. They checked for everything."

He shook his head, obviously trying to reconcile the autopsy finding with his brother's final words. His knuckles were bone-white on the steering wheel.

"The cause of death," she said, "was SCD—sudden cardiac death."

"Heart attack?"

"Yes. But the pathologist was surprised."

"Why?"

"SCD is quite rare in someone as young as Kyle. Also, Kyle was in excellent health. And the autopsy didn't find the coronary disease or weakness normally present with SCD."

"Kyle has never had heart problems. Hell, he ran marathons."

"I know," she said. "His death makes no sense to me either. Unfortunately, SCD just happens sometimes."

Reed looked devastated.

"I banked everything on a finding that Kyle was poisoned," he said. "Without that finding, Detective Beachum can't justify an investigation. Without an investigation, many people will die Friday. Now, their lives...." His eyes dimmed.

"Their lives what?"

"Depend on me."

"Only if you believe Kyle was poisoned."

He paused a moment, then looked at her. "I believe he was."

She felt a cold, sinking sensation in the pit of her stomach as she realized that changing Reed's mind would prove very difficult, if not impossible.

She took a deep breath and leaned back. Checking the side mirror, she noticed the dark Lincoln automobile had moved up close to them.

The two large men, faces darkened by the tinted glass, seemed to be staring straight at their car.

Three

"A little good news," Hallie said, closing her cell phone and knowing Reed would welcome *any* good news.

"What's that?" He steered around a tight curve.

"Dr. McDonald will review his findings if we drive over now."

"Terrific," he said, hope flickering in his eyes.

"Something might have been missed the first time around," she said.

"Something *was* missed," Reed said. "Either lab technicians accidentally switched the tests, or botched the results, or diagnostic equipment malfunctioned."

"Or Dr. McDonald forgot something," she added, doubting he did.

Reed thumped his hand against his forehead. "*I* forgot something."

"What?"

"A sixty-million-dollar anti-smoking ad campaign our agency is pitching for. I forgot to brief the creative team."

"Who's the campaign aimed at?"

"Teenagers."

"Tough audience?"

"Very savvy. We need commercials that break through the clutter. Commercials that visually grab teens. But...."

"But what?"

"I'm focused on grabbing the bastard who poisoned Kyle."

Hallie held back, not wanting to remind him that the autopsy found no indication of poison. How could she help him accept the autopsy's heart attack? Maybe if she eliminated all other possible causes....

"So who would want to kill him?" she asked.

Reed shrugged. "I've been asking myself that question for two days. Only one answer makes sense. The man he phoned me about Sunday. Kyle had met him that day and was worried about him. Kyle must have discovered something. Probably something to do with Friday. So the man murdered him."

She nodded without agreeing.

They passed a yellow school bus with smiling kids from Emmett Mount Carmel School and she thought of Kyle's daughters with sadness. Their father would never attend their graduations or weddings, never hold their babies.

In the side mirror, she watched the school bus fade as the dark blue Lincoln passed it. The two stone-faced men now wore sunglasses and baseball hats. Not your typical Lincoln attire. And why were they wearing sunglasses on an overcast day?

"Maybe Detective Beachum came up with something," Reed said.

"What's his number?"

Reed fished Woody Beachum's card from his pocket and handed it to her. She dialed and pushed the car's speaker button.

Hallie liked the large, pink-faced detective with understanding pale-blue eyes. His brown sport coat had been stretched over a bowling-ball paunch that mushroomed into a massive chest and shoulders. A narrow red tie had snagged on a button and stuck out like a dog's tongue. His brown Hush Puppies and pants cuffs were dotted with cigarette ashes.

"Woody Beachum."

"It's Reed and Hallie," Reed said.

"How're you holding up?"

"Not bad, considering we're driving back from the funeral home."

"There are better places to drive back from," Beachum said with genuine sympathy. "How's your brother's wife and daughters doing?"

"The daughters better than the wife."

"That's not uncommon."

Reed paused a moment. "Detective, did your forensic people uncover anything suspicious in Kyle's Tahoe, or even in my house?"

Beachum rustled some papers. "I'm afraid not, Reed. They went over everything twice. Found absolutely nothing that even remotely suggests foul play."

Hallie watched Reed slump further into his seat.

"Did you check Kyle's cell phone calls Sunday?" Reed said.

"Yes. He made two cell phone calls. One to his home, and one to you. He received no calls."

"What about his home phone?"

"Three calls. One from his wife's mother. One from the Salvation Army. One from the elderly woman next door. Also, I just spoke with Doc McDonald out at the Oakland County Morgue."

"So did I," Hallie said.

"Then you know," Beachum said, "that he found no trace of poison. He's

17

fixed Kyle's cause of death as a heart attack."

"SCD," Hallie said. "Sudden cardiac death."

"Did he suggest what caused Kyle's SCD?" Reed asked.

"No," Beachum said. "He said on rare occasions seemingly healthy young people simply drop dead."

"Autopsies can be wrong," Reed said.

"Yes, but rarely with Doc McDonald."

Hallie watched Reed as he seemed to steel himself to ask the big question.

"So, Detective, can you investigate even though the official cause of death is a heart attack?"

Beachum exhaled slowly. "Well, it depends on all the circumstances. In this case, Dr. Homer McDonald, the best we've got, conducted an extremely thorough autopsy. He found absolutely no evidence of poison. Also, forensics found nothing even remotely suspicious in your house or in Kyle's car or on his clothing. Bottom line, nothing even hints at poisoning."

Hallie realized Beachum was not going to investigate, a decision that would frustrate Reed even more.

"We have one thing," Reed said.

"What?"

"My brother *said* he was poisoned."

Beachum rustled his papers again. "I'm sure he *believed* he was. But again, the only *evidence* says heart attack."

Reed looked like he was being hammered into the seat. "My brother believed something else."

"What's that?"

"That his murderer will kill *many* more people this coming Friday. *Two* days from now."

Beachum remained silent.

"Why was he so precise—*Friday?*" Reed continued. "The answer is clear. He was warning me and the police to save them."

Hallie knew Reed was shifting some responsibility to the police in the hope that Beachum might reconsider.

Reed continued, "Kyle should have said, 'Tell Anne I love her.' Instead, with his last breath he warned us that *many* people, hundreds, thousands maybe, will *die!* He said 'many' like it was a *lot* of people!"

Hallie admitted to herself that she too was puzzled that Kyle—right in the middle of a heart attack—would talk about many deaths Friday. He had not seemed delusional. He'd seemed *focused.*

"Your brother have any enemies?" Beachum asked.

"Not that I know."

"Gamble a lot?"

"Superbowl, office baseball pools, stuff like that."

"Belong to any extreme political or religious cults?"

"Not that I'm aware of."

"Did he have an affair or fire some crazy guy at the office?"

"Not that he mentioned."

Beachum was silent for several moments, then lit a cigarette and drew heavily. "So basically you want me to believe that your brother—who was loved at the office, loved at home, didn't gamble, didn't fool around, didn't belong to any bizarre political or religious groups, and didn't have enemies— was poisoned by some guy who doesn't leave a shred of evidence?"

Reed appeared to understand how weak his case was. "Yes."

"Your logic sure would make a prosecutor drool," he said sarcastically.

"I know, it's not so great," Reed said. "I worked part-time at the Ann Arbor police station during college. You police have the toughest job in the world."

Beachum chuckled and whooshed out air like Jonah's pet whale. "It used to be tough, Reed. Now it's flat-out crazy. Use too much force, you're prosecuted. Too little, you're dead. Hell, I've got a serial rapist attacking every few weeks, a phone company imposter robbing old women, and a caseload I can't keep up with. We can't just commit people without *some* piece of evidence."

Hallie watched Reed sigh and open his window a bit. The wind blew his hair over his eyes and she brushed it back.

"Tell you what," Beachum said, clearing his throat. "I'll ask forensics to recheck some things, and let you know."

"Thank you, Detective."

They hung up.

Hallie looked at Reed. Clearly, he was demoralized by Beachum's refusal to investigate. "Beachum's decision is understandable from a *police* perspective," she said.

"Yeah, but it leaves me with a lousy choice."

"What's that?"

"*I* have to try to carry out my brother's dying request. I have to prevent Friday's deaths. Which leaves me just two days."

"Reed...." Hallie said, hoping to divert him from a self-deceptive path that would further frustrate him. "Nothing in the autopsy or police forensics supports Kyle's words. He may have been delusional."

Reed started to speak, then stared back at the road ahead.

She knew her changed diagnosis bothered him and wanted him to

19

understand. "As a physician, I've learned to trust medical facts, autopsies. They're more reliable than doctors' opinions."

"I understand, Hallie. But as a brother, I've learned to trust Kyle. And the autopsy findings could be wrong."

It's possible, she thought, *but I doubt it.*

They were silent as Reed exited I-75 and headed west toward the Oakland County Morgue. Hours of chatting with mourners had made her throat dry and scratchy. A big, cool Coke would taste wonderful. Ahead, a 7-Eleven store called out to her.

"You thirsty?" she asked, pointing to the store.

"My throat is like chalk."

Reed pulled in and parked facing a beautiful black Harley Davidson.

Suddenly, behind her, she heard tires squeal. Her rearview mirror filled up with a dark blue car—the Lincoln. It had blocked the TrailBlazer in.

Both Lincoln doors opened, the two men rushed toward them, gunmetal glinting in their hands.

"Hang on!" Reed shouted.

Her heart slammed against her chest.

He threw the TrailBlazer into gear, bulldozed the Harley to the side and floored the accelerator. The men ran after them. She ducked as a muffled gunshot shattered a Cadillac headlamp beside her.

Reed sped toward the exit as the men ran back to their Lincoln.

"What do they *want*?" Hallie asked.

"Us. Dead, probably."

Reed careened down the first side street, then turned at the next corner and hid behind some thick evergreens. Seconds later, Hallie saw the Lincoln slow at the side street. The men looked in their direction, but she was certain they couldn't see them through the thick evergreens.

The Lincoln moved ahead, stopped—then sped toward them.

"*Damn!* They saw my brake lights," Reed said. He hit the gas, squealed around the next corner and raced down a wide residential street that curved like a half moon. He cornered onto a straightaway, accelerated, then sped around another long, gradual bend in the opposite direction.

Hallie saw nowhere to hide. To her right were low, single-story ranch houses. To the left, a five-foot-high wire fence bordered an enormous open field filled with large pools of rainwater.

"Reed!"

"What?"

It was too late. He'd already sped past the Dead End sign—directly toward a thick forest that stood like the Great Wall of China. She searched the trees for an opening, but saw none. In the mirror, the dark Lincoln roared toward them like an angry rhino.

They were trapped.

Adrenalin shot through her, hardening every muscle in her body.

Reed kept glancing at the fence beside them.

"Cover your face," he said.

She placed her arms over her face as Reed suddenly swerved wide and slammed the TrailBlazer into a padlocked gate in the fence. The vehicle smashed through, but not without whipping their heads forward and back, then two-wheeling down onto soft ground. He shifted into four-wheel drive and sped ahead, kicking up chunks of soggy turf. One hundred yards later, he blasted into a wide, fender-deep pool of rainwater, roostertailing water up behind them like a speedboat.

The Lincoln raced through the gate and came after them.

Reed's TrailBlazer churned out of the water as the Lincoln sped toward it. She watched the big car skid to a stop, its front tires sliding into the pool up to the fender. Backing up, the car began fishtailing and spinning its tires. The driver rocked the Lincoln back and forth, digging deeper.

Watching the Lincoln get stuck, Hallie leaned back and exhaled. She saw her fingernail indentations in the center console.

Reed drove from the field onto a side street. With any luck, she thought, the Lincoln drivers were mired up to their necks.

She took another deep breath and tried to calm herself. Two men had just tried to *kill* them. Why? Did they want money? Reed's shiny new TrailBlazer? They couldn't possibly be related to Kyle's death, since he'd died from SCD.

"Let's tell Detective Beachum," Reed said.

Hallie grabbed the phone and dialed Beachum's number.

"Detective Beachum, please," she said. "It's urgent."

"Detective Beachum just went out," a man said.

"Please try his beeper. It's very important!"

"Yes, ma'am."

Moments later, he came back on.

"He's turned it off, sir. He does that a lot when he's in the field."

Reed thumped the shift handle.

"Please have him call Reed Kincaid immediately," Hallie said. She gave him Reed's cell phone number and hers, and hung up.

Ahead, she saw a paving crew pouring concrete as a crane swung a massive chunk of sewer into position. To avoid traffic, Reed turned down a side street, then handed her a file that had slid between the seats. He placed his hand on hers and said, "You okay?"

As she started to answer, tires squealed behind her.

Turning, she saw the mud-caked Lincoln careen around a corner and race toward them.

Reed floored the accelerator. Cornering on two wheels, he sped toward the next cross street. Halfway down, her stomach turned to stone. Concrete abutments blocked the road ahead. Behind the abutments, two parked construction cranes hovered, their hooks dangling in the wind like gallows ropes.

Reed skidded to a stop.

They were blocked from all angles. The Lincoln raced toward them. Hallie gripped the armrest, her eyes glued to the side mirror.

Reed spun the TrailBlazer around.

"Crouch down, he said.

What's he doing? she thought.

He floored the accelerator and sped directly at the Lincoln. Scrunching down, Hallie held her breath.

The men in the Lincoln stared at them.

Reed drove straight toward them. They were only three hundred feet ahead and closing fast. The confused driver shouted something. His passenger shouted back angrily at him.

Two hundred feet.

Hallie's heart slammed into her throat.

Ninety feet.

Reed's misjudged them! "Reed!"

Then she saw it, the blink of fear in the Lincoln driver's eyes. The man jerked the car left.

Reed swerved the opposite direction, careened through the factory gate and raced across the empty parking lot.

Behind her she heard tires screeching to a stop. Looking back, she saw the big Lincoln spin around and take up the chase.

Reed sped behind the factory into the massive back lot where she saw an EXIT sign two hundred feet ahead. But the EXIT led to a narrow street that looked clogged with construction equipment. A perfect place to get trapped.

At the last second, Reed steered through the entrance of the plant warehouse and parked in a dark corner facing the entrance.

Twenty-five seconds later, the Lincoln roared by, heading toward the EXIT.

Slowly, Hallie let her breath out.

"You okay?" he asked.

Her heart was pounding so loudly she barely heard him. "Sort of," she whispered.

"Let's wait a bit."

She stared at the entrance, listening, waiting, expecting the big Lincoln to come into view at any second. Overhead, she heard wind whistling through the rafters.

Why are they still pursuing us?

A large crow swooped down to a nearby, chemical drum and defiantly stared at her.

She strained to hear any sound of the Lincoln. Would the men soon realize their mistake, double back and wait outside? Or had they *already* doubled back? Were they stepping through the darkness toward them now?

Suddenly, from behind, a loud snap.

Four

Another snap behind her....

Hallie spun around and stared into the warehouse shadows. She saw only darkness. Outside, the wind suddenly whipped up and gusted through the entrance, buckling the aluminum wall, *snapping* it.

Only the wind, she realized, relaxing a bit.

Still, the wind made it impossible to hear. The two men could be sneaking up behind them. She looked at the large crow on the chemical drum. He stared back as though anxiously awaiting her execution.

"See anyone?" Reed asked.

"It's too dark to see."

Snap, snap....

"Let's get out of here," she said.

"Crouch down. You check right. I'll check left."

She scooted down and tightened her seatbelt.

Slowly, Reed drove toward the entrance. They looked outside and saw no Lincoln. Creeping into the daylight, they saw the parking lot was empty. Reed sped across the cracked asphalt to the side street.

Okay so far, she thought.

They checked driveways, alleys, between houses, behind stores, and two minutes later, they merged into traffic on northbound Telegraph Road, heading toward the morgue in Pontiac. Fortunately, the morgue was located right next to the Oakland County Sheriff's Office, which should keep their attackers away. Slowly, Hallie felt the tension begin to drain from her body.

"What's going on?" she asked.

"They want us dead."

"Why?"

"Kyle."

That doesn't make sense, except to you, Reed, she thought. "But the autopsy says Kyle died from *natural* causes, sudden cardiac arrest."

"Kyle begs to differ. You heard him, Hallie."

"But I also heard Dr. McDonald."

24

He shrugged. "I simply believe my brother."

And nothing will change your mind, she realized. Ahead, a large gray cloud swept past, blocking the sun. A light mist began to dot the windshield. The wind picked up, bending a row of evergreens toward the road that was crowded with large trucks, vans and SUVs. A red Corvette swept past her, leaves swirling after it.

"There's the morgue," Hallie said, pointing ahead to the modern building located in the sprawling Oakland County government complex on north Telegraph Road in the outskirts of Pontiac. Reed drove onto a winding road, pulled in and parked in a slot about one hundred feet from the entrance. They waited, watching for the Lincoln.

After a couple of minutes and no Lincolns, they got out. A damp wind chilled her to the bone as they walked across the lot, stepping on wet leaves that looked like giant cornflakes. Staring ahead at the distinctive brick building, she realized that its pale, cool stones were like the pale, cool cadavers inside.

They entered the morgue's reception area, and Hallie was again reminded how it looked more like a successful doctor's suite. The display cases, however, reminded you this was a House of Death. They contained the actual objects that had killed real people: a hangman's noose, a black pistol, drug needles, a knife, a tiny toy ball that choked a baby to death.

"This way," Hallie said, leading Reed over to a reception window. An attractive, raven-haired woman with a sunny smile and pink cheeks greeted them. Her nametag read Kathy. She looked like she should be baking warm pies instead of directing people to cold cadavers. She directed them to Dr. McDonald's autopsy room.

As they walked down the hallway, Hallie felt the air turn cool and thick. The acrid scent of disinfectant stung her nasal passages. She envisioned bleached-white corpses peeled open like sardine tins and wondered if Reed could stomach the sight of autopsied bodies.

"If you're not used to them, autopsies can be kind of upsetting," she said.

"As in throwing up?"

"That and passing out. Would you rather wait out here?"

"I'd rather hear what Dr. McDonald says."

"If you start to feel woozy, tell me," she said.

"Tarzan strong," he said, thumping his chest.

Jane hope so, she thought, leading him down to a set of steel doors with a tag that read *Dr. Homer McDonald.* They put on green gowns, slippers and masks. Pushing through the doors, they entered the large autopsy room. Ceiling lights and ultraviolet wall bulbs hit her like a Death Valley sun. She

25

blinked and saw two stainless steel tables surrounded by sinks, counters and X-ray view boxes. The familiar smell of death, sour and sticky, stiffened the air.

Beside her, Reed looked as though maggots were crawling on his skin.

On one table, an older male cadaver, dull, waxy gray, bald, US Navy tattoo on his left arm, was being autopsied by two doctors wearing hoods and white plastic aprons. At the other table, two doctors were jack-knifed over the pale, ashen corpse of a young woman. One doctor, magnifying glass to his eye, examined something above her ear.

Buzzing filled Hallie's ears. Turning, she saw bone dust spray from the old man's skull as a pathologist leaned into his Stryker saw. She swore she smelled bone, and suddenly remembered that a med school professor had told her that all odors are particulate.

Hallie led Reed over to the young woman, whose chest cavity was splayed open with a sprawling incision from the shoulders, under the breasts to the center of her chest, and then straight down to the pubic bone. Her body cavity appeared empty. Purple-red organs were stacked in steel dishes.

Hallie heard a sucking sound. She looked down and saw water with bits of stuff swirling into a drain. Beside her, Reed's eyes began to swirl. She prayed he didn't pass out.

"Dr. McDonald?" Hallie said.

A slight, stooped older man turned slowly and removed his goggles. He squinted at her through drooping eyelids that could not conceal warm silvery-blue eyes. His pale skin almost matched the cadaver's. Tufts of gray hair stuck out like stalks above his ears. He had a kind, grandfatherly aura, which vanished when she saw the bloody scalpel with which the good doctor was carving the woman's brownish-red liver.

"Yes. May I help you?" His voice was as soft as melting butter.

"I'm Hallie Mara. You told me to come find you even if you were on autopsy."

"Ah yes, of course, Doctor." He smiled and his cheeks pinked up a bit. "I knew your father, Kyo. A splendid surgeon."

Splendid father, too, she thought, wishing he was around to help her with this situation.

"Thank you, Doctor. This is Reed Kincaid. You autopsied his brother, Kyle."

Dr. McDonald's eyes dimmed. "Ah yes … I'm sorry for you, Reed. Your brother was so young. Like this poor woman. Heart attack." He gestured toward the corpse. "Cocaine induced. Only twenty-eight."

Hallie looked down at her gray, thin face and wondered how many more young lives drugs would take to an early grave.

"Doctor," Hallie said, "you mentioned we might review Kyle's autopsy?"

"Certainly."

He gestured for his young female assistant to finish. Stripping off his bloodstained gloves, mask and gown, he led them down a hall to his office, a wide room filled with cabinets, a desk and small round table. They sat at the table. On the desk, Hallie saw a family photo of McDonald, probably his wife and children and a gaggle of grinning grandkids at a lakeside cottage. Beside the photo sat an enormous jar of red cinnamon jelly beans. Dr. McDonald offered them some, but they declined. He tossed a couple in his mouth, and the sugar pumped a little more pink into his cheeks. He opened a drawer, fingered through the files, and finally pulled one out.

"Doctor," Hallie said, "we witnessed Kyle Kincaid's death. I believe the police told you that Kyle, as he died, whispered that a man had poisoned him."

"They did."

"And that many more people would die Friday?"

"Yes. And because of the urgency we did a very comprehensive medical-legal autopsy. We also enlisted a number of labs to greatly expedite the results."

"And they found no evidence of any poison?" Hallie asked.

He nodded. "None whatsoever."

"You conducted a full toxicity workup?"

"Oh yes, quite extensive," he said. "We checked the most common poisons. For example, cyanide poisoning was not indicated. His whole blood, carboxy hemoglobin, gastric contents, tissues and urine were all normal."

"The heavy metals?"

"Absent."

"Strychnine?"

"*Nada*. No traces. Also, we found no street drugs, ethyl alcohol, or methanol. His electrolytes were fine. We checked for botulism, carbon monoxide, PCP, opiates, cocaine, you name it. All negative." He tossed a few more jelly beans in his mouth and chewed, making his gums look bloody.

Hallie hoped Reed remembered what she'd told him, that Dr. McDonald was one of the most respected forensic pathologists in the state. He was known for reporting the facts, even when, on occasion, the social elite or corporate heavy breathers exerted considerable pressure on him to record a more socially acceptable cause of death.

"What about arsenic?" she asked.

"Well, our bodies normally have a little arsenic. Kyle's tissue and fluid levels were normal."

He flipped a page. "We even performed multiple esoteric analysis."

"Like what?" she asked.

He ran his finger down the page. "Oh, let's see here ... snake venom, curare, and several other exotic poisons...."

"And?"

"All negative."

Hallie was impressed at the extent of McDonald's tests. "Doctor, are there any lethal poisons that toxicology tests would not normally detect?"

McDonald tapped the stem of his glasses against his lip. "Well, of course there's succinylcholine. Sneaky stuff. Kills you, then politely decomposes in the body. A regular autopsy won't pick up sux. But a fella down in Toledo developed a new test for it. He called me this morning. Succinylcholine was not present."

Hallie realized she was running out of questions.

Reed leaned forward. "Doctor, what do you think caused Kyle's cardiac arrest?"

Dr. McDonald rubbed his eyelids for several seconds and shook his head. "It's a mystery, son. It just happens sometimes. We can't always explain Mother Nature. She simply has a mind of her own on occasion."

"Isn't thirty-three quite young for sudden cardiac death?" Reed asked.

"Far too young," McDonald said solemnly. "The death rate for coronary heart disease among white males twenty-five to thirty-four is only *one* in ten thousand. Quite rare, but it happens. That young Russian skater. And a while back, a Detroit Lions wide receiver. In their twenties. Bad arteries. Genetic defect."

"And Kyle's arteries?" Hallie asked.

"You could drive a truck through them. No pulmonary fibrosis. No *cor pulmonale*."

Hallie shook her head from side to side, realizing that the heart attack made no sense. "Doctor, did anything about this autopsy puzzle you?"

Dr. McDonald started to grab some more jellybeans, then paused and scanned the report. His finger stopped halfway down the page. "Well, I did find some hemolysis."

"What's hemolysis?" Reed asked.

"Basically a rupturing of the red blood cells," McDonald said.

"What causes it?"

"A number of things. Intrinsic abnormalities of the red blood cell contents, like enzymes, or membrane structure. Or it's caused by extrinsic problems like serum antibodies, arsine gas or infectious agents. In your brother's case, we found none of these. So the hemolysis is puzzling."

The phone rang. Dr. McDonald picked up, listened intently, then began discussing assignments and scheduling with a colleague.

Clearly, Hallie realized, McDonald's team had conducted extensive toxicology testing. Seemingly, nothing had been excluded. She noticed that Reed looked even more discouraged. Painful as this was, it might be the only way for him to accept that his brother was not poisoned.

McDonald hung up and ran his finger along the jelly bean jar.

"Doctor," Hallie said, "earlier today at the funeral home, I learned from Kyle's colleague, the medical director of Dunne Corporation, of two other recent young SCD deaths in the Grand Blanc area. There could be even more we don't know about. Have you experienced an abnormal number of young SCD cases recently?"

He frowned. "Abnormal number? No. Are you suggesting a connection?"

"No, but in that small town it seems like a lot of young SCD cases in a short time."

He nodded. "Three does, doesn't it. Probably coincidence. But let me ask around."

"Thank you, Doctor," Hallie said.

"My pleasure."

Dr. McDonald faced Reed with sad, heavy eyes. "I wish we could give you the evidence you seek, Reed. But we simply found nothing that suggests your brother died from unnatural causes. I'll call you with the result of a minor test tomorrow. But I don't expect it will alter our findings."

Hallie watched the last ray of hope fade from Reed's eyes. They thanked Dr. McDonald again and left the Oakland County Morgue.

Minutes later, as Reed drove her toward Genetique Laboratories, she noticed his large, powerful hand. She thought back to when she'd first touched it two months ago. They'd shaken hands when he'd visited Genetique to interview her for a public service commercial on Alzheimer research.

After the interview, she gave him a quick tour, during which he'd asked her to be in the commercial. She'd suggested her boss, Rex Randall, but Reed had said that Randall came off a bit too aggressive. How right he was. So reluctantly, she'd agreed.

Shooting the commercial had turned out to be fun, and after the 'wrap' they'd gone out for coffee at Starbucks. The coffee had led to dinner, which led to many dinners, which led to the most wonderful two months of her life. She'd been attracted to him from the start, to his easy charm, his intelligence, his boyish good looks and sense of humor. She'd also been fascinated by his intuitive grasp of things, so different from her methodical, scientific decision making.

At first, she'd felt herself holding back a bit. Nothing new there. She'd become the Queen of Holding Back. For good reason: David Harrington. The memory of their painful breakup had taught her an important lesson: Always keep a part of yourself uncommitted, a safety valve.

Everyone needs a place to retreat to when the inevitable rejection broadsides you.

Five

Hallie noticed that Reed seemed deep in thought as he drove her toward Genetique Laboratory. Probably, he was trying to understand the autopsy finding in light of his brother's dying words. She wanted to help him accept the finding but wasn't sure she could. He seemed uptight, his neck muscles scrunched up.

She reached over and began to rub his neck.

"Ahhh...." he purred.

"Thinking about Kyle?"

He nodded.

"Try to remember the good times."

"Vengeance would be a good time," he said with a weak smile. She felt his neck muscles loosen a bit. "But I'll probably remember Kyle mostly for the not-so-good times. He was always there for me."

She turned and looked at him. "When your parents...?"

He nodded. "I can still see the Michigan fullback leaping for a touchdown, still hear the crowd roar, still hear the loudspeaker call Kyle and me to Stadium Security."

She noticed his eyes glaze over.

"Mom and Dad had just left us an hour earlier," Reed continued. "An asphalt truck ran a stop sign and slammed into their open convertible. Buried them in the hot asphalt. Burned eighty percent of their bodies. They survived for almost two years at the University of Michigan Burn Center. Medical insurance handled many expenses. But over time, hospital bills exhausted our family savings."

They passed a blue van stuffed with wide-eyed kids waving shiny birthday balloons.

"Since their deaths, Kyle's been my only family," Reed continued. "I grew up trying to be like him."

"You're not too shabby as yourself, you know."

"But a tad shabby, right?"

She smiled. "Hey, being honored as one of *Advertising Age*'s twenty

31

hottest young creative directors isn't exactly chopped liver."

"I got lucky."

"You got good, thanks to your eighty-hour workweeks. But sometimes I think...." She stopped, realizing now was not the time to get into this.

"Sometimes you think what?"

Too late, she realized. "Sometimes I think you work too hard."

"Hey, it's not work if you love it."

"And it's not love if *all* you do is work."

"What is it, Dr. Laura?"

She smiled.

"Tell me, tell me...."

She shrugged. "Maybe some kind of work junkie thing."

He smiled. "You're probably right. Some colleagues have suggested I'm a workaholic at times. Probably am. I'm not quite sure why. Mostly to do the job well, but sometimes to let work's narcotic numbness soothe my problem-du-jour. The more I work, the less problems intrude. The less they intrude, the smaller they seem. Maybe hard work is cheap therapy."

"Maybe. But you told me it cost you big once."

He cheeks grew a little pink. "It did...."

Reed had briefly confided that he'd been serious with someone named Anna Marie. She'd apparently wanted more of a commitment than he could promise at the time. A month later, she accepted a job in Portland. He said it had hurt, but that now he was over Anna Marie. Hallie wondered if he really was over her.

"All I know is I get caught up in my work at times," Reed said. "Kyle did too. Maybe it's genetic."

"Maybe his heart attack was too."

She felt his neck muscles tighten again.

"If my brother says he was poisoned, he was."

Still not budging, she realized. They drove in silence for several moments. "I'm sure he believed he was, Reed. But there's simply no evidence."

"There is."

"What?"

"His eyes. His voice. Kyle *knew*. He was warning me. He was asking me to save the people who'll die this Friday."

The passion in his voice jarred her.

"And," he continued, "some men just tried to kill us."

"Yes, but I'm confused about whether they're related in any way to Kyle's death." She needed facts, and so far, not one single fact connected the Lincoln to Kyle's death.

Reed's cell phone rang and Hallie punched the speaker button.

"Hello," Reed said.

"Detective Woody Beachum. I just got in. What's going on?"

"Two men in a dark blue Lincoln just blocked my TrailBlazer. They shot at us."

Beachum paused several moments. "Where?"

"Strip mall, near Pontiac, just off I 75."

"You get the license number?"

"No time."

Hallie heard the click of Beachum's cigarette lighter, followed by a deep draw.

"Been a few carjackers in that area," Beachum said.

"They weren't carjackers."

"How do you know?"

"They shot *at* the TrailBlazer. And at *us*. They used silencers, a sign of professional hit. They pursued us for more than two miles."

Beachum exhaled slowly. "Crazed druggies maybe. You and Hallie are probably well dressed from the funeral home. Maybe they wanted your money."

"They wanted us dead." Reed's face reddened.

"I hear you. But even so, that's Pontiac's jurisdiction. I'll ask a buddy there if they've had any dark blue Lincolns involved in robberies or carjackings and get back to you."

"I think they're connected to Kyle's murder."

Beachum paused several moments. "Again, Reed, all I have is an autopsy that says heart attack. I just can't investigate without more."

"I'll find more," Reed said with icy determination as they hung up.

Will you? Hallie wondered. Looking out the window, she saw the clouds were low and thick, hovering over them like a gray blanket. Light rain began to sprinkle the windshield and the air felt cooler.

"You seemed to know the morgue well," Reed said.

Too well, she thought, closing her eyes. "I'll never forget it." Her mind drifted back many years.

"Your dad?"

"Kevin, my brother."

She'd briefly mentioned to Reed that Kevin had died young, but she hadn't told him the painful details.

"He was eighteen," she said, her throat tightening. "I was fourteen and idolized him. My parents and I were escorted into a room. The attendant lifted the sheet. Kevin's bruised, swollen face stared up at me. I'll never

33

forget it." She closed her eyes, remembering Kevin's dull, lifeless, swollen eyes, his beautiful face lacerated nearly beyond recognition.

Gently, Reed placed a hand on her shoulder.

"Police theorized he was pulled from his car and beaten with a metal pipe or baseball bat. Murdered."

"Murdered brothers...." he said, shaking his head.

"What?"

"We could have better things in common."

She agreed.

"Who did it?"

"The police never found out."

"Robbery?"

"They left his money."

"So what was the motive?"

"The police never established one. But I did."

"What?"

She felt the old pain, the emptiness, the hot anger rush back. "Kevin was beaten to death simply because he looked Asian. Thousands of auto workers had just been laid off due to Japanese imports. Three days earlier, two drunk rednecks clubbed a Chinese tourist to death. Kevin's death taught me what extreme racism is, what could happen to me simply because I'm part Asian. His death completely changed my understanding of racial prejudice."

They passed an abandoned auto assembly plant with broken windows, then a cement mixer shifting gears. When the noise faded, Reed asked, "May I ask how?"

She stared at him and wondered how to answer him diplomatically. "Don't take this personally, but it taught me that most Caucasians unconsciously harbor, whether they know it or not, some degree of anti-Asian sentiment."

Reed seemed to think about that a few moments. "You're probably right. Most Caucasians, I suspect, like all ethnic groups, are naturally biased a bit toward their own kind in subtle ways."

"It's the not-so-subtle guys that scare mc. Frankly, when I pass an auto plant that had layoffs due to Asian imports, I get nervous. And sometimes, when I'm alone, I'm afraid I'll be attacked."

Reed brushed hair from her eyes. "Simple solution."

"What?"

"I'll hang around."

She smiled. "I can live with that." *For life,* she thought, surprising herself and wondering if he'd read her mind.

She thought back to when they'd first met, just two months ago. From the start, they were at ease with each other. He was warm, fun to be with and made every aspect of her life richer and fuller.

And just a week ago, they'd made love for the first time. She could still feel the magic of that night, the marriage of their souls, the sense of oneness she'd felt with him, a kind of inner warmth and peace she'd never known before.

They were driving back from Chicago. As they entered I 94, a light rain began to fall. Near Battle Creek, the rain became ice, turning I 94 into a skating rink. The radio warned of "extremely hazardous conditions." Motels blinked "No Vacancies." They exited and crept down ice-slick roads to the tiny village of Beadle Lake, where they took the last room at Considine's B&B. Their hosts provided warm chicken sandwiches, delicious raspberry-apple-pie with homemade ice cream and a bottle of heady Leelanau Peninsula Merlot. They finished the wine and food with little trouble.

"You take the bed," Reed said. "I'll take the sofa."

"You're six-two. I'll take the sofa."

"Flip you for it."

"Okay."

"Heads," she said, flipping her two-headed coin. "I win. The bed's yours."

He shrugged and plopped into the bed. She disappeared into the bathroom for a minute, came out, turned off the light and settled down on the sofa. Despite the effects of wine and food, she lay awake thinking how much she wanted to wrap her arms around him. Five minutes later, she wrapped her arms around him.

"I slid right off that weensy sofa," she whispered, snuggling closer.

"Keep on slidin', you hussy."

The hussy kept on slidin'.

Looking into his eyes, she kissed his lips gently, and he returned her kiss, caressing her neck and shoulders with his fingers. They removed their bed clothes. The soft streetlight filtered through the lace curtains and revealed the magnificent contours of his powerful shoulders and body. He cupped her breasts, then feathered her nipples and she arched her back in pleasure. They kissed harder, deeper. His hands slipped around her and stroked her back. She kissed his eyes, then traced every muscle of his body with her fingers. Her hand moved down his stomach, caressed him, and gently she guided him into her. They moved in unison, slowly, then faster, feeling the pleasure build, holding back. She sighed softly, and soon her sigh became a tiny cry as they came together, silently, then violently, melting into waves of ecstasy unlike anything she'd known. When the shudders subsided, she rested against him weakly, breathing into his chest, knowing that her life had just changed.

Now, she looked over at those same warm blue eyes, dimmed by sadness, and was again overwhelmed with love and concern for him.

Reed pulled out of his lane to pass a Humane Society truck stuffed with dogs and cats. The sad-faced animals stared out at her.

"Many of them will be put down in days," she said, pointing to an old golden Lab.

He nodded. "So will many people."

She suddenly realized how heavily his brother's dying words weighed down on Reed. She knew what she had to do. She had to help him look for evidence Kyle was murdered, even though she didn't believe the evidence existed.

"I'm going to talk to a pal," she said. "Ameen's an excellent pathologist at Detroit Memorial. I'll ask him to check Kyle's autopsy. Maybe he'll see something Doctor McDonald or the labs missed."

His face brightened instantly. "Thank you."

He reached over and placed his hand on her cheek. She watched the sun brighten his firm, sculpted cheekbones and bathe his face with its healthiest glow in days.

She glanced at the side mirror and froze. A dark Lincoln swerved in behind them.

"Reed!"

"Relax. It's maroon."

Six

"Handle them," the man said, after Luca Corsa confessed that Hallie Mara and Reed Kincaid had escaped at the 7-Eleven.

"Today?" Corsa asked.

"Yes," the man said and hung up. Calmly, he fingered the phone. Luca Corsa would handle things. What he lacked in social graces and intelligence, he made up for in more admirable traits, like a total absence of morals, Neanderthal strength, and most of all, a pathological pursuit of his prey. Luca Corsa delivered. Always. And he would deliver Reed Kincaid and the woman to their eternal resting place very soon.

Pushing the phone aside, the man stood and stretched his six-foot-three frame.

Unfortunate, he thought, *that Kyle Kincaid didn't simply die in silence. The good news is the police are not involved. Which means he revealed nothing significant about Friday to his brother. Nor did he reveal my name.*

The man stroked his beard, then stepped onto a small elevator, pushed the button and descended thirty-seven feet beneath his home. He stepped out into a small room and picked up the hood of his Drager HazMat suit. He blew static dust from its mirror-like visor and stared into his own eyes. Despite their dark circles, the result of eighteen-hour days, his eyes burned with intensity. He'd waited years for what he would unleash this Friday.

Nothing can compare to it. Not even 9/11. The day of penance and atonement is at hand.

He touched his jaw, feeling the familiar indentation left by his father's pipe wrench. He traced the indentation to the scar on his nose, another souvenir of daddy's rage. Despite the scars, women said his face was handsome, had character.

Not for long, ladies. My face won't exist in nine days. I won't exist.

He stepped into his HazMat suit and felt his heart pump faster. Ironic, he thought, since he was about to test something that stopped hearts.

He walked over to his laboratory door and rotated the large wheel. The airlock hissed open. He moved inside, looked around the large, brilliantly illuminated laboratory and felt a delicious sense of power. It was *his* laboratory. All built with a fraction of fees paid by political groups and oil-rich Middle-East fanatics, fools who fought over grains of sand and paid handsomely for his very special products.

Only he knew of his lab's existence. The construction crew was sworn to secrecy, and the secret had died with them three days after completing the lab. He remembered the newspaper headline: CONSTRUCTION WORKERS DIE IN TOXIC POISONING ACCIDENT.

Toxic poisoning, yes. Accident, no.

He inserted the orange, ceiling-tracked air hose into his suit nozzle and felt cool air wash over his skin. Strolling past stainless steel tables, he noted the culture dishes, pipette racks and two new Olympus Tokyo microscopes. He checked the gauges on his large walk-in incubators and the long row of Beckman Vitra centrifuges. Everything was in order, clean. The way he liked it.

Unlocking a yellow biohazard container, he removed a device with a long, modified syringe and an inflated rubber bag. He carried the device past cages filled with skittish monkeys and stopped at a glass-enclosed cage where canines 37 and 38, golden Labradors, ran toward him. They were excited to see him. After all, he'd raised them since they were pups.

"Dinner tonight is very special, 37," he whispered to the closest dog.

Tails wagging, they nuzzled eagerly around the trap door, expecting a treat. He inserted the syringe needle through a tiny slot in the door and they approached the needle.

He clicked his stopwatch and squeezed the rubber bag, swirling the vapor into their cage, then removed the needle. The dogs sniffed and wrinkled their brows, clearly disappointed there was no food.

Circling the cage, they looked up at him every few seconds, confused. Soon their tails wagged slower. Then 37 froze, stared at the floor and tilted his head, disoriented. He wobbled a moment and collapsed. Seconds later, 38 slumped to the floor, his lips pulled back in a macabre grin.

The man watched how they choked, how their paws trembled, how their little eyes jerked about.

Funny about the eyes, he thought. *Sometimes they freeze, sometimes they zigzag like ping-pong balls.*

37 crawled toward him, whimpering, eyes pleading. Then 38 crept forward, staring up at him. He stared back, wondering what the animals were thinking. *Do they know they are dying?*

He watched their mouths gasp for air. He watched their lustrous, golden fur rise and fall, knowing that beneath it, their lungs were begging for air, their hearts racing out of control, perhaps bursting. He watched their jaws snap like windup toys. Bloody vomit and feces stained the white tile floor.

Magnificent, he thought.

Seconds later their eyes locked open and their soft, golden fur went still.

Staring down at them, he felt a strange, indefinable tug, a faint echo of some emotion, perhaps sadness, or something he might have once felt as a young child. The feeling was quickly bulldozed away by the warm adrenaline rush he always felt when he harvested life. An abnormal feeling, he knew. Abnormally *wonderful.*

Never more wonderful than one evening a few years ago in his father's Des Moines apartment. His mind drifted back to that rainy December night. After twenty-three years of no contact, daddy dearest had invited him to visit, saying he wanted to right the wrongs of the past. The bastard didn't realize that some wrongs can never be made right. Like beatings and burnings. Like abusing and abandoning his mother. Like causing her suicide.

He'd accepted his father's invitation. After dinner, and after his father's pathetic 'I made a couple mistakes' apology, he handed him a large scotch. He watched his father sip it and smile. He watched the smile fade, his face darken, his eyes grow fearful and then start pleading.

He watched his father die very slowly and painfully, begging for help.

Such a beautiful Kodak moment....

Now, looking at the dead golden Labradors, he realized *America's* beautiful Kodak moment was drawing near.

"You did not die in vain," he whispered to the dead dogs. "Your deaths have just shown me that *thousands upon thousands* of traitors to America will die exactly like you did in just three days."

Seven

Wednesday, 8:20 a.m.

Reed felt like a door had just slammed in his face.

Dr. McDonald had informed him that not only had the final toxicology test come back negative, but that his fellow pathologists were reporting normal levels of sudden cardiac death among young adults.

And five minutes ago, the police door banged shut. Detective Beachum told him that technicians had re-examined the forensic evidence from Kyle's clothing and car, and from Reed's house, and found nothing suspicious.

Slam, bam, no investigation.

Now what? Reed wondered, sipping coffee in his home office. *Why can't they find some shred of evidence?*

He stood and walked to the window. Clouds were rolling across the sky in a furious rage, like dirty, balled-up sweat socks. The wind spun his garage weathervane and pulled dark leaves from an ancient oak where two blackbirds squawked down at the neighbor's gray cat. Near the cat was a concrete slab where Kyle and he'd planned to put up a basketball backboard for some one-on-one.

More than anything, Reed wanted some serious one-on-one with Kyle's killer.

He slumped into his chair and closed his eyes. How the hell could someone poison Kyle without leaving a trace of evidence? It made no sense. He replayed Kyle's final moments, second by second, word by word. He saw his brother's panicked eyes, felt his trembling body, heard his pleading words. *True words.*

Kyle was murdered. He was not hallucinating! He was telling me a man will kill many people on Friday. And begging me to stop the man.

"And I've done nothing!" he said aloud.

He stood quickly, rattling the coffee mug, and began pacing beside the bookshelves, his frustration mushrooming into desperation. How could *he* find evidence Kyle was murdered if experts couldn't? His last hope was

40

Hallie's pathologist friend, Dr. Ameen Howrani, who'd agreed to review Kyle's autopsy. Maybe Dr. Howrani would uncover something.

He looked at the photo of Hallie on his desk and felt his spirits brighten. Her smile did that to him. And it had since they'd met two months ago. She had redefined his life.

So had events of the last few days. He realized now that the real world didn't exactly check in with his agenda. Assassins didn't phone ahead to warn you. The only sure thing in his life was the breath he was taking *this second*. So what's the lesson? Do and say what's right now, and undo and un-say what's wrong now, while you still can. Easier said than done. But probably done easier than most people realized.

For so long, my game plan made sense, he thought. First came career, which begot financial stability, which begot marriage and family. But he'd begotten stuck in the career part, he now realized. Career was his passion and nourishment, but as it turned out, his self-deception.

Maybe even my self-destruction, Hallie, if you hadn't come along. He ran his finger along the silver frame of her photo.

Checking his watch, Reed realized it was time to go see Dr. Howrani. As he walked toward the door, the phone rang and he picked up.

"Hastings," said a familiar, squeaky voice.

Damn. The last person Reed wanted to talk to now was Huey Hastings III, a.k.a. Baby Huey. The agency's Director of Account Services was an obese, pompous man with soot-gray eyes. He was also a highly ambitious, highly despised, not highly principled individual whose mission was to replace the retiring agency president in two years. In the meantime, Hastings wanted to remove all other contenders, which included Reed and just about anyone else who could sit up and not drool.

"What's up, Huey?" Reed envisioned Hastings's blue Brooks Brothers blazer, and beige slacks with a crease that could slice bread.

"I was talking to Thurston about our Mason Industries commercials."

Reed sensed trouble. Hastings always insisted on revising commercials to *his* liking to make them *better*. The problem was, he couldn't recognize 'better' if it jumped off the screen and bit him in his massive ass.

"Thurston feels as I do," Hastings continued, "that the creativity needs to be dialed down a bit."

"Like a thermostat?"

"Right. It's just a tad too creative."

"But Huey, remember what Mason Industries asked us to do?"

Huey did not appear to remember.

"They asked us," Reed continued, "to develop 'very creative, very

41

original, slightly provocative commercials—so they get *noticed.*' Their words. Remember?"

Again, Huey's memory appeared to fail him.

"Well," Huey said, "it's simply a question of degree. Thurston and I are just talking about a little tune-up."

Reed felt heat rise in his face. "Tune-up? You just said 'dial down.' Which is it, up or down?"

"For chrissakes, Kincaid. You know what I mean."

"No, Huey, I don't. And right now I have a … personal situation."

"*Business* is personal."

"You probably haven't heard."

"Heard what?"

Reed swallowed hard, surprised at how painful it still was to tell people. "My brother suddenly passed away two days ago. He'd never been sick a day in his life."

Silence. For the first time in Reed's memory, Huey Hastings III appeared uncertain what to say. "Oh … I've been traveling. My condolences, of course." Spoken with all the sensitivity of mud.

"Thanks, Huey."

"I'm sure we can hold the meeting off for a couple days."

Baby Huey was all heart.

"That would be good."

"I'll call."

"Right."

They hung up. Reed wrote down 'Huey meeting,' and exhaled slowly. He had to watch Hastings. The man wanted to discredit him in the agency, and ultimately replace him with a creative director that he could browbeat. Hastings had already complained to top management about him, and they'd listened. They *had* to. Hastings's father was CEO of Mason Industries, the agency's second-largest account, nearly one hundred ninety million dollars. Huey, the evil offspring, was a major problem.

Unlike you, Hallie, he thought, smiling at her photo. He'd never forget how she'd helped him through the pain of the last few days, sacrificing her own work.

He loved her passion for work, but oddly, it reminded him of Anna Marie. Another lifetime, but only three years ago. He pictured Anna's smiling face on the Channel Four News. The city was swept away by her award-winning journalism and stunning beauty. He was too. They dated for several months. She became serious very fast and said she wanted a commitment from him. He explained that he simply wasn't ready, partly because her career would jerk her from city to city every few years, creating a weekend relationship or marriage. Four weeks later she took the anchor spot at a major Portland station. Her departure had been painful, and for a long time he'd wondered if he'd made the right decision. Four months later, she married the station general manager.

Now, thinking of Hallie, he knew he couldn't thank the general manager enough.

Reed stood and looked down at his 'Huey' note. He'd have to deal with him later. And his job.

Assuming he still had one.

Eight

"You think Dr. Howrani might find something?" Reed asked.

"It's always possible," Hallie said, doubting it, but still trying to give Reed a ray of hope.

She was escorting him down the gleaming marble hallway in Detroit Memorial Hospital, heading toward Genetique Laboratories, which was connected by several passageways to the teaching hospital. Her pathologist friend, Dr. Ameen Howrani, had kindly agreed, despite his crushing workload, to review Kyle's autopsy and the other SCD autopsies. Dr. Howrani had promised to get back to her, probably late tonight or tomorrow morning.

"How're things going here?" Reed asked, pointing to a large blue *Genetique Laboratories* sign.

Hallie hesitated, not wanting to burden him with a certain problem in the office. "Busy as always...."

"How's the Alzheimer research?" he asked.

"Going well. We're seeing medical breakthroughs. Estrogen and nonsteroidal anti-inflammatory drugs help. Aricept seems to delay placement in nursing homes by up to two years. And our hope, of course, is that we'll soon be able to significantly slow down the onset of Alzheimer and control it better."

"That would be terrific."

"Yes. And in time, stem cell research might lead to treatments that help cure it." She felt herself growing thrilled yet again at the prospect. The thought of giving patients back their minds and memories motivated her day after day.

They entered the laboratory.

"Ah ... the lovely couple," said Dr. Diedre De Bakker, Hallie's assistant and good friend, working at a nearby lab bench.

Hallie cherished De Bakker. A Belgian-born molecular geneticist, Diedre was a willowy thirty-two-year-old who looked like she belonged on a *Vogue* cover rather than hunched over a microscope. Her thick titian-brown hair was pulled back in a chignon, allowing the lab lights to flatter her elegant milky-white cheeks and large china-blue eyes that were as warm as her personality.

"Your flowers were very thoughtful, Diedre," Reed said. "Thank you."

"You're quite welcome, Reed," she said, depositing liquid into a row of pipettes.

Diedre was a godsend, Hallie reminded herself once more. Brilliant, creative, organized and fun. A rare combination which permitted Hallie to delegate many day-to-day operations to her, while she focused on strategic direction, interfaced with management and kept their overbearing boss from harassing the lab team.

"How're things going?" Hallie asked.

Diedre handed her a clipboard. "Better than our competitors, I hope."

Reed straightened up. "Speaking of competitors, my agency's competing for that anti-smoking campaign I mentioned. Is there a phone I might use?"

"Sure. In there," Hallie said, pointing to a nearby cubicle. "Just hit nine. I'll be reading these." She tapped the stack of papers on the clipboard.

Reed moved into the small cubicle and settled in as Hallie walked over to her desk and sat down.

She studied a DNA map that displayed rows of tiny black smudges, some circled in red, then a chart that tracked Alzheimer's in an extended Mormon family. As she started to read about a new pharmaceutical for immune system disorders, she heard the click of a man's shoes on the parquet floor. Her body tensed up. Turning, she saw her boss, Rex Randall, walking toward her.

Randall was called T. Rex by those who disliked him, which included three ex-wives, four children, co-workers, and most of western civilization.

"Everything's on schedule?" Rex Randall demanded. Rex demanded as often as most people inhaled.

"Yes," Hallie said.

She looked at Randall, a tall, slim man with dark, close-set reptilian eyes that oozed ego and reminded her of a cobra planning to strike. His veal-gray lips were always stretched in a sneer, as though reminding you he should be talking to someone far more important.

"Then we'll recommend our Gen-Est2 estrogen replacement to Bio-Chron Tuesday," Randall said. His eyes gleamed as he appeared to calculate the influx of juicy new revenue. He raked his bony fingers through slicked-back black hair.

"Only after more testing, Rex."

"Why more?" He appeared shocked.

You know why, Hallie thought. "Our Gen-Est2 findings are not yet conclusive."

Randall's jaw line hardened. "Don't you get it?"

"Get what?"

"I want something by next Tuesday. Something I can sell to Bio-Chron. This is a *business!*"

"I understand, but—"

"But nothing! The future of Genetique depends on it."

Hallie felt her frustration heating up and stared hard into his cold, slitty eyes. "It also depends on something else, Rex."

"What?"

"Accuracy." She was troubled that Reed was overhearing this.

"Jesus Christ, I realize that!" T. Rex huffed. "Get it clear, Doctor. I *will* have something on Tuesday. Anything less is unacceptable performance. And speaking of performance, your evaluation is coming up soon." Randall thrust his jaw out belligerently, turned and stormed toward the lab door.

Hallie watched Reed stand up, fearing he might run over and punch out Randall. Fortunately, Reed strolled over to her as Randall's wingtips echoed down the hall.

He stared at her a moment. "You okay?"

She shrugged. "Yeah."

"Nice guy."

"A real peach."

"And I know where to cram the pits," Diedre said from the corner.

Everyone laughed.

"You put up with that attitude often?" Reed asked.

"No. Just a few times a day," she said, half-smiling, but still upset by Randall's threatening remarks and that Reed had witnessed the unpleasant scene.

"You're earning your money working for that jerk," Reed said.

"Not for much longer, if the jerk has his way."

Nine

Walking into Hallie's office, Reed stopped, looked around and shook his head.

"What's wrong?" she asked.

"Your office. It's...."

"Too female?"

"*Immaculate*," he said.

Hallie noticed a notepad, pen and a some lab gloves out of place. "It's not *that* neat."

"Your desk is uncluttered; mine looks like tornado damage. Your files are organized; mine require a posse to find them."

"Mr. Messy and Ms. Neat?" she said.

"Do opposites attract?"

"Perchance," she said, smiling and knowing she'd be attracted to Reed if spaghetti hung from his ears.

She checked a vase of fresh daisies beside a photo of her parents, brother and herself waving from a cruise ship. Behind the daisies was a Japanese painting, *Moonlight on the River Sheba*, a gift she cherished from her grandmother in Kyoto, whom she loved deeply, despite spending little time with her. An unread stack of *JAMA* magazines sat on the window ledge.

"The guy amazes me," she said, hurrying to her desk.

"T. Rex?"

"No. Ameen Howrani. Look—he's already reviewed the autopsies." She pointed to a stack of files on her chair, walked over and picked up the cover sheet and read it aloud.

> Hallie, Reed,
> I reviewed your autopsies. Nothing extraordinary, except for the unexplained hemolysis in Kyle's case and two others, for which I would hope the pathologists have since identified a cause.
> But in canvassing hospitals for similar SCD, I found

47

something that greatly concerns me. Review the new
autopsies here, then call me ASAP.

Ameen

Hallie felt her stomach tighten. Ameen Howrani *had* found something. As
she scanned his autopsy notes, she understood his concern. When she
finished, she stared at Reed a moment, trying to digest what she'd just read.
Quickly, she phoned Ameen and hit the speaker button.

Howrani picked up on the first ring.

"Ameen, it's Hallie and Reed."

"Listen, you may have uncovered something." His voice was tight with
emotion.

"What?"

"I'm not quite sure," Howrani said, "but I called some hospitals in the
Detroit metro area. Only one had a three-month rate of young SCD cases
marginally higher than normal."

"Statistically acceptable."

"Right. But Grand Blanc Valley Hospital is not. They have a significantly
higher number of young-adult-to-mid-age SCD cases. The hospital e-mailed
me some autopsies. You'll find them in my stack. Bottom line, the number
of SCD cases is *way* too high."

"How can you be sure?" Reed asked.

"Statistics. Roughly one percent of a city's population dies each year.
Grand Blanc township has a population of 33,250. That means roughly 333
people die annually."

"Do the statistics suggest what percent are young adults?" Hallie asked.

"Yes—and what percent of young adults die from SCD."

"What percent?"

"Less than one percent of all deaths."

"Which means," Hallie said, "that approximately three young adults in the
Grand Blanc area would die of SCD this year."

"Correct."

"So how many died?" Hallie asked.

"Seven."

"Maybe it's an exceptional year?" she said.

"An exceptional *three* months!"

"Seven SCDs in three months?" she whispered, feeling like she'd been
kicked in the stomach.

"Yes."

"At this rate," Reed said, "*twenty-eight* young people in that area will die from SCD in a year." The color drained from his face.

"That's the trend," Dr. Howrani said.

"Incredible," Hallie said, writing furiously on a pad. "Thank God it's just *this* hospital."

Ameen's silence terrified her.

"I wish it were," he said.

The hairs on the back of her neck began to rise. She didn't want to hear about more deaths.

"Flint General," Howrani said, "a few miles away, also has a significantly higher-than-normal incidence of young SCD."

Hallie leaned toward the speaker. "Ameen, as far as you know, is this problem confined to Kyle's area?"

"Yes. But we've only checked one other area. Detroit."

"How should we proceed?" Hallie asked.

"I'm canvassing other hospitals in the state," Howrani said. "We must quickly determine what's causing the SCD—natural causes, or, as you suggest, Reed, something or some person. I'll get back to you."

"Thank you, Ameen," she said, hanging up. Hallie realized the loud thumping in her ears was her pulse. Reed was writing down the SCD statistics, which he would give to Detective Beachum.

She rubbed her temples, shocked by what she'd just heard. What was causing so many young SCD deaths? "It's times like this when I wish my father were still here."

"He sort of is," Reed said, nodding toward her father's University of Michigan Medical School photo on the wall.

She turned and saw her dad's kind everything-will-be-fine eyes. As always, they calmed her.

"He taught me so much," she said, "About life, and being half-Asian in a Caucasian culture, and mostly to always pursue the truth." She wished Reed had known her father. They would have liked each other enormously.

"What would he have suggested now?" Reed asked.

Good question, she thought, looking back at the photo. "Dad would have said, 'Hallie, do your research first. Get the facts.'" Suddenly, her memory sparked. "That's it!"

"What's it?"

"Research," she said, standing and sliding her finger along the photo to a smiling young man with a thatch of unruly black hair. "Dr. Brendan Bryant, a brilliant researcher. My dad's best pal in med school."

"So...?"

"So," she said, flipping through her phone book and dialing, "maybe he's still at the Centers for Disease Control in Atlanta and will look at these cases."

Reed's eyes lit up. "The CDC could be our big break."

Hallie punched the speaker button and was immediately connected to Dr. Bryant's office. The phone rang several times and she feared she'd be tossed into voice mail.

"Brendan Bryant," said a raspy voice with the hint of an Irish brogue.

"Doctor Bryant, this is Hallie. Kyo's daughter."

"Saints preserve us! How grand to hear from you, Hallie. How are you?"

"Just fine, Doctor."

"And what might you be doing these days?"

"I'm a molecular geneticist working on Alzheimer's at Genetique Laboratories. We're affiliated with Detroit Memorial, a teaching hospital."

"Good for you. Your father would be very proud."

After more catching up, Hallie explained the circumstances of Kyle's death, his autopsy finding, the other SCD cases, what Dr. Ameen Howrani had discovered, and finally Kyle's warning of many deaths Friday.

When she finished, Doctor Bryant was silent so long she thought she might have been disconnected.

"Where are these autopsy reports?" Dr. Bryant finally asked.

"I have many of them."

"How fast can you get them to Atlanta?"

She glanced at her watch. "Tonight."

"Tonight?"

"Yes, I think there's a Delta flight in a while. Could you see me?"

"Of course, Hallie. Come right to the CDC. I'm working late."

They hung up.

Reed high-fived her over the desk. "If the CDC discovers something, Detective Beachum will *have* to investigate."

She nodded, then phoned Delta and booked an Atlanta flight departing in an hour and fifty minutes. "I have to leave now to make the flight."

"I'll drop you off."

"Can you come?"

He started to say yes, then seemed to remember something. "I'd like to, but I told Anne I'd drive up and see how she and the kids are doing, help with funeral arrangements."

"That's far more important."

Reed nodded, but his eyes suddenly grew serious.

"What's wrong?" she asked.

"Nothing."

"Tell me."

"You're traveling alone."

"Hey, I'm over twenty-one."

"So are the guys in the Lincoln."

She frowned. "But they aren't in Atlanta. Besides, Anne and the girls need you now."

He nodded, then looked outside. "I'm going to tell Anne what Kyle's last words were."

Hallie thought about how it would hurt Anne, but she knew it was the right thing to do. "It will upset her, but she deserves to know."

"And she might know if Kyle had any enemies."

Hallie nodded, then glanced at her wall clock. "We should leave now." She scooped up the stack of autopsy reports, then walked to a nearby closet and took out a small packed suitcase she kept for overnighters at the lab.

"If I miss the late flight back, I'll stay at the Marriott near the airport."

"I'll call you there or leave a message on your answering machine."

They left Genetique. As Reed drove onto I-94, Hallie phoned and made her Marriott reservation. She found herself checking for the blue Lincoln and studying any vehicle that got too close. She also noticed Reed checking cars.

Forty-five minutes later, Reed at her side, Hallie purchased her ticket in Detroit's massive, new 97-gate McNamara terminal. They walked to the passenger screening checkpoint, waited briefly, then kissed goodbye.

He stood there smiling as she moved through the metal detector and headed toward her gate with some end-of-day business travelers and noisy students.

She turned to wave back at him, but her view was blocked by a tall man with thick shoulders and sunglasses. The man had stood directly behind her in the ticket check-in line. He seemed to stare at her as though he knew her.

Is he following me? she wondered.

She was still wondering as he disappeared around a corner.

Ten

Reed drove into the familiar residential area southwest of Grand Blanc. He moved slowly past a row of distinguished Williamsburg Colonials and Tudors, then a neo-Mediterranean home with a red tile roof and attractive arched windows.

The upscale houses were tucked neatly into expensively landscaped lawns sprinkled with leaves. He noticed some beautiful mums flaunting their final splurge of yellow before winter shriveled them brown.

Ahead, a Chevy van pulled into a driveway and a soccer mom unloaded six giggling, blue-jerseyed pre-teen girls. As he passed a Lincoln Navigator, a Cadillac Escalade and a yellow Humvee, he wondered when exactly family station wagons had evolved into troop-carrying invasion vehicles.

Redwood decks jutted out behind many homes. Behind one, a domed swimming pool glowed in the darkness like a half-buried light bulb. Affluence. The good life.

Now, less good for Anne and her daughters.

Less good for me. Who ripped you away from us, Kyle?

Reed anguished over how to share Kyle's last words with Anne. It would cause her fresh pain, yet she had a right to know and would want to know. She might also know if Kyle had enemies. Yesterday, when he'd asked her whom Kyle had met Sunday, she didn't know. He'd ask her again today. Perhaps they'd find the man's name in Kyle's business agenda or notes.

He turned in at the red mailbox with the Mickey Mouse sticker, turned off the car and stared at Kyle's home. The attractive two-story house had wide, arched windows over the entrance. The doors opened onto a large gray slate foyer, which led to a living room and then to a cozy family room where Reed had enjoyed many good times. He watched a large maple leaf cartwheel past a Japanese yew and lodge beneath Kyle's office window.

Grabbing a large shopping bag, Reed stepped from the car and walked toward the door. He breathed in the rich, sweet aroma of burning leaves.

The front door opened and he saw Anne and the two young girls framed in soft light. Anne's appearance crushed the air from his lungs. She looked even more distraught than yesterday. Her pale face contrasted with the dark blue dress hanging loosely on her thin frame. Strands of honey-blond hair had fallen over her red, haunted eyes. The full weight of her loss was sinking in, and sinking her with it.

Clutching her hands were Haley and Tess, five and four. Their eyes, fortunately, did not yet register the depth of their loss. That pain, cruel and intense, would be felt later in their lives.

They all stared at him, wanting him to be Kyle.

He wanted to be Kyle for them, and he even felt a tinge of guilt that he wasn't.

His guilt quickly turned to anger, and he curled his hands into fists. He knew that however long it took, whatever the personal price, he would bring Kyle's killer to justice.

"Uncle Reed," Tess squealed, melting his rage.

She ran toward him, her auburn pigtails bouncing off her freckled cheeks. Beside her, Haley ran, smiling Kyle's smile.

"Look what I found for you guys." He swung the large shopping bag from behind his back and watched their furry little heads burrow inside.

"Freddie Teddy is for you, Tess. And Mr. Yappy is Haley's."

"Thanks, Uncle Reed," they shouted, scurrying into the house with the bag.

"You didn't have to do that," Anne said, forcing a smile.

"Toys B' Me."

He held her in his arms.

"You look a little better," he lied.

"I look awful," she said, leading him inside to the foyer. "But I can still whip up a good sandwich."

"Sounds great," he lied again, following her into the spacious kitchen with its white cabinets, built-in appliances and large antique French spice chest. They walked over to the circular glass table where Kyle and the family had always gathered for meals.

He stared at *the* chair—his brother's high-backed wooden chair—where Kyle had spooned green pea goop back into Tess's mouth, stuck a bandage on Haley's knee, talked and laughed. A good-times chair. Reed couldn't bring himself to sit in it.

Plopping down into the next chair, Reed watched Anne, her face as white as the cabinets, place dishes on the dark green marble island. The heavy scent of lilies hung in the air, reminding him of the funeral he dreaded tomorrow.

"It's nice of you to drive up, Reed. But we're managing. Really." Her pink-rimmed eyes suggested otherwise. "And we'll get through this, right?"

"Right. And if we don't, he'll come back and nag us."

She smiled, but sadness quickly reclaimed her face.

He reached over, took her hand and guided her into Kyle's chair. "After Mom and Dad died," he said, "Kyle and I found only two things helped."

"What?"

"Time. And more time." He didn't mention that even today, time had only made the loss somewhat more bearable.

She stared back and nodded. "Time ... I've got."

She stood, opened the refrigerator, pulled out a tray of chicken and roastbeef sandwiches and brought them over to the table. Beside it, she placed a large serving tray of kosher dill pickles, Dijon mustard, mayonnaise, sliced onions and juicy tomatoes. The scent of fresh food awakened his taste buds and he could hear his brother demanding he eat. He loaded up a chicken sandwich and bit into it. It tasted delicious.

"How about a beer?"

"Sounds great."

"In the can?"

"No, I'll drink it here."

She smiled, her eyes flashing almost normal, and handed him a can of Fosters. "Just like your brother. Never let an entendre go undoubled."

"Curse of the Kincaids."

They talked about the funeral arrangements, trying to adjust to life without Kyle, the girls, her real estate career. Talking seemed to distract her, and gradually her eyes brightened and her natural confidence surfaced a bit. *Now might be the time,* he thought. He took a long swig of beer, fortifying himself.

"Anne, it's amazing, but *everyone* I talked to really liked Kyle."

She nodded. "For him, making friends was like breathing."

"But everybody has some enemies."

"Kyle did."

Reed's grip tightened on the beer can. "Who?"

"The newsboy," she said. "The kid always tosses the paper near the sprinkler. And we've told him at least ten times."

Reed relaxed. "Did Kyle have any serious enemies?"

She toyed with the corner of a napkin. "Serious? None that I'm aware of."

"No one he seemed especially worried about recently?"

"No." Her eyes locked on Reed's. "Why do you ask?"

Now or never, he knew. He chugged down more beer. "Anne, I have something to tell you."

She stared at him oddly, as though part of her didn't want to hear, then walked over and eased back into Kyle's chair.

Reed began telling her Kyle's final words and watched her eyes glaze over, then moisten with fresh pain. He hated the tear sliding down her cheek, hated that he'd caused it, hated Kyle's killer. When he finished, he held Anne's hands and they sat in silence for several moments. The kids' voices filtered in from the other room.

She blinked and whispered, "Kyle believed he was murdered?"

He nodded.

"Do you believe him?"

"Yes."

She stared at him. "But he *was* sick Saturday and Sunday morning, and the autopsy said heart attack."

"I think someone *caused* his sickness and heart attack."

A slow red mounted her cheeks and her lower lip began to quiver. She stood and paced beside the counter, her eyes filling. "Reed, my God, I can't believe this. Why didn't you tell me?"

"Anne, I thought the shock of his death, the funeral, the girls … you had so much to deal with."

She stared through him for several long moments. Finally, she nodded that she understood. Reed breathed out in relief.

"I also wanted to give you *proof*!" he said.

"Have you found proof?"

"No."

"Have the police?"

"They're not investigating his death."

"What?" She stopped pacing and turned toward him, her eyes filled with something approaching outrage.

"They need evidence first. I'm trying to find some."

"I'll help," she said with an icy determination he'd never heard from her before. Clearly, some inner switch had just transformed her grief into full-blown revenge. Kyle's killer didn't know it yet, but he had another angry, tenacious adversary.

"I hope you can, Anne."

"But how?"

"Were you able to remember the name of the person Kyle met Sunday?"

She closed her eyes a moment. "No. But maybe the name's in his planner." She grabbed the planner from the spice chest and flipped to Sunday, November 9. The page was blank. They flipped through the past three months and found only meeting times and names of attendees.

"Was Kyle having serious difficulty with anyone at work?"

She paused. "Not that he mentioned."

"Kyle told me he kept notes on his laptop."

"He did. It's in the study."

They hurried down the hallway and stepped into the small study. Instantly, Reed felt his brother's presence. The room was dominated by an antique burled elm desk stacked with files and huge bookshelves crammed with chemistry books, pharmacognosy periodicals, biochemical and medical magazines. The smell of books reminded him of Kyle.

On a shelf he saw a photo of Kyle and him, laughing, ages nineteen and sixteen, with their parents at Mackinac Island in a horse-drawn carriage in front of the Grand Hotel. They were laughing. A terrific family vacation. Their last one together.

They searched the desk files and found no hint that Kyle was worried about anyone.

"Where's the laptop?" Reed asked.

"Far from tiny fingers." She walked to a nearby closet shelf, lifted Kyle's bulky green sweater and slid out an HP laptop. "Kyle found Tess sticking Old Maid cards in the disk slot. Thank God it still works."

She flipped the laptop open, turned it on and sat down. The screen booted up to the prompt. She typed in a command, the computer cranked into the software program, and then flashed: *Enter Password.*

Reed felt his neck muscles tighten.

"Don't worry," she said. "The password is 'wombat.'"

He relaxed, thinking only his brother would dream up 'wombat.'

She typed in the letters and pressed Enter.

The screen flashed *Invalid Password.*

Reed's palms grew moist. Perhaps she'd typed it wrong.

"I'm sure it's 'wombat,'" Anne said, staring at the screen. She tried again. *Invalid Password.*

She tried it with all caps.

Invalid Password.

"He changed the password. We're blocked," Reed said, a knot forming in his throat.

They tried the kids' names, birthdays, plus a long list of possible passwords for the next five minutes. None worked. He remembered that there were ways to circumvent passwords and phoned his agency computer guru. The guru's voice mail said he was hiking in California. Reed left a message to call.

"Sometimes," Anne said, "Kyle took the laptop to work. Maybe Meg, his assistant, knows the password?" She flipped the address file to Meg Haney's number and started to dial.

"Wait," Reed said.

Her hand froze on the phone and she looked at him, puzzled. "What's wrong?"

"Meg seems very loyal to Kyle," he said, "but ... you never know."

Anne stared back. "Meg's like family. Kyle trusted her completely. She was devoted to him."

Reed recalled Meg's tears and obvious sorrow at the funeral home. "Okay, but she should not mention this to anyone."

Anne nodded, dialed and hit the speaker button. Meg Haney picked up on the third ring.

"Meg, it's Anne. I'm here with Reed, Kyle's brother. We wondered if Kyle told you the new password for his laptop?"

"No. But his office computer password is CHEMGUY. Maybe it's the same."

"'CHEMGUY,' one word, all caps?"

"Yes."

Reed typed it and hit Enter. The screen flashed—*Invalid Password*. His knuckles whitened on the laptop. "Maybe his office computer can tell us something."

"Meg," Anne said, "Reed needs to check Kyle's office computer files. It's very important. Can you meet him there now?"

"Well, sure, but why check Kyle's *office* computer?"

Reed nodded for Anne to explain. "Meg, this will sound unbelievable, and you should not mention it to anyone, but Kyle may have been...." Her eyes teared up and she took a deep breath. "Kyle may have been ... murdered."

Meg Haney gasped. "My God, Anne. What are you saying? Who on earth would want to murder Kyle?"

"We're trying to find out."

Haney began breathing rapidly. "This is just so incredible. Reed, I'll meet you in fifteen minutes in the lobby of Dunne's Administration Building. We can go through Kyle's documents. Some deal with confidential new products. I'll have to review those myself."

"I understand," Reed said.

They hung up and Reed faced Anne. "I'll call when we're finished."

"I'll be waiting," Anne said, her eyes alive with new purpose.

As they walked toward the front door, the girls rushed from the family room and latched on to his legs like monkeys.

"Don't go, Uncle Reed," they pleaded, as he stiff-legged them to the door.

"I have to," he said, scooping them up into his arms. Two wet kisses slid into his ears. He hugged Anne for several moments, then headed out into the cool night air.

Driving away, he waved back at them in the doorway and blinked moist eyes.

For the first time in his life he wanted to kill someone.

Eleven

Hallie bounced hard as her taxi hit a pothole on Clifton Road. Her burly, dark-haired driver apologized and slowed down as he passed the parking decks of Emory University.

She was impressed with Atlanta's sprawling Federal Centers for Disease Control and Prevention complex. She recalled that over one hundred institutions in the area focused on biomedical research and technology and that nearly five thousand medical specialists worked in the CDC Atlanta facilities—more medical expertise in one location than anywhere else in the world. The serene, academic surroundings gave her a needed sense of calm.

They also gave her hope. Behind the brick walls, CDC medical professionals performed miracles, prevented outbreaks of deadly diseases and contained epidemics that threatened Americans and the peoples of the world. And the CDC often did it with scanty information.

I have one scanty fact, she thought. A high incidence of SCD cases in a small area of Michigan. Kyle's claim of poisoning, his warning about Friday and a link between Kyle's death and the Lincoln were all unsubstantiated. Somehow, she had to persuade Dr. Bryant that the SCD deaths alone warranted CDC investigation.

She paid the driver and stepped from the taxi. A mild breeze swept her hair back. Beside her, another taxi rolled to a stop. As she turned toward it, the heavyset passenger buried his face in the *Racing News.*

She walked past thick concrete barriers, obviously an anti-terrorism security blockade, then a large white sign with *C D C* in blue letters.

Inside, she walked over to the receptionist, a muscular blond guard with a sparkling diamond ear stud. He looked up from a *Gray's Anatomy* medical schoolbook and smiled at her. She was surprised to see the word *chowa,* Japanese for 'harmony,' tattooed on his bulging forearm.

On a whim, she said in Japanese that she was here to see Dr. Brendan Bryant. In flawless Japanese, he asked her to sign in.

"I'm impressed," she said in English, smiling.

"Tokyo-born and raised. Papa-san in Navy." He smiled and handed her a visitor's badge with her name already on it. "Doctor Bryant pre-approved your visit."

She took it and put it on. "Thank you."

He then inspected her overnight bag and briefcase and swept her with a metal detector. "Your escort will be right down. Please have a seat," he said in Japanese.

She thanked him, walked through the tastefully decorated lobby and settled into a large, comfortable brown chair. She thought back to her three visits to Japan as a teenager. Brief family trips for her father's medical conferences. She'd enjoyed the trips immensely, but always wished she could have stayed much longer, absorbing the richness and warmth of her Japanese heritage. It was a part of her she wanted to know more about. Now, she wondered sadly if she'd ever get the chance.

Suddenly, a dark shadow crept onto her lap. Looking up, she saw a towering man with tribal scars on his ebony cheeks. His way-too-short white medical coat stretched over a skinny six-foot-nine frame. He smiled down at her, then introduced himself.

"Dr. Fred Baraza. Out of Uganda."

"Dr. Hallie Mara. Out of Michigan."

Smiling, they shook hands. As they walked down long, clean corridors and elevated walkways, she couldn't help but notice numerous video cameras. "What's with all the TV monitors and motion sensors?"

"Bioterrorists. They'd love to snatch our nasty little bugs."

A chill run down her spine.

Moments later, Dr. Baraza led her into Dr. Bryant's office and bid her a good day. Dr. Bryant was on the phone, speaking French. When he saw her, his face brightened and gestured her into the leather chair opposite his desk. His smoke-gray eyes, as gentle as ever, were still framed by bushy black brows. But his thatch of unruly black hair was now unruly white and scrunched oddly to the side like he'd been wearing a helmet.

He toyed with an old, empty pipe shaped like a walrus head. The head balanced itself on two long white tusks. Gazing up at the wall photos, she saw Dr. Bryant with a group of skeletal children in an African jungle hospital. To its right was the University of Michigan Med School photo with Bryant and her father.

"*Merci, et à demain, Chloé,*" Dr. Bryant said, hanging up and smiling. "Hallie, look at you." He came around the side of the desk and swept her into a gigantic hug. "Thank goodness you're a personal friend."

"Why?"

"Because I can tell you how absolutely beautiful you are without getting my derrière litigated."

She felt herself blush as they sat down.

"You're as lovely as your mother."

"Thank you, Doctor Bryant," she said, thinking no one could be as lovely as her mother, whom she'd forgotten to phone about Atlanta. She'd call her later.

Bryant glanced up at the med school photo and his eyes dimmed. "I still miss him, too."

"It's hard not to miss a perfect father," she said.

"With the imperfect gene...."

She nodded, remembering how her dad had grown progressively weaker, how his muscles withered, eyelids drooped, speech slurred, lungs and heart stopped one day, and how his death from Lou Gehrig's disease had devastated her.

"So now you're a molecular geneticist, studying the little chromosomes and their naughty genes." He placed his fountain pen on a yellow legal pad and leaned forward. "Let's have a look at your strange SCD cases."

She handed him the files. Perching bifocals on his nose, he began reading. As he did, he jotted notes. For several minutes he studied the autopsies and asked her questions she was able to answer. He flipped rapidly from one report to another, then back again. Finally, he closed the last report, took a deep breath and stared out the window for several moments.

"Most interesting," he said, fingering his walrus pipe. "But we don't have much to hang our hats on, do we?"

"No."

"Nothing medically that even remotely suggests death from unnatural causes. No forensic evidence."

"None," she said. Her stomach clenched as she realized he couldn't commit CDC resources without proof of a *serious* health concern. She'd wasted his time. Reed would be devastated.

"Yet," he said, tapping the autopsies with his pipe, "there's something about these cases, taken as a whole, that feels wrong."

Her stomach unclenched a bit.

"Your suspicions are not without foundation," he continued. "The very high incidence of SCD in this small area in a short period of time, the victims' apparent lack of cardiovascular disease, and their relatively young age concern me."

"And they were found without extensive searching," she added.

"Exactly," he said, peering over his bifocals at an autopsy. "One puzzle, though."

"What's that?"

"The hemolysis in Kyle Kinkaid's autopsy and some others."

"Kyle's pathologist was puzzled by it too."

The phone rang and Dr. Bryant picked up. She watched his eyes narrow as he gnawed on his pipe stem. He nodded slowly, listened some more, thanked the caller, then hung up and looked at her. "Some related news. After you phoned me, we asked fourteen major metro hospitals nationwide to take a cursory look at recent young SCD cases."

Hallie held her breath, praying the problem was not national.

"In these hospitals," Bryant said, "SCD among young adults is well within statistical norms."

She felt her neck muscles relax.

"Which suggests," Doctor Bryant continued, "that this high incidence of SCD might be confined to the thumb area of Michigan." Bryant doodled on his paper, then turned his eyes toward her. "Now, you mentioned that this Kyle Kincaid, as he was dying, said someone poisoned him?"

"Yes."

"And that many more people will die Friday?"

She nodded.

"Do you believe him?"

"I believe *he* believed it. But as you see, the autopsy doesn't support poisoning."

Bryant nodded and glanced back at Kyle's autopsy. "Have the police found any hint of murder? Or any link between these cases?"

"No. The police won't investigate until they have evidence of foul play."

"Ah, I see." Dougal Bryant stared out his window again and rubbed his pipe stem along his lower lip. "Well, clearly, Hallie, this abnormally high incidence of SCD cases warrants further examination. However, proving someone is causing them is another matter. I'll phone our CDC Michigan representative and ask her to inform the Michigan Department of Health. I'll also assign one of our best young medical officers to work with you."

"Thank you, Doctor." She felt like sandbags had been yanked from her shoulders.

He dialed a number and asked someone to come to his office. One minute later, the door opened and Bryant introduced her to Dr. Kundan Shah, a short, thin man, about thirty-five. Large, intelligent eyes and a thick mustache dominated his handsome face. His thick black hair was combed back off his high forehead, giving him a scholarly appearance. A loose-fitting tan shirt and slacks complimented his honey-brown skin.

As Dr. Bryant explained the SCD cases, Dr. Shah made notes and seemed eager to help. Hallie glanced at her watch and realized she'd missed the last flight to Detroit.

"Hallie," Dr. Bryant said, "why don't you join Margaret and me for dinner with some friends. Margaret would love to see you. You could even stay with us. We have lots of room."

"That's very kind, Dr. Bryant, but I've reserved a room at the airport Marriott. And I really have to finish some paperwork tonight. Also, my flight leaves at 6:45 a.m."

"I'll try to get on that flight," Dr. Shah said.

"Very well, then," Dr. Bryant said. "You youngsters go solve this problem. It gives me an uneasy feeling. Call me the instant you learn anything."

Dr. Bryant escorted her back to the lobby, where she thanked him again and caught a taxi. Twenty-five minutes later, it pulled up in front of the tall, gray Marriott. She paid the driver, grabbed her overnight bag and copies of the autopsies, and walked toward the entrance. The night air felt much cooler. Overhead a 747 roared into the night sky.

She passed a middle-aged couple wearing formal attire and found herself enveloped with the pleasant scent of perfume and cologne. The woman's velvet dress, an attractive full-length plum color, had a fitted top and an angular hem that hung down one side. She looked stunning. Hallie couldn't remember the last time she'd gone to a formal social event. Before Reed, the highlight of her social week was shopping at Kroger on Singles' Night.

Reed would be delighted the CDC would look into the cases, and he'd use the news to persuade Detective Beachum to investigate. What if, she wondered, Dr. Shah's investigation determined that Kyle *had* in fact been murdered, that Reed had been right all along?

She knew she sometimes relied too heavily on scientific evidence. Her training had taught her to base decisions on medical facts. But facts, like autopsies, could be incomplete, or flawed, or misleading. Perhaps an unknown new poison had killed Kyle and conveniently decomposed in his body, leaving no trace. And maybe the Lincoln thugs *were* linked to his death.

Kyle's eyes suddenly flashed in her mind. He was obviously terrified of dying. But he had seemed more terrified of what would happen Friday.

Shivering, she walked into the hotel lobby. As she turned toward the reception desk, she froze.

It's David! she thought, staring at the tall, handsome businessman at the newsstand. *It's him!*

Then he turned and she saw his eyes were brown. Not David. But the similarity was astonishing.

David Harrington II. Her mind raced back to their wonderful relationship and their painful split. A split initiated by his Boston Brahmin mother. The woman had threatened to disinherit him if he dared bring "that Oriental girl into our family. Surely, David, you can find someone more like us," mom had demanded. At first, David had been outraged by mommy dearest's ultimatum. But eventually he'd caved in to her threats. Hallie had never felt so devastated. She'd cared a great deal for him, thought she loved him. Retrospectively, it was better to discover David's silver umbilical cord *before* she considered marriage. Now, she viewed the David relationship as one of life's tough lessons. She also saw it as just one more anti-Asian sword to swallow.

Now, she watched the David-clone straighten his Armani suit, enter an elevator and disappear, just like the original.

* * *

From his cab window, Luca Corsa had watched Dr. Hallie Mara walk into the hotel. Classy chick. The way her firm ass moved with that no-bullshit stroll. Nice, long legs, too. Real wraparounds.

She reminded him of Mai Dinh. Poor Mai Dinh. Frankie Vecchio brings her back from Saigon, then last year he trades her in for a Vegas bimbo with big boobs and an IQ you could count on your thumbs. Hey Luca, he says, take Mai Dinh for a real long swim. Luca didn't want to. He'd kind of liked Mai Dinh himself and had even thought about keeping her. But nobody double-crossed Frankie Vecchio. And ten grand's better than ten holes in your head. Far as Corsa knew, Mai Dinh was still tied to the Mack truck axle two hundred feet under Lake Huron twenty miles off Grand Bend.

Corsa hurried into the lobby, stood near some businessmen, and watched Hallie check in. She signed the card, then followed a zitty-faced bellhop carrying her bag into an elevator.

Corsa walked over to the young, blonde receptionist. Cute face, big melons. Nice package.

"Hi there. Can you tell me if Doctor Hallie Mara has checked in yet? She just left something at the CDC."

The receptionist glanced toward the elevator. "Oh, you just missed her, sir. She's going up to her room now."

"What room's that?"

"Sorry, sir, we can't give out that information."

"Can I call her room?"

"Certainly. The house phone's on that counter. Just ask the operator to ring her room."

"Thanks. By the way, could I see that copy of *USA Today* on that table there?"

"Of course, sir."

As she turned and walked toward the paper, Corsa glanced down at Hallie's registration card and saw Room 607.

The receptionist handed Corsa the newspaper. "Keep it with our compliments, sir."

"Gee, thanks."

Corsa strolled over to the house phone and pretended to call the operator. Quickly, he hung up and entered an elevator. He got off on the sixth floor and walked toward her room. As the bellhop came out, Corsa strolled by, glimpsing the layout of the room and the door lock. Piece of cake.

He walked down to an exit stairwell, flipped open his cell phone and dialed. "She just checked in the Marriott."

"She still have the files she had on the plane?"

"Yeah."

"Take them."

"Right."

"And handle her."

"With pleasure."

Twelve

"Thanks for coming right over, Meg," Reed said, hurrying with Meg Haney down a long, gleaming hallway in Dunne Corporation. He hoped Kyle's files would uncover some hint of who was behind his death, or at least point them in a direction.

"I couldn't get here fast enough," she said, scooching horn-rimmed glasses up her nose. Her brown eyes looked puffy and red from crying.

As they walked, Reed listened to Meg's left tennis shoe squeak with each step. Her slight limp, which Kyle had told him was sustained in a mountain biking accident, didn't slow her one bit. She looked hell-bent on identifying Kyle's murderer, and if she got the chance, maybe doing him some serious bodily harm.

Fluorescent ceiling lamps highlighted her thick, reddish hair. Her blue sweatshirt portrayed Beethoven's stern face, but her ample breasts had curled the maestro's lips into a raunchy grin. Despite Meg's full figure, which filled every stitch of her Levi's, Reed found her very attractive. His brother had considered her a terrific friend and by far his most capable assistant ever.

"It's just so unbelievable, Reed. Everyone worshiped Kyle."

"With one notable exception."

She stared at him, then nodded, anger flashing in her eyes.

They hurried past a massive wall design of the periodic table of chemical elements in red, green, gray, yellow and purple groups, then past large oil portraits of Madame Curie, Albert Einstein, Jonas Salk and others. Reed wondered if Kyle would have ever discovered something that warranted his portrait on the wall.

They stepped onto an airport-like moving walkway that whisked them down a long, narrow hallway. Thirty seconds later, they stepped into the Research and Development department. Meg ushered him toward a door name-tagged *Kyle Kincaid.*

"I haven't touched anything," she said, moving into Kyle's office. "It hurts even to come in here." She blew her nose with a damp Kleenex.

His office looked the same to Reed. Bookshelves with textbooks and

66

reference volumes, walls with awards and plaques, a desk with neat files and computer, a connecting laboratory with computer screens glowing in the dark.

Reed's eyes moistened when he saw the photo of Kyle and him in sweat-drenched jogging clothes holding Evian bottles and a six-pack of Bud. They'd just run the twenty-six-mile Detroit Marathon and achieved their goal: they were still alive.

"Meg, was Kyle in any kind of political battle here?"

"Kyle was above office politics."

"That's not really possible, is it?"

"It was with Kyle's talent."

Reed nodded. "That kind of talent can breed jealousy."

"Everyone was jealous," she said, gesturing toward the other offices. "But not enough to kill him. Kyle always spread the glory, always said his discoveries were team breakthroughs."

She sat at Kyle's computer and flipped the power on. The screen sprang to life and booted up to the words, *Enter Password.* She typed "CHEMGUY" and pushed Enter. Instantly the computer cranked itself into a main list of seven subdirectories that appeared to contain at least two hundred documents. Reed relaxed a bit.

Meg pushed Enter to retrieve a recent document. He listened to the computer crank it up. The cranking stopped—and they found themselves staring at a blank white screen.

Reed's pulse kicked up a notch.

"That's strange," Meg said, fingering her turquoise bracelet.

"Why?"

"Kyle worked on this document last week."

"Maybe he deleted it."

"No. It's important."

"Try another."

She retrieved a second document.

Reed leaned forward and watched another empty white screen emerge. Three more documents came up blank. He felt his throat go dry.

"This is insane," she said. "I pulled up two of these documents on *this* computer yesterday!"

"Did your network crash today?"

"No."

"Virus problems?"

"Not as of six o'clock this evening." Puzzled, she stared at the screen.

Reed wondered if a Dunne computer expert might be able to retrieve the lost files.

"Wait!" Meg said, hurrying into her adjoining office. She sat down and flipped on her computer.

"Backup files?" Reed asked, pulling a chair over.

"Yes. Our network automatically copies all files. I can access Kyle's backups from here."

Reed's hope resurfaced.

She retrieved one of her own memos and Reed relaxed as several beautiful paragraphs popped onto the screen. Then, using Kyle's password, Meg entered the company network and entered his backup files.

She brought up a document.

Blank.

Reed slumped down in his chair. She tried four more. Empty white screens. He realized what had happened and felt a dull pain spread across his forehead.

Meg leaned forward, confused. "This is not possible. His backup files have also been destroyed by something."

"By some*one*."

She stared at him.

"Who has access to Kyle's computer files?" he asked.

"Only Kyle and me."

"Who can enter the Research Department?"

"Only those with this pass." She held up a red and green pass with her photo and Dunne Corporation logo. Reed realized that any ad agency art director could duplicate it in twenty minutes.

"The pass is mandatory," she said. "And the computers are well protected."

"Not for a hacker."

"But we have excellent firewalls."

"So did the Pentagon."

Her face turned chalk-white, then she nodded. "I have to inform computer security."

"And I have to inform Detective Beachum."

As Meg called security, Reed walked into Kyle's office and phoned Beachum. The desk officer told him that Beachum was out and not answering his home phone or pager. Reed asked her to have Beachum call him, then hung up.

Frustrated, he walked back into Meg's office and looked out the window. Heavy clouds swept across the night sky. The wind whipsawed some maple trees near a large water fountain. "I think Kyle kept personal notes on his laptop at home."

Meg nodded.

"I'll have to find a way around his password tomorrow."

"And I'll see if anyone else here lost their files."

"Be careful, Meg. Don't mention Kyle's last words. You could be talking to his killer."

She stared at him a moment. "I'll be careful."

Minutes later, they signed out of the lobby and walked toward their cars. Something popped loudly behind them. Reed spun around and saw a line of international flags snapping in the wind. Since the Lincoln, every sharp sound spooked him.

As they neared their vehicles, he watched a leaf swirl above the fountain where cascading water slammed it hard into the water. He felt like the leaf; his hope kept getting lifted, doused and slammed down.

He walked Meg to her car, thanked her, watched her drive off, then got in his car.

Later, on I-75, he phoned Anne. He explained that Kyle's computer files had been deleted and asked her to hide Kyle's laptop in a safe place. Tomorrow, after the funeral, they would try to get around the password.

Glancing at his watch, he realized Hallie had probably missed the last flight home. He called information for the Atlanta airport Marriott and they put the call through. The hotel operator said Hallie had not checked in.

He hung up and stared into his headlight shafts. Black clouds hung low in the night sky. Thunder popped loud, reminding him of the gunshot at the 7-Eleven yesterday.

Again, he wondered—did one of those hitmen follow her to Atlanta?

* * *

In his underground laboratory he stared at the fascinating liquid in the enclosed glass bottle. The liquid fascinated and terrified him.

Just one pint of Botulism Type A, if properly dispersed into a city's water system, under certain circumstances, would easily kill a million or more people.

Next week, he would ship a twenty-five-gallon drum of Type A to his special customer, an al Qaeda unit in Yemen. What astounded him was *how* the al Qaeda group planned to use the Type A. Against their *own people* ... at *The Hajj*, in Mecca, the holiest Muslim site. The end, they said, justifies the means.

The end was obvious: dethrone the Saudi King and his royal family and replace them with a fundamentalist Islamic government.

Go right ahead, he thought as he placed the glass vial in a rack, leaned back in his chair and envisioned what would soon happen in Saudi Arabia.

Summer ... the *Hajj* ... hundreds of thousands of Muslim pilgrims, crammed together, circling the sacred *Kaaba* seven times, perspiring in the blazing sun, accepting free bottles of *Jedda Gold Water* from smiling al Qaeda operatives, guzzling down the cool, refreshing water that would end their lives....

Hours later they would feel weak and dizzy. Their vision would blur, their mouth would dry out like cotton, their lungs would cease to breathe.

Then, mercifully, death would take them.

30,000 bottles of water. 30,000 corpses.

Not bad ....

But only half as many as I will harvest here in America Friday.

Thirteen

Hallie stifled a big yawn as she underlined a report at her hotel room desk. Stretching, she noticed she'd also underlined the sleeve of her tatty nightgown. Loose threads hung from it like spaghetti. *My Shroud of Turin,* she thought, noticing a wide split near the shoulder.

She turned back to the report. It was encouraging. The results confirmed that certain cholesterol-lowering drugs might reduce the risk of the Alzheimer's disease. It also found that the antibody m2666 almost immediately improved memory in mice. *And maybe humans soon,* she prayed. Hopeful news.

The kind of hopeful news Rex Randall was hammering her for. Something he could sell in Tuesday's meeting with Bio-Chron.

Sorry, Rex, but my lab reports, while encouraging, don't support selling anything yet. They support only more research. Which would further infuriate T. Rex. He'd already left three voice mails demanding she report to his office. She left him one, explaining she'd see him first thing in the morning.

The phone rang and she grabbed it, hoping it was Reed. She wanted to tell him about the CDC's decision to investigate. Earlier, when she'd tried to leave a message, his cell and home phone voice mail were full, probably crammed with condolences for Kyle.

"Hello?" she said.

No response. She heard faint music, the soft clink of glass. Perhaps he was calling from a restaurant.

"Reed?"

Still no one spoke. Another clink of glass. The ding of a cash register. Did she hear breathing ... soft, raspy? Was she imagining it? She pressed her ear harder against the receiver.

There, she did hear breathing now, muted and deep.

"Who is this?" she asked.

Silence.

She felt the hairs on the back of her neck rise. "Can you hear me?"

Nothing.

She waited a few seconds, then hung up. Did a technical malfunction prevent the caller from hearing her? Was it a cell phone glitch? She'd experienced those problems before.

Or was someone trying to frighten her?

Shivering, she pulled her nightgown closer around her and continued reading the report. Minutes later, she felt her eyelids growing heavy. She yawned, lay down on the bed and opened another report. But soon her eyelids were drooping and jerking open and drooping....

Thump!

She bolted awake.

Thump thump thump!

Someone at the door.

She sat up. "Who is it?" She cleared her throat, wondering who would possibly disturb her at this late hour. Did they need her for a medical emergency?

"Room delivery, ma'am." A deep, male voice.

She walked to the door, questioning why they hadn't called her first. Perhaps her phone was still not working correctly.

"Special order, ma'am. Flowers. The sender insisted we bring 'em to you tonight."

"Flowers?"

"Yes, ma'am."

Only Reed and Dr. Bryant knew she was here. They had no reason to send her flowers, unless they were just being nice, which came naturally to them.

"Long box, ma'am. Pretty roses, I bet."

She squinted through the peephole and saw a long white flower box in the hands of a large man. He wore a Marriott room service jacket and rose-tinted glasses. The peephole lens made the man's neck mushroom out of his thick shoulders.

"The desk called earlier, ma'am, but your phone wasn't workin'."

So they couldn't hear me, she realized.

She flipped back the dead bolt, cracked open the door, started to unhook the chain, then something told her to leave it on a moment. Inching the door open, she got a better look at the man. He was huge, with blond hair and a beard. His neck arteries bulged like computer cables and his shoulders nearly split the seams of the Marriott coat. His fat fish lips bent in a strange smile. And even though there was no way she could have seen the man before, his dark eyes seemed vaguely familiar.

His gaze slid to her nightgown and lingered a bit. She inched back.

"Who sent them?" she asked.

He looked at a small white card. "Ah … says here, 'A secret admirer.'"

A secret admirer? Atlanta? Midnight? This was all wrong. "I think there's been a mistake. I don't have a secret admirer in Atlanta."

"Says here, 'Deliver to Doctor Hallie Mara.'"

She was puzzled. Reed and Dougal Bryant wouldn't use "Doctor." Curiosity nibbled at her. She should just open the damn door, take the flowers and see who sent them. She reached to take the chain off, then paused again.

"Is there a card inside?" she asked.

"Ah … lemme see." He opened the box and fingered through the folds of green paper. "No card, ma'am."

Probably beneath the flowers, she thought. She started to unlock the chain, then paused as she heard an airplane roar overhead. "Oh, I just realized…."

"What's that, ma'am?"

"I'm catching a plane in a few hours. The flowers will just die. Please keep them yourself. Or give them to a charity."

This seemed to confuse him. "Ah … okay. Just sign this here Refused Form. That way, I don't get in no trouble."

"Sure," she said, happy to relieve her growing uneasiness with the man and get back to bed.

He held the pen just beyond the crack in the door. Keeping the chain on, she opened the door another inch and reached for the pen.

Suddenly, his meaty fingers grabbed her wrist.

"What are you doing?" She tried to yank her arm back, but his fingers dug in.

His eyes crazed, he slammed his massive body against the door and the chain's hinges loosened.

"Stop!"

Again the man's thick shoulder pounded into the door, popping off three hinges. Only one remained.

As she started to scream, the door smashed against her chest, crushing the wind from her and knocking her back into the closet. She hit some wood hangers and fell in the corner, dazed. The man's shadow moved into the room.

My God, he's got a gun! With a silencer!

Her mind racing, she grabbed a heavy wooden hanger and held her breath. Her heart jackhammered into her throat.

Slowly, the man leaned into the dark closet.

73

She smashed the wood hanger hard against his head.

"Bitch!" he shouted, jerking back.

She hadn't even dazed him. His hands groped angrily and he caught her arm. She swung the hanger again, but it bounced off his muscular bicep. She kicked for his groin, missed.

Yanking hard, she ripped free, leaving the sleeve of her tattered nightgown in his fingers.

Confused, he looked down at the sleeve.

She slammed the closet door hard against his shoulder, jumped into the bathroom and locked the door.

"Help!" she screamed.

He fired three muffled shots. Chunks of the bathroom door sprayed splinters into her neck. She groaned, pretending to be shot, then stepped into the tub and flattened her back against the wall.

Two more bullets blasted through the door. She moaned again and remained silent, praying he'd leave if he thought he'd hit her. Another bullet blew out a chunk near the doorknob.

Slowly, the knob started to turn.

Fourteen

Rain, baby, rain! Reed thought as he stared through his rain-slick windshield into the hazy shafts of his headlights. The rain pounded the roof like pebbles.

A typhoon couldn't dampen his spirits. He had important news for Woody Beachum: Kyle's computer files had been wiped out as deliberately as the attempt by the men in the Lincoln to wipe out Hallie and him. Beachum would have to see some connection to Kyle's death, or at least be suspicious enough to initiate a preliminary investigation.

Unfortunately, Beachum wasn't answering his home phone.

Reed drove past a big vehicle hauler that sprayed up thick sheets of water onto the windshield.

Wondering if Hallie was successful at the CDC, he called the Marriott and asked for her room.

"Sorry, sir," the operator said, "we have no one registered under that name."

"When she checks in, please have her call Reed's cell phone."

"Sir, we show no reservation in her name."

"Are you certain?"

"Yes, sir."

"This is the Marriott near the airport?"

"Yes, sir."

"She made her reservation this evening," Reed said.

"Our computer shows all reservations made within the last few minutes," the operator said with pride. "But we have a lot of vacancies. When she checks in, we'll give her your message."

"Thank you." He hung up, wondering why her reservation hadn't shown up.

As he climbed a long, gradual hill, he realized Hallie and Dr. Bryant might be working late at the CDC. He called information, got the CDC number and was connected.

"Centers for Disease Control and Prevention," said a deep voice with a southern accent.

"I'm looking for Dr. Hallie Mara. She visited Dr. Bryant this evening."

"Mahrah?"

"M-a-r-a."

"Just a moment, please." Reed heard pages flipping. "She signed out about two hours ago."

Reed grew concerned. "How long from the CDC to the airport area?"

"At that time, reckon on thirty minutes or so."

She should have checked into the hotel by now, Reed realized.

"Is Dr. Bryant still there?"

"He left about the same time."

"Can you give me Dr. Bryant's home phone number?"

"Gotta be a medical emergency."

Reed's knuckles whitened on the steering wheel. "I've got a very serious medical situation here."

The man sighed. "All right then."

He gave Reed the number. Reed dialed it. After about fifteen rings, Reed felt heat crawl up his face. The good doctor didn't believe in answering machines. Reed thumped the phone down on the seat. Another dead end.

Okay, what are the possibilities? he wondered. She and Bryant had gone to verify something in a lab. Or they were consulting with a colleague. Or they were having dinner. Or she wasn't near a phone. Or she was in a taxi heading to the Marriott.

Or … she's in danger.

Fifteen

Her heart pounding, Hallie's eyes remained riveted on the doorknob. It had *held* despite the last shot. But for some reason, he hadn't fired into the door in thirty seconds.

Has he left?

Does he think I'm dead?

Suddenly, she heard the sound of a new clip being shoved into his handgun, then....

Thump!

A chunk of wood split off near the doorknob.

He's coming in!

She had nothing to protect herself. He would kill her. Her life, Reed, everything flashed through her mind. She leaned far away from the door and suddenly saw it, partly hidden behind the shower curtain—*a phone.* She grabbed it, clicked the receiver loudly so he'd hear, punched Operator and started yelling as it rang.

No one picked up. She continued shouting anyway.

"A man's shooting at me. Room 607. He's wearing a Marriott coat. Blond with a beard. What? Security men are on this floor now? *Hurry!* Room 607!"

Silence.

Then footsteps thudded ran down the hallway. Was it her attacker running away? Or pretending to? Or a hotel guest running from him? No, her attacker wanted her *dead!* He was right outside. He would turn the knob, bolt in and end her life.

Seconds passed, then a minute. Was he hiding in her room? She heard hallway doors clicking open, guests whispering.

Is it safe?

She waited. More voices. Slowly, she opened the door and looked around. Her room was empty. She leaned into the hall and saw hotel guests in pajamas peering from their doors, questioning each other.

Hallie hurried back to the phone and heard the anxious operator asking, "Are you all right?"

* * *

Luca Corsa headed down the stairwell. Two floors down, he yanked off the room-service coat and bow tie and tossed them behind a large potted fern. Then he shoved his beard, tinted glasses and the flower box into a trash bin and ran down to the ground floor.

As he entered the lobby, he blended in with some rowdies staggering from the bar. Ahead he saw the desk manager directing two security guards to the elevators.

Corsa strolled out the hotel entrance, climbed into a taxi and told the driver to take him into the city.

The bitch had outmaneuvered him. Clearly, she was a worthy prey. Which made the game even more exciting. He'd make sure she died extra painfully. And even though he didn't get her files, he'd tell the boss he didn't see any. Which was sort of true.

Corsa leaned back, pulled out a silver flask and gulped several mouthfuls of Jack Daniels. Damn, it tasted good. Like drinking liquid gold. He chugged down some more. The cab hit a bump and he spilled some on his crotch, sending a sweet little tingle through his groin. He lit a cigarette and took a deep, rich drag.

Cracking the window, the wind flicked a cigarette spark onto the seat beside him. He rubbed it out and noticed a slit in the cushion. Suddenly, his mind raced back to another slit cushion. Back when he was eleven. Back to the night Bitch-Momma, a street whore, had sent some old bastard into Corsa's bedroom to have a little fun. Anything to feed her coke habit. When Corsa told the old jerk to get lost, the guy went crazy, swung a knife at him, slit his sofa-bed cushion wide open. Corsa grabbed the switchblade and sliced away. Old bastard ran out of the trailer screaming and bleeding like a stuck pig, holding his nuts on. Even now, years later, Corsa got a good warm feeling just remembering.

Bitch-Momma kicked him out of the house that night. Raining like a monsoon. Thunder and lightning. Cold as hell. She didn't give a shit. He slept under the porch. Left in the morning. Never saw her again. Never wanted to. Never heard that she asked about him. Never felt anything but pure happiness when he heard she'd died painfully from syphilis at thirty-eight.

The slut got off easy.

Sixteen

Reed took a deep breath and let it out slowly. Even though Hallie was in Atlanta, far from the men in the Lincoln, Reed was increasingly worried about where she was now right now.

At least I know where one person is, he thought, checking the rearview mirror. The vehicle behind him had maintained the same distance for the last ten miles. Fortunately, its high-set headlights ruled out his friends in the Lincoln.

Lightning flashed as he drove up a rain-slick hill. Rising over the crest, he quickly swerved to avoid a chunk of truck tire. Rain pummeled the windshield as thunder rumbled across the sky. He was trapped in a deafening storm that suggested Mother Nature was sending even more menacing weather soon.

Is Hallie flying back in this storm?

He called Delta and learned that the last flight to Detroit departed while she was at the CDC.

Hugging a bend, he glanced down into a dark ravine. He pulled out to pass a sixteen-wheeler. One second later, the truck splattered what looked like a *tsunami* onto his windshield. He turned the wiper speed to high.

The phone rang and he grabbed it.

"Hallie?"

"Woody Beachum."

"Oh, Detective, thanks for getting back. I've got something."

"What's that?"

"Someone destroyed Kyle's office computer files."

Beachum cleared his throat. "Computer problem?"

"A *person* problem."

"How do you know?"

"Only *his* files were destroyed."

"Maybe an angry co-worker?"

"His secretary says everyone liked him," Reed said.

Reed heard the click of a lighter, followed by a deep intake of breath. He felt guilty that he always caused Beachum to light up. The guy was overweight, overworked, over fifty, over two packs a day, and probably overdue for a heart attack.

"So," Beachum said, exhaling, "if everyone liked him, it must have been a computer problem."

Reed gripped the wheel tighter. "Or his killer deleted files he didn't want anyone else to see."

Beachum huffed out air and wheezed himself into a throaty cough. "Reed, all I know is that the autopsy says your brother died of natural causes."

"Autopsies can be wrong."

"Yes, but Doc McDonald is the best."

Clearly, Beachum wasn't budging. Reed slumped back against the headrest. "So the fact that my brother says he was poisoned, the fact that two men in a Lincoln tried to shoot Hallie and me, and the fact that someone just deleted only Kyle's computer files are unrelated events that just happened coincidentally in the last three days?"

Beachum clicked his lighter top a few times. "It appears so."

Not to me, Reed thought, shaking his head. Beachum wanted more evidence and Reed had no idea where to find it. "Tomorrow I'm checking Kyle's home computer."

"Let me know if you find anything."

"I will."

They hung up.

Frustrated, Reed stared ahead as lightning bleached the southern sky. The storm was intensifying as fast as his sense of desperation.

Driving beneath an overpass, he glimpsed a police car hiding beside an overpass ramp, waiting for speeders. In the mirror the police car didn't move, even though Reed was six miles over the limit. But wonder of wonders, the vehicle behind him had moved to within a hundred yards. Watch the cop, pal.

A half mile further, Reed noticed the vehicle, a white delivery van, had closed to within thirty yards and was moving closer.

Reed started up a rain-sleek hill. Lightning exploded, silhouetting the hill's tree-lined summit, and he gripped the wheel tighter. Behind him, the van drew closer. Above its windshield read *Norma's Bakery.* The van eased into the passing lane, crept alongside, started to pass.

Then it slowed.

Then it inched forward.

Reed glanced over. Big man driving. Big smile. And a big surprise, as the bastard intentionally jerked the van right into the front of Reed's TrailBlazer.

Reed swerved, but it was too late. He was off the road, losing control, careening onto the narrow shoulder. He steered back but realized he was steering air, heading over the shoulder down into a ravine. His heart in his throat, Reed slammed against the door as the Blazer bounced down the hill, rolled sideways, striking huge rocks, flipping him around like a rag doll. The air bag engulfed his face as the vehicle cascaded, bounced off a tree, then struck bottom hard. A crumpled Doublemint wrapper floated down, or was it up?

Catching his breath, he moved his arms and legs. Everything worked, except his head, in which he felt incredible pressure; the result, he realized, of hanging upside down in his seatbelt. He unclicked the belt and dropped hard onto his shoulder.

Beside him, he saw weeds and muddy water inches from his face. He lunged against the door but it wouldn't budge.

A light flickered onto the windshield.

He looked around the airbag and saw a flashlight beam swaying down the hill toward him.

He's coming down, making sure I'm dead.

Reed pushed the door again. *Jammed!*

The gleaming flashlight beam swept closer.

Crawling over to the passenger door, he found it locked. He flipped the power-door locks. Dead. He manually unlocked the door and pushed. Jammed shut, thanks to a massive dent in the panel.

Bright light flooded the windshield.

He climbed into the backseat, unlocked a door and pushed it open a foot. Squeezing out, he kept low, clawing mud, hurrying toward the cover of nearby trees. Behind him, he heard footsteps crunching twigs. Reed looked back and saw it was same big man.

Reed reached the trees and ran, the flashlight beam streaking across his arm.

"Wait!" Big Man shouted. "I came to help."

Sure, Reed thought, racing into the forest shadows, sprinting over soggy leaves and fallen branches. Big Man ran after him, seemingly very serious about helping.

Reed slipped, and a branch cut the corner of his mouth. He tasted warm, salty blood as he jumped over a log and ran down into a gully. Big Man was keeping up, helped by his flashlight.

Beside Reed, something *thumped* into a tree.

Bullets!

Reed sprinted faster. Another *thump* and bark stung his ear. He ran behind some evergreens and soon found himself in a clearing. He ran faster, knowing the open area made him an easier target.

Two bullets hissed past his left ear.

A flash of lightning.

Another *thump*.

A rainwater puddle exploded beside him.

Legs pumping like pistons, he ran through the rain toward the forest's darkness one hundred yards ahead. He glanced back and saw Big Man dropping back a bit, his weight finally slowing him down.

Running at full speed, Reed disappeared into the forest, looking for thicker cover, but seeing none.

Suddenly, his left foot slammed into a leaf-covered stump. He fell, clutching his arch. He got up, put his foot down, and felt sharp pain radiate through it. He looked back. The flashlight was closer—only fifty yards behind him.

Reed hobbled ahead, unable to run, looking for a place to hide. The trees were too thin, bushes too obvious. Limping a few feet further, a long, sharp thorn raked his knuckles, but he saw the shadowy recesses of a small ditch. Maybe....

Quickly, he dragged two fallen limbs over to the ditch, slid down into it, and pulled the leafy branches over his head. He was squatting in icy, ankle-deep water. A foul odor wafted into his nostrils. He turned and saw the rotten carcass of a racoon three feet away. From the racoon's stomach, a rat lifted its head, bloody intestines dripping from its teeth. The rat stared at him. Reed stared back, breathing heavily. Finally, the rat dragged the intestines and the racoon down a hole.

Exhaling, Reed listened. Footsteps pounded onto the forest floor, then slowed to a walk. Moments later they came to a stop. The flashlight beam swept the trees overhead.

He heard the man breathing, loud at first, then fainter. Then he heard nothing, except his own pulse pounding against his temples. More silence. Sixty seconds, ninety. No flashlight beams. Maybe Big Man had headed back.

Then a twig snapped a few feet away.

Seventeen

"Could I look at those?" Dr. Kundan Shah asked, pointing at the autopsy files in Hallie's lap.

"Please do," she said, hoping he found something the others had missed.

Dr. Shah took the files, flipped open the top one and began reading.

Hallie looked out the window of the Delta flight as it taxied into position for takeoff. Seconds later, the 737 raced down the runway and soared into the inky morning sky, Atlanta's lights creeping past below.

The cabin lights flickered back on and she noticed the purple bruises on her wrist, souvenirs from her attacker. She could still see his crazed eyes, still feel splinters from the bathroom door sting her neck.

Easing her aisle seat back, she tried to relax. It was impossible. She was too worried about Reed. He'd said he'd leave a message at the Marriott or on her home answering machine. He'd done neither. And he wasn't answering his home or cell phones. Something was wrong.

She thought back to last night. The fact that her assailant knew her name and tried to kill her suggested more than a random attack. The fact that his gun had a silencer suggested more than an amateurish robbery. Everything suggested that he was a pro, a hitman somehow connected to her CDC visit and the SCD deaths, and, therefore, to Kyle's death.

Which led her to conclude that Kyle *was* in fact poisoned. And even more terrifying, *that many more people will be slaughtered tomorrow.*

She wanted to phone Reed and tell him what had happened, but the phone in her row was being used by a loud, obese businessman in the window seat.

She noticed a green file on Dr. Shah's lap. "Your work travels with you?"

He smiled. "Afraid so. The curse of a CDC medical officer. But this file needs my attention. It reports on a petrochemical plant accident in a village in southwest Kashmir. It also outlines medical procedures for treating victims of a mass chemical weapon attack. The attack is based on a rather frightening rumor."

"What's that?"

"Apparently, massive amounts of a chemical weapon were purchased in Asia by an arms dealer. The dealer then resold it to someone in the US."

"An al Qaeda cell?" she asked.

"No. An individual. Not al Qaeda."

"Is the weapon already in the US?"

"Yes. It got in well before the tighter security following September 11 and the Iraq war."

She swallowed a dry throat.

"The study also suggests the weapon's probable delivery system."

"What is it?"

Shah shrugged. "Haven't read that section yet. But whatever the delivery system, a chemical weapon attack terrifies me."

"Me too." She leaned back, closed her eyes and thought about the horrific implications of a chemical weapon attack. Victims, doctors and nurses cramming hospital ER rooms, helpless to prevent most deaths. Dead patients on gurneys. Body bags on floors. Total chaos.

Turbulence shook the aircraft and her eyes shot open. Coming toward her was a large, thick-chested man. Same build as her attacker, but not him.

Still, he could be on this flight.

She looked across the aisle and saw three women. Behind them, a young couple with a baby. Behind them, Asian businessmen.

Is he behind me?

Peering back through the seat gap, she saw the wrinkled hands of an elderly couple. Her view to the front was blocked by the high seatbacks.

She knew her imagination was in high gear, but so was her survival instinct. She tried to calm herself by thinking of Reed, but it only made her more anxious. Why hadn't he called or left a message? She had important things to tell him. Unfortunately, the phone in her aisle was still permanently cradled in the jowls of the loud businessman. He'd been talking on it since take-off. She leaned over, giving him her best smile.

"Will you be using the phone long?" she asked, smiling, but with a touch of urgency.

The man puffed up like a cobra, clearly annoyed that she dared request *his* phone. "At least thirty minutes," he said. "Probably more." He returned to tongue-lashing an underling.

T. Rexes are everywhere, she thought. She signaled a passing stewardess. "Is there a phone I might use? It's quite urgent."

The young woman turned and scanned the aircraft. "Last seat in first class."

"Thank you."

Hallie told Shah she was going to make some calls, stood and started toward first class. A few steps later she froze.

Her attacker was sitting only three rows ahead. Aisle seat. Same bull neck, thick shoulders, huge fingers, sunglasses hiding his eyes. He was staring blankly at the seat in front. Her heart slammed into her throat. She started to return to her seat, then paused.

Is it really him?

She had to get closer to be positive. If it was him, she'd go back, call the police and have him arrested on arrival.

She moved a bit closer to the man, to the row behind him, then just behind his shoulder. She paused. People were staring at her. Had *he* seen her?

The man's hand was moving slowly along his waist.

He's reaching for a weapon.... No. Security would have caught it.

Or *missed* it.

If she could just see his eyes, she'd know. She inched closer, glanced down at his hands, and froze. The man's fingers were gliding over a page of braille. Beside the book was a white cane. A blind man. A beardless, blind man.

Feeling a little chagrined, she walked ahead to first class and sat in the last aisle seat. No one was seated next to her. She phoned Reed's home, cell phone and office but got no answer. She phoned her office, but he'd still left no message. T. Rex, of course, had left two more see-me-or-die messages.

Maybe Reed had stayed overnight at Anne's. By now, she and the girls would probably be up. Hallie took out her palm pilot, found Anne's number and dialed.

"Hello."

"Anne, it's Hallie."

"Oh, Hallie, how'd it go at the CDC?"

"Reed told you?"

"He told me everything." Hallie heard the pain in her voice.

"The CDC is investigating."

"That's terrific."

"Yes. Listen, Anne, is Reed there?"

"No. He drove back last night."

Panic squeezed Hallie's chest.

"We tried to get into Kyle's laptop computer," Anne said, "but couldn't get around the password. So Reed drove to Dunne Corporation, where he and Meg Haney tried to enter Kyle's computer files. But someone had deleted them."

"Really?" Hallie said. *Another unexplained event.* "Did you talk to Reed after he left Dunne?"

"Yes. He called me from I-75. He was driving back to Birmingham."

Hallie's throat closed as she tried another painful swallow.

"Hallie, is something wrong?"

"Oh no," she said, knowing something was terribly wrong, that Reed was in trouble. But she refused to burden Anne with more distress on the day of her husband's funeral. "Reed's probably on the way to his office."

"You tried his cell phone?"

"Yes. He must have turned it off."

"If he calls here, I'll have him phone you right away."

"At my office, please," Hallie said, "We'll see you later today." *At the funeral,* she added to herself.

"Okay."

As they hung up, Hallie suddenly imagined two caskets at the funeral: Kyle's and Reed's. She forced the image from her mind and stared out at the dark gray clouds sliding past. Where was Reed? Maybe his secretary, Lori, knew. Lori tended to arrive early. Hallie dialed Reed's office.

"Reed Kincaid's office," Lori said, her voice tense.

"Lori, this is Hallie. Has Reed—"

"Oh, Hallie…."

Something is wrong, she realized.

"I've been trying to reach you," Lori whispered. "The state police just called."

Hallie slumped back in the seat, her pulse pounding over the roar of the aircraft.

"There's been an accident."

Hallie opened her mouth to speak, couldn't.

"They found Reed's TrailBlazer near I-75. It rolled down into a ravine."

Her mind spinning, Hallie forced herself to whisper, "How's Reed?"

"We don't know."

"What?"

"He wasn't anywhere near the Blazer."

Hallie pictured Reed injured, lying in a field.

"The police found fresh footprints leading away from the Blazer. Two sets of footprints. The men were running."

"Reed was running from someone."

"That's what the police think."

"Why?" Hallie asked, swallowing.

"They found fresh bullet holes in some trees."

Hallie closed her eyes. "Maybe hunters' bullets?"

"Handgun bullets, the police said .38 caliber."

Hallie massaged her temples. She didn't want to hear any more. Turbulence suddenly shook the aircraft again and she was tossed hard against the armrest.

"Hallie, I'm very worried."

Fighting her own panic, Hallie said, "I am, too, Lori, but Reed is very resourceful. If he *ran*, he wasn't hurt too badly. And he's run marathons before, so he's in good shape. Also, it was dark. Maybe he's hiding." Hallie said the words as much for herself as Lori.

"I'm sure you're right."

"Call my office if you hear anything," Hallie said.

"Okay...."

They hung up.

Hallie felt something digging into her palms. She looked down and saw it was her fingernails. She took a deep breath and listened to the hum of the jet engines for a moment.

She didn't want to be on this flight. She also didn't want to get off this flight and be greeted with news that would devastate her life.

Feeling nauseated, she stood and walked slowly back down the aisle toward her seat.

* * *

As she walked toward him, Luca Corsa clenched his braille book so hard he separated several pages from the binding. He moved his fingers, pretending to read, but felt like pulling out the razor-sharp plastic shiv in his cane and crudely *gutting* the bitch wide open as she walked by.

But no. He still had to get his hands on her files.

Then he'd get his hands on *her*. She'd embarrassed him bad. Faking being shot and all. For that, she would die soon, very painfully. He'd make sure of that.

Maybe he should just do her in the airport.

Who would suspect a blind man?

87

Eighteen

Reed pushed aside an evergreen bough and felt fat, icy dewdrops slide down his neck and back. He shivered, turned up the collar of his muddy suitcoat and squished ahead through the rain-soaked forest. The air was heavy and damp, the ground spongy and smelling like wet, rotten wood. Nearby, a bird trumpeted the arrival of dawn, a sliver of ruby red chasing an inky sky.

After hiding in the branch-covered ditch for two hours, and determining his armed attacker was not lying in wait, Reed had crawled out and trudged through the forest. In the darkness, he'd lost his way twice. Finally, he'd glimpsed I-75 and walked parallel with it, staying far enough away to avoid being seen. His bruised ankle was walkable, thanks partly to soaking it in the icy ditch water for two hours. The rest of his body felt like someone had pounded it with a sledgehammer.

Black and blue evidence that someone wants me dead, he thought. *Evidence that Detective Beachum will have to link to Kyle's destroyed computer files and the Lincoln.*

But first Reed needed a phone.

Suddenly two huge crows swooped down within inches of his head, squawking angrily at his invasion. He shooed them away and slushed ahead through ankle-deep rainwater.

Minutes later, he discovered America: The yellow arches of a McDonald's. In the parking lot he saw two Chevy pickups, a Tracker, a BMW and a Taurus. No white vans. No blue Lincolns.

As he limped inside, customers glanced at his bloodied face, mud-caked suit and shoes, and returned to their food unimpressed, as though they regularly ate with pig wrestlers.

He walked over to the pay phone and called Beachum's office. The detective was not in yet. He phoned the local police, explained his incident, and they agreed to pick him up immediately. Then he called the Atlanta Marriott.

"Has Doctor Mara checked out yet?"

"Just a moment, please," said the operator. Moments later, "Sir, no one with that name checked in last night."

Reed sagged against the wall. He was right. They had pursued her to Atlanta. After all, they had even more reason to kill her. Her medical knowledge and her CDC visit might prove Kyle was poisoned.

"Sir."

"Yes?"

"Did you try the other Marriott?"

"What?"

"The other Marriott, sir. It's also near the airport."

"There's *another* Marriott near the airport?"

"Yes, sir. She may have stayed there. I can check."

"Please," he said, his hope rekindling. He should have known there'd be more than one Marriott near the airport. Marriotts were drawn to airports like bugs to a patio zapper.

"She checked out early this morning," the operator said.

He felt like a barbell was yanked off his chest. "Thank you more than you'll ever know."

"You're quite welcome, sir."

Grinning, he hung up, hurried over and ordered a large coffee. The attendant, "Amy," with freckles and brown hair, stared at his bloody face, muddy clothes and bizarre grin and took a step back. Apparently, she pegged him for a fast-food whacko about to whip out an AK-47 and riddle her hash browns, because she served his coffee in under ten seconds.

Behind him, he heard snickering.

Turning, Reed noticed two young executive types hunched over their power breakfasts laughing at his muddy clothes. One was a large, beefy-faced blond. The other a skinny, pencil-nosed guy. Both had starched white shirts and red ties, serious blue suits and gleaming hair slicked back. They chuckled again at his appearance. Yuppies mocking poor Mr. Mud. Not very nice.

Laugh on, guys. I just want to drink this nice, hot coffee.

As Reed walked by, Beef Face tripped him slightly on purpose. Hot coffee spilled onto Reed's fingers and pain rocketed up his arm.

"Oops, sorry, pal," Beef Face said, winking at Pencil Nose. "Didn't you read the sign? No street bums allowed."

This caused Pencil Nose to laugh so hard that a wad of mucus actually shot out one nostril and hung there. Astonished, he quickly sniffed it back in, except for a gob which perched on his eyebrow like a hanging maggot.

Reed took a deep breath and counted to five. He really didn't need these jerks. A car crash, a man shooting at him, a twisted ankle, assorted cuts and bruises and a cold night in ditch water had lowered his pissed-off level to minus ten.

As he leaned over to suggest they grow up, Beef Face again accidentally-on-purpose bumped Reed's elbow, spilling more coffee.

"Whoops again," Beef Face said, acting surprised, winking at Pencil Nose.

Pencil Nose was convulsed with giggles.

Beef Face searched nearby customers for laughs. Instead, they stared back disgusted, like they'd seen him pull this stunt often.

Show time, Reed thought. Smiling into Beef Face's eyes, he quickly grabbed the large man's hand and twisted it behind the man's back in an armlock. Beef Face's eyes shot open as he realized he couldn't move.

"Whoops," Reed said.

Then using his elbow, Reed tipped Beef Face's coffee onto his McMuffin, turning it to mush and sending a stream of hot coffee down onto the man's crotch.

"Whoops again," Reed said.

Beef Face's cheeks turned as red as a baboon's butt.

"Tell me," Reed asked, "is McDonald's coffee as hot as they say?"

A vein on Beef Face's forehead bulged. As he started to swing his other hand, Reed twisted harder and the man emitted dainty little bird-like chirps.

Pencil Nose looked like he'd swallowed Draino.

Leaning closer, Reed whispered, "In one minute, my fellow police officers will walk in that door. If you're still here, they'll arrest you for assaulting an undercover officer—me. We'll inform your employer. Possible jail time with gentlemen who prefer gentlemen. You getting this?"

Beef Face nodded like a woodpecker. Reed released the man's arm, walked to the next booth and sat down to the applause of smiling customers.

Wiping hot coffee from his crotch, Beef Face, followed by Pencil Nose, scurried outside, jumped in a BMW and sped toward the exit. They braked fast as a Waterford police car pulled in.

The policeman took Reed to a nearby station, where he explained how he'd been forced off I-75 and chased. They gave him the cell phone from his car. He tried to call Hallie, but the battery was dead. They drove him home, where he checked his phone messages for one from Hallie—but it was crammed full of condolences for Kyle. He showered, changed into a dark blue suit for Kyle's funeral, then taxied to the agency to pick up another company vehicle.

As he walked into his office, the phone rang.

"Reed Kincaid."

"Reed?" Hallie's voice was an octave higher than normal.

"The very one. Where are you?"

"My lab. Reed, are you all right?"

"The main parts still work, thank God!"

"I've been so worried...."

"A guy drove me off I-75. But I'm fine." He fingered the scab on his lip and flexed his bruised ankle. "I'm sure the incident is connected to Kyle's death. The guy shot at me."

Hallie was silent for several seconds. "Me too."

Her words one-two punched him. He dropped into his chair and the office seemed to tilt. "Jesus, what happened?"

As she told him, every muscle in his body hardened. The bastards *had* followed her to Atlanta and tried to kill her!

"But I'm fine," she said, her tone hinting otherwise.

Reed knew she was still in danger. "Hallie, they think you know how Kyle was poisoned. Or how the other people will die tomorrow."

"I don't."

"But they *think* you do."

She was silent for several moments.

Reed continued. "They probably assume you showed evidence to the CDC and may still have it. Did the attacker take any files from your hotel room?"

"No. He ran away when I screamed for help on the bathroom phone."

"So he's probably still after the files."

"Maybe."

"And he's after *you*...." He hoped she grasped the danger she was in.

"Possibly."

"I have a suggestion," he said.

"What?"

"A police safe house. Just until after Friday."

"But Reed, everything has changed now. *I* believe Kyle. I believe many people will die Friday. I want to help prevent their deaths. And remember one thing."

"What?"

"They tried to kill you, too. How about a safe house for you?"

She had him there. "I hear you. But my cop-street-smarts are back," *sort of*, he added to himself, rubbing his sore lip.

"And I know some karate and self-defense," she shot back. "Also, I've got to prepare for a crucial meeting Tuesday."

"These people are professional killers, Hallie."

"Tell me about it," she said with her iron-lady voice. He knew the voice, loved her for it and knew it was useless to try to change her mind.

"Another suggestion, Doctor."

"Suggest away, Mr. Kincaid."

"A police bodyguard."

"Do you really need one?" she asked, a smile in her voice.

"For *you*, ma'am. I'll ask Beachum."

"Okay," she said, "but only if he's got a cute butt."

"Beachum fills the bill."

"The bodyguard."

"Deal," he said. "Speaking of Beachum, how quickly can you grace his office?"

She paused. "Give me thirty minutes."

"Please have someone drive you."

"I'll see."

"Please...."

"Save me, Popeye, save me!"

"Okay, Olive Oil, *I'll* pick you up."

"Never mind. Someone will drive me."

"Thank you."

They hung up. Reed asked his secretary, Lori, to hold all calls and not to mention he was in the agency. He quickly walked down and checked with his creative team working on the pitch for the teenage anti-smoking campaign. He felt guilty for not spending more time with them, but knew he'd been too distracted to help. He entered the conference room, and the team quickly took him through the television commercial concepts they'd plastered on the walls. One really grabbed his attention.

The commercial opened up with the camera looking down on an eleven-year-old boy and girl, lying on their backs, side by side, on a white floor. They're shirtless. Suddenly, large drops of a black, oily substance begin to drip onto their bare white chests. The thick, black liquid drips faster, covers their chests, blanketing their necks, arms, spilling onto the floor.

A voice-over announcer says, "If these 11-year-olds started smoking today and smoked a pack a day for the rest of their lives, gallons of thick black tar like this—over *fifty gallons* of thick black tar and nicotine—will enter their lungs ... and eventually cause cancer, which can lead to their early deaths."

The camera pulls back slowly to reveal their bodies and the floor of a gymnasium covered with thick black tar. "So don't start smoking. But if you do—quit, and don't quit quitting." Fade to black.

Reed felt the commercial would grab teenagers visually and drive home the message. He complimented the creative team and headed down to the office of his friend, Barb Rennick, who ran the company car pool.

"What?" she said.

"I need fast."

She reached in her drawer, took out some keys and tossed them to him.

"A new black GMC Typhoon III," she said, "sort of a Corvette in SUV clothing."

* * *

As Diedre De Bakker pulled up to the quaint red brick Birmingham police station, Hallie scanned the area for Reed but didn't see him. He was probably already inside.

"Thanks again, Diedre," she said, getting out.

"You're welcome, boss lady. And don't worry about things at the lab."

"I'll worry about one thing."

"What?"

"T. Rex haranguing you."

Diedre smiled. "Didn't you know?"

"What?"

"We Belgians are harangue-proof."

Hallie laughed as Diedre drove off. Again, she realized how fortunate she was to work with a brilliant colleague who was also a good friend.

"Hey you!"

Turning around, she saw Reed step from a new black SUV across the street. She walked over to him, and they embraced each other in silence, knowing how incredibly fortunate they were to be in each other's arms.

They hurried inside the station, where a curly-haired young patrolman escorted them to Beachum's office. Beachum was on the phone and gestured for them to help themselves at his coffee machine. They poured two cups and sat in wooden chairs with faded blue cushions.

She noticed the walls were decorated with citations and photos of a younger, thinner, dark-haired Beachum shaking hands with two former mayors, Governor Jennifer Grandholm and police dignitaries. In one photo, Beachum, around thirty-five, embraced a smiling woman and young girl, perhaps wife and daughter, at Disneyworld. In another photo, the same girl wore a cap and gown from Michigan State University. A wood-framed photo portrayed Beachum smiling from a row of men and women holding certificates from the FBI Training Academy.

She caught the scent of cigarette smoke wafting over from a butt-stuffed ashtray on the windowsill. Case folders dominated the oak desk, and his dusty computer looked like it might never have been turned on. Beside it, a transparent evidence bag revealed a woman's blouse, shredded and bloody. Another bag held a bloodstained eight-inch knife. She noticed Reed staring at the knife.

Beachum hung up and nodded toward the phone. "The Waterford police. They say you're lucky to be alive, Reed."

"They're smart as whips."

"They figure the guy in the white van was a carjacker."

Reed shook his head from side to side. "A very persistent carjacker. I think he drove the blue Lincoln yesterday. He shot at me both days. Did the Pontiac police report any carjackings with a blue Lincoln or white van?"

"Nope." Woody Beachum stared at Reed, then stuffed a Camel in his mouth. "Sorry about this nasty habit. Tried the patch. Damn thing reminded me how much I like cigarettes." He lit it, drew hard and exhaled toward a slightly opened window, where a wind current magically pulled the smoke outside.

"A man also shot at me," Hallie said.

Beachum sputtered out smoke. "When?"

"Last night in Atlanta. He posed as a room service man and brought flowers to my hotel room. He fired several shots at me through the bathroom door. When I called security, he escaped. But he left these." She pushed up her sleeve, revealing ugly black bruises above her wrist.

Beachum's eyes narrowed on the bruises as smoke curled from his nostrils. Suddenly, his face reddened. He sat up and crushed out his cigarette. "Too damn much!"

"What?" Hallie asked.

"Coincidence," Beachum said. "When you two investigate Kyle's death in different cities on the same night and both of you become murder targets, are attacked and shot at two days in a row, and when your brother's computer files are deleted, well, that's not coincidence. That's someone trying to stop you from poking around Kyle's death."

Finally, Hallie realized, *Beachum's turned the corner.* The big detective was suddenly all business. It was like somebody had pulled a lever inside him. He jabbed two digits on his phone. "Bob, pull Ned Martin and Deke Larsen over to work with me on the Kincaid case. Larsen should guard Dr. Hallie Mara, starting now." Beachum looked at Hallie for agreement.

She nodded and noticed Reed visibly relax.

Beachum hung up. "Hallie, may I ask why you were in Atlanta?"

"To ask the CDC to investigate several sudden cardiac deaths like Kyle's."

"And...?"

"They agreed too. They think the high number of SCD deaths similar to Kyle's warrant further investigation. They've assigned a medical examiner, Doctor Shah, who flew back with me. He's at Genetique working with Detroit Memorial Hospital on the cases."

"Good," Beachum said, raking his fingers through thinning, gray hair. "This whole situation is giving me bad vibes. Someone clearly does not want you sniffing around Kyle's death."

"Or the deaths tomorrow," Reed added.

Beachum bit his lower lip. "Your brother said 'kill *many* Friday'?"

Reed nodded.

Beachum looked at Hallie. "There's a strong likelihood your attacker followed you across state lines to Atlanta. That means I'm calling in a pal, the Special Agent in Charge at the Detroit FBI office."

Her hope surged. The FBI and the CDC brought awesome investigative and forensic resources to the case. Awesome was needed.

As they stood to leave, Beachum asked them not to mention anything about Friday to anyone. He walked them into the hall and introduced them to Corporal Deke Larsen, a young, handsome, powerfully built officer with thick brown hair and a small v-shaped scar on his chin. Walking outside, Larsen hurried ahead to an unmarked police car.

"Cute buns," Hallie whispered to Reed, gesturing toward Larsen.

"Hairline suggests he's a eunuch."

She smiled. "Only one way to find out."

"Slut."

She laughed and kissed Reed on the cheek.

Suddenly, they both grew serious again.

"Pick you up around eleven for the funeral?" he said.

She nodded, then got into the car with Larsen. They drove off toward Genetique. Larsen seemed like a pleasant young man, and she was relieved to have his protection.

But she also knew that anyone who arranged assassinations in two cities on one night could easily get around one police bodyguard.

Nineteen

Driving away from the station, Reed racked his brain over who was behind Kyle's death. One candidate kept coming to mind above all others—the man Kyle phoned him about. Was he a co-worker? Casual acquaintance? Friend? Stranger?

Detective Beachum's check of Kyle's phone calls Sunday turned up no viable candidates. Perhaps Kyle's laptop files would reveal the name, but first he had to get around the password. Unfortunately, his agency computer guru was out camping somewhere in northern California.

Reed stopped at a red light and found himself sucking in foul bus exhaust fumes. He speed-dialed his office for voice mail. There were two bad-news calls from Huey Hastings demanding a meeting tomorrow. The third call hit pay dirt—Earl the Pearl, the company computer guru, had left a number. Reed dialed it, and after four rings Earl picked up.

"How's the camping?" Reed asked.

"White...."

"What?"

"Three feet of snow. Avalanche warnings. I'm back at the lodge, where I picked up your message. Whose computer you want to break into?"

"My brother's."

"PC or MAC?"

"PC."

"Got a pencil?"

"Sure," Reed said, pulling into a Kmart lot. He parked and wrote down Earl's detailed instructions, plus the name of some software programs Earl's secretary would give him.

"Think these'll work?" Reed asked.

"Depends on how many passwords, secret codes and anti-tampering barriers your brother has added."

"What if he added a lot?"

"Big problem. Even experts might not be able to penetrate the hard drive."

They hung up. Reed drove back onto the road, where a gravel hauler swung in front of him. Pebbles pinged off his windshield. As he passed the hauler, his cell phone rang. He picked up, thinking Earl forgot something.

"Huey Hastings."

America's leading Butt-Head, Reed thought. "What's up, Huey?"

"The Mason Industries meeting with Thurston Maybury. Two o'clock tomorrow. Maybury's conference room."

"I can't make it, Huey. Please set it up for this weekend or any time next week."

"Too late."

"Why?"

"I want to meet Friday afternoon."

"I can't meet before Saturday."

"Why not?" Hastings demanded, as though meetings should happen when he ordained, and that one day after a brother's funeral should be business as usual.

Reed remembered Beachum's request to not mention anything about Friday. "It's hard to explain," Reed said.

"This is serious! I insist we meet!"

"Huey...."

"Yes?"

"After Friday."

Reed heard Baby Huey huffing like a toddler denied candy. "I refuse to do business this way!" Hastings shouted, slamming the phone down.

"So try another business, melon-head!" Reed said aloud to himself. His cheeks felt hot. Hastings was a piece of work, undoubtedly already calling Thurston Maybury to complain. By not attending the meeting, Reed was weakening his position on the Mason Industries account, and maybe even in the agency. So be it. He'd have to handle Hastings and his career *after* Friday.

Reed was more than a little surprised by his so-be-it attitude. A week ago, nothing would have kept him from the meeting. Career first. Always. But recent events—like bullets aimed at him—had quickly rearranged his priorities in life. Priority number one was keeping Hallie and himself alive. Everything else, like his job and meetings, had slid way down his list.

He stopped for a red light and found himself walled-in by two vehicle haulers carrying shiny new red Corvettes. The sunlight reflected off them onto the scab on his hand which was healing. So was his ankle, he realized, flexing it.

His phone rang and he prayed it wasn't Hastings again.

"Reed ... it's Anne." She sounded excited.

"Everything okay?" He was surprised she even had his cell phone number.

"Yes, but I just remembered something."

"What?"

"About three weeks ago, Kyle was concerned about someone. A man he'd given freelance work to."

Reed sat up straight. "How concerned?"

"Quite concerned."

"Threatened?"

"More like very worried. Kyle visited the man's home to drop off a report and saw something there. It alarmed him."

Reed's heart rate kicked up a notch. "What was it?"

"He didn't say."

"Did he mention the man's name?"

"No."

"Where's he live?"

"I don't know. But Kyle was back within two hours."

"What kind of freelance work?"

"Kyle didn't mention."

"Maybe he kept notes."

"If he did, they'd be in his laptop," she said.

Ahead, Reed saw road work slowing traffic. "After the funeral and after everyone leaves your home, we'll try to get into his laptop."

"I'll *make* them leave." Her words were hard, determined. Clearly, she'd channeled her pain into finding the man who caused it.

After hanging up, Reed felt his hope surge. Clues were trickling in. Kyle had been worried about someone. No, more than worried ... *alarmed!* Alarmed about his own safety perhaps.

And even more alarmed about what would happen Friday.

Twenty

Father Matthew Harmon, eighty-two, tufts of white hair flapping like angel wings in the gusty, chilly November winds of Mount Hope Cemetery, leaned over Kyle's casket and wheezed, "May perpetual light shine upon him."

And if you have time, Lord, shine some light on his killer, Hallie thought.

She held Reed's hand as the old priest sprinkled holy water onto Kyle's mahogany casket. The droplets skidded down the gleaming side, where she saw the reflection of black-clad mourners and gray tombstones. A painful scene she knew was forever etched in Reed's memory.

Hazy shafts of sunshine forced their way through bony black trees and blanketed the casket in gold.

Leaning closer to Reed, Hallie felt her shoes squish into the rain-soaked grass. Beside him, Anne clutched the girls' hands, doing well one moment, losing it the next. Her eyes, although brimming with tears, seemed focused beyond this painful moment. Perhaps to an uncertain life without Kyle, or raising daughters without Kyle, or finding Kyle's killer.

"You okay?" Hallie whispered to Reed.

He shook his head no.

She understood. She had felt the same excruciating emptiness at her brother Kevin's funeral. Two brothers, Kevin and Kyle, young and innocent, ripped away unfairly from those who loved them. How incredibly tragic and cruel. She eased her arm around Reed's shoulder and again was overwhelmed with love for him. Over the last few days she'd grown even closer to him. She'd seen him handle great pain with dignity, and comfort Anne and the girls with great gentleness. She would never forget his kindness and compassion for them.

Looking around at the more than two hundred mourners surrounding them, Hallie couldn't help but wonder, *Is Kyle's murderer one of them?*

Many she recognized from the funeral home: Kyle's business colleagues, friends, neighbors. All looked devastated by the unfair loss of a young friend, and sobered by life's fragility.

"*In nomine patri, e filii, e spiritu sancti,*" the priest monotoned, making

99

the Sign of the Cross over the casket. He gestured that the service had ended, then stared into the pit a moment, an old man perhaps realizing this black earth would soon call him home. Quickly, he shuffled over to Anne, consoled her and the girls, then hurried away, the two altar boys waddling after him like ducklings.

Hallie turned to Reed, who was staring down at the casket. Part of him, she knew, still could not accept the finality of Kyle's death.

The pain in his eyes caused hers to moisten. The scene blurred into dull browns and yellows. Sounds faded and the wind grew still, leaving her with the raw, numbing finality of death.

She saw people walking toward the vehicles. "Everyone's leaving," she whispered.

He nodded, but stood there like his shoes were bolted to the ground. Finally, he forced one foot forward, then the other. They followed Anne and her family as the mourners strolled slowly toward the limos and cars fifty yards away. Couples approached Anne and offered their condolences. She stopped and spoke briefly with each but appeared eager, like Hallie knew Reed was, to get back home and search Kyle's laptop files.

Hallie saw Kyle's good friend, Dr. Dan Katcavage, Dunne Chemical's medical director, walking toward them. He looked like he had at the funeral home, as though he'd lost his last friend on earth. The portly man wore the same wrinkled blue suit and stained red tie he'd worn yesterday. She liked the frumpy man with sleepy blue eyes and elephantine ears that actually drooped a bit at the top.

Katcavage scratched his hair, sending an avalanche of dandruff onto his lapels.

"Hell, if anyone should have a heart attack, I should," Dr. Katcavage said. "I'm fat as a pig, smoke two packs a day and get less exercise than a Dutch elm. But last week, I promised Kyle I'd stop smoking. Got the patch yesterday."

"Good for you, Dan," Reed said.

"Next week I'll invent the food patch," he said, thumping his large belly, where a chili stain had found refuge beside an ink smudge.

Hallie smiled.

"Take care, you two," he said, shaking hands with Reed and her. She watched him lumber off toward some colleagues, one of whom was Philip Lambe, another friend of Kyle's, chatting with Father Harmon. Lambe, a tall, bearded man, said goodbye to the priest and walked toward them. Two days ago at the funeral home, Lambe had kindly offered to ask his doctor friends about similar SCD cases.

Lambe's grief-stricken face was dominated by sad, deep-set eyes. A charcoal single-breasted suit hung comfortably on his broad shoulders. He stepped around a small pool of rainwater and shook hands with Reed, then Hallie.

"Thank you for coming, Phil," Reed said.

He shrugged. "Kyle was a pal."

"He had many," Reed said, gesturing toward the mourners.

"We should all be so lucky. Listen, Reed, after we talked, I checked with colleagues in some hospitals. Their records suggest normal SCD rates among young adults."

"Are the hospitals in this area?" Hallie asked.

"No. Over in Ann Arbor and Battle Creek. But this afternoon I'm meeting with a friend, Dr. Brooks, over at Port Huron Mercy. I'll ask him to check around."

"Thanks, Phil. And let us know," Hallie said.

"Glad to." Lambe smiled and waved to someone over her shoulder.

She appreciated Lambe's willingness to help.

"You mentioned you worked with Kyle at ChemSKan?" Reed said.

"For about two years. Great times." Lambe smiled as though recalling the great times.

"Do you remember if Kyle had difficulty with anyone there?" Reed asked. "Any enemies?"

Lambe's eyebrows climbed higher. "Enemies? No, not that I recall. Kyle was so easy to work with. But it's been a while. Let me think about it."

"We'd appreciate it," Reed said.

"No problem."

Hallie noticed Lambe's right hand was badly scarred, apparently from burns, and that the small finger had withered.

"Forgive my scientific curiosity," Lambe said, "but first you're worried about the SCD cases, and now whether Kyle had enemies. One might conclude you feel something's wrong."

Hallie and Reed glanced at each other, remembering Beachum's request to not mention anything.

"We were concerned," Hallie said, "that the high number of SCD cases might be a statewide medical problem."

"A valid concern," Lambe said, nodding. "But the enemy thing?"

"Oh, that," Reed said, obviously scrambling for something believable. "Well, someone deleted Kyle's office computer files. All of them."

Lambe's eyes widened in shock. "But why?"

"We're not sure."

Lambe shook his head from side to side. "Probably professional sabotage. It's rampant, you know. Happened to me twice. Anything to prevent someone else from getting a Nobel."

"It's possible," Hallie said.

"Let me think more about ChemSKan," Lambe said. "We did have a couple of very aggressive guys over there. I'll call you tomorrow."

Too late, she thought. "Could you possibly call today?"

"Today?"

"It would really help," Reed said.

"Sure," Lambe said, but was clearly puzzled by the urgency. "Where can I reach you?"

"I'll be at Anne's house for a few hours," Reed said, "then at home." He wrote the phone numbers on a piece of paper and handed it to Lambe. "If I'm not home, just leave a message."

"Of course," he said, shaking hands. "Again, Reed, my condolences."

"Thanks, Phil."

As Lambe strolled away, Hallie pointed toward the waiting limousine. "It's time."

Reed nodded. She watched him glance back at the gravesite, as though hoping one last time that he'd awaken from a nightmare and discover Kyle was still alive.

A gust of wind blew blood-red leaves across the grass. One flew to the edge of the pit, teetered, then fell into the pit and stayed there, buried with Kyle.

Like part of Reed.

Twenty-One

"Thank you for the rhubarb pie, Mrs. Yancy," Anne said, helping the elderly neighbor and her gabby sister, the last mourners, out the front door.

Finally, Reed thought, waving goodbye to the friendly women.

"I'll get the laptop," Anne said as they hurried down the hall. In Kyle's study, she placed the laptop on the desk in front of him. Reed spread out the instructions and software from his agency computer guru.

"Anne, did you remember the name of the man Kyle was worried about?"

"No. He only mumbled his nickname once. None of the names in his agenda rang a bell. Maybe I'll recognize it in the computer files."

"*If* we get in." Reed turned on the laptop as Anne pulled a chair beside him.

"What are our chances?"

Reed shrugged. "Depends on how many passwords and barriers Kyle set up."

Her eyes narrowed. "What if nothing works?"

He feared the same thing. "Then experts have to remove the hard drive. They'll try special password clues to get around the anti-tampering barriers."

"Which will take more time than we have?"

"Probably."

Following Earl's written instructions, Reed tried various scenarios for twenty minutes. Nothing worked. Each failed attempt twisted his stomach tighter. He took out the Norton Disk Editor and started reading the directions.

Tess toddled in, dragging Snoopy by his remaining ear. "Mommy, can we have Domino's Pizza tonight?"

"Sure, honey, later."

"Just cheese, Mommy. No pepper ponies."

"Okay, no pepperoni."

"What are you and Uncle Reed doing?"

"We're trying to get into Daddy's computer."

"You're too big."

"We just want to turn it on, honey."

"You want to make it all white?"

"Yes," Anne said, gently ushering her toward the family room.

"Sset, Uncle Reed," she said, squiggling away.

"I am sitting, honey," Reed said.

"No, sset! Daddy showed me!" She jammed Snoopy into Reed's crotch hard enough to vasectomize him, then tapped her chubby three-year-old finger on S-S-E-T and hit Enter. "My name backwards—see!"

The computer cranked into the most beautiful white screen he'd ever seen. *We're in.*

"From the fingers of babes," he said, swooping Tess into his arms and kissing her. "Who's the smartest Tess of all?"

"Me," she said, happily giggling.

"And who's going to buy you and Haley more presents?"

"Uncle Reed!"

"Right!"

She scampered into the den to tell her sister the good news.

He entered the computer's main directory and they began scanning the documents alphabetically. They searched for anything out of the ordinary. Most documents dealt with chemical reports and scientific papers for Dunne Corporation. Some were articles for trade journals like *Journal of Biochemistry*. Anne and he scoured individual names for any hint of conflict. Plenty of names, no conflicts. They searched older files from ChemSKan for fifteen minutes. Nothing.

Nearly two hours later, Reed rubbed his eyes and looked out the large window at the heavy, dark clouds hanging low in the evening sky. He remembered last night in the cold, wet ditch, and that the man who put him there was still looking for him, and that the other hitman was still looking for Hallie. Fortunately, she and her bodyguard were back at Genetique.

Reed looked back at the computer screen. They'd worked down to 'S.' He was beginning to fear their search would turn up nothing when he noticed an odd document named "Squirrel."

"You have squirrels in the attic?"

Anne frowned. "No...."

Reed retrieved the document. As the words flashed onto the screen, his heart started pounding.

Tim,
Squirrel worries me. I recently gave him a freelance assignment. When I visited his home, I noticed mail order forms for botulism A and other toxic cultures on his desk. I

asked him why he needs botulism A? He said he's working with some USAMRIID scientists on a secret defense project, a new weapon that can nail anyone in minutes.

When he left his office to answer the doorbell, I noticed an open file on his desk. The file name was *Shikei*. In the file it mentioned a toxic agent called *Korusu* which has a "kill rate of thousands." He's testing it nationally Friday, November 14. When he came back to his office, I asked him about *Korusu*. He was shocked the file was on his desk. He closed it quickly and said *Korusu* was just a new herbicide he was working on. But he was *very* worried I'd seen that file. *Too* worried for a herbicide. Back home, I phoned a friend at USAMRIID. They have no record of him ever working for them.

Tim, I'm concerned. You know Squirrel. He's smart enough to make deadly biological or chemical weapons. Is he crazy enough to use them? And why kill thousands of *weeds* on one day—Friday the 14th? I've called him three times to discuss this *Korusu* stuff. He says there's nothing to talk about. Two days ago I called him again and he went ballistic. Said I was harassing him. Something's very wrong. Call me asap. I think we should talk to the police.

Kyle

"'...*very* worried Kyle had seen the file,'" Reed repeated.

"Worried enough to murder?" Anne whispered, her eyes brimming with tears.

Reed nodded and placed his hand on hers. "And tomorrow, Friday, November 14th, he's testing this *Korusu*'s kill rate. Everything fits."

"So does Squirrel!" Anne said, drying her eyes.

"Why?"

"*That*'s the nickname Kyle used."

"What's his real name?"

"Kyle didn't say."

"Who's this Tim?"

"Probably Tim McMillan, Kyle's good friend at ChemSKan. His number's right here." Anne fanned through Kyle's phone book, punched the speaker button and dialed.

Tim McMillan answered on the third ring.

"Tim, it's Anne Kincaid."

"Anne," he said, clearly surprised. "I just got in from Singapore. My God, I'm still in shock. How are *you*?"

"Managing, Tim, sort of. And I'd like to thank you and Marnie for the beautiful flowers."

"Oh ... sure," he said softly. "Anne, if you or the girls need anything...."

"Actually, I do need your help. I'm here with Kyle's brother, Reed. We have a few questions."

"Sure."

"Did Kyle recently send you a note about someone named Squirrel?"

McMillan paused. "He might have. I was just now going through six inches of mail."

Reed heard McMillan rustling papers.

"Do you know this Squirrel?" Anne asked.

"Hard not to. ChemSKan fired him six years ago. Brilliant biochemist. But a real headcase. Worked his own agenda, occasionally got around to his ChemSKan assignments. Very competitive."

"Competitive enough to kill?" she asked.

McMillan cleared his throat. "Sorry. For a moment I thought you'd said kill."

"I did."

McMillan gasped. "Anne, are you suggesting Kyle was murdered?"

Her eyes moistened. "It's quite possible, Tim."

"My God," McMillan whispered. "Squirrel was a whacko, but crazy enough to kill Kyle? Hell, Kyle was much nicer to the guy than anyone in the company."

Anne's lower lip began to quiver and she fought back tears. Reed leaned toward the phone and introduced himself. McMillan asked him to read Kyle's note. Reed read it slowly. When he finished, Tim McMillan was silent for several moments.

"That's absolutely incredible," McMillan said in hushed amazement. "Kyle sounded terrified."

"Tim," Reed asked, "what's Squirrel's name?"

"Squirrel? His name is Philip Lambe."

Reed bolted forward. He'd obviously misunderstood him. "Did you say Lambe?"

"Yes."

"Tall, bearded guy? Strange eyes, scarred hand?"

"You know him?"

Reed felt like he'd been kicked hard in the stomach. His mind was reeling. "I just spoke with Lambe at the funeral. He claimed he's been helping us check for other SCD cases. But obviously, he's been keeping tabs on what we know."

"Did you tell him the police are investigating?" Anne asked.

"No. But he'll assume they are."

"What else does he know?" Anne asked.

Reed thought a moment. "I told him that someone destroyed Kyle's office computer files."

"Anything else?"

"I asked him if Kyle had enemies at ChemSKan."

"What'd he say?"

"He said he'd think about it and get back to me. Then Hallie and I ... we told him we needed to know *today*."

"So he realizes we know about *tomorrow*," Anne said.

Reed nodded and turned back to the phone. "Tim, any idea where Lambe works or lives now?"

"No. But our Human Resources people might know. Hang on, I'll ask."

As he waited, Reed's frustration grew, knowing how easily Lambe had deceived him.

McMillan came back on. "All HR knows is his address of six years ago."

"What is it?"

"Thirty-seven Drummond Road. West of Grand Blanc."

Reed wrote it down. "Thanks, Tim. Do you remember anything else about Lambe?"

Tim McMillan paused. "Not much. But he always had animals shipped to his home. Mice, monkeys. Dogs. Test animals, we assumed."

"He has a laboratory?"

"He must. But we never saw it at his home."

"Anything else?"

"Money. The guy had tons of it. Best cars. Best clothes."

"Where's the money come from?"

"Don't know. But he took a lot of trips to Europe and the Middle East."

"The trips and money connected?"

"Possibly."

"Maybe it's family money?" Anne suggested.

"He has no family. Once, after a few drinks, he told me he had a horrific childhood. Grew up in Japan. Father was a colonel in the military. A real psycho. Alcoholic. Abusive. Deserted the family. Shortly after his father left, his mother committed suicide."

"That could damage a kid," Reed said.

"Lambe is damaged. But brilliant. Also very charming if need be. The more I think about it, Lambe may be capable of anything under the right circumstances. You should be very careful."

"We will," Anne said.

They hung up.

Reed felt excited. He had a suspect, Philip Lambe, a man who'd easily misled him at the funeral. A man his brother was very worried about.

"I've got to tell Detective Beachum," he said, grabbing the phone. He called the Birmingham police station and was told that Beachum was in court.

"Can you please beep him?" he asked, drumming his fingers.

"Got to be an emergency," the female desk officer said.

"It is."

She sighed heavily. "Hang on then!" She put him on hold.

He stood and paced until she came back on the line two minutes later. "He's not answering his beeper."

Reed's neck muscles tightened. "Please tell him to call Reed Kincaid immediately. It's urgent." He gave her his cell and home numbers and hung up.

He said goodbye to Anne and the girls and took the laptop so the police could search it for more information on Lambe.

Near I-75, he pulled into a Mobil station and filled the Typhoon's tank. He walked inside and paid the hulking red-haired cashier, whose shirt identified him as 'Burnell.' The man's gold nostril ring worked nicely with the gold dragon tattoo on his neck. His beard looked like a rusty Brillo pad. Behind him, Reed saw a wall map of the Grand Blanc area.

"You know where Drummond Road is?"

Burnell turned and thumped an oily finger on the map. "Take that exit. 'bout two miles down, turn left at Cecil's Paint. Yer on 'er."

"Thanks."

Reed decided to drive by and see if Lambe still lived there and save the police some time. Pulling out of the station, he checked the mirror and saw no other cars. A second later, vehicle lights flicked on in a parking lot. The vehicle followed him onto the road, and moments later street lights revealed it was an older Jeep. Reed automatically switched to code red.

All vehicles were guilty until proven innocent.

He turned right and the Jeep followed. He drove onto I-75, still trailed by the Jeep. Traffic was light, and Reed increased speed. The Jeep increased speed. He slowed, the Jeep slowed.

Show time....

He floored the Typhoon III and his head snapped back like he'd been bumped from behind. He couldn't believe the power. In seconds he was doing one hundred fifteen miles per hour.

The Jeep faded. Quickly, he put more than a half mile between himself and the Jeep. He maintained one twenty MPH, hoping police radar wouldn't pick him up.

When he no longer saw the Jeep, he bolted off an exit and hid behind a Burger King billboard. Fifty seconds later, the Jeep sped past. When it faded from sight, Reed drove to the other side of the freeway and headed back.

Back toward 37 Drummond Road.

Twenty-Two

My lovely angels of death, he thought as he gazed lovingly at the exquisite castor bean plants in his sprawling greenhouse near Grand Blanc.

The flowering plants, hundreds of them, looked magnificent. Over six feet tall, their black-purple foliage was in full bloom. He strolled over to one and felt its spiny seed pod. Soon the pod would split into three sections. Then the sections would burst open and release their glimmering seeds, each with its own intricate, unique design. Gorgeous seeds.

Drop-dead gorgeous. They were, after all, the most deadly seeds on earth.

Philip Lambe enjoyed serene moments like this, nurturing his delicate young plants from infancy to their lethal ripeness. Soon he'd harvest the seedlings to produce enough fresh ricin to eliminate a good-sized city.

Fingering a leaf, he realized the plants could benefit from more sunlight. He reached over and increased the wattage of the overhead halogens. As he adjusted the timer, his cell phone buzzed.

He removed the phone from his pocket and answered.

"Lambe."

He heard car phone static.

"Uh ... Reed Kincaid ... sorta got away," Manny Gómez said in a naughty-boy voice. "He left his brother's house with a laptop. I followed him. But...."

Lambe exhaled slowly. It was unfortunate he'd had to use a dysfunctional idiot like Gómez. But Luca Corsa had insisted only Gómez was available on such short notice.

"How did he get away?" Lambe asked.

"Uh ... well see, he's d-drivin' a Typhoon III back toward Detroit. He floored it. Thing's a rocket. My Jeep couldn't—"

"He knows you're following him?" Lambe asked, his pulse rate creeping up.

"Uh ... well, yeah, he does," Gómez confessed.

Lambe considered the implications for a moment. "Nothing changes. Handle him at his home."

"You got it," Gómez said.

"What about Hallie Mara and the CDC doctor?" Lambe asked.

"Ah, Luca's doing 'em at that ... Gennituck place."

"Inform me when he has."

"Right. Oh, yeah, and somethin' else...."

Lambe took a deep breath and prepared himself for more unpleasant news.

"Luca told me to tell you somethin.'"

Lambe waited, his impatience mounting.

"Ah, geez, it was just in my brain."

Your brain was fried by a crack pipe, years ago. "Well?"

"I'm tryin'—"

"Try harder!" Lambe cranked fire into his voice. He heard tires squealing, horns blaring.

"Asshole!" Gómez shouted. "Oh, not you, Mr. L. Some guy in a pickup jus—"

"I understand."

"Oh, now I remember. When Luca was moppin' the floor, he heard that Dr. Shah and the Jap lady talkin' about one of Dr. Shah's files, a green file. It was about some kinda biology thing. Or maybe it was chemical stuff, like a weapon or somethin', you know. Anyway, this guy in the Midwest, he bought a bunch of the stuff from one of them like A-rab or slant-eye countries."

Lambe's body straightened. Could it be *his* weapon? If it was, there was always a possibility, remote as it was, that the authorities might connect it to him.

"Did it name the weapon?" Lambe asked.

"Yeah. And maybe how the guy's gonna use it."

Impossible, Lambe thought, sliding his finger along the silky leaf of a purple orchid. The file couldn't possibly reveal *how* he would deliver his weapon. Only he knew the unique delivery system. And even if weapon delivery experts brainstormed for a year, they couldn't begin to imagine it. Still, the file might inconvenience him a bit.

"Tell Luca to get the file at all costs. Do you understand?"

"Uh-huh."

"No exceptions."

"Got it!"

"Bring me the file."

"Where you gonna be at?" Gómez asked.

"Home. I'm driving there now."

Twenty-Three

Reed watched a panther-shaped black cloud sweep across the sky and swallow a yellow moon. Leaves swirled in his headlights as humid air seeped through the vents and fat drops of rain splotched onto the windshield.

Seconds later, Mother Nature started throwing fastballs. Lightning flashed and the downpour started pinging the roof like marbles. Visibility dropped to a hundred feet, then fifty. Cars pulled off the road. Reed slowed to fifteen miles per hour, his wipers slapping away thick sheets of rain.

A mile further, Drummond Road narrowed into a country lane. From the rainy darkness, large old houses emerged like deformed, shimmering faces. They were set back from the road and surrounded by tall, skeletal trees. He passed a gray three-story house, a red-brick grade school, then what looked like an abandoned feed store.

Entering a forest, long, spidery branches arched over him, creating a shadowy, dripping passageway. Moments later, lightning bleached an old wood house. His headlight beams swept over the mailbox—number 31. A quarter mile further, he passed number 32.

If Lambe still lives at 37, I'll phone Beachum and wait for the police.

A half mile further, he saw number 35, a gray farm house with a rusty International Harvester tractor sunk in muck up to its axle.

Reed thumped across a wood-plank bridge, water roaring a few feet below. A hundred yards further, the road bent left and his headlight beams crept onto an oversized black mailbox.

He squinted at the gold reflective numbers—37. Inching closer, he watched rain spill over *LAMBE*.

Reed's heart pumped furiously. He parked, turned the lights off and phoned Beachum.

"Has Detective Beachum called in yet?"

"No, sir," said the woman desk officer.

"Please try his beeper again."

112

"Hang on."

Three long minutes later, she came back on. "He's still not answering."

Reed squeezed his cell phone harder.

"If he calls in," she said, "I'll have him call you immediately, first thing."

"My cell phone, please. It's *extremely* urgent."

He hung up.

Lightning flashed, illuminating the large old house. It sat back off the road about two hundred feet and was tucked into a forest of evergreens and maples which cast long, fingery shadows over the front door. The wood-frame house, probably built in the twenties, had three stories, an enormous bay window, a third-floor balcony and intricate filigree borders along the roof. Thick green shrubs were planted close to the house like a security fence. The driveway snaked alongside tall hedges to a three-car garage in back.

No lights were on. Lambe was out.

Old house, old locks. Reed knew old locks thanks to Arnie Waynert, an Ann Arbor cop who'd taught him how to open most of them.

I can probably get inside in seconds, Reed thought.

But unarmed.

Logic said wait for the police. His gut said break in. Beachum was a slave to legal procedure, required to observe the Is-There-Sufficient-Cause and Who-Has-Jurisdiction games. Was it Birmingham, where Kyle was murdered, or Genesee county, where Lambe lived? Or maybe even Oakland county, where Lambe's thug drove Reed off I 75? Sorting everything out might take lawyers and judges a week to issue a search warrant.

Tomorrow people would die.

Information in the house might save them.

I'm going in.

He drove down the road about one hundred yards, turned up a swampy forest path and flicked off the lights. He needed something to pick the lock. Searching the glove box, he found only a Bic pen and the owner's manual. The center armrest compartment revealed a roadmap and a package of Wrigley's Doublemint. He crawled into the back, checked the seat pockets and found a quarter and a pocket comb. Useless.

The luggage area contained just the spare tire, but as he turned, something glinted beside the tire. Squinting, he saw two large paperclips. Maybe if he bent them into the shape Arnie taught him, they might throw the bolt. He slipped them into his pocket.

Stepping outside, he walked smack into a soggy evergreen which drenched him with cold raindrops. He shivered, then hurried through the forest to Lambe's backyard and over to the garage window to see if a car was inside. A thick curtain blocked his view.

Lambe could be in the house.

Watching me now.

Reed looked at the house, saw no one in the windows. Squishing through the grass, he bent down and studied the backdoor lock. It *was* an old rim-type. He took his thinnest key, slid it in, turned and jiggled. Nothing. He tried another long, narrow key without success.

Beside him, rain from the gutter splashed into a massive puddle. He took out the paperclips, bent one into the appropriate T-shape, then bent the other and inserted them into the keyhole. Using one clip, he felt for the lock mechanism, found it, then scooched it slightly higher. When the height felt right, he gently nudged the bolt with the other clip.

The bolt wouldn't budge.

He tried again.

Nothing.

Hard rain stung his eyes, blurring his vision. He raised the lock mechanism a fraction, jiggled the other clip. Still no movement. The damn thing was probably rusty.

As he eased one clip out, it caught the lock mechanism—and seemed to nudge the bolt a bit. Delicately, he pulled and felt the bolt drop into place. He was in.

But would *going* in trigger an alarm? Only one way to find out. Slowly, he turned the handle, pushed in and listened. Only rain.

He stepped into a dark kitchen and looked around. No motion detectors, but what if he'd triggered a silent alarm? Nearby a refrigerator hummed. He saw mail on the table, walked over and flipped through the stack: a phone bill addressed to "P. Lambe," a bubble-pack envelope filled with bulky containers from a company called *Biologiekultur Firma* in Berlin, some junk mail.

To the left, he saw a narrow hallway. He walked down it to a spacious living room with a dark antique credenza, gray leather sofas, expensive-looking chairs, gleaming oak table. The walls were covered with Japanese art, a Chagall, and a Salvador Dalí of melting watches. The watches reminded him that Lambe could walk in any second.

Above him, ceiling boards creaked oddly, and suddenly Reed felt a draft.

Did a door open?

Lambe had every legal right to shoot him as an intruder.

Quickly, Reed moved down a side hall past a closet to a door. He twisted the knob and stepped inside what looked like an office. The dark room smelled musty and sour. In the corner sat a massive seven-foot armoire with its door slightly ajar. A large wood desk held a computer and neatly stacked files.

He moved slowly across plush carpet over to a wall-length shelf filled with books on chemistry, Japanese global trade, biological weapons, auto industry statistics, computer architecture design, and what looked like a large, murky specimen jar.

Lightning flashed—illuminating the jar—and Reed found himself staring into the single eye of a young male fetus with a grotesquely misshapen head. The umbilical cord was twisted around his limbless body. Small one-inch nubs hung from his shoulders.

Reed swallowed hard and hurried over to the desk. He removed the crystal paperweight from atop a stack of folders and looked into the top file. It dealt with fertilizers for Laotian rice farmers. Another contained research for Tigres Limited in Damascus.

Above him, the floorboards snapped again.

Slow. Like someone walking.

Quickly, Reed opened another file, some kind of plastic experiment for a Los Angeles firm called Petro-Tek. On the other side of the desk he saw a folder for NorthStar Signal, a pager-beeper company. The next file contained microscope invoices. The next, a Homeland Security report on weapons of mass destruction, and beside it the *9/11 Commission Report*.

Suddenly, the air smelled of rain and something creaked in the hall.

Is Lambe out there?

Opening a side drawer, he found pencils, a box of Cuban Boliva cigars, a Mont Blanc pen and pencil. He pulled the bottom drawer. Locked.

Why?

He eased his paper clips into the keyhole and jiggled. Nothing. He lifted the drawer handle and jiggled again. No luck. Twisting the clip a fraction, he lifted, shook hard and the old lock shifted. He yanked the drawer open, rattling pens, then flipped through a stack of folders with chemical labels. Nothing suspicious.

Then he saw it. Hidden in the back of the drawer. A gray folder. He opened it and read.

R.C. Test (Toxin: R.C.)
27 test subjects:

S.M.	8/16	R.S.	9/30	E.R.	11/1
R.T.	8/29	T.Y.	10/6	T.N.	11/3
N.R.	8/30	E.B.	10/12	M.K.	11/4
E.R.	9/3	W.B.	10/16	L.N.	11/4
T.H.	9/13	G.H.	10/20	L.R.	11/4
B.M.	9/21	P.G.	10/28	P.V.	11/6
W.K.	9/23	H.B.	10/29	K.K.	11/9
N.M.	9/26	S.T.	10/30	D.F.	11/9
A.C.	9/28	P.G.	10/31	S.C.	11/9

Test Completed
Autopsies: Cause of Death—SCD

The Shikei
November 14

Ten cities: (Korusu: <u>(CH3-P(=O)(-F)(-OCH(CH332)</u>
- Delivery system operational
Tested, successful
- Estimated harvest—60,000 deaths

Reed's heart pounded in his ears. He slumped against the desk and tried to blink away some of the zeros. They remained.

"Sixty thousand people...." He felt a vein throbbing on his forehead. Scanning the list of initials on the *R.C. Test,* he froze on *K.K. 11/9.*

Kyle Kincaid! November 9. The day he died!

A loud thud. Car door.

Lambe....

Reed glanced at the folder. Taking it was illegal seizure. Inadmissible. Better to have the police take it, along with Lambe and more evidence, into custody. Reed replaced the folder exactly as he'd found it and shut the drawer.

Feet thumped onto the front porch, keys jingled.

Reed hurried from the office, closed the door and moved down the hall past the living room. The front door squeaked open as Reed nudged a kitchen chair.

Did Lambe hear?

The front door slammed shut.

Silently, Reed closed the backdoor and ran into the woods. He glanced back and saw the lights go on in the front hall, then seconds later in the study, then the kitchen, then he heard the backdoor open.

Lambe knew someone had been inside.

Reed jumped in the Typhoon and drove onto Drummond Road, speeding away from Lambe's house. A quarter mile further, he skidded to a stop at a stone fence. Dead end. He had to drive back past Lambe's house.

He turned around and floored it, wipers sweeping away sheets of rain. As he approached Lambe's house, two headlights sprang from the driveway like leopard eyes.

Lambe raced toward him on the one-lane road. The man would block the road and take target practice at him.

Reed was trapped.

He slid to a stop, hunting for some way out.

Lambe sped toward him, then fish-tailed his Jaguar to a sideways stop, blocking the road.

Reed saw only one choice. He slammed the Typhoon into low-four-wheel drive, drove down into the marshy field and clawed ahead through the muck.

Lambe jumped out and fired three shots. The bullets thwacked into the back end of the Typhoon.

Reed ducked down and steered hard left to avoid some trees—just as two bullets ripped into the Typhoon engine.

Twenty-Four

Easing his .38 back in its shoulder holster, Philip Lambe let the icy rain wash over his face. He took a long, deep breath and relaxed his muscles, slowed his pulse down, took control. Mind over emotion, as always.

He watched Reed Kincaid's taillights vanish into the night.

You will also vanish tonight, Kincaid. Manny awaits you.

Lambe got back in his car and drove back to his house. Inside, he inspected the hidden entrance to his subterranean laboratory. He ran his fingers along the entrance base and felt the black filament was not broken. Kincaid had not entered the hidden lab.

In his office, Lambe looked around. The folders on his desk were in order, paperweights on top, chair unmoved. As he turned, he saw it. The pencil was *crooked!*

He grabbed the drawer. Unlocked!

Opening it, he saw that the gray *Shikei* folder was an inch too far left. He flipped through and found the third page out of sequence.

Rechecking the pages, he realized Kincaid had taken none, but he had learned some basic *Shikei* details. The weapon's name, *Korusu*. And that it would kill sixty thousand people.

But he failed to learn what *Korusu* was, since he wouldn't have understood *Korusu's* formula. Nor did he learn who would be killed or which ten American cities would be hit.

And most important, Kincaid did not learn the uniquely ingenious *way* the *Korusu* would reach its deserving victims. Bottom line, he learned nothing that could stop the *Shikei.*

But you will learn one thing more, Kincaid. Something your brother learned. How it feels to die in great pain.

Lambe called Manny Gómez in the van.

"Kincaid just broke into my house."

"But I seen him headin'—"

"He doubled back here."

"Bastard's gonna pay—"

118

"Or I don't," Lambe said. "Wait for him at his home. Eliminate him. And take the laptop."

"Right."

Lambe hung up. He knew he should leave now. Kincaid might have already informed the police. Even though he couldn't justify his illegal entry, or prove he found clear evidence of a serious crime, the police might believe him and arrive any second.

Taking the gray *Shikei* file, Lambe hurried upstairs and placed it in his prepacked suitcase. From his bedroom wall safe he took forty-eight thousand dollars in cash, plus four separate sets of ID: Passports with matching credit cards, drivers' licenses, birth certificates and voter registration cards.

He rushed outside, where the rain had eased to a gentle mist. Quickly, he installed Florida plates on his Jaguar and drove onto Drummond Road.

Pausing a moment, he stared back at the house. His home for eight years, longer than any house he'd ever lived in. He should probably feel some attachment to it, but he felt nothing. It was wood, nails and mortar. A place where he'd created very special biological and chemical products for clients who'd stuffed millions into his Curaçao and Cayman Island bank accounts. A place that had given him blissful isolation and pleasure.

And a place that would soon give him one final pleasure.

Smiling, he drove on down Drummond Road toward his destination. There, he'd wait until it was time to launch his *Shikei.* But along the way, he'd do a little housecleaning, so to speak.

Twenty minutes later, Lambe parked directly across the street from a large, neo-Mediterranean home in the affluent suburb of Potter's Creek, southwest of Flint. Nearby, spacious Tudors and Colonials bordered the rolling hills of a pine-studded golf course. He relaxed, knowing his Florida plates would deflect police interest.

Lambe studied the white three-story house. Its orange-tile roof covered over five thousand square feet. The home was expensively landscaped with tall evergreens standing like sentinels at the sides. On the far left was a glassed-in sun room and a garage with a gray-brick walkway curving up to the front doors.

Luxury. Opulence. Wealth. Stolen by the home's owner.

Stolen partly from me.

Lambe leaned back and let the hypnotic melody of Ravel's *Bolero* work its magic. *A perfect view,* he thought as he gazed through the enormous arched windows. Focusing powerful binoculars, he watched a tall, attractive blonde woman about thirty-five, wearing an expensive lime-green sweatsuit, stroll into view. He recalled her. The perfect corporate wife, all smiles and giggles at the boss's dumb jokes.

Lambe was surprised to see a young boy around three, and a girl, five, wearing pajamas, toddle into view. Yesterday, when Gómez had posed as a gas company serviceman and deposited a device in the furnace ventilator shaft, he'd seen no hint of children. But then, Gómez wouldn't recognize children in a day-care center.

Too late, Lambe thought. This would have to be a family affair. Besides, "family" was a myth, a cruel illusion, a collection of similarly chromosomed individuals who pretended affection for each other, but in a life-and-death crisis sold each other out.

"Family...." he muttered aloud into the car's darkness.

The word had held no meaning for him since Taka Hoshi, the Nip slut, had seduced his father into leaving the marital home. Lambe had only been nine. Secretly, he'd rejoiced that his abusive father had left them, but he was enraged by the anguish it caused his mother.

Headlights flashed in Lambe's mirror, and he watched a silver Lexus LX470 sweep into the driveway. Wilson Stockman stepped from the expensive SUV. Scrawny, fortyish, Ichabod Crane re-incarnated. He rolled a tan Hartmann suitcase toward the house.

A tailored brown suit drooped like a Sears tent on Stockman's tall, bony frame. He bent down to move a red tricycle from the sidewalk, and pathetic wisps of stringy hair fell down over his scrawny forehead. He looked exhausted.

Rest is coming, Stockman.

He entered the house and kissed his wife, who took his suitcase. The kids swarmed him and he bent down and hugged them. The young boy pointed to a page in a coloring book. Stockman smiled and rumpled the kid's hair.

Lambe felt a rare stab of envy. When his father came home, Lambe had hidden and prayed the bastard drank himself into oblivion.

Grabbing his cell phone, Lambe called Stockman's home and watched the wife pick up.

"Is Wilson there?"

"Yes, just a moment."

She handed the phone to Stockman.

"Hello." Same stupid, squeaky voice.

"Long time no talk, Wilson."

"Who is this?" Stockman smiled, looking puzzled.

"You've enjoyed your meteoric rise in Trans-Linc, haven't you?"

Stockman tilted his head. "John, is this you?"

"Not John."

"Eric?"

"You're very good, Stockman. Mostly at recognizing the genius of others, like mine."

Less smile now.

"Who the hell is this?"

Lambe fine-tuned the binoculars on Stockman's eyes and saw them tighten with concern.

"You feared quite rightly, Stockman, that I would be promoted over you. So you lied to management, didn't you? You said my formula didn't have the tensile strength and heat tolerances for all computer applications. You said your formula did. You lied, Stockman."

Stockman's eyes flickered with recognition.

"And," Lambe continued, "your lies resulted in my termination, didn't they?"

"Lambe, is this you?"

The recognition warmed Lambe like a sip of single malt scotch. "Guess what, Stockman?"

"What?" Stockman looked irritated now, bored.

"Termination's a two-way street."

Fear flickered in Stockman's eyes.

Lambe enjoyed seeing the fear. He hung up, then picked up a modified garage opener and rubbed its cool plastic against his cheek.

Stockman faced his wife and twirled his finger around his temple as though the caller was crazy. Then he laughed.

Lambe did not appreciate the laugh. Angrily, he jammed his thumb down hard on the garage opener button. A small blue light came on, indicating the special device Gómez left in the Stockman's ventilation shaft was now releasing its toxin.

Clicking on his stopwatch, Lambe leaned back and enjoyed the close-up view. The Stockmans sat watching the large-screen television. Watching their last show. He wondered what it was. Too bad he didn't have a video camera to capture the next few minutes. Family snuff films might be a hot new product.

Predictably, the small boy coughed first. He rubbed his throat and eyes and swallowed with obvious difficulty.

Lambe checked his stopwatch—only sixty-eight seconds. Amazingly fast. The ventilator fan must be running. Moments later, the young girl rubbed her eyes and throat. The wife coughed and pointed at her son, who slid off the sofa.

Stockman moved toward his children, then stopped and clutched his chest.

His face was a wonderful shade of crimson.

"Painful, isn't it, Stockman?" Lambe whispered. "So is termination."

Stockman's lips yanked back over his teeth in a bizarre grin as he clutched his throat and began to gag.

Lambe enjoyed their obscene gyrations … a sweet little dance of death, enhanced even more by *Bolero*'s mounting crescendo. The music seemed to have been written exclusively for the magnificent denouement before him.

The wife collapsed, vomiting on the sofa, which Lambe noticed was a marvelous beige Thayer Coggin, the exact color and style he'd been shopping for. He wondered where she'd bought it.

The boy's tiny fingers quivered down the picture window, leaving streaks of bloody vomit. Stockman, purple-faced now, fell to his knees. He crawled toward the still bodies of his wife and children, then jerked oddly. Seconds later, his body went still.

Lambe clicked his stopwatch. Two minutes, forty-seven seconds. Remarkable. Much faster than he'd estimated. He opened a small notebook and wrote "2:47" beside Stockman's name.

Sitting back, he savored this wonderful moment, letting the exquisite pleasure surge through him, strengthening him. His senses were razor sharp. He saw a small worm crawling beneath a thin leaf, smelled damp night air seeping through the vent, heard a bird chattering in the large oak tree fifty feet away.

Only death made him this alive.

He knew he should feel something for the children, but he didn't.

Feelings got in the way.

Twenty-Five

Speeding down I-75, Reed rechecked the Typhoon's oil and temperature gauges. Normal. Lambe's bullets, somewhere in the vehicle's engine, had not affected the Typhoon's powerful engine. So far.

Reed was sure Lambe had recognized him. But if not, he'd figure it out when he talked to the driver of the Jeep.

Ahead, Reed saw a livestock truck stuffed with cattle. As he pulled out to pass, a cow stared out at him with sad eyes, as though somehow she sensed she was heading for the slaughterhouse.

Humans are headed for Lambe's slaughterhouse tomorrow, Reed thought. Sixty thousand men, women and children. Innocent people.

Why, Lambe? What did these people do to you? Why are you killing them?

He dialed Beachum's home phone again. No answer. "Damn!" he said aloud, tossing the phone back on the seat.

Time was beyond critical. Beachum had to brief state and federal authorities, who had to mobilize a maze of agencies like Homeland Security, the FBI and others—and he had to do it in hours.

A dull pain began to migrate above Reed's eyes.

He phoned the Birmingham police station again and was told Beachum was still not answering his pager. The second he hung up, it struck him. Beachum could be dead. Lambe might have learned Beachum was investigating and had him killed. What's one cop when you're killing thousands of people?

Reed decided to phone Genetique and explain everything to Hallie, who could tell Officer Larsen, her bodyguard. He called, but got Hallie's voice mail and left a message.

What now? he wondered.

Drive to Genetique and brief Larsen in person.

He tuned the radio dial to 98.7 FM, hoping the light jazz might help him think better. The music didn't help.

What if Lambe launches his Shikei early? I should have taken the damn file. It might have saved lives.

Staring into his headlight beams, he remembered the Tokyo subway nerve gas deaths. Authorities said the *Aum Shinrikyo* doomsday cult responsible had stockpiled enough chemicals to kill *ten million* people. Experts said al Qaeda, rogue states and other terrorist groups probably had enough nerve gas and biological agents to kill millions more.

Did anyone doubt they'd use it?

Ahead, Reed saw a poster for tomorrow's Britney Spears concert at Ford Field. Sixty thousand kids and parents crammed together, swaying to the beat, clapping their hands, singing their lungs out—then filling those same lungs with the air from a self-contained ventilation system.

Was Ford Field one of Lambe's gas chambers?

Twenty-Six

Reed hurried toward Genetique's lobby entrance. Through the tinted window, he saw the elderly security guard, Maynard, wave to him, then punch a number on the desk phone.

Reed pushed through the revolving door and entered the long, rectangular lobby with its gray marble floor and paneled walls. He passed a massive wall painting of DNA, two multi-colored chains twisting around each other, and a blue-and-red diagram captioned *Genetically Engineered Insulin.* Nearby, a large man in a tan chair read *Environmental Health Perspectives.*

Reed signed in at Maynard's desk, a gleaming chunk of marble that wrapped around the guard like a black granite skirt.

"She's a comin' down," Maynard said. He stuffed the last two inches of a chili-drenched hotdog into his mouth, leaving mustard skids on his lip. Splotches of chili and onion adorned his gray uniform. Behind him, an "Athens Coney Island" bag seeped grease onto the sports page of the *Detroit Free Press.*

"Thanks, Maynard."

Maynard nodded, wiped chili from his chin. "Three to two, Red Wings." He nodded toward his tiny desktop television, flinging his thick silver hair nearly down to his gray mustache.

"Them Rooskies skate like old Gordie Howe." Maynard pointed at the screen. "Hey—Blackhawks high-sticking!" He cleared his throat like gravel shaking in a can, then crammed four slippery French fries into his mouth.

* * *

The elevator hissed open and Hallie led Officer Deke Larsen into the lobby. She saw Reed talking with Maynard. When Reed spun around, she knew something was terribly wrong. She hurried over.

"Did you hear my voice mail?" Reed asked, clearly agitated about something as he hurried them toward the corner.

"No," she said. "We've been in the lab."

"Kyle *was* murdered."

She felt the air rush out of her. "How?"

"With something called R.C."

She searched her memory but came up empty.

"What's this R.C.?" Larsen asked, flipping open his notebook.

"I don't know," Reed said.

"Nor do I," Hallie said. "How'd you learn this?"

"Anne and I found notes in Kyle's laptop. The notes implicate Philip Lambe."

She blinked, wondering if Reed misspoke. "The man—"

"Yes. The man at the funeral."

She couldn't believe it. "But Lambe was helping us."

"We've been helping *him*! Telling him what we know."

"Are you *sure* it's Lambe?" she asked.

"He just shot at me."

Her heart rate raced into high gear. "My God, Reed!"

"Kyle was worried about a file he'd seen at Lambe's house. I tried to reach Beachum but couldn't. So I drove over to Lambe's home and broke in."

Larsen stopped writing and looked at Reed.

"I found Lambe's file. It contained Kyle's initials and the date he died on a list of twenty-seven R.C. test victims."

"Twenty-seven victims?" Larsen repeated, his eyebrows climbing.

"It gets *much* worse."

How on earth could it get worse? Hallie wondered.

Reed led them over to the farthest corner and checked to make sure no one was listening. "Tomorrow," he whispered, locking on her eyes, "Lambe will unleash a biological or chemical weapon that he estimates will kill 60,000 people in minutes."

Hallie felt her knees weaken and slumped against the wall. She couldn't speak. Larsen looked like he'd been zapped with a stun gun.

"Sixty *thousand?*" Hallie whispered.

"With some weapon called *Korusu.*"

"Kill," Hallie said.

"What?"

"*Korusu* means 'kill' in Japanese."

The lobby phone rang. Maynard picked up and signaled Hallie. "For you, Doc."

She walked over, talked briefly, then returned. "That's Dr. Shah, the CDC medical officer I flew back with. You should tell him everything immediately."

Reed nodded.

Larsen pulled out his cell phone. "I'm going to stay here and phone Beachum. We've got to brief Washington."

"Beachum's not answering his phone or pager," Reed said.

Larsen rolled his eyes. "He turns the damn things off. Why does he even have them? What's Lambe's address?"

Reed gave it to him and described the desk drawer where he'd found the gray *Shikei* file. Larsen walked to the window and dialed as Hallie and Reed stepped into an elevator. Moments later, she led him into the lab, where Dr. Shah looked up from his microscope.

"Ah, there you are," Shah said with a clipped Indian accent.

She introduced him to Reed and they shook hands.

Shah's dark, intelligent eyes seemed to sense her fear. "Hallie, what's wrong?"

"Reed should explain."

As Reed told Dr. Shah what he'd found, Hallie watched the small man shake his head as though he'd long expected the bad news. He dropped in his chair and stared at the floor. "Even before 9/11, I knew this day would come—*before* we could adequately protect all our citizens."

No one spoke for several moments.

Dr. Shah took a couple of deep breaths. Then, leaning forward, he seemed to shift gears deep inside. He stood up, ramrod straight, and looked at them with steel in his eyes. "This bastard won't win! We'll discover what R.C. is, and how he delivered it. Once we know that, we might be able to help save lives tomorrow. I was just about to check Kyle's serum sample."

"For what?" Hallie asked.

"His red blood cells. To see if they matched the cells in this microphotograph." He pointed to a large photograph in a textbook, then squinted into a microscope.

She watched Shah study Kyle's cells for several moments, then look at the large microphotograph, then Kyle's cells again.

"Voilà!" Shah said.

"Match?"

"You tell me."

Hallie walked over, brushed back hair from her eyes, squinted into the microscope, then at the photo, then repeated the process. "Definite match. Hemolysis. What percent of red blood cells would you estimate are ruptured?"

"Roughly twenty to thirty percent are lysed, kind of broken open," Shah said. "But it's *how* they're ruptured that reminds me of something."

"Of what?" Hallie asked.

"An infection I saw in a small Peruvian Indian village."

"Was it lethal?"

"Killed half the village."

"What caused the infection?"

"Bartonella. Carried by sand flies."

"Could sand flies be up here?" Reed asked.

"Too far north. They're usually in Peru, Ecuador, Colombia. Did Kyle travel to those countries recently?"

"No," Reed said. "So what caused Kyle's hemolysis?"

Shah shrugged. "Nothing in the autopsies suggests a cause."

Outside the lab door, Hallie noticed a large red-headed janitor roll a mop and bucket past, then begin swabbing the hall floor with disinfectant.

"Humm ... I see 'retinal hemorrhage' in this report," Shah said, rubbing his chin. "I also saw retinal hemorrhage in the first and second reports."

"And *renal* failure in the reports I checked," Hallie said.

"Renal?" Dr. Shah seemed surprised and turned toward her. "I hadn't noticed renal." Quickly, he paged through his reports and paused. "You're right. Renal failure is in these as well. And two had hemorrhagic gastroenteritis, plus complaints of a burning throat just before seizures and death." Shah's brow tightened as though fitting together the pieces of a puzzle.

Hallie noticed Reed looked a bit lost, like a six-year-old in med school.

Behind her, she heard pantyhose swishing together like sheets of sandpaper. Hallie turned and saw a plump, double-chinned lab technician in a white coat. Her brown hair was pulled back so tight it yanked her eyes into hyphens. Her nametag read "Mary Jean."

"You'll find this interesting, Doctor," Mary Jean said to Dr. Shah, handing him a folder. "Your final toxicology report."

"Thank you, Mary Jean."

She nodded and swished back down the hall.

Shah scanned the tox report and his eyes shot open. "Good Lord...."

Hallie leaned closer, trying to see the report.

"What?" Reed asked.

"Toxalbumin and phytotoxin," Dr. Shah said. "Traces of both were found in the four serum samples we tested here, including Kyle's."

"Toxalbumin?" Reed asked.

"Plant proteins. Extremely toxic."

"Could they cause the hemolysis?" Hallie asked.

"Could and did." Shah stood and paced alongside his bench, rubbing his forehead, obviously trying to remember something. "I *know* I've seen this cluster of symptoms before."

"Recently?" Hallie asked.

"No. Years ago."

"Africa? Asia?"

"No."

"Middle East?"

"No. It was rainy and cool."

Shah walked to the door and back a few times. Then he stopped and stared at something on the lab bench. "Yes, yes, that's it!" He hurried over and grabbed a syringe.

"What's it?" Hallie asked.

"London, years ago. The Russians placed a syringe like this on the end of an umbrella and injected a Soviet defector in the leg."

"With what?" Reed asked.

"Ricin!" Shah's face relaxed with the puzzle solved.

Hallie knew ricin was an absolutely terrifying poison. She felt her throat tighten.

"Saddam Hussein stockpiled ricin," Reed said.

"Yes," Shah said. "You know how deadly cyanide is."

Reed nodded.

"Ricin is six hundred times more deadly. Comes from the castor bean plant."

"What happened to the Russian defector?" Reed asked.

"Poor man died."

"So ricin may have caused my brother's death and these other test deaths?" Reed asked.

"All symptoms fit."

"But," Reed said, "Dr. McDonald said Kyle was not injected,"

"Ricin can be ingested. Perhaps even inhaled," Shah said. "Just last summer, a woman drove back from Mexico chewing on a necklace of castor bean seeds. It killed her."

Hallie swallowed, noticing her throat was a little scratchy.

"Ricin," Dr. Shah said, "Absolutely terrifying stuff. Officially it's *ricinus communis.*"

Reed bolted out of his chair. "R.C.! Rici...."

"What?" Shah asked.

"R.C.," Hallie said. "The letters Reed saw in Lambe's file," "R.C. stands for *ricinus communis.*"

Dr. Shah's large eyes brightened. "Yes! You've got it!"

The phone rang. Shah grabbed it and listened. "Thank you, Doctor. I'll walk right over." He hung up. "That was Doctor Rowles over at the hospital lab. His samples are ready. We need to see if they match these."

Shah stood. "Please come along. We shall discuss tomorrow's medical procedures. There's so much to do." He bounded toward the door, Hallie and Reed trying to keep up. Entering the hall, Shah nearly collided with the burly janitor mopping the floor.

"Oh, sorry," Shah said.

"No problem, Doc," the janitor said. He continued swabbing pine-scented disinfectant over the floor.

Hallie, Reed and Dr. Shah hurried down the hall to the elevators.

* * *

Wringing out the mop, Luca Corsa adjusted his fake red beard and ponytail. He hated them. They were hot and sticky and itched like hell. But they did the job. The bitch didn't recognize him. Glancing down the hall, he watched her and the two men get on the elevator and head up.

He reached in his pocket and carefully touched the eye drop bottle.

Above all, Lambe had warned him, *don't touch the contents!*

His hand began to tremble a bit.

Corsa entered Shah's lab and reminded himself to be extremely careful. He checked his gloves and saw no holes. He unscrewed the top of the bottle and delicately dabbed the substance on the two microscopes. Then he swabbed some on the phone and the other locations.

Places they were sure to touch.

If only I could stay and watch....

Twenty-Seven

Hallie and Reed could barely keep up with Dr. Shah as he hurried down the Detroit Memorial corridor with the new blood serum samples from Dr. Rowles. Hallie noticed that Shah cradled the samples like they were newborn infants.

Reed turned to her. "So now we see if these samples also contain toxalbumin?"

"Right."

"Why didn't Kyle's toxicology tests find the toxalbumin?"

"Autopsies test for the most likely poisons," she said. "Toxalbumin from the castor bean plant is virtually nonexistent this far north. Lambe knew they wouldn't test for it."

Passing one room, Hallie was overwhelmed by the scent of disinfectant and hair spray. She passed an anorexic-thin blonde teenager inching her walker down the hall, then an elderly man on a gurney, grumbling about a conspiracy between Richard Nixon and the pope.

As they stepped off the elevator into the hallway at Genetique, her nostrils were once again overwhelmed, this time by pine-scented disinfectant, which the janitor had apparently spilled all over the place.

They walked back into the small lab. Hallie sat in front of her microscope while Shah located himself next to his. Reed settled in by the phone.

"We've got to figure out how the victims were exposed to ricin," Shah said as he prepared a new sample for his microscope. "*How* is very important."

"But tomorrow he's using *Korusu*," Reed said. "Do you think *Korusu* is ricin?"

"It's possible, but I don't think so."

"Why not?"

"Ricin is not the most practical weapon to kill 60,000 people. There are better weapons of mass destruction, WMDs."

"But he may use his ricin *delivery* system," Hallie suggested.

"Yes."

"And if we discover the delivery system," Reed said, "we steer people away from it."

"Precisely," Shah said. He gestured for Hallie to check the open textbook. "Read how ricin works while I prepare this sample for us."

She pushed her microscope to the side a bit, then read from the textbook. "Says here that ricin acts as proteolytic enzymes, breaking down critical proteins."

"Which break down other functions," Shah said.

"Like breathing," she added.

"Exactly," Shah said. "*In vitro*, as few as ten ricin molecules bound to a glycroteind surface receptor of HeLa cells in culture can kill the cell. Toxicity level of six."

"A high level?" Reed asked.

"The highest, Reed. As I mentioned, ricin is six hundred times more poisonous than cyanide. Just seventy micrograms could kill a person."

"How much is seventy micrograms?"

"Like a few grains of salt."

Hallie was shocked that so little ricin could kill. "Where do castor bean plants grow?"

"Warm, sunny climates, like in the Southwest."

Hallie watched Shah settle in at his microscope and slide the sample into position. He squinted into the eyepiece, then frowned. "That's strange...."

"What is?" she asked.

"Focus is off. I must have nudged it." He fine-tuned the focus knob, then yanked his fingers away. "What's this?"

Hallie watched Shah rub a clear substance between his fingers.

"Lubricating oil?" she suggested.

Shah sniffed it. "No. No scent."

"Water condensation?" Reed said.

"No. Too viscous."

Hallie looked up at the ceiling and saw nothing dripping.

Shah shrugged and wiped the stuff into his palms. He adjusted the focus knob again, picking up more substance, and rubbed it on his lab coat.

"What about Lambe's delivery system?" Hallie asked. "What are our chances of stopping it tomorrow?"

"Depends on so many things," Shah said. "The delivery system itself, where the victims are located, whether *Korusu* is a chemical or biological weapon, and other variables."

"But won't the government's new security measures help?" Reed asked.

"They'll help some, Reed. But unfortunately, despite the post-9/11 security improvements, Homeland Security, the new intelligence czar, and everything else, most Americans are still seriously unprotected against *all* types of biological or chemical attacks."

"Why?" Reed asked, obviously puzzled.

Dr. Shah frowned and cleared his throat. "Too many biological and chemical weapons out there. Too much easy access to them. Too many terrorists willing to use them. And frankly, too many years when Congress downplayed warnings from biological and chemical experts."

"And ignored the warnings," Hallie said.

Shah nodded. "And now they're trying to play catch up."

Hallie watched frustration tighten his face.

"The sad reality," Shah said in a soft voice, "is that a skilled terrorist with the right weapon and a new, unpredictable delivery system can kill thousands in any city in America."

"Or any *ten* cities...." Reed said.

Shah nodded and sighed with obvious, tired resignation.

Hallie noticed that the man's eyes were pink. Clearly, he was exhausted from a lack of sleep. He'd flown back from Iraq two days ago, where he'd probably worked around the clock, squinting into other microscopes. Then he'd flown back to Atlanta, then up to Michigan.

She turned a page and read, "Chewing ricin seeds causes severe burning, nausea, vomiting, circulatory collapse and death. Thank God the plant doesn't grow in northern climates like Michigan."

"Lambe might import the seeds," Shah said, clearing his throat.

"Or grow the plant in greenhouses?" Reed suggested.

"Also possi—" Shah coughed loudly, then again.

"Or buy ricin in weaponized form," Hallie said.

Shah started to respond, then stopped. Hallie noticed Shah was having great difficulty breathing in air.

"My goodness," Shah said. He swallowed in obvious pain and rubbed his throat. His face darkened quickly. "What's happening here? My eyes ... so hot ... can't breathe...." He coughed and blinked several times, then gripped his throat again, grimacing in obvious pain.

Hallie realized something was terribly wrong.

Shah's eyes were now crimson, zigzagging, panicked. Kyle's attack flashed in her mind.

"Kundan...?" Hallie said, hurrying to his side. "What's wrong?"

Shah opened his mouth to speak, couldn't. Perspiration drenched his face. He clutched his chest and slumped toward the floor. Reed caught him and eased him down on his back.

"What is it, Kundan?" Hallie asked, cradling his head.

Dr. Shah stared at his fingers, then the microscope, then at Hallie. "Micro … don't touch…."

"The oily stuff?" Hallie said.

Shah nodded, then suddenly his body began to jerk as though locked in the jaws of a shark. Reed shielded Shah's head from hitting the metal file cabinet, but the man suddenly jack-knifed forward like someone was driving stakes into his chest. Bloody froth slid from his lips.

"ER," Hallie said, reaching for the phone.

Reed grabbed her wrist. "*Wait!*"

"What's wrong?"

"Look—the phone's wet! The oily stuff maybe."

She saw the numbers gleaming with something moist.

Reed ripped off a piece of paper towel and wiped the numbers dry, then wrapped another piece around the wet receiver. She punched in the Detroit Memorial ER number with a pencil and asked for a trauma team STAT.

Shah fell unconscious.

Hallie began CPR and ninety seconds later the Detroit Memorial team burst into the lab, lifted Shah onto a gurney and rushed him toward the hospital. She grabbed a sheet of paper and wrote "Do Not Enter! Lethal Biohazard," then taped it to the door and locked it. Her heart was racing as they hurried down the hall toward the hospital.

Suddenly, Hallie felt dizzy. The hallway seemed to sway. She stopped, leaned against the wall and took a deep breath. Swallowing, she realized her throat hurt. She rubbed her neck, coughed, and started to panic, fearing the worst.

"What's wrong?" Reed asked, his eyes wild with fear.

"My throat's … warm." She looked back toward the lab. "I touched the other microscope."

"No…." Reed held her face.

She swallowed hard and felt her cheeks redden. Then it hit her. "I remember now."

"Remember what?"

"I woke up with this sore throat."

"Jesus, Hallie," he said, pulling her into his arms.

"Sorry," she said, holding him tight. "I only touched my microscope's base."

Turning, they hurried toward Detroit Memorial. When they entered the ER, Hallie saw the medical team working frantically to save Dr. Shah.

"Clear!" a doctor shouted.

She watched Shah's body jerk up and collapse hard on the table, but the heart monitor remained flat. Again, they placed the paddles on his chest.

"Hit it!" The green line remained flat.

The trauma team tried again. Then again. Hallie sensed they'd already defibrillated him several times without success. The lead doctor, Aleta Brown, a tall, attractive friend of Hallie's, looked up at her colleagues. They stared back, nodded, then slowly drifted away. A nurse looked at the clock and wrote down the time.

Hallie watched Dr. Brown, turn and face her.

"Hallie, I'm sorry...."

Hallie felt her knees grow weak. "He touched something in the lab."

"My guess is he had a massive stroke," Dr. Brown said.

"The substance he touched killed him, Aleta," Hallie said.

"*Touched*?" Dr. Brown said, staring at her as though she was losing it. "That doesn't sound very plausible, Hallie."

"His last words to us were 'don't touch ... mic....' A minute earlier, he'd touched a clear, oily substance on the microscope, then rubbed it into his hands. A minute later, he collapsed. Five minutes later, he's dead."

Dr. Brown's large brown eyes stared back.

"It must be a chemical toxin," Hallie explained. "Get a sample from his hands, Aleta. But wear gloves."

Dr. Brown blinked twice, then spun around toward her colleagues. "Everyone away from the body now! Do not touch his hands! Bag them immediately!"

The team, puzzled, backed further away from Shah's corpse.

Dr. Brown turned to Hallie. "We'll go over everything in the lab."

"Thanks, Aleta."

Dr. Brown placed her arm on Hallie's. "You okay, Hallie? You're white as chalk."

No, I'm not okay, she thought. *I'm devastated. I asked for CDC help and now this man is dead.* "I'll be fine. It's just that he was a wonderful man."

Dr. Brown nodded, then turned and hurried back to her team.

In silence, Hallie and Reed walked down the hall to the elevator. She stared at the floor, trying to absorb what had just happened. She felt Reed's arm go around her shoulders and leaned into him.

"I should have warned Kundan more," she whispered.

"Dr. Shah was doing his job."

"But *I* involved him."

"And he succeeded in identifying ricin."

She agreed, but it did little to assuage her growing sense of guilt.

They returned to her office, shut the door and sat in silence for several moments. There was nothing to say. She pictured Dr. Shah getting excited about his discovery. She remembered herself moving the other microscope, which may have had the substance on it. She remembered Reed stopping her from touching the phone, which *had* the substance on it.

"I'll tell Detective Beachum," Reed said.

"And I'll tell Officer Larsen."

He nodded. "Can you leave now?"

She blinked and nodded slowly. "I just have to brief Diedre, then I'll come."

"With Officer Larsen."

"Yes."

Hallie gazed out the window at the dark, crooked branch of an oak tree. A lone, brown leaf twisted in the wind but held on. *She* had to hang on too. Despite the attempts on their lives, and now Shah's death, she had to help make certain Dr. Shah and Kyle had not died in vain. No matter what it took, *she* had to help stop Lambe tomorrow.

The phone rang, and Hallie flinched. She punched the speaker.

"Hallie. It's Brendan Bryant in Atlanta. Is Dr. Shah there?"

Twenty-Eight

Reed drove toward Birmingham, agonizing over the death of Dr. Shah, a dedicated, compassionate man who'd just given his own life so that others might live tomorrow. Now, those lives hung like thick, heavy chains around Reed's neck.

Whose are these people?

Men and women working in offices? Parents playing with their kids, making dinner, making love? *Whoever they are, they'll never see their future. Nor will I, if Lambe has his way.*

Which means I need my .38.

Reed decided to drive by his house and check for the Jeep. If it wasn't there, he'd go in and get his gun, then brief Detective Beachum at the police station.

Minutes later, he turned down his dark, narrow street and waved to a young couple, jogger friends, in yellow reflective vests. As he approached his driveway, he saw several cars clustered in front of the Heltberg home two doors down. Third Heltberg party this week. He saw a Buick, BMW, Jaguar, Corvette and a Cadillac Escalade. No Jeeps, vans or Lincolns. In the picture window, Bjorn Heltberg delivered a punch line to wine-sipping partygoers who exploded with laughter. Someday, Heltberg's liver would explode.

Behind his home, Reed crunched down a narrow gravel drive and parked the Typhoon. He scanned his darkened backyard and saw no odd shadows. No hint of human movement.

He got out and locked the door. Another burst of raucous laughter rocketed over from the Heltberg party, followed by Canada geese honking their arrival at nearby Quarton Pond. He stepped onto his driveway and walked along the tall hedge toward the rear door.

Then a twig cracked. Loud, as though stepped on.

Every muscle in his body stiffened.

A huge man with a very serious handgun stepped from behind the hedge. Mean, olive-pit eyes squinted from deep in his fleshy face. A gold chain glinted around his neck. His massive shoulders and chest fused into a thick torso. He stood about six-four, weighed maybe two forty and looked like a concrete barrier.

"You got one fast truck, Kincaid. But it ain't as fast as my bullets is, if you get my drift."

Reed got his drift. He also recognized him as the Big Man who drove him off I-75.

"You also broke into a guy's house. Snoopin' where you got no fuckin' right."

Big Man was not here to lecture on American jurisprudence. "Let's talk about this," Reed said, his mind racing.

"'bout what?"

"Money. How much they paying you?"

His thick lips bent with pride. "A big chunk."

"Five grand?"

"The fuck you say?"

I've insulted him. "Fifteen?"

"Twenty!" he said proudly, jutting his jaw out, revealing an ugly zigzag scar along his Adam's apple.

"I'll give you thirty grand. Cash. You walk away clean. No murder one on your head."

Big Man's smile exposed stubby, yellow teeth. "You don't git it."

"Get what?"

"I'm pulling twenty for you, plus another twenty for helpin' wax your Jap chick."

Reed's heart slammed against his chest. "Listen, I'll give you fifty thousand dollars to stay away from her and me. Fifty thousand cash in your hand! My banker will bring the money over *now!*" Reed had no idea where to get that much cash now.

Big Man's thick brow scrunched up as though considering the offer. "Fifty big ones is kinda nice. But see, the boss ain't the kinda guy what you double-cross."

"Say I never showed up."

"He'd figger it out. "And I'd just hafta come after you again. Nothin' personal, you unnerstand."

Reed understood his chances were sliding faster than the sweat down his neck. Panic started to claw through him. Suddenly, an idea came to him. If it worked, great. If it didn't....

He inched slowly toward his neighbor's driveway just a few feet away. "There's something you should know."

"Yeah? What's that?"

"You don't want to do this job."

Big Man smirked as though this had better be good. "How's come I don't?"

"That big elm tree behind you."

"What about it?"

"This morning," Reed said, "the police installed a tiny surveillance camera in it."

"And I'm Madonna's left tit."

"They installed it after you drove me off I-75. They're watching this live."

"Bullshit!" Big Man rolled his eyes, tightened his silencer and seemed to grow impatient.

Keep him talking, Reed thought. "They offered a bodyguard," Reed said, easing closer to the driveway. "But I told them no."

"You was kinda wrong." He grinned.

"I was. But the cops are on the way by now."

"Nice try, Kincaid. I checked things out good. I never seen no camera."

"It's only an inch wide. But you can see its lens reflecting just above that large branch on the left."

Uncertainty flickered in the Big Man's eyes.

"You can also see where its red electrical wire taps into the power line."

More uncertainty.

Keeping his gun on Reed, Big Man stepped a couple of feet to the left, then turned around to look.

Reed jumped onto the neighbor's drive, triggering the Night Guard security system—and drenching the entire area in brilliant halogen spotlights.

Running, Reed glanced back. Big Man spun around, squinted into the blinding lights and fired off two muffled shots in Reed's direction. Chunks of garage siding bounced off Reed's back.

The huge man ran after him.

Reed raced in and out of shadows, hoping his erratic moves made him a difficult target. Behind him, two more *thumps*. Bullets whooshed past his ear.

Remembering how fast this large man ran last night, Reed sprinted onto a street and alongside a row of protective elms. He saw a side street and sprinted all out, pulling a little further away.

Behind him—*thump!*

A yard lamp exploded beside him.

Turning the corner, he found himself on a well-lit street.

Too well lit. He'd be a sitting duck. Searching for a hiding place, he saw a half-constructed house on his left. He ran into the open garage, then stepped through a roughed-in kitchen cluttered with wood scraps. Hurrying along a wall, he felt a nail rip into his forearm and warm blood trickle down.

He climbed the roughed-in stairs to the second floor, entered a bedroom and peeked out a small window toward the street.

Big Man sprinted around the corner, ran down the street a few feet, then stopped cold. He scanned the area, his massive chest rising and falling. From his pocket, he took a penlight and aimed the beam along the ground. The light froze on a fresh footprint in the mud.

Mine, Reed realized.

Big Man moved to the next footprint, then the next, tracking Reed's footsteps into the garage. Seconds later, Reed heard him scuff across the kitchen floor, then move from room to room.

Reed saw moonlight pouring through a nearby window. In the middle of the moonlight was his fresh, muddy footprint. Big Man could follow his wet prints upstairs to this room. Reed needed some kind of a weapon. A metal pipe, a chunk of wood, a large nail, anything. He found nothing.

He was trapped. If he moved, a floorboard might squeak and reveal his location. Sweat covered his body. A full minute passed without a sound. Maybe he was confused by all the workers' muddy footprints. Maybe he'd left. The wind suddenly gusted through the windows, creaking some floorboards and wall studs.

Reed waited another minute in silence and considered leaving.

Then a shoe thumped on the stairs. And another. Big Man *was* coming upstairs—following Reed's prints.

Reed moved into a dark closet beside the window and waited.

The footsteps hit the top of the stairs, shuffled down the hallway, and stopped outside Reed's room.

A floorboard creaked nearby.

Where is he?

Silence.

Then footsteps moved on down the hall. *He's NOT following my footprints.* Reed breathed out slowly.

Big Man checked two more rooms, slammed doors, then stopped at Reed's door again. The penlight beam swept into the room along the wall and window.

He sees my footprint....

Big Man stepped into the room, but his shadow covered Reed's footprint like a huge oil slick.

Reed's heart pounded into his throat. Perspiration dripped onto the sawdust on the floor. He had one chance. Surprise him, knock him off balance and run downstairs—without getting shot. Timing would mean life or death.

Inching back further in the closet, Reed's heel touched something. He reached down and felt a scrap of two-by-four. Six inches long, but better than nothing. He grabbed the wood.

Big Man took a step closer. His shadow spread even larger. He was just outside the closet. Three feet away, wheezing beer breath.

He knows I'm here!

Silence....

Suddenly a floorboard creaked on the other side of the room.

Big Man hurried over toward the sound.

He's turned his back.

Quickly, Reed leaned forward and threw the wood through the open window. It hit the ground and thudded onto something metal.

The man rushed over to the window and looked down. Then he ran from the room, headed downstairs and outside. Reed heard him searching beneath the window, and circling the house. He began cursing and throwing construction materials around.

Then it became quiet.

Reed waited several minutes, listening, hearing nothing, wondering if Big Man was lying in wait, maybe watching the garage opening. Finally, Reed stepped to the window and looked out. Below, he saw the stack of metal pipes the wood scrap hit. Beside it, some rain-soggy grass.

He stepped onto the sill, jumped down to the grass and rolled up into a kneeling position. He listened but heard nothing. He stood and sprinted down the street toward Birmingham's shopping district. Big Man was nowhere in sight.

Reed ran down Maple Road past Dick O'Dow's Pub, where some departing happy-hour yuppies cheered loudly for the jogger in a muddy business suit. One minute later, he entered the vestibule of the Birmingham police station and signaled to the desk officer inside. The young policewoman stared at his sweaty face and clothes, then signaled him in.

"Detective Beachum," he gasped.

"Hasn't called in."

"Try Deke Larsen."

"He's not answering his pager either."

Twenty-Nine

Hallie sat at her desk, staring at Dr. Shah's tattered tan raincoat hanging on a corner rack. The hem had been ripped away—not unlike his life. She was numbed by the loss of the gentle, talented man who'd worked beside her until just thirty minutes ago.

Kundan, please forgive me....

She felt hollowed out and cauterized, as cold, heavy grief pressed down on her. She would never forget Kundan Shah and the pain in his eyes. Nor would she forget Dr. Bryant's pain when she told him of Shah's death. Bryant, his voice cracking, had whispered that "Shah was one of the CDC's best young epidemologists."

Was.... The word ran shivers down her spine.

She sipped cool tea, then walked over and pulled on a sweater. Too much was happening too fast. Her life seemed to be spinning out of control. Days ago, she'd been tracking chromosomes for killer genes. Now, killers were tracking her.

Her phone rang and she picked up.

"Hallie, it's Brendan Bryant again. I just briefed the military's biological and chemical weapon experts at USAMRIID and Aberdeen Proving Grounds. Their teams are landing at Detroit City Airport in about twenty minutes. They need to see your autopsies and Doctor Shah's ... findings." Again, Bryant's voice faltered.

"I'll have everything ready for them," she said.

"They're working with Homeland Security, the FBI and local police. They want you and Reed to brief them. A Detective Woody Beachum will take you both to the crisis team location."

"Reed and I are meeting Beachum in thirty minutes."

"Good. Hallie, one last thing."

"Yes?"

"Washington and Homeland Security have placed top security status on this. Please don't mention it to anyone. The White House fears premature, inaccurate media exposure could create panic. They don't want any unnecessary deaths."

"I understand."

Hallie hung up and glanced at her watch. She and Officer Larsen should leave now for the Beachum meeting. She phoned Diedre De Bakker and explained she'd be out. As usual, Diedre had everything moving along well in the lab for Tuesday's meeting. Hallie gathered the autopsy files, then picked up Shah's ricin notes and her purse.

Behind her, wingtips clicked to a stop. Turning, she saw Rex Randall, arms on hips, blocking her door, staring at her files.

"Now where?" he demanded.

"A personal matter, Rex."

His eyes hardened. "Didn't I make it clear to you?"

"Make what clear?"

"Genetique matters take precedence until Tuesday."

"They are. The team is going all out."

"Too bad *you're* not," he said.

"Actually, Rex, I am going out."

His face reddened. "Your job is *here,* cracking the whip over these people."

"Last week you said to empower them."

"Screw empowerment!" Randall shouted, puffing a vein up on his forehead. "I want results. And I want you *here* making sure I damn well get them! Is that not clear?"

"Clear as the crystal on your Rolex." She knew she was about to lose it and took a deep breath to calm herself. She also knew that Randall would whine to Gretchen Nordstrom, President of Genetique, a young widow who'd managed the company quite well since her husband's death four years ago. Randall had her ear, and if the rumors were true, he had pursued everything below it, but without success.

"What the hell's more important than our research?" Randall demanded, staring at the files in her hand.

Hallie remembered Dr. Bryant's mandate for secrecy. Still, she felt she owed Genetique an explanation for her absence. "Rex, the CDC has asked me not to mention—"

"The CDC? My, my." He raised his eyebrows skeptically.

"I'm involved with something that will affect many lives in the next twenty-four hours."

"And I suppose Alzheimer's won't?"

Hallie's patience was drained. She'd been working seventy-hour-weeks on a cure for Alzheimer's and still had two weeks of unused vacation she'd never get around to. "Yes, Rex, it will, unfortunately. And that concerns me greatly. But this other situation threatens *many* lives right at the present. Washington has asked us not to discuss this."

"Washington…?" He sneered down his thin aquiline nose at her. "Next you'll tell me the White House is involved!"

"It is."

Randall's jaw muscles hardened into angry little knots. "Bullshit! I refuse to entertain your delusions."

"Then entertain your own."

Randall's face went dark. "If you are not working here with the others this evening, you leave me no choice but to question your commitment to and your future at Genetique. Understand?"

She held Randall's stare and suddenly realized what she'd denied for too long, that a long-term working relationship with Rex Randall demeaned her intelligence. It was time to play hardball.

"I understand, Rex."

"Finally," he said, storming away in victory.

"Rex?"

He stopped, glanced at his watch, annoyed. "Now what?"

"Actually, *I've* been reevaluating my future here. I'll let Gretchen know what I decide in two weeks. If I leave, I'll tell her there's only one reason."

The hint of concern crept into his eyes. "And that is?"

"A guy with wingtips and vile nasal hair."

T. Rex's fingers shot up to his nostrils. Hallie swept past him and into the hallway, nearly bumping into Diedre De Bakker, who was bent over laughing. They hurried away as T. Rex stormed off angrily in the other direction.

"He *is* a nasal hair," Diedre whispered, "a most heinous and vile one!"

Hallie smiled, but she worried about what venom T. Rex would spew out about her to Gretchen Nordstrom. "Diedre, I'm on this CDC crisis until Friday night."

"Not to worry. I'm watching the store," Diedre said. Then she grew serious. "Hallie…."

"Yes?"

"You've had some very close calls recently."

Hallie shrugged. "I know."

"Be careful. Please."

Hallie saw her friend's concern. "I will. Besides, I have a cute police bodyguard downstairs."

Diedre's eyes widened. "How cute?"

"Very, but...."

"But what?"

"Reed thinks he's a eunuch."

"The perfect man. Does he do back rubs?"

Laughing, Hallie entered an elevator and headed down to the lobby. She stepped off and looked around for Deke Larsen. The Cute Eunuch was nowhere in sight. Maynard, the guard, explained that Larsen had gone out to check her car ten minutes ago. Hallie decided it was safe to go find him, since the lot was well lit and required ID-card entry.

She stepped outside and a blast of cold wind hit her face. Shivering, she walked ahead, looking for Larsen near her vehicle. He wasn't there. Nor was he near his car. She scanned the lot and saw only a white-coated lab technician hurrying toward the back entrance.

She had to leave. USAMRIID experts were waiting for her. But she'd promised Reed she'd come with Larsen. Her stomach began to churn. She decided to give Larsen ten more minutes.

Returning to the lobby, she sat down and reviewed the autopsies again. She made notes of what Shah said and outlined how best to present the facts. Eleven minutes later, Larsen still hadn't shown up. She called Reed's cell phone but got no answer. She phoned the Birmingham police station, but Beachum was not in. Frustrated, she tossed her cell phone into her purse and walked over to Maynard.

"Please tell Officer Larsen that I had to leave for an important meeting at Detective Beachum's office. I'll see him there."

"Will do," Maynard said, still glued to the Red Wings game.

Hallie walked back outside. The wind blew harder and the overhanging trees seemed to swoop down close to her. Long, fingery shadows swept between the cars. As she passed a red Pontiac, a willow branch lashed out at her and she ducked away.

Quickly, she opened her trunk, took out a windbreaker and put it on. Then she placed her files and purse inside and closed the lid.

Behind her, something clicked. She spun around and saw nothing. Perhaps a car engine was cooling down. She hurried to her driver's door.

Two more loud clicks.

Without looking back, she beeped her car open, jumped in, locked the doors and looked around. Nothing.

She checked the rearview mirror, half expecting a man's head to creep up in her backseat. She waited ... her heart pounding. No one.

Slowly, she released the air from her lungs, took several breaths and calmed herself. She drove out of the lot and, moments later, steered onto the entrance of I-75. Traffic seemed heavier than usual, perhaps a sporting event or an auto-plant shift change. She saw no Lincolns.

As she drove, she rehearsed what she'd tell the experts: the similarities between the SCD deaths, the hemolysis link, the ricin, what Dr. Shah had said, how he died, what Kyle said, how he died.

She passed a slow-moving garbage truck as a clunker drifted in front of her. In her side mirror, she saw a dark Mercedes pull in behind her. The Mercedes pulled out to pass, crept even, then maintained her pace.

She slowed a bit. The Mercedes slowed.

She glanced over and froze—her Atlanta assassin was aiming a gun at her head.

She hit the brakes as bullets thudded into her front fender. Heart pounding, she realized she was blocked in front by the clunker and a semi-trailer ahead. She darted to the third lane and braked hard, causing a driver behind her to honk.

To cut off the shooter's angle, she swung back into his lane, but two cars *behind* the Mercedes. Trucks wedged in the Mercedes for the moment. She saw an exit, two hundred yards ahead. She had to take it, even though doing so would briefly give the shooter an angle.

The exit rushed toward her, one hundred yards ... fifty ... twenty....

She jerked her Volvo into the exit lane. Two bullets ripped into her left fender—barely missing an Exxon gas tanker that had appeared beside her. She was inches from cremation.

She heard another shot, horns honking, tires squealing.

She passed the Exxon tanker and barreled up the ramp doing ninety. Seeing no Mercedes in the mirror, she eased of the gas a bit.

Suddenly the dark Mercedes swerved from behind the Exxon tanker, careened up the grass onto the ramp and raced after her.

She sped through two green lights, slowed at a red light on St. Aubin, checked traffic, then ran the light. She grabbed for her phone to call 911 and realized it was in her purse in the trunk.

The Mercedes, one hundred yards back, was gaining.

She drove past abandoned stores, deserted homes, cars up on concrete blocks, discarded tires, fences clogged with yellowed newspapers. She slowed at a red light, barely missing a produce truck. Honking nonstop, she tried to warn drivers and draw the police.

The Mercedes blasted through the red light and pulled closer.

Quickly, she turned down a side street of crumbling apartments. The Mercedes skidded past, then backed up. Before the Mercedes driver could see her, she'd veered down a narrow alley and sped ahead.

No Mercedes in the mirror. She followed the alley around a curve and screeched to a stop.

She was staring into the Mercedes's headlights. The big car rocketed toward her.

Jamming into reverse, she raced backward down the alley, nicked a garbage can, skidded out into the street and sped ahead. Perspiration blanketed her skin, and her palms began to slip on the steering wheel.

She had one hope—find a passageway too narrow for the Mercedes.

Moments later, she saw a possibility. Turning down the alley, she followed it, making excellent speed until she skidded to a stop at a parked UPS van that blocked most of the alley.

Quickly, she gauged the narrow gap between the van and the building.

Maybe, she thought.

Pulling beside the van, she scraped through, leaving silver paint on the van's mirror. She sped on down the alley as the big Mercedes screeched to a stop at the UPS van. The big car's left front grille tried to bulldoze the heavy van, but couldn't. The Mercedes was blocked.

"Yes!" she shouted.

Two hundred feet later all hope vanished. She dead-ended at a chain fence. Behind her, two huge men jumped from the Mercedes.

She got out and ran along the fence.

Glancing back, she saw them search her car for something, then run after her.

Gunmetal glinted in their hands.

* * *

"Where the hell you been?" Reed asked Woody Beachum with more irritation than he intended. Reed was frustrated that the detective had been unreachable, but greatly relieved he was alive.

They hurried into Beachum's office and sat down.

"Looking for a murder witness."

"We may have a murder *victim.*"

"You?" Beachum stared at Reed's muddy clothes.

"Hallie." Reed wiped sweat from his face. "They're still trying to kill her and I can't locate her."

"Larsen's guarding her."

"Not according to Genetique's guard. He hasn't seen Larsen for forty-five minutes. Hallie waited for Larsen, then left by herself to come here. Did Larsen phone you about tomorrow?"

147

"Maybe. I haven't picked up my voice mail. I'll beep him."

"I tried. He's not answering it."

"He always answers it," Beachum said, frowning. He dialed Larsen's beeper and waited for him to call in. Reed stared at the phone, the silence intensifying his fear and giving rise to a frightening possibility: Dead phone, dead cop.

"What about tomorrow?" Beachum asked, staring at the phone.

"Kyle was murdered. And tomorrow his murderer is killing...." Reed still found it hard to say, "he's killing sixty ... thousand ... people."

Beachum fell back as though kicked in the chest. He stuffed a Camel in his mouth, lit it, drew a quarter-inch of ash and blew out clouds of smoke. "Talk!"

As Reed explained everything, Beachum's face grew crimson.

"Who the hell's Philip Lambe?"

"A biochemist Kyle once worked with."

"Where's Lambe now?"

"Lives near Grand Blanc. I broke into his house."

Beachum coughed out smoke. "We can't use anything you found as evidence."

"Then we'll have other evidence."

"What?"

"Thousands of corpses."

Beachum huffed out another thick shaft of smoke, accidentally sprinkling ashes onto his desk. "Which ten cities is Lambe targeting?"

"The file didn't say."

Beachum grabbed the phone and began to brief someone.

Reed's mind drifted to Hallie. *Where is she?* She'd left Genetique nearly sixty minutes ago to come here. The drive was thirty minutes. There'd been no reports of traffic jams or accidents. There was no road construction along the route. She didn't answer her home phone or cell phone, which she always had with her.

She was out there alone. She was in trouble.

Thirty

Sprinting along the schoolyard fence, Hallie heard two muffled shots rip into the garbage can beside her. A huge rat jumped out, brushed her ankle and crawled beneath some rotten tomatoes.

She ran past a row of dark, abandoned stores, their doors hanging open. *If I enter one, I'm trapped!*

Her lungs were bursting, and she knew she couldn't sprint at the same pace much longer. Turning a corner, she slipped, but quickly regained her balance. She glanced back and saw the men were gaining on her.

A muffled *thump!* Beside her a tricycle seat exploded.

She ran past an abandoned refrigerator, then around two large cast iron garbage dumpsters, thankful for their brief protection.

Suddenly her foot skidded on a flattened beer can and she fell, scraping her knee. Getting up, she slipped again, but she recovered her balance and raced ahead.

But the men were much closer.

Then she heard it. A familiar, rhythmic thumping. Something hitting concrete. A ball bouncing. *People.* She ran toward the sound. Seconds later, she saw several men playing basketball on a dimly lit school yard court inside the fence, two hundred feet away. She sprinted through the gate toward them.

"Help!"

Bullets splashed muddy water onto her calves.

"Help me!"

The basketball players stared at her.

She pointed back at her attackers. "Trying ... kill me!"

A tall, muscular ball player, perspiration dripping from his ebony face, looked at her, then at her attackers, then nodded to a small man in a wheelchair.

The wheelchair man flipped a red blanket off his legs and unleashed several shots from an automatic rifle. Chunks of mud splattered onto her attackers as they crashed into each other trying to stop.

149

The tall black man stepped forward. "You got ten seconds to be gone!"

Her attackers seemed frozen.

"One, two, *ten!*"

The tall black man nodded.

Four men on the sideline yanked weapons from their coats and fired, spattering more muddy water and muck onto her attackers.

The attackers turned and ran. One slipped and fell into the other, knocking them both down. They scrambled up and limped toward the gate. Hallie watched them disappear down the alley like roaches scurrying for cover of darkness.

She exhaled slowly and turned to the tall man beside her. His light brown eyes watched the alley with amazing calm, as though he was enjoying a sunset. Perspiration dripped from his shaved head onto a thin, gray scar on his knuckles and then trickled down the basketball.

"Thank you," she said, knowing her words were pitifully inadequate.

"Hood's going to the dogs," he said, smiling with lots of perfect white teeth. He bounced the basketball and palmed it in one hand.

"My car's down the alley where they ran," she said, pointing. She noticed her hand was shaking and he noticed it too.

"You're safe now," he said gently.

"Thank you."

"Us minorities got to hang together, right?" Another easy smile.

"Right...."

"Name's Luther," he said, offering his hand.

"Hallie," she said, shaking it.

"Like Berry?"

"Yes, but she got all the looks."

"You're looking just fine, but a little muddy," he said, laughing.

She laughed and brushed a clump of mud from her dress.

He raised two fingers. Instantly two large midnight-blue BMWs purred to life and drove up beside him.

"Luther's Escorts at your service, Hallie. Like us to walk you back to your car, nice and easy?"

"I'd like that very much, Luther, and thank you."

One BMW pulled in front and one behind.

Luther walked beside her dribbling the basketball. His armed pals in the two BMWs crawled along like Secret Service agents. When they reached her Volvo, she fished twenty-four dollars from her purse and offered it to Luther. He declined, saying business was real good. She decided not to ask him what business. Instead she handed him her card. "Luther, if you or your friends ever need help at Detroit Memorial Hospital, ask for me."

He smiled, then his eyes dimmed. "Expect we'll be needin' that, Doctor."

She thanked him again, got in her Volvo and drove off. The big BMWs escorted her to the relative safety of Woodward Avenue, where she waved goodbye and drove toward Birmingham. She suspected any car that came within five feet of her.

Two miles later, a dark Mercedes pulled in several cars behind her. She couldn't tell if it was the same one.

* * *

"Earth to Kincaid!" Beachum said, waving his hand in front of Reed's eyes.

Reed blinked. "What...?" He was lost in worry about Hallie. He'd called her car, home and office again with no luck. She was in trouble. His neck muscles felt like they were being squeezed in a vice.

"What's Lambe's R.C. test all about?" Beachum said, lighting a cigarette even though a fresh one burned in the ashtray.

"Lambe listed twenty-seven sets of initials and dates. I found Kyle's initials and the date he died."

Beachum made notes and huffed smoke toward the window. The phone rang. Beachum answered, listened and then hung up. "Kyle's laptop wasn't in the Typhoon at your house."

"The bastard went back and got it."

Reed heard an ambulance, siren blaring, racing down Woodward Avenue. Was Hallie in an accident?

Beachum's phone rang again and he hit the speaker button. "Beachum."

Reed heard cell-phone static. *It's Hallie....*

"Woody, it's Drew Manning."

Reed's hope sank again.

"You heard what's coming down?" Manning asked.

"Just found out."

"Deke Larsen phoned me when he couldn't reach you. Some psycho plans to kill *sixty* thousand people tomorrow."

"Yeah. In ten US cities."

"Any idea what he's using?" Manning asked.

"Some kind of biological or chemical weapon, according to the guy who uncovered all this, Reed Kincaid. I'm with him now."

"Reed ... I'm Drew Manning, special agent in charge of the Detroit FBI office. We need to talk to you and Dr. Hallie Mara."

I need to talk to her more, Reed thought.

151

"You too, Woody," Manning continued. "We've formed a crisis team, consisting of our people, Homeland Security, the USAMRIID experts from Fort Detrick and Aberdeen Proving Ground and the CDC. We'll be linked to our Washington crisis group and the director. We're meeting in twenty-five minutes. We need you all there."

"At your bureau office?" Beachum asked.

"No. The Huron Room at the Ren Cen Marriott. And keep that confidential."

"Why the Marriott?"

"The media watch our place like hawks. They'd see the high activity level, count the pizzas, know something big was up. Broadcast the story, cause chaos. Maybe spook Lambe into pulling the trigger early."

Maybe he already did, Reed thought.

"We'll see you there," Beachum said.

Beachum hung up and a young officer with a bushy red flattop stuck his head in the door and nodded toward the lobby. "There's a Hallie in—"

Reed bolted past the officer, ran down the hall and saw her leaning on the counter in the reception area. He'd never felt so relieved to see anyone in his life. She turned and her eyes found his. He knew instantly something had happened. Her face was pale, her hair pushed to the side. She seemed a bit shaken and muddy, but unhurt, except for a scraped knee.

Reed hurried over and she moved into his arms.

"The Atlanta guy really doesn't like me," she whispered.

Her words felt like a kick in the gut. "Where the hell's Larsen?" Reed asked.

Beachum lumbered up beside them.

"Officer Larsen wasn't around. I waited for him, but Dr. Bryant told me I had to brief government people. I was late, so I left."

As she explained how she'd run from her pursuers, how they shot at her, how she found the basketball players, Reed felt his anger grow. He never should have left her alone. He'd known she was a target. Once again, he was not there to protect her. Once again, she'd almost been killed. Once again, she'd been lucky to escape with her life. From now on, he wouldn't let her out of his sight.

Woody Beachum turned to the young officer with the flattop. "Jesse, you and Big Tom get over to Genetique fast. Something's happened to Deke." Jesse bolted down the hallway.

Reed glanced at his watch. "We should leave for the Ren Cen."

"You guys are riding with me," Beachum said. "Too damn many people planning your funerals."

Twenty minutes later, Reed saw the illuminated towers of the Renaissance Center, electronic stalagmites jutting into the night blackness. The view of the four cylindrical columns surrounding the majestic central tower always seemed to calm him. They stood like Roman sentries watching over the city, guarding it against harm.

But how can you guard against weapons you can't even see or hear?

Thirty-One

You are mine, sweet lady, Luca Corsa thought as he followed the Jap chick, Reed Kincaid and the big cop, Beachum, through the crowded Marriott Hotel lobby.

Tweaking his dark handlebar moustache, Corsa blew dust from his wraparound sunglasses. As he squeezed through a group of rowdy conventioneers, someone bumped him from behind. He spun around but couldn't figure out which jerk did it. Corsa hated being touched, especially from behind. It reminded him of years ago when some bastard pushed him onto a crowded Manhattan subway car. Corsa had turned around and popped the guy's finger back—snapped the bone. The wuss screamed like a baby. Even now, Corsa got a nice warm feeling remembering how the finger snapped like a stick of chalk.

Corsa wove his way through the crowd. *Just like the old days,* he thought. Crowds had been his only source of income when he was a kid. Hell, he could pick five wallets in the next fifty feet. But picking pockets was for low-rollers. He'd come way up in the world.

Keeping his eyes on the Jap, he squeezed through some executive dudes bragging about their auto parts, a few chic broads with cell phones glued to their ears, group leaders shouting directions to nearby Greektown restaurants and the casinos, convention dweebs demanding everybody wear ID badges. Businessmen. Shriners. Geeks.

He walked a little further and smelled aftershave and booze in a group of noisy plumbers with red fezzes and blood-bourbon levels near a hundred. Guys who worked with their hands. Like him.

He passed a table filled with Delta Faucet nametags and slipped one labeled "Ned" into his pocket. Ned, a good name. Solid, American. Like him. He walked behind a potted fern and pinned the tag on his lapel. From another table, he took a red fez and pushed it down on his head.

No way the Jap broad would recognize him. His fez, name tag, big handlebar stash and sunglasses made him a genuine plumber.

He followed Dr. Mara and the others into an elevator filled with sloshed conventioneers and maneuvered himself right behind her. He leaned close and smelled her hair. Nice and fresh.

He stared down at her long, thin neck. He could just *snap* it now! The bitch had really pissed him off. Christ, he'd pumped bullets through her hotel bathroom door, heard her moan, then calling security, then she didn't touch the nerve agent stuff on the microscope, then Manny told him those nigger basketball players saved her ass. This kitty's nine lives were way used up.

Corsa realized his stiletto was only two inches from her spine. He could stick her so easy right now. *Just stick her and move behind the guy next to me. As she falls, I act real shocked. So easy ....*

But no, Lambe wanted her green file real bad, and she wasn't carrying it. She probably left it back at her lab. And besides, stabbing was way too kind for her. She had to feel *pain,* lots of pain, when she died.

"Our floor," Beachum said, stepping out.

Two Shriners stumbled off and headed left. Corsa, acting drunk, wobbled down the hall, trailing the Jap, Kincaid and Beachum. Corsa pretended to check rooms against a card in his hand. To the right, he saw the massive open center area with lots of shadowy hallways and balconies. He loved the Ren Cen. It was made for his kind of work. He could whack a guy, stuff him in an alcove, and drive to Chicago before anyone found the body.

Ahead, the big cop knocked on the Huron Room door.

Corsa staggered toward the room as a muscular dude with blond eyebrows and a gun bulge under his coat stepped out. The blond checked Beachum's badge, spoke to someone in the room, then motioned them inside.

Strolling past, Corsa glanced into the large conference room. He saw at least fifteen serious types working with laptops and cell phones around a big table. Behind them were guys and broads, most talking on phones. Cops. He could smell them like sharks smell blood. He hated them. Always had. Cheap bastards made his old lady spread her legs for free, then strutted around in their tight-ass blue uniforms and I'm-God attitude. He'd love to toss a few grenades into the room, whip up a little cop soup.

But Lambe just wanted him to report who they were. Simple report. Cops. Assholes.

Corsa swayed on down the hall. He took the escalator to the lobby, pulled out his cell phone and dialed Lambe.

"They're in the Huron Room at the Marriott."

"Who else is in the room?"

"Cops."

"What kind?" Lambe asked.

"Locals, FBI types."

155

"Any scientists or medical types?"

Corsa wondered what scientists or medical types looked like. "Yeah, maybe."

"Did the woman bring Shah's green file?"

"Nope. Just some white ones."

"If she returns to Genetique, you know what to do."

"Uh-huh." Luca said, praying she returned. "Then she's mine?"

"Then she's yours."

Thirty-Two

Woody Beachum coughed, then stuck a thick black hunk of chewing tobacco into his mouth and tongued it over to his jaw.

"Kills germs," he whispered, smiling at Hallie and Reed.

And detectives, Hallie almost reminded him.

Beachum's mood and hers had brightened moments ago when they'd learned Deke Larsen was found alive, but dazed from a hard whack on the head. The good news had brought only brief relief to the crisis team members surrounding her and Reed in the Renaissance Center conference room.

The team's objective was clear. They had to stop a brilliant, driven psychopath, a maniac poised to exterminate sixty thousand innocent people in ten unidentified US cities in a few hours.

They sat in a war room. The walls displayed large, detailed maps of all major US cities. Beside each map was a list of the city's most populated office buildings, sports stadiums, malls and convention centers that held more than two thousand people. FBI agents, police and assistants hovered over cell phones and laptops. Agents checked credentials and frisked everyone who entered. Tension crackled through the room like static electricity.

Hallie was impressed with how quickly the FBI had transformed the room into a sophisticated command center with open lines to key personnel nationwide. She smelled freshly brewed coffee and knew caffeine would be as necessary as air tonight.

She and Reed sat at a sprawling walnut conference table near Beachum's friend, Drew Manning, the special agent in charge of the large Detroit FBI office. Manning had been appointed crisis team leader. Other team members had settled in around the table, their serious-faced assistants sitting behind them.

Manning, who Beachum told her wasn't a worrier, looked damn worried. In his early forties, Drew Manning was a tall, broad-shouldered man who reminded Hallie of a muscular Kevin Spacey. His chiseled, handsome face was taut. Strands of dark brown hair had fallen over his forehead and he kept clasping and unclasping his hands as though the full responsibility for stopping the disaster rested squarely on his broad shoulders, which of course it did, as well as the rest of them. Hallie felt the pressure weighing down on her more heavily with each minute.

She leaned close to Beachum. "You know Manning?"

"About fifteen years. Met him at the FBI training academy. Smart. Great guy. One of the most rapidly promoted agents in Bureau history."

"So why's he here?" Reed asked.

Beachum's eyes dimmed. "Wife died of cancer three years ago. He told the brass, 'Transfer me out of DC, or I'll retire.' One month later, he landed in Detroit. It's a top FBI spot, and the busiest border crossing between Canada and the USA."

A phone rang beside Manning. Beachum had told her it was the open line to Washington's FBI Headquarters and the special Hazardous Materials Response Unit group. A young female agent handed it to Manning.

"Director Hatcher, sir."

The room quieted.

Manning looked around the table. "Folks, please ask the director anything you want." He punched the speaker button.

"Manning."

"Drew, it's Fred."

"We've got you on the speaker phone, sir," Manning said, "so we can all hear each other."

"Good."

Hallie remembered a CNN profile of Frederick Lee Hatcher, the FBI director, a tall, lean man, working in his Washington office. His intelligence and integrity had drilled holes through FBI critics, as had his bureau successes. His ongoing war against terrorists had grown increasingly effective, and crimes of violence had declined significantly under his aegis.

"What's the status, Drew?" Director Hatcher asked uneasily.

"The same, sir."

"Think Lambe is still in your area?"

Manning shrugged. "Hard to say. But no one using his name has left area airports, bus or train stations. We've got several thousand police in five bordering states and Canada looking for his Jaguar."

"Good."

Hallie heard familiarity in their voices and sensed that Hatcher and Manning were friends, an advantage in the critical hours ahead.

158

Hatcher cleared his throat. "Everyone here in DC has been properly briefed: the National Intelligence Director, the Director of Homeland Security, The Attorney General, the White House, the SOLIC group, the Army, the Commander in Chief of the Joint Forces. Everyone."

"Yes, sir."

"And Homeland Security just raised the risk advisory to orange—*HIGH!* They're informing appropriate federal, state and local authorities.

"Makes sense."

"Who's with you now?" Hatcher asked.

Manning looked around the table. "We have Doctor Janet McKay, an expert in weapons of mass destruction, from the military's Aberdeen Proving Ground. Also, Doctor Darren Livingstone, a weapon delivery specialist from USAMRIID. Their Chemical Biological Rapid Response teams are here too. We also have Homeland Security, the CDC and FEMA people. Plus Reed Kincaid, Dr. Hallie Mara and Detective Woody Beachum, the individuals who uncovered this. They've just briefed us."

"Good. Am I on the speaker?"

"You are, sir."

"In that case, I'd like to say something. Ladies and gentlemen, we've been handed the worst potential slaughter of Americans in our history. September 11's three thousand deaths sickened our nation. Tomorrow, *sixty* thousand deaths could rip our country apart. Consider the consequences; many people will refuse to go to work, parents will refuse to send children to school, business will stop and our nation will freeze in its tracks."

Nervous coughs rattled around the room.

"Before people will feel safe," Hatcher continued, "the government will have to implement massive security measures. It may take weeks, months. That will devastate our economy and thousands of jobs will be lost."

Heads nodded in agreement.

"What I'm saying is that *together* we must stop Philip Lambe. Our inter-agency political turf wars just ceased. We have one purpose, to stop Lambe and his delivery system tomorrow."

Tomorrow, Hallie noticed, began in two and a half hours.

"If we fail," Hatcher said, "the FBI will take a lot of the heat. We'll live with that. But if anyone has been counterproductive, I'll spread the fecal matter commensurately. We're in this together, and we'll succeed together, because frankly, failure is not an option. Is this clear?"

A chorus of yesses filled the room. Hatcher's tone suggested that he would crucify anyone playing turf politics.

"Good, now if you need *anything*, just ask."

"We will, sir," Manning said.

The conference call was over.

Two seconds later, Manning's cell phone rang. He listened a few moments, then flipped the phoned shut. "That's our team at Lambe's house."

"Did they find the gray *Shikei* file?" Reed asked.

"It wasn't in the desk drawer."

Hallie watched Reed's hands curl into fists. "I should have taken the damn file," he whispered to her.

"That file name," Manning said, *"Shee…?"*

"S-h-i-k-e-i." Reed spelled it out.

"It's Japanese," Hallie said, "for 'death penalty.'"

"And the other word?" Manning asked. "The word for his weapon … *Kor—?"*

"Korusu," Hallie said. "It means 'kill.'"

Manning wrote it down. "So Lambe has decreed a death penalty for sixty thousand people. The question is who? And why?"

No one offered answers.

"And why did he use *Japanese* words?" Hallie asked.

"We know he spent his early years in Japan," Manning said, "and he's fluent in Japanese."

Hallie nodded, but she wondered if there was a more personal reason. Had his years in Japan angered him toward the country or the Japanese? If so, was he targeting them? And if he was, how could he isolate them in ten US cities?

"Did they find any lab equipment?" asked Dr. Janet McKay, the expert from Aberdeen. She was an attractive woman in her late thirties with thick auburn hair that framed large, pale-green eyes. Her face, Aubrey Hepburn delicate, was taut with concern. She wore a blue *Université Paris* sweatshirt and Nike Air Maxes, which, along with her trim figure, suggested she was no stranger to exercise. "You know, things like pipettes, sterilizers?"

"An old microscope in a kitchen cabinet," Manning said. "How big a lab does he need?"

"A room this size is plenty big," Dr. McKay said.

"To make what?" Manning asked.

"Toxins that can kill hundreds of thousands."

"Which toxins?" Hallie asked.

"He has a wide choice, Hallie," McKay said. "For example, Type-A botulinus toxin, about the most lethal substance known."

"How could he disperse it?" Manning asked.

"Lots of ways. Water, for example. If placed into the water system under certain circumstances, and at prime locations, Type-A botulinus toxin could kill the five million people in this greater metro area."

Everyone stared at Dr. McKay, waiting for her to qualify her statement. When she didn't, a sickening hush fell over the room.

"Wouldn't Lambe need a lot of lab equipment?" Drew Manning asked.

"All he needs for a biological agent are some cultures, incubators, a bioreactor tank, things like that. The equipment's relatively easy to get. And unfortunately, so are many biological cultures."

"How easy?" Manning asked.

"Mail-order easy," she said.

Hallie was shocked. "You mean like ordering videos and CDs?"

"Almost that easy, Hallie," McKay said, clearly frustrated.

"Welcome to America," Reed said, "where you do slammer time for marijuana, but it's okay to walk around with a biological culture that kills millions."

Manning nodded in agreement. "What other biological weapons should we worry about?"

McKay's face grew more serious. "Smallpox, of course."

"But I read we have enough new vaccine for nearly everyone," Manning said.

"Yes, but...." McKay's eyes grew dark.

"But what?"

"The new vaccine may not work."

"Why?" Hallie asked, confused. She'd recently read in *JAMA* that the new vaccine was effective against smallpox.

McKay paused and whispered, "We've heard rumors about a ... *new* pox. A *genetically-engineered* smallpox. A kind of *superpox*."

Hallie understood the implications immediately and felt nauseated. "And then our vaccine won't stop it?"

"No, it won't," McKay said.

The silence felt like someone hit the mute button.

Manning leaned forward on the table. "Are you saying that even if we all got the new smallpox vaccine, we could still get this new superpox smallpox?"

"Yes," McKay said, her voice quivering. "And it would spread unstoppably, like wildfire across the country."

The room was quiet as a graveyard.

Hallie felt perspiration dot her upper lip.

"We've warned Congress about these biological and chemical threats for years," McKay said. "But they were too damn busy politicking."

"It took September 11 to get their attention," Manning said.

Janet McKay nodded. "Actually, tragedies help. Out of the rubble of 9/11 are *finally* coming safeguards we'd been begging Congress to give us for years."

"Against biological weapons?" Manning asked.

"Yes."

"And nerve agents?"

McKay nodded.

Hallie watched Janet McKay's eyes close when she heard 'nerve agents.' Beachum had said McKay's husband and seven-year-old daughter died in her arms from a nerve gas accident on a Middle East field trip four years ago.

McKay turned to Reed. "Did you see any hint of a laboratory at Lambe's?"

"No," Reed said. "But I only saw the ground floor. The house is large, three stories, perhaps with a basement."

"Small basement," Manning said. "Furnace. Workshop. Small gym with weights. The weight settings suggest Lambe's very strong. Upstairs, five bedrooms. One used. No hint of a lab. We're checking to see if he purchased lab equipment."

"Knowing the equipment would help," McKay said.

Manning stood and walked alongside the table, his body rigid with tension. He stopped and looked at Dr. McKay. "What about chemical weapons? Could Lambe make them?"

"Yes," McKay said. "Some are very simple to produce. The more sophisticated ones require complex manufacturing."

"But he could buy chemical agents, right?" Manning asked.

"He could buy just about anything in weaponized form," McKay said, "Biological or chemical. In fact, there's a rumor someone in the US purchased large quantities of a weaponized chemical agent a while ago in Asia."

"From whom?" Manning asked.

"Maybe from the Japanese religious cult, Aum Shinrikyo. Or from al-Qaeda. A French informant in Beirut was about to tell us who, but...." McKay closed her eyes.

"But what?" Manning asked.

She shrugged. "Police found his head in a laundromat dryer."

Hallie watched several people touch their necks.

Drew Manning walked to the end of the table and faced the group. "So, we know that a man named Philip Lambe is planning to exact his *Shikei*—his death penalty—to kill thousands in ten US cities using a weapon called *Korusu*—in a few hours."

The group nodded.

"So the big question is, *how?*" Manning said. "How can Lambe deliver *Korusu* to his victims? What are his options? Hallie, did Dr. Shah determine how Lambe delivered ricin to his test victims?"

"No," Hallie said. "He was just starting to work on that."

Manning nodded. "How can Lambe deliver *Korusu?*"

Janet McKay gestured to her colleague, Dr. Darren Livingstone, whose bio sheet said he had thirty-six years experience with the delivery systems of biological and chemical weapons. Leaning forward, the sixty-four-year-old man rested bony elbows on the table and took a slow, deep breath. His thin face was dominated by serious eyes, which seemed to have been sucked deep into their sockets. Long, arthritic fingers flicked wisps of silver hair off his rimless glasses. He looked like a man who sensed the guillotine dropping toward his neck but was too exhausted to move.

"Depends on what *Korusu* is," Livingstone said, cracking his bony knuckles. "But in general, Lambe has many delivery options. What we call vectors. Like water."

"How would he get *Korusu* into water?" Manning asked.

"Many ways. For example, his teams break into the city waterworks—"

"Whoa!" Woody Beachum said. "City waterworks are well guarded since 9/11."

"That's true," Livingstone said, "but there are still gaps in water security in some cities. And sleepy guards at three a.m. might not hold off a large, well-trained team of terrorists."

Hallie sensed Dr. Livingstone was right.

"Once the terrorists are inside," Livingstone continued, "they shut down the water purification and pollution detection systems. Then they dump the *Korusu* into the water. A few hours later people are brushing their teeth, taking showers, drinking water and coffee. Depending on what *Korusu* is, many people could be dead by noon."

Hallie swallowed, knowing she showered, brushed her teeth, drank water and coffee every morning.

"Or the terrorists could back-siphon chemicals or biotoxins into the water system *closer* to their targets," Livingstone continued.

"Closer to suburbs and large buildings?" Manning asked.

"Yes."

"Could *Korusu* be Type-A botulism?" Manning asked.

"Very possible," Livingstone said. "*Korusu* could also be a nerve agent."

Manning punched the speaker button on the open phone and briefed Director Hatcher's assistant. The assistant informed him that security teams had already been deployed to the municipal waterworks in all major US cities as well as most reservoirs in surrounding suburbs.

Manning hung up and faced Livingstone. "Doctor, how else can Lambe strike?"

"Many ways. Homemade mortar tubes, for example. Pack a few kilograms of *Korusu* into the tubes, then fire them at crowded city streets."

"But people would see them setting up mortar tubes," Reed said.

"Not if they fire from open windows, Reed. Or from rooftops, or the backs of open trucks."

Hallie realized Livingstone was right.

"The mortar shells burst on impact," Livingstone continued, "dispersing a respirable aerosol over a large area. Winds spread the aerosol. Building ventilators and cars suck it inside. People breathe it in...." Livingstone shrugged as though little could be done.

Again, silence blanketed the room.

"There must be an easier way to reach sixty thousand people," Manning said.

"Large office buildings," Livingstone said. "Thousands of people, enclosed. A perfect environment. With enough toxin or nerve agent in the ventilation system, it could kill almost everyone that breathed it."

"But we're inspecting major office buildings," Manning said.

"Yes, but even if they're clean now," Livingstone said, "someone could introduce *Korusu* into the systems tomorrow."

"Don't big buildings have bio-chemical detection systems?" Manning asked.

"Some do," Livingstone said. "But not nearly enough."

Manning's eyes tightened in frustration. "There's simply no sure way to guard every ventilator opening in every major building in every major city in the next few hours."

Dr. Livingstone nodded agreement. "Another possibility is stadiums." He glanced at his notes. "Tomorrow evening, there are one-hundred and ninety-three major sporting events, concerts or shows inside *enclosed* stadiums. Hundreds of thousands of people packed together."

Hallie envisioned the sixty-five thousand kids packed together at tomorrow's Ford Field concert.

Manning turned to a young blond assistant. "Nate, contact all these enclosed stadiums. Tell them we're inspecting their ventilation, heating and cooling systems, then positioning guards on the vents before they let the public in."

"They'll ask questions."

"Tell them it's a matter of public health. And tell them *not* to inform the media."

Nate nodded. "What if they refuse?"

"Failure to comply will cancel all stadium events for one week while their entire stadium, kitchen and food facilities are inspected by federal, CDC and state health officials."

Nate's eyes widened. "Can we do that?"

"Probably not. But tell them anyway."

The agent hurried from the room.

Hallie was relieved that Manning was going to do whatever it took to protect lives in the next twenty-four hours. Diplomacy and protocol could take a fast hike south.

"How else can Lambe strike?" Manning asked Livingstone.

The old man rubbed his tired, pink eyes and took a deep breath. "Trucks equipped with *Korusu* generators could drive through crowded city streets. The driver flips a switch and the generator expels the *Korusu* fumes out fake exhaust pipes. The fumes look like truck exhaust."

Hallie felt a sinking sensation in her stomach as she envisioned men, women and children dropping dead on streets.

"What the hell can we do?" Reed asked.

"Issue a few million gas masks if we had them," Livingstone said.

"Let's issue the gas masks we have," Reed said.

"Which ten US cities get them?" Livingstone said.

No one answered.

"And *who* in those cities get them?"

Again, silence.

Hallie was sickened by how vulnerable and unprotected most Americans still were for a massive biological and chemical attack.

"Crop dusters," Janet McKay said, "could also disperse toxins over crowded cities."

"But we have restricted airspace zones," Beachum said.

"Apparently not *that* restricted," McKay said, "a Cessna recently passed within one mile of the White House. It took Air Force F-16s *eleven minutes* to intercept it!"

Hallie shook her head in disbelief.

"Despite the restricted airspace zones," McKay continued, "determined crop duster pilots could probably spread some *Korusu* over busy city streets *before* Air Force planes intercepted them. People breathe it, and again, building ventilators and cars pull it inside."

Manning lifted his six-foot-two, two-hundred-pound frame, walked to the front of the table and looked at the group. His face revealed the unspoken reality that Lambe might be unstoppable.

"Our challenge is difficult. How will Lambe strike? Will he put *Korusu* in water? In mortar tubes fired at busy streets? In the ventilation systems of office buildings? In enclosed stadiums? In trucks that spew it onto pedestrians? In humans infected with an unstoppable new superpox? In aircraft that disperse it over crowded cities?"

Or, Hallie wondered, *has he found some new, unpredictable, totally unimaginable way to strike?* She felt like needles were piercing her neck. Each delivery system mentioned pushed them deeper.

Manning continued, "We must use every asset at our disposal to discover and destroy his delivery system. At the same time, we must find Lambe and stop him. Failing that, we must identify his intended victims and move them out of harm's way. If we succeed on any of these, we stop him."

But even as Manning spoke with great passion, Hallie felt their chances slipping away like grains of sand. Lambe was hiding, and they had no idea where. He had a delivery system, and they had no hint what it was. He had had months to plan his attack, and they had hours to stop it.

Lambe held all the aces.

Thirty-Three

Philip Lambe steered his Jaguar up to the parking lot booth of the older city airport and punched out his ticket. The booth attendant, a withered man with a silver-gray ponytail and ear studs, stared slack-jawed at a small television tuned to *America's Most Wanted*.

America's Most Wanted *is right in front of you, moron!*

Lambe drove into the lot and saw it was three-quarters full and dimly lit by yellow lamps overhead. He parked near the far corner, leaned back and waited.

He ran his fingers over the wood shift knob and soft leather. The car had served him well and would again tonight. The police would find it *after* his Michigan license plate was put back on, in about an hour. They would assume he'd taken a flight, successfully escaped and canceled his *Shikei*. Police always assumed the logical, the easy explanation, the one that gave them more time for doughnuts.

Cops were Silly Putty. You molded them to your needs, and right now he needed them stretching their resources across the country, checking out flights and scouring the cities for him, and that was precisely what they would do.

Meanwhile, he'd be nearby, savoring the minutes until he pushed Enter on his computer, launching his *Shikei*.

In the rearview mirror, Lambe saw the black limousine purr to a stop, right on time. Maurice, the French-Canadian chauffeur, got out and strolled up to his window. Maurice's curly dark hair framed raisin-like eyes and a nose flattened by too many hockey pucks.

Lambe scanned the lot, saw no one watching, then handed Maurice his Michigan license plate. "Install this on my Jaguar in one hour, then lose the Florida plate."

"Sure thing, Mr. Smith," Maurice said, tipping his hat. He opened Lambe's door.

Lambe stepped out, stretched his tall frame and inhaled cool, crisp air deep into his lungs. It refreshed him, as did the sweet scent of burning leaves wafting in from the neighborhood. Walking toward the limo, he heard the ping of metal. He turned and saw a young, skinny boy, around ten, with a long-stemmed screwdriver poised on a car's hubcap.

Lambe felt his body tense. The screwdriver looked similar to one he remembered from years ago. Remembered with great pain. The boy slid the screwdriver into his back pocket and stared at Lambe with fear, the kind carved into his psyche early in life by those who were supposed to love him, but didn't. Lambe knew that fear well. The boy's light brown face was bruised and swollen beneath his left eye, where a three-inch scab curved up to a bandaged ear.

"How much you get for the hubcaps?" Lambe asked.

The young boy stared back like a trapped animal, obviously realizing Lambe blocked his exit. "These ones, twenty-five dollar each. Cash."

Lambe peeled off two hundred-dollar bills and tossed them on the ground. The boy's feral eyes narrowed, then he snatched the money and examined it.

"Who's beating you?" Lambe asked.

The kid stared back, apparently deciding whether to answer.

"Somebody used to beat me, too," Lambe said.

The boy blinked, then nodded sadly as though maybe he'd deserved his beatings.

"Your father?" Lambe asked.

"He gone."

"The man you give your hubcaps to?"

The boy shrugged a maybe. "Bring in three bill a day, I don't git whupped."

Lambe peeled off five one-hundred dollar bills and tossed them on the ground. Wide-eyed, the boy scooped up the money and crammed it in his pocket.

"Don't do no sex," the boy said.

"You don't have to."

Suspicion lingered in the boy's eyes. "Why you gimme money?"

Because life's been unfair to you, Lambe thought. *Because you never had a chance.* "I got reasons. Good ones. The money's yours."

Lambe turned, strolled over to the limo and settled into the luxurious rear seat. He felt the kid's eyes still staring at him. Lambe didn't know exactly why he helped him. Now and then, when he saw a kid in trouble, he felt an odd kinship, a vague urge to help. The urge never lasted long.

As Maurice drove out of the parking lot, Lambe grabbed the tumbler filled with Glenfiddich scotch. He swallowed a third, leaned back and let the heat rush through his body, relaxing him, melting away the last vestige of concern. Soothing classical music, Brahms' *Der Jäger*, seeped from the overhead speakers. He sunk his feet into the plush carpeted footrest. The lap of luxury felt good. He deserved it.

The boy's screwdriver flashed back in Lambe's mind. So similar to the one his father had used that night when Lambe was seven. He could still hear his father, drunk and crazed, screaming, "This will teach you to not leave toys out!"

Then he stabbed the screwdriver through Lambe's hand, and twisted the end, severing tendons and nerves. Then he'd 'cleansed' the bleeding wound with scalding water from a tea kettle. Lambe had passed out when he smelled his own flesh burning.

Now, Lambe looked down at the remnant of that night—the grotesque purple scars and atrophied small finger of his right hand. He felt the rage again, even though he'd repaid his father for this mutilation and many others.

Lambe swallowed the rest of his scotch. Tonight was too important to dwell on the demons of his youth. Tonight was for celebrating. Everything he'd planned for years, his *Shikei,* was about to take place. It was, he reminded himself with pleasure, the defining moment of his life.

And a defining moment for thousands, Lambe thought, as he gazed out at the skyscrapers passing by.

He poured two more inches of Glenfiddich over the crushed ice.

Everything was still on schedule. His ingenious ten-city *Shikei* delivery system was tested and in place. A delivery system so brilliant and unimaginable that even weapons' experts couldn't anticipate it. He alone knew how *Korusu* would strike people. He alone knew which people would be killed. He alone knew how quickly and painfully they would die.

And he alone could activate the *Shikei*. Once activated, not even he could stop it.

"The FBI crisis team is a joke," he whispered to himself. "You have too many questions, and too little time to get answers."

Sipping more whiskey, he smiled as he reviewed his escape plans. The majestic Ambassador Bridge would take him to Windsor, Canada. There, as Armand Toussaint, he'd fly to Montreal and then to Brazil. In Sao Paolo, he'd assume his new identity.

Then, from his special hideaway, he'd sit back and enjoy watching the police authorities of the world try to find him.

A man who no longer existed.

Thirty-Four

Thursday 11:06 p.m.

"Suicide pilots," Janet McKay said, checking an item in her notebook.

Hallie closed her eyes, remembering the horror of 747s spearing the World Trade Center towers.

"But we have no-fly zones," Manning said. "If terrorists fly an aircraft into it, the Air Force will blast it out of the air."

"*Exactly* what a *suicide* pilot wants," McKay said. "The blast spreads his lethal toxin over the city."

Hallie watched Manning's jaw tighten with frustration.

"Then we'll ground most planes," Manning said, signaling a young, dark-haired agent. "Anna, call the director's office. Tell them we recommend only commercial and private aircraft inspected by Chemical-Biological personnel be allowed to fly within five miles of large metro areas tomorrow. And put more sky marshals on each flight. Everything else is grounded."

Anna nodded and flipped open her cell phone.

Hallie noticed that everyone spoke softer. Many had slumped further into their seats, their eyes desperately searching each other for any hint of hope.

Hallie wondered what Lambe's intended victims had done to deserve death. "Any thoughts on whom Lambe is targeting?"

Manning opened an FBI folder. "This preliminary psych profile indicates that he's demonstrated a dislike of Japanese, Arabs, Catholics, Jews, Wasps, Blacks. No one's safe."

"Does he hate one group more than the others?" Reed asked.

Manning checked notes in front of him. "This profile suggests a strong dislike for the Japanese. We don't know why. We're getting a more detailed profile in one hour, but in the meantime, let's assume he hates them more than the others."

"Are there 60,000 Japanese nationals in the USA?" Hallie asked.

"There are nearly 60,000 Japanese nationals in the US, plus 800,000 citizens of Japanese heritage," Manning said. "They live mostly in major US cities."

170

"How could he hit just them?" Hallie asked.

The group pondered the question for several moments.

"The post office," Dr. Janet McKay said.

Hallie turned toward her. "Like the anthrax letters?"

"Right."

"But the post office sanitizes letters now," Manning said.

"Sanitizing may not stop *everything*," McKay said.

"What can get through?"

McKay paused. "We've heard of a new, highly absorbent nerve agent compound that can apparently be impregnated into paper. When you take the letter out, the moisture in your fingers absorbs the toxic agent. The toxin gets into your blood. Thirty minutes later … you're dead."

"Jesus," Manning groaned. "You're telling me *touching* the letter can kill you?"

"It's possible, but remote," McKay said. "Lambe would need some *very* expensive equipment to manufacture this agent and then impregnate it into the paper."

"Eight-and-a-half million dollars were deposited into his Grand Cayman bank accounts. Another three million in Curaçao, plus six million in two Swiss banks," Manning said.

McKay slumped in her seat. "Probably enough to buy the finished product."

Manning rubbed his eyes. "Nate, brief the Postmaster General. Tell him to prepare for the possibility of canceling mail delivery tomorrow."

"He'll raise major hell," Nate said.

"Not as much hell as the families of 60,000 dead Americans or Japanese nationals in the USA."

Hallie sipped her cool, bitter coffee. The longer she sat there, the more desperate she felt. Resignation was moving through the team members like a cold, dark glacier, freezing all hope. Despite the massive police dragnet, the exhaustive high-tech forensic scrutiny of Lambe's home, and the expertise of chemical and biological weapon scientists, the crisis team still had nothing concrete, except less time.

The minutes—and their options—were ticking away fast. She glanced at Reed, knowing he was still angry with himself for not taking the *Shikei* folder at Lambe's house.

"Bingo!" shouted a young red-haired agent, snapping shut her cell phone. Everyone turned as though she offered water on a desert.

"We've found Lambe's laboratory," she said.

"Where?" Janet McKay asked.

"*Beneath* his basement."

"Doctor Livingstone and I need to see it *now*," McKay said, standing and grabbing her leather satchel.

"Let's go," Manning said, heading toward the door. Suddenly, he stopped and faced Reed. "You went through Lambe's desk files."

Reed nodded.

"Would you notice anything missing?"

Reed paused. "I think so."

"A missing file might give us a clue. We need you there." More command than request.

Hallie pictured Reed walking unprotected into Lambe's lab. The place was probably swarming with deadly toxins.

"Promise you won't go in the lab," she said, as he stood.

He took her hands in his. "Promise," he said and left.

* * *

Outside, Reed and the others exited the Ren Cen and hurried toward the river. Shards of a frigid river wind knifed through to his skin. He looked over at Casino Windsor's spectacular string of jewel-like lights. An ore freighter slid past, extinguishing the casino lights one by one.

Lives will be extinguished one by one tomorrow, he thought.

Manning pointed out the FBI's mobile Fly Away Laboratory and explained that it held twelve suites of analytical instruments and scientists standing by to identify any biological, chemical or radiological materials found in Lambe's lab.

As the group moved to an open area, Reed heard the rhythmic thwak of three helicopters, rotors churning slowly. They hurried over and boarded the nearest Bell chopper and strapped themselves in. The other two choppers were filled with Chemical Biological Rapid Response teams wearing yellow HazMat suits.

The helicopters clipped upward into the night sky and skimmed along the shimmering river. The chopper banked left and headed north toward Grand Blanc at 120 miles per hour. Minutes later, he saw hundreds of lakes, many surrounded by tiny dock lights flickering like fireflies. To the east, he saw larger lakes, pools of silver in the moonlight, and he recalled reading that Michigan had over 11,000 lakes, more than any other state except Alaska. Soon, the lakes gave way to dark forests and farms. A solitary car crept down a winding country road.

Suddenly, a red light began flashing. Reed turned and saw it was a wall phone. Manning grabbed it, listened a few moments and hung up. "We got Lambe's Jaguar."

"Where?" Reed asked.

"Detroit City Airport."

"Which flight?"

"None."

Reed stared at him.

"He wanted us to think he took one. A parking lot attendant saw him park, get in a chauffeured limo and drive off. We're checking all dark limos in the metro area, but there are hundreds."

"So Lambe's probably somewhere in the area," Reed said.

"Let's hope so."

Reed noticed Janet McKay rubbing a lotion on her hands. He assumed it was some kind of protection. He leaned over. "Any idea what you might find in his lab?"

"We assume the worst, Reed."

"Which is?" Manning asked.

"Biosafety Level 4. The most lethal. Viruses like Ebola and Lassa."

Manning, who was scanning a document entitled *Operation Iraqi Freedom, Chemical Weapons* said, "Chemical weapons like VX nerve gas are horrifically fast."

"Death in a few minutes...." McKay whispered, then closed her eyes and turned toward her window, obviously remembering.

Reed wanted to divert her mind. "Could *Korusu* be a virus?"

She turned back, her eyes a little moist. "Easily."

"What if it's Ebola?" Reed asked.

"We pray," she said. "The Ebola virus attacks every organ in the human body. Your blood clots, dead spots appear in the brain, liver, kidneys. Skin becomes so flimsy it can be pulled off. Eyeballs fill up with blood, the nose bleeds. Necrosis crawls over the internal organs. The liver swells and turns yellow, then liquefies and goes putrid. Testicles swell, nipples bleed."

Reed's stomach churned like a washing machine. "All from one tiny virus?"

She nodded. "A tiny virus that replicates into millions of tiny viruses and then devours the host body in hours."

Hours, Reed thought. *How many hours before Lambe strikes?*

Thirty-Five

"*There!*" the co-pilot said, excited, pointing ahead.

"Where?" Reed asked, squinting into the thick forest canopy that blanketed the rural countryside like a black shroud.

"Two o'clock."

Leaning forward, Reed saw nothing, then glimpsed a flicker of light through the branches. Seconds later, the helicopter banked hard left and swept down like a giant predator over Lambe's house. The gabled roof tucked into small turrets at the corners. All curtains and blinds were shut, but light from inside still filtered out. Floodlights bleached the grounds white and reflected off the rambling frame structure, except for a few crevices where light couldn't penetrate. Yellow crime scene tape surrounded the estate, as did several police cars flashing red and blue lights across Drummond Road.

The chopper searchlight moved along the roof and froze on a satellite communications dish. Near the dish, Reed saw two lidded smokestacks.

"What are those?" Reed asked, pointing the smokestacks out to McKay.

"For his lab."

The three helicopters glided over Drummond Road and nestled into the grassy field. Reed watched the biohazard teams deplane and hurry toward the house like a swarm of yellow-jackets.

"What are they carrying?" Reed asked.

"HHAs," McKay said. "Hand-Held Assay devices. Some identify the presence of the most common bioweapons. The three men on the left are carrying CAMs—Chemical Agent Monitors—that give us an instant reading of chemical weapons. The black camera-like devices scan the air for everything—from toxic methane to chemical and biological agents to traces of explosives."

McKay, Manning and Reed jumped from their chopper. The rotor's icy downwash sent shivers down Reed's back. He flipped up his collar and headed toward the house, his feet sinking into rain puddles.

A young woman wearing a dark FBI jacket and khaki slacks jogged toward them. The cold wind had reddened her cheeks and tousled her short blond hair. Drew Manning introduced her as Special Agent Lori Holloway.

"Has anyone entered the lab?" Janet McKay asked her.

"Not yet," Agent Holloway said.

"Good. Doctor Livingstone and I'll go in now."

Holloway led them inside through a spacious marble foyer to a seven-foot tall glass case displaying rows of exquisite Japanese figurines. She eased the case away from the wall, revealing a narrow elevator. They squeezed into it, descended and seconds later stepped out into a brightly lit room. Reed saw several white HazMat suits on hooks beside an enormous bookcase filled with chemical and biology textbooks.

"Lambe's lab is in there," Agent Holloway said, pointing to a wall-length window.

They hurried over and looked in at the massive laboratory.

"Serious stuff," McKay whispered.

Livingstone nodded and breathed out slowly. "Let's suit up."

A USAMRIID team member opened a case with two orange biohazard suits and helmets. McKay quickly searched her suit for tiny holes. She pulled on her latex gloves, then she and Livingstone carefully stepped into their suits.

"We found something," Manning said, closing his cell phone.

"What?" Reed said.

"Something buried in the woods behind the house. I'll go take a look. When I get back, Reed, you and I'll check Lambe's office files." Manning entered the elevator and headed upstairs.

Janet McKay placed a three-inch black box on a table. "Through this speaker-recorder, I'll tell you what we see in the lab, Reed." A little dampness appeared on her faceplate and she flipped on her suit's air system. Within seconds the vapor cleared and her suit seemed to puff up.

Livingstone walked to the lab door and spun the large brass wheel. The airlock door hissed open and they stepped inside the decontamination chamber. Seconds later, they moved into the main laboratory.

Despite the fact that they were experts wearing protective suits, Reed felt an unfounded, but real sense they were in danger.

* * *

Philip Lambe's fingers froze on his laptop.

Why is it beeping?

He grew concerned as the beeping continued. The laptop had to function perfectly. It was, after all, his backup launch system for the *Shikei*. He checked but saw nothing amiss.

Then, slowly, his lips twisted into a smile. Reaching down, he opened his briefcase. Flashing up at him was a small gray electronic device beeping like he'd known it would one day.

"Well, well," he whispered to himself, smiling. "So someone's knocking at my chamber door. I've been expecting you."

He could see it all now. Several HazMat-suited people walking through his laboratory. Biochemists and scientists, he prayed, not the doltish police. The scientists would recognize the beauty surrounding them. They would appreciate his genius, his laboratory's unique sophistication. They would be envious, of course. And best of all, they would be extremely worried.

Stroll around, browse, my friends. You may even find some helpful information. If only you could use it.

Philip Lambe gazed down at the electronic device, picked it up, then flipped its tiny red switch.

Smiling, he leaned back and visualized with almost sexual gratification what was about to happen.

* * *

Above the lab door, Reed noticed a red light flash on. He assumed it indicated that people were in the lab. But who would Lambe signal? Did others work with him? Reed doubted it. Lambe's profile didn't suggest a team approach. He was a loner. Especially in *his* laboratory. The red light began to bother Reed.

He watched McKay and Livingstone walk deeper into the enormous laboratory. The gleaming state-of-the-art equipment indicated Lambe had unlimited funds. Reed saw three mini-lab suites along one wall. From the ceiling, a coiled air hose dangled like an orange slinky. Four stainless-steel lab benches held bulky, box-like devices labeled incubators. A large gray tank that McKay called a bioreactor could be used to create biological weapons. In one corner sat two large vats, and nearby a seven-foot-tall stainless steel door that looked like a meat freezer door.

"Death factory," Livingstone hissed from the speaker box.

"Biological or chemical?" Reed asked.

"Both," he said.

Suddenly, animal cries erupted from the speaker box. McKay and Livingstone hurried to an alcove. Reed moved left and saw caged monkeys, their long, sharp teeth bared, shaking their cages and shrieking at McKay and Livingstone.

"They're terrified," McKay said.

"Of that!" Livingstone said, pointing at something Reed couldn't see.

"Of what?" Reed asked.

"Dead monkeys," Livingstone said, "male and female, autopsied on a table. Jesus, the bastard cut them wide open right in front of the others."

"Crab-eating monkeys," McKay whispered. "We'll send someone back for blood samples. He may have tested *Korusu* on them."

Livingstone walked over and opened the seven-foot steel freezer-like door. Inside, Reed saw dozens of stainless steel cylinders stacked like large thermos bottles. Livingstone picked one up and tried to remove the top, but couldn't.

He shook it gently. "Liquid."

They tried several more cylinders but couldn't get the sealed tops off.

"Labels?" Reed asked.

"Don't see any," Livingstone said, checking another.

As Livingstone placed a container back on a top shelf, McKay pointed at the container's bottom. "Got a label," she said.

"What?" Reed asked.

She leaned closer and read, "*Korusu!*"

"Yes!" Reed said, pumping a victory fist in the air and feeling a tremendous sense of relief.

Livingstone cradled the container like it was a ticking bomb as they hurried back into the main laboratory.

"Any hint of the delivery system?" Reed asked.

"Not yet," McKay said, looking around.

They opened several drawers, lifted out pipettes and lab dishes. From one drawer, McKay removed a long, two-inch wide black object about the size of a thick ruler.

"Is it solid?" Reed asked.

"No. Hollow plastic," she said, turning it over. She shrugged and placed it back in the drawer.

Reed looked up and saw that the red light above the lab door had gone off. *Why off if they are still in the lab?* The red light began to worry him even more.

"Got something," McKay said, lifting a black notebook from a drawer. She began flipping through the pages.

"His lab notes!" Livingstone said, excited.

McKay's gloved finger paged awkwardly through the notebook. "Notes in English and what looks like Japanese." About halfway through, they both slammed their fingers onto a page.

177

"The *Shikei!*" McKay said, excited. "Friday, November 14th. Ten cities. The *Shikei* body count estimate: Sixty thousand."

"Which cities?" Reed asked.

"No names on this page."

"Anything else?" Reed asked.

"A diagram," Livingstone said. "Central structure that seems to be linked to ten units. The ten cities maybe. Also a ten-word list in Japanese. The cities maybe."

Reed's hope soared as he realized Hallie could read the Japanese.

"We're bringing the book and *Korusu* out now," McKay said.

The sooner the better, Reed thought, checking the red light. He was surprised to see it flash on again and begin to fade on and off slowly.

Reed couldn't shake the overpowering sense that Lambe somehow knew they were here and had set a trap for them.

The sooner everybody gets the hell out of this house, he thought, *the better.*

Dr. Livingstone placed the notebook in a large plastic bag, then he and McKay stepped into the small decontamination chamber. They turned on the decon shower and liquid jets drenched their suits. Ultraviolet lights turned them purple in the dark, glistening chamber. Moments later, they stepped out of the lab, shut the airlock door and began to remove their suits.

Behind him, Reed heard the elevator swish open. He turned and saw Manning.

"What'd you find outside?" Reed asked.

"Bones. Dog, monkey … and a human femur. Anything here?"

"*Korusu!*" Reed said, pointing to the container in Livingstone's hands.

"Terrific!" Manning's face brightened for the first time in hours.

Reed heard a soft sputter, then a hiss. He checked to see if the airlock door was leaking, but the door was shut tight. The hissing grew louder and a fine white mist began to sprinkle onto a nearby bookshelf. Looking up, he saw the mist spraying down from ceiling fire-extinguisher nozzles.

"Get back!" McKay shouted, pointing at the nozzles. "Put on those HazMat suits *FAST!* Don't breathe the mist!"

Reed's heart pounded against his chest. He grabbed a nearby suit, yanked it on and zipped up. McKay handed a suit to Manning.

After suiting up, they crowded into the corner. The white mist sprayed thicker and swirled toward them.

McKay checked Manning's hood. "No filter," she said. She grabbed his gloved hand and placed it over the respirator hole. "Keep your hand here. Don't breathe until we're upstairs."

Manning nodded, eyes white beneath the visor.

Reed followed the others through the snowy mist to the elevator. They crammed on and headed up.

When they stepped off, Reed felt his blood stop. The white mist was spewing down from all nozzles. Agent Holloway was reaching up toward one.

"Get back!" McKay shouted at her.

"What?" Holloway asked.

"The mist can kill you."

Holloway backed up, then clutched her throat and began to cough. *She's breathed it*, Reed realized. They had to get her outside fast. McKay grabbed a small throw rug and placed it over Holloway's head, then hurried her into the corner where the mist seemed lighter.

"Everybody outside!" Manning shouted as he and Reed ran to the door.

Reed turned the knob and pulled. It wouldn't budge. He saw a thick deadbolt glinting in the door jamb. He looked for the deadbolt knob. There was none.

"He's bolted it electronically!" Reed shouted as white dust sprinkled onto his visor. His HazMat suit suddenly felt like a furnace. Sweat poured down his face and neck.

"Backdoor!" Manning shouted.

"Bolted!" someone yelled back.

The bastard's trapped us in his death chamber! Reed realized.

He felt nauseated and his mouth was chalk dry. *Did I breathe some?* He swallowed hard. Beside him, an agent began coughing.

Agent Holloway was gasping now, clutching her neck, slumping toward the floor. Outside, Reed saw agents gesturing to bring the battering ram. *Holloway won't last that long.*

"Get Holloway," Reed shouted to Manning.

Manning nodded.

Reed picked up a large lounge chair, carried it a few feet, then heaved it through the eight-foot bay window. The window shattered, flinging jagged shards of glass back into the room. Outside air whooshed in, swirling the poison mist around them like a tornado.

Manning lifted Holloway, stepped through the window and carried her far away from the house. Reed helped Livingstone, still clutching the *Korusu* canister, through the window and outside onto the lawn.

Behind him, Reed heard something rip. Looking back, he saw Janet McKay halfway through the window, staring at the shard of glass that had just ripped through her sleeve. As she stepped forward, the rip caught on the window handle. Trying to free herself, she twisted the handle deeper into her suit.

She yanked but couldn't untangle herself. She was trapped, and Reed realized her ventilator was sucking the deadly mist through the rip into her suit—and probably into her lungs.

Reed ran to get her—when suddenly Manning jumped onto the window sill and lifted McKay in his arms. He yanked hard, snapping the handle off, then carried her out near Agent Holloway.

Terrified, McKay wriggled out of her suit and ripped open the shoulder of her blouse. Reed saw her skin was not cut. She relaxed and turned to Manning. "You saved my life, Drew."

"Just one public servant helping another."

"*This* public servant needs us more," Reed said, rushing over to Agent Holloway.

McKay hurried over. Lori Holloway's face was a sickly gray, her eyes tight with pain. Reed feared she'd fall unconscious any second.

"Can you breathe?" McKay asked.

Holloway slapped her leg several times and Reed wondered if she was starting a seizure. She slapped her thigh again, where he noticed an odd bulge in her pocket. He reached into Holloway's pocket and came out with a small atomizer. He handed it to McKay.

Quickly, McKay pinched Holloway's jaws open and sprayed the atomizer medication into the young woman's throat. Within seconds, Reed was relieved as Holloway's breathing and color improved miraculously.

"Asthma...." Holloway gasped. "Couldn't breathe."

"Which saved your life, Lori," McKay said. "Just relax."

Holloway managed a faint "Thank you" as two policemen lifted her into the back of an ambulance.

McKay turned to the local police chief. "Get everybody far away from the house fast! Evacuate all homes within two miles. The wind will spread this killer mist!"

The chief turned and shouted to his officers.

Suddenly, the icy wind knifed through Reed's sweat-soaked clothes, and he began to shiver. Reed, McKay, Manning and Livingstone hurried to their chopper and boarded.

The chopper lifted into the night sky and Reed breathed out slowly. They'd escaped Lambe's insanity. Barely.

Janet McKay leaned over and placed her hand on Manning's arm. "Thank you again, Drew."

Manning blushed a bit and shrugged. "You're welcome, Janet."

The group settled in and began to relax.

Until the explosion.

The chopper rocked wildly. Reed knew they were going down. He grabbed the arm rests, thought of Hallie, watched his life fast-forward. Then, amazingly, the aircraft leveled off and everything seemed normal.

"What the hell was that?" Manning asked, staring out the window.

Reed looked outside and saw that the back half of Lambe's house had been blown off. The rest was engulfed in fifty-foot tongues of fire. Smoke and flames leapt from windows, setting nearby trees on fire. Policemen and HazMat team members ran for their lives.

Stunned, Reed watched the house burn like a scene from Dante's *Inferno*.

Near the garage, two policemen lay face down on the ground, their backs ablaze.

Thirty-Six

Friday, 4:45 a.m.

The conference room door swung open. Hallie spun around and watched Drew Manning, Dr. McKay and Dr. Livingstone walk in wearing very serious faces.

Where's Reed? Did something happen?

She'd been worried sick about him since she'd heard about the fiery explosion and injuries at Lambe's house. Did he get burned, or inhale some poison mist?

Seconds later, Reed breezed through the door, looking fine, although pink. Her anxieties melted as he sat down beside her and they embraced. She touched his face and damp hair.

"Your hair's wet? she said.

"Anti-contamination showers. Scrubbed hard with their bug-killer soap."

"You look sandblasted," Hallie said.

"Feel like it." He yawned. "And a little tired."

She felt exhausted too. Her mind was sluggish, her eyes dry, her back muscles stiff as wood. The scent of strong coffee hung over the room and trays of toasted bagels, Philly cream cheese, lox, tomatoes and sliced Bermuda onions sat untouched.

She noticed everyone was whispering now. Their grim, dark faces reflected the reality that they were out of time and nearly out of hope.

It was Friday. Lambe's day. And they still had no leads on his whereabouts, his delivery system, or his target cities. They had some *Korusu*, the weapon, but Hallie wondered whether its identification, expected any minute, would matter much. *Korusu* killed people. That was known.

The unknowns—*how it would be delivered to its victims, in which ten cities, and who he was targeting*—might have been answered in the book found in Lambe's lab. But unfortunately Dr. Livingstone dropped the book in his panic to escape Lambe's house, and it was incinerated in the fire.

"More coffee?"

Hallie looked up and saw a thirtyish, freckle-faced male agent holding a large pot.

"Thank you," she said. Caffeine was today's drug of choice, even though her stomach lining felt like Swiss cheese.

She sipped some and looked up at the wall where Lambe's face, enlarged to poster size, glared down at her. Hallie stared into his dark, empty eyes, their unfathomed evil seemed so obvious now. How had she missed it?

Manning hung up the open line to Washington. "That was Director Hatcher. Homeland Security has just elevated the national risk advisory to red, the *highest*: *SEVERE*. They're sending out the general information to all federal, state and local authorities."

"Why *general* information?" Woody Beachum asked.

"We don't have specifics, Woody. We don't know the weapon, the cities, or even the delivery system."

"How will they inform the public?" Hallie asked

"They're still debating that. They've got a couple of hours before people wake up."

Hallie asked Manning, "Did you read Agent Whitlock's profile on Lambe?"

"I only scanned it," Manning said. He turned to Agent Merle Whitlock, a terrorism specialist with the FBI's Behavioral Science Section.

Whitlock was a short, plump man with a massive, egg-shaped head, rimless glasses and small, pouty mouth. His bio sheet, which Hallie had read, said he held a law degree from Harvard, degrees in Asian studies from the University of Hawaii and a Ph.D. in criminal psychology. He'd begun his career profiling serial killers, but after 9/11 he had switched to profiling terrorists. His hobbies included comparing the mating habits of primitive tribes along the Amazon's Xingu River, and ballroom dancing with his sister, Myrna Faye, a professional wrestler.

Whitlock fingered the long, thin wisps of brown hair spanning his bald dome and jawed a serious wad of bubble gum. In front of him, Hallie noticed he'd made an extremely neat stack of Double Bubble wrappers.

"Merle," Manning said, "can you slide a couple copies of Lambe's profile over here?"

"*Preliminary* profile," Whitlock corrected in a high, squeaky voice, then slid two copies across the table.

Earlier, Hallie and Reed had paged through the quickly compiled profile and found it revealing.

"What's your take on him?" Manning asked Whitlock.

Merle Whitlock shrugged, then fingered his soft, fleshy lip, revealing pink bubble gum inside. "Professionally, Lambe is a brilliant biochemist who's demonstrated formidable depth and diversity in chemical, biological, medical and industrial disciplines. His greatest attribute would appear to be inventiveness. He's exceptionally skilled at adaptation, creating new and better applications based on existing products, methodologies and materials. New ways of doing things."

"Including new biological and chemical weapons?" Dr. McKay said.

Whitlock nodded. "*And* their delivery systems, I would think."

Hallie worried increasingly that Lambe's delivery system might be something completely unexpected. Perhaps even different in each city.

"Lambe's a psychopathic loner," Whitlock continued. "Angry at the world for wrongs he believes it committed against him. Rules mean nothing. He does not associate guilt with his antisocial behavior. Right is what he wants. Wrong is what's in the way."

"Any close friends?" Manning asked.

"Not that we know. But he can be very friendly and helpful if it serves him."

Hallie recalled how friendly and helpful Lambe was at the funeral.

"What's your net net on the guy?" Manning asked.

Whitlock stopped chewing and stared at the table. "Very bad. Lambe's brilliant. Angry. Focused. A highly functioning psycho. The worst combination. Absolutely the worst." Whitlock's eyelid began to flicker.

"His early life looks traumatic as hell," Manning said.

Whitlock nodded. "The Japan years especially."

"Starting with his father's desertion?" Manning asked.

"No, no. Much earlier. Daddy was quite the sadistic bastard."

Hallie remembered reading about the father, Karl Lambe, and turned to the page. "It says here that when Lambe was seven, his father held his arm under scalding water until Lambe passed out. Left hideous scars on his hand, and on his psyche, I imagine."

"Quite right," Whitlock said, nodding at Hallie's insight. "Japanese hospitals document that Lambe was admitted on several occasions. Broken jaw, two broken fingers, fractured arm, two ripped-off toenails, and the burned hand. His father claimed they were accidents or sports injuries. Lambe agreed, probably out of fear. But a nurse strongly suspected it was psycho daddy's work."

"So today Lambe pays back America instead of daddy," Manning said.

"Actually, he probably paid back daddy," Whitlock said, tidying a gum wrapper. "Daddy died of sea wasp poisoning about six years ago."

"It happens," McKay said.

"Not in Iowa," Whitlock said, taking off his thick glasses and rubbing them hard with a tissue. "In brief, Lambe's intellect, his arsenal of weapons, his vendettas, and his unfathomable rage are a horrifying combination. He's the most frightening, well-financed, *evil* terrorist we've faced since Bin Laden. And he's here among us." Whitlock's eyelid twitched wildly as he crammed another chunk of bubble gum into his mouth.

"His father deserted him and his mother," Hallie said. "Six months later, his mother committed suicide."

"Lambe found her," Whitlock said, chewing hard. "Holiday Inn near Kansas City. He was ten when he found mom floating in a bathtub of blood."

Several people stopped what they were doing and stared at Whitlock.

"Desertion and suicide," Whitlock said, "scud missiles through the kid's psyche. Extreme parental abuse. After that, he bounced from foster home to foster home. Some were cruel environments, two with documented sexual abuse."

"But," Manning said, reading from the report, "his school grades remained excellent."

Whitlock nodded. "School was his refuge. His 171 IQ helped protect his self-esteem. Sort of leveled life's playing field a bit."

Hallie turned to a page. "Full scholarship at Stanford. *Summa cum laude* in biochemistry."

"Professors and fellow students recall him as a brilliant loner," Whitlock said.

Shades of the Unabomber, Hallie thought.

"Any love life?" Manning asked.

"Prostitutes mostly," Whitlock said. "A few lived with him briefly. The one we talked to left because she didn't enjoy the rough stuff."

"Rough stuff?" Manning asked.

"Ropes and rape." Whitlock popped a large bubble, blushed, then peeled the gum off his lips.

Hallie glanced at another page. "He worked for many biochemical firms, plus Ford, Chrysler and Delphi Automotive. They all released him. Why?"

Whitlock frowned. "Guy at Chrysler said Lambe always worked his own agenda. Used the company labs for personal experiments. His company work was shoved aside. Same story at Delphi and Ford. But Lambe always blamed other things for his dismissals."

"Like what?" Hallie said.

"Bad managers, Japanese and Korean import car sales."

"Were his complaints justified?" Reed asked.

"No. His dismissals were his own doing, according to his co-workers. He made enemies."

"Individuals or groups?" Manning asked.

"Both," Whitlock said, arranging a thin strand of hair back across his gleaming scalp. "At one time or another, Philip Lambe has demonstrated hatred of virtually all ethnic and political groups."

"But with a special hatred for the Japanese?" Manning asked.

"It would appear so."

"So it's not unreasonable," Manning said, "to assume he might strike Japanese business buildings, offices and facilities."

Whitlock nodded. "How many are there?"

Manning turned to an assistant bent over her laptop. She nodded and tapped something into it. Two seconds later, she said, "Over 4,445 Japanese affiliates now operate in the USA."

Manning nodded. "Okay, get extra police protection for the largest Japanese affiliate offices and assembly plants, those with the biggest worker populations. And give them all a heads-up warning."

The assistant nodded, flipped open her phone and gave the order.

I'm half Japanese, Lambe. Do you hate me only half as much? Hallie wondered. Her neck and shoulder muscles were cramped from sitting for several hours. She'd give anything for a brief walk or jog, anything to pump blood through her body and brain.

The conference room door opened.

All eyes turned to a thin military man with a matched set of eagles on his shirt lapels, a bird colonel who looked his rank. He also looked as though he'd just witnessed a train wreck.

It's started! Hallie feared.

The bird colonel handed Janet McKay a piece of paper. As she read, color drained from her face. She gave the paper to Dr. Livingstone, who scanned it and closed his eyes.

"We've confirmed what *Korusu* is," McKay whispered.

Everyone waited.

"*Korusu* is a sarin compound."

Hallie felt sickened. She knew sarin. Death would be painful and fast.

"A nerve gas," McKay said. "In chemical terms it's called methylphosphoryldifluoride (DF)+ isopropanol."

"*Extremely* deadly," Livingstone added, massaging his temples.

"The gas used in the Tokyo subway incident?" Hallie said.

"Yes, but Lambe's *Korusu* sarin is more deadly," McKay said, reading the paper.

"How bad?" Manning asked.

McKay hesitated. "One drop on your skin can kill you. So can breathing a small amount of its vapors."

"You can't see it, smell it or taste it," Livingstone said.

Hallie felt the ceiling ventilator fan blowing air down on her that she couldn't see, smell or taste.

"How can Lambe deliver this *Korusu* sarin?" Manning asked.

"Aerosol or liquid are the primary delivery vectors," Livingstone said.

"How does sarin work?" Reed asked.

McKay swallowed. "Basically, it interrupts your nerve impulses. Shuts down your body systems. Your diaphragm can't pump your lungs and you suffocate from respiratory paralysis."

Hallie closed her eyes, imagining the pain sarin victims would feel.

"What about symptoms?" Manning asked.

McKay spoke in a whisper. "Your nose starts to run. Your vision blurs. Your breathing becomes difficult. Your chest feels like someone's crushing it. Soon you can barely see. You feel nauseated, sweat profusely and become disoriented. Finally, you can't breathe, you convulse and die from SLUDD."

"SLUDD?" Reed asked.

"SLUDD stands for salivation, lacrimation, urination, defecation and death. Basically, you suffocate and choke to death on your vomit."

Several people cleared their throat.

Manning asked, "How much time from exposure to death?"

Dr. McKay hesitated. "Minutes."

"Fifteen?"

"Three, maybe," McKay said, "but Lambe's *Korusu* sarin may be even faster."

"Bottom line," Hallie said, "there's no time for medical treatment."

"No," McKay said, "not unless people carried atropine and injected themselves immediately."

"Are there enough injectors for all cities?" Hallie asked.

"Not nearly enough. The CDC has eight National Pharmaceutical Stockpiles throughout the country. But they have only *limited* supplies of atropine injectors."

"Let's get those we have to major cities in the next few hours," Manning said.

"New York, Boston, DC, and other major cities already have some atropine now," McKay continued, "but America has over one hundred cities with populations over 200,000 or more. Which cities do we send our limited stockpile supply to? Which hospitals in the cities? Which citizens get them?"

No one offered a suggestion.

"Have the CDC decide the best way," Manning said.

McKay and Livingstone nodded.

"Let's also distribute the protective masks," Manning said.

"Again, Drew, there are not enough masks for *all* civilians," McKay said with some anger. "Not enough detection and warning systems, not enough mass sheltering locations."

The door swung open and Hallie watched Agent Dan LaCage rush in, nervous and wide-eyed, carrying another note.

Again, Hallie's stomach froze. *It's started....*

"We found a link between the sixteen test victims," LaCage said.

A hush fell over the room.

"Each victim worked on a computer several hours the day they died."

Dr. Livingstone leaned forward on his elbows. "Are you suggesting *computers* might be *how* Lambe delivers *Korusu?*"

"I'm just reporting facts," LaCage said.

"*Could* computers deliver *Korusu* sarin?" Manning asked.

"Yes," McKay said. "If the sarin is encased in something, it could handle the computer's thermal environment."

"What about computers, Bradleigh?" Manning turned toward Agent Rob Bradleigh, an FBI computer expert. "Could computers be programmed to release sarin?"

All eyes swung to Rob Bradleigh, who cleared his throat. A tall, hefty man with the whitest skin Hallie had ever seen, Bradleigh had recently built a new FBI Intranet system with several anti-tampering devices and firewalls which so far had thwarted invasion by hackers. A brilliant hacker himself, Bradleigh had done jail time for breaking into Pentagon computers. The FBI engineered his parole on condition that he hack for them on issues of national security.

"Yes, computers could be programmed to release the sarin. A Japanese company has the technology," Bradleigh said, his eyes twinkling like tiny blue marbles. "And they could all release *Korusu* on one day."

Hallie felt her mouth go dry.

"How?" Manning asked.

Bradleigh hoisted his considerable girth up onto his amazingly tiny feet and waddled over to the drawing of Lambe's network. "First, some kind of *Korusu* unit had to be installed in the computers. Then it's simple. Programming triggers the *Korusu*'s release today."

"You mean a computer virus could trigger the release today?" Hallie asked.

"Right. Or maybe a SPAM-like E-mail triggers the release."

"But wait," Livingstone said, "how the hell could Lambe get *Korusu* sarin units inside sixty thousand computers?" Livingstone asked.

No one answered.

"Maybe during manufacturing," Reed said.

"But how?"

"Maybe Lambe persuaded the manufacturer that the unit was some kind of anti-virus device or extra memory or whatever. Assembly line workers install it without knowing."

"But the manufacturer would examine the units closely," Livingstone persisted.

"The first few prototypes," Reed said. "Which could have been legitimate."

Livingstone nodded slowly. "And the rest contain *Korusu*...."

Reed nodded.

"Once the *Korusu* is released," Janet McKay said, "it floats out through the computer vents. Remember, you can't smell it or see it. If you're using your computer, or sitting nearby, you would inhale it. In minutes, you're...."

Hallie watched several people lean away from their laptops.

"Agent LaCage," Manning said, "dismantle the test victims' computers fast. If we find *Korusu* sarin, a media blast tells people not to turn on their computers today."

Bradleigh cleared his throat. "We may still have a problem."

Hallie didn't want to hear the problem.

"What?" Manning asked.

"Lambe may have programmed sarin to seep out even if people don't turn them on."

Thirty-Seven

Friday, 5:58 a.m.

"Special Agent Manning," said an excited blonde agent leaning across the conference table, her dark silk blouse stretched tightly against her full bosom.

Hallie watched Manning put down his coffee mug and face the agent.

"For you, sir," she said, sliding her cell phone down to him.

Manning grabbed the phone and listened. Quickly, his eyes grew serious.

Please God, no.... Hallie thought.

Manning snapped shut the phone and slowly looked up at them. "The twenty-five largest US cities and their suburban reservoirs report water is normal."

Sighs of relief rolled across the table.

Hallie watched Manning relax. The man's face was drained from stress and lack of sleep. Less than twelve hours ago, the most frightening terrorist threat in US history had been nailed to his back. If he failed, there'd be awesome pressure to scapegoat him. Washington craved scapegoats like junkies crave a fix. But Hallie sensed Manning could care less about blame. What mattered to him was saving the innocent lives locked in the cross hairs of Lambe's insanity.

Hallie rubbed her eyes. They felt dry and scratchy, the result of only seven hours total sleep in the last three days. She popped another No Doz tablet into her mouth and gulped it down with lukewarm coffee.

Fear, she noticed, had again tightened all faces. Nerves were stretched to the breaking point. Each phone call silenced the room. Every visitor spun heads. Each team member knew it was only a matter of time.

Manning walked over to the large photo of Philip Lambe. "Okay, one more time, assume you're Lambe. You're delivering sarin to sixty thousand people today. You *know* they will eventually get physically close to your sarin delivery system. What is it? Let's start in the morning."

"Subways, trains, buses and cars," Janet McKay said.

"All possibilities," Manning said, nodding. "But do we feel those are

190

Lambe's easiest, most practical way to kill *sixty* thousand?"

Most heads shook no.

"Too many delivery units," Livingstone said.

Heads nodded.

Hallie agreed too, but she worried about the group's tendency to assume Lambe would use a practical delivery system. Her instinct told her otherwise, that Lambe would strike in an original, ingenious way, a way the experts would never consider. And the more she thought about it, the more terrified she felt.

"Once people are at the office," McKay continued, "they get close to heating and air-conditioning vents, computers, elevators, water coolers, printers, copiers, whatever."

Hallie noticed the FBI Washington phone flashing.

Manning pushed the speaker button. "Manning here."

"Any news, Drew?" Director Hatcher asked.

"The same, sir. How's Washington?"

"We're fighting the usual gang of butt-covering presidential advisors." Director Hatcher's voice sounded strained. "No reports of deaths yet?"

"No, sir."

"And Lambe?"

"Still no leads." Manning wiped perspiration from his lip.

"In four minutes, I'm briefing the President. What can I tell him?"

Tell him today's slaughter may cost him his reelection, Hallie thought.

"Lambe has a number of options, sir," Manning said. "First, as you know, large office buildings. Thousands of people congregated together. He places sarin in ventilation systems. This may be his most practical option."

"But we're inspecting large buildings."

"Right, sir. But sarin can be carried in briefcases, lunch boxes, whatever, at the last minute."

Hatcher was silent.

"He could also hit enclosed stadiums," Manning said.

"What are we doing?"

"The Rapid Response Team personnel are crawling through stadium ventilation systems now. We'll guard the systems before and during the games."

"Maybe we should cancel the games if we haven't caught Lambe by game time."

"Agreed."

"What about subways?"

"Our new advanced detection systems for New York, Chicago, DC,

Boston and Los Angeles are working well. In other cities, we have personnel walking through commuter trains with our new CAMs detection units. But we don't have enough units. So uniformed officers are patrolling the cars, checking unattended packages and briefcases."

"Airports?"

"Again, sir, our anti-terrorist systems are working, plus we have personnel with CAMs walking through the terminals now."

Hallie heard Hatcher shuffling papers.

"Any other possible delivery systems?" Hatcher asked.

"Food," Manning said.

"Sarin in food?"

"Anything's possible with Lambe."

Director Hatcher mumbled a string of obscenities to himself.

"But McDonald's," Manning said, "Burger King, Wendy's, KFC, Taco Bell, and all other major chains are working with the CDC, spot-checking food this morning."

Hallie swallowed as she envisioned children dying in their parents' arms in fast-food restaurants. A vein thumped at the side of her head. She tried to relax but knew the only thing that would relax her was stopping the crazed psychopath, Lambe.

Director Hatcher sighed heavily in the speaker box.

"Sir?" Manning asked.

"Yes?"

"Something wrong, sir?"

Hatcher cleared his throat. "The world, Drew."

Manning nodded.

"After 9/11," Hatcher said, "Congress said they'd act *immediately!* They took several *months* to make airports and flying marginally safer. So terrorists shifted to anthrax, biological and chemical weapons, threats of smallpox, threats of nuclear suitcase bombs, dirty bombs...."

"Frankly," Hatcher continued, "the weapons' menu and the terrorists who have access to these weapons is growing faster than our ability to defend against them, thanks in part to Congress's failure to pass adequate funding."

"I agree."

"For too many years," Hatcher continued, his voice growing more passionate, "Congress didn't have the intellectual depth to comprehend that biological and chemical terrorist threats were real, or the courage to put aside partisan politics and do something about it. Some members still don't get it."

What part of September 11 don't they understand? Hallie wanted to shout.

"Congress slept!" Hatcher sounded angry. "They failed to fix a federal system that had *forty-three* separate organizations responsible for protecting against terrorism. They failed to fix the fifteen independent federal intelligence-gathering organizations that didn't even have to share information. They failed to allocate sufficient funds to USAMRIID and Aberdeen Proving Ground. And they failed to provide enough treatment and antidotes for all Americans who become exposed to chemical and biological weapons. Bottom line, they failed the people who elected them."

"Yes, sir," Manning said.

"They did succeed, however, at fully funding certain things."

"What's that, sir?"

"Their fat pork barrel projects."

"Yes, sir."

Hallie heard and sympathized with the hot, pent-up rage in Director Hatcher's voice.

"As a result of their dereliction, thousands may die in the next few hours," Hatcher said. "Other than that everything's swell...."

Hallie watched Manning massage his temples.

"You think Lambe's still holed up in your area?" Hatcher asked.

"Probably, sir. He knows thousands of police are looking for him. Largest manhunt in Detroit since the disappearance of Jimmy Hoffa."

Let's hope we're more successful finding Lambe, Hallie thought.

"Drew, the White House has agreed to quietly move military units into the major cities. Mostly around hospitals and medical centers. At the first hint of panic, they'll establish control."

"Makes sense."

"So does a stay-home curfew."

"I agree," Manning said.

"We're considering a curfew now. But some presidential advisors are dead set against it."

"On what basis?" Manning asked, clearly puzzled.

"They see a curfew as caving in to Lambe. Bringing America to its knees."

Hallie couldn't believe it and whispered to Reed, "Would they prefer bringing sixty-thousand Americans to their graves?"

"Do these advisors remember 9/11, sir?" Manning said, red-faced. "Have they ever seen thousands of dead bodies?"

"Most wouldn't recognize a dead body if they slept with it."

"Where's the President on this?" Manning asked.

"With us. But these guys are very persuasive. They want him perceived as hanging tough. In a few weeks he announces for reelection."

"When will he decide on a home curfew?"

"By 6:35 this morning. But the majority is against the curfew."

A possibility occurred to Hallie and she signaled Manning, who gestured for him to speak. "Director, this is Hallie Mara."

"Yes, Hallie...."

"The home curfew may also pose a risk."

Hallie saw puzzled faces turn toward her.

"What risk?" Hatcher asked, his voice tight.

"*Korusu* sarin might be *in* the homes."

Hatcher cleared his throat. "In sixty thousand homes? How can Lambe do that? We've suspended mail delivery today."

"We've also considered that he may have somehow implanted sarin inside computers," Hallie said. "The computers are programmed to release the sarin today."

"Is that possible?" Hatcher asked with alarm.

"Yes, sir," Janet McKay said. "The sarin might have been installed during assembly. All Lambe's test victims worked on computers the day they died."

Hatcher paused. "Jesus, we've got a lose-lose situation. People die if they stay home or go out."

Suddenly a cup shattered on a floor, piercing the pent-up tension. Everyone spun around and saw a red-faced male agent lean out of the kitchenette. "Sorry...."

"I want Lambe now!" Hatcher said.

"Yes, sir," Manning said.

The room was silent for several seconds.

Hatcher cleared his throat again. "What are the chances we caused Lambe to postpone today?"

"Probably zero, sir."

Hallie felt her last ember of hope fade.

"And our chance of finding him in time?" Hatcher asked.

Manning shrugged. "If he stays holed up, maybe five percent."

Hatcher exhaled long and hard. "Do your best, Drew."

"Yes, sir."

Hallie hated hearing the desperation in Director Hatcher's voice, hated Congress for its years of ego-driven partisan debates. Now Congress could debate something else.

What to do with the bodies?

Thirty-Eight

Hallie and Reed walked out of the conference room during a five-minute break and headed toward the Ren Cen's cavernous, multi-tiered atrium.

If only, she thought, *we could keep on walking away from this insanity and pretend it wasn't happening.* But it was happening. And she knew the team wouldn't give up until they stopped Lambe or he won.

But time was in his favor. With each passing minute, she knew their chances to prevent the attack, *and* the horrific pain it would inflict on people, were dwindling away.

Lambe was winning. Everyone knew it. And there wasn't a damn thing they could do about it. A quick glance at Reed told her he was equally numbed by the impending slaughter.

"You okay?" she said as they approached the balcony overlooking the cavernous atrium.

"It's these deadly weapons...."

"What about them?"

"Anyone can get them. It's just overwhelming."

She nodded.

They leaned against the balcony and looked down into the vast central court surrounded by the Ren Cen's massive towers. The thick gray concrete walls always reminded her of an enclosed futuristic city in which people, like well-dressed robots, scurried along on walkways, escalators and elevators. She watched people with briefcases on the lower levels, stroll into coffee shops. Men and women rushed to their offices, hotel guests window-shopped, seniors shuffled along on morning walks, guides directed tourists.

She'd read that seventeen thousand people entered the Ren Cen towers each day. Towers of *people,* all breathing air circulated by central air systems.

Air we can't see, or smell, or taste, she reminded herself.

Will it soon be laced with sarin?

Below her, a young guard helped an elderly, silver-haired couple who seemed lost. He pointed them back where they'd come from. They nodded and drifted away. Hallie studied the guard. Toothpick skinny. Short. He'd have no chance against trained terrorists who sealed doors, disabled elevators, and unleashed toxins into the ventilation systems.

Hallie rested her head on Reed's shoulder. He put his arm around her, and she realized how wonderfully safe she always felt with him near. She also realized, thanks to her recent, life-sobering experiences, that she loved him in a way she'd never loved anyone before. He had altered her life profoundly, and whether he knew it or not, he was now an integral part to it, a part she did not think she could live without. Did he need her that much? Could his love for her possibly be that deep?

The balcony's cool concrete soothed her caffeine-jittery stomach. Looking down to the level below, she watched an attractive brunette businesswoman hand a green folder to a tall man.

Suddenly something clicked in her mind. She pointed below.

"What?" Reed asked.

"That brunette down there."

"What about her?"

"Her green folder," Hallie said. "Dr. Shah had a green folder. It reports on someone here in the Midwest who bought a chemical weapon from Asia. A massive amount. The report also contained schematics of the delivery system. Maybe it's linked to Lambe."

"Where is the file?" Reed asked.

"In Shah's briefcase in the lab where he...." Her stomach clenched at the memory of Shah's collapse.

"Can we get in?"

She reached into her coat pocket and pulled out the lab key.

They hurried to the nearest FBI agent, a well-built crew-cut man named Walters, and Hallie explained the situation. Walters' eyes shot open. "You think the file's connected to Lambe?"

"It's possible," Hallie said.

Agent Walters rushed into the conference room and briefed Manning, then returned with a tall, curly haired agent named Ramírez, whose muscles were on the verge of bursting the seams of his dark blue suit coat.

"We'll drive," Walters said.

Fourteen minutes later, Walters steered his silver Buick into the Genetique Laboratories lot and parked next to a red Chevy Cavalier with a Daffy Duck sticker on the bumper.

Hallie led the group inside, where Agent Ramírez announced he would watch the lobby entrance. She took Reed and Agent Walters down to the lower level, then hurried down the long corridor toward Shah's lab. She saw yellow crime scene tape and an official yellow biohazard sign on the door.

From a nearby room, she grabbed two white HazMat suits and handed one to Reed.

Agent Walters saw the suits and swallowed hard. "I'll keep watch out here."

Hallie nodded, then helped Reed into his suit.

"The last time I wore one of these," Reed said, "bad stuff happened."

"So the odds favor good stuff," she said, checking his suit, then hers, for holes.

She unlocked the door and they entered the lab.

Transparent biohazard bags covered the microscopes and phone. She looked at where Shah collapsed and again felt her heart ache for the man. Turning, she scanned the room for the briefcase and noticed it wasn't where she'd last seen it. She checked the shelf above and behind the cabinets and saw no sign of it. Reed shrugged that he hadn't found it either.

"Maybe someone took it to your office," Reed said.

"Nothing should have been removed from here."

They searched again, opening file drawers and cabinets. Her HazMat suit suddenly felt like a steam room. Perspiration moistened her skin. She watched Reed climb on a chair and check the top of a cabinet, then shake his head. Nothing.

"Let's check my office," she said.

Stepping down, Reed stopped and pointed to an angular shadow behind a box of pipettes between the bench and wall. He reached in, moved the pipette box and pulled out Shah's briefcase. Its leather handle, she noticed, was stained with perspiration. How many years did Dr. Shah work to make the world safer?

Reed snapped open the briefcase.

"There it is," she said, lifting out the green folder.

Quickly, they left the lab, and she locked the door. They pulled off their bulky suits and stepped into the hall. Hallie didn't see Agent Walters.

"Walters should be here," Reed said, sounding concerned.

"Maybe he's in the restroom."

Behind her, she heard an odd click.

She turned around and looked into the barrel of a handgun. The huge man holding it wore a white medical coat with an MD badge and thick, horn-rimmed glasses. Beside him stood another large man in a white coat with a gun.

"Agent Walters won't be joining us," said Horn Rims. "Nor will Agent Ramírez." He pulled the .38 from Reed's shoulder holster, then snatched the green file out of Hallie's hands.

"Walk to the rear service entrance," the other man said. "Act real normal."

This is not happening, Hallie thought as Reed and she walked slowly down the long, dimly lit hallway. She prayed that Diedre, T. Rex or anyone else would walk out and see them. Passing a partly open janitor's closet, she saw Walters, his lips smeared with blood, and beside him, Ramírez, slumped against a bucket.

Horn-Rims smiled, closed the door and pushed them forward.

Outside, they were forced into a black Ford van with tinted windows. They drove out of the lot and headed east along the Detroit River.

We're useless to them, Hallie realized. *They have the green file. They have Reed's gun. They're taking us somewhere to kill us.* She looked into the rearview mirror and felt like she'd been slapped.

"Got away in Atlanta, didn'cha?" the bullnecked driver said, smiling. "Not this time, bitch."

Thirty-Nine

A one-way trip, Reed realized.

They drove past the Belle Isle Bridge, heading east on Jefferson, hugging the river bank. He slouched down, acting defeated and submissive, hoping to catch his captors off guard. All he needed was the right moment, a split second to overpower one and yank his gun away. No easy task, considering his smallest opponent outweighed him by thirty pounds.

The driver, Luca, had a neck that looked like he'd swallowed a football. Reed recognized him as the man who'd been behind Hallie in the airport ticket line, then followed her to Atlanta and attacked her. His olive pit eyes glared at her every few seconds, taunting her.

Beside Hallie sat a tall, silent man named Nick, stroking the barrel of a .45 Magnum. Beneath his left eye, a dark cyst puffed out like a small prune. On his neck, a swastika tattoo was visible among acne scars.

Reed sat in the third row, next to Big Man, a.k.a. Manny, the muscular dolt who'd driven him off I-75, and later tried to shoot him in the driveway. Manny was clearly thrilled to see him again. Wiry black hair crept over the gold chain on his neck. The dim-witted man constantly scratched his neck with the business end of his .38 even though the safety was off. One deep chuckhole could lobotomize the fool or worse.

Manny leaned over close to Reed, revealing stubby, yellow teeth. "No escape this time, pal." His breath smelled like warm garbage.

They stopped at a red light and a furniture truck rolled up beside them. Reed looked over at the truck's passenger and started to signal him. Suddenly, the truck pulled ahead into the left-turn lane.

Then—manna from heaven. A big, beautiful Detroit police patrol car eased to a stop next to him. The driver, a young black officer sipped coffee, then faced Reed.

Reed started to mouth 'Help!' when Manny's cold, hard .38 pushed deep into his ribs. "Look straight ahead, asshole. Real normal."

Reed looked ahead real normal.

The cop's flasher came on.

He recognizes us! Reed thought. *Manning issued an APB!*

"Don't say nothin'!" Manny said, jabbing his gun so hard Reed flinched.

Suddenly, the police car sped off down Jefferson. In disbelief, Reed watched it race ahead, flasher and siren fading away … like all hope.

"Stupid fuckin' pigs!" Nick said, laughing.

"Musta smelled doughnuts," Luca quipped.

Manny and Nick cackled like hyenas.

The light turned green and Luca drove on down East Jefferson. As they approached an older, blighted area known for the occasional body dump, Luca slowed down a bit. People disappeared among the area's abandoned buildings and shadowy alleys. Anyone walking its dark, deserted streets at night remained upright about as long as an NFL running back. Reed grew anxious.

But Luca drove past the area.

Soon the palatial estates of Grosse Pointe swept into view. Not exactly Murder City. Reed had attended elegant parties in some of the magnificent mansions overlooking the blue waters of Lake St. Clair. They passed mammoth fifty-room English, Tudor, Georgian and French Provençal homes with sprawling gardens, elegant dining rooms, libraries with gold-leaf ceilings, sun rooms and guest cottages, all built in the early decades of the 1900s. Many estates were built by the original automotive barons, the Fords, the Dodges, the Fisher Brothers, whose assembly lines had put America —and to some extent the world—on wheels. Today, many automotive descendants still lived there, but their new neighbors included pizza, high-tech and furniture barons—and apparently some thugs, Reed realized, as Luca turned down a driveway.

The drive wound through tall evergreens and led to a large three-story English Renaissance house overlooking the lake. The home's fieldstone base extended up to ornate woodwork and high-arched windows facing the water. Lush, manicured landscaping was tucked around two massive bay windows like a mink stole hugging firm breasts. In back, Reed saw a large white yacht rocking gently in the royal blue lake stretching towards the hazy Canadian shoreline. Luca drove into a massive underground garage and parked between a new Lexus and Mercedes.

Inside the mansion, Luca led them past a full-size bronze statue of a nude woman pouring water from a jar. Reed saw several Japanese paintings and glass tables adorned with expensive *objets d'art*, all coordinated nicely with custom-made white leather sofas and chairs.

Nick whispered something to Luca, then disappeared down a stairwell.

Hallie and Reed were ushered down a hall to a long, pine-paneled room with a panoramic view of the lake. More leather sofas and chairs and an antique roll-top desk. Reed saw a closed door beside him and at the end of the room a mini-laboratory with microscope and lab equipment. Next to the mini-lab was a huge, wall-mounted ant farm and beside it, a steel door.

Luca walked to the desk, rolled up the top and grabbed a palm-sized cell phone. He punched in one digit and faced the lake.

"They're here," Luca said. "Yeah, I got it." He listened, mumbled a few "uh-huhs," then flipped the phone closed.

Seconds later, Reed watched the steel door click open.

"Nice of you to drop by," Philip Lambe said, stepping into the room. "You left in such a hurry last night." He wore a charcoal turtleneck sweater and slacks, but had made no attempt to alter his appearance.

Manny handed Lambe the green file. He scanned the pages, then snapped the file shut. "So someone couldn't keep a secret. Most unfortunate. His family will miss him."

Lambe strolled over to the massive ant farm and stared through the glass at hundreds of ants crawling through tunnels in the sandy soil.

"Army ants," Lambe said. "Delightful beasts. Devour everything. Plant, animal. Been known to consume pigs, horses … even humans. Imagine that, being eaten alive by thousands of vicious little bites. Slow, painful.…" Lambe's eyes glazed over. "But some ants, like people, make very bad decisions. When they do, they must suffer the consequences."

Lambe traced his finger along a jagged tunnel that forked in two directions. "You see, right here the ants have a decision to make: enter the new chamber, or continue in the main one. Entering the new chamber is a bad decision, like this little fellow is about to make."

Reed watched a brownish ant inspect the entrance to the new chamber, then slowly creep in. Suddenly a gray mist puffed onto it. The ant stopped, then tumbled down onto a pile of what appeared to be hundreds of dead ants.

"Bad decision," Lambe said, smiling. "Paid with his life."

Reed said nothing, waited.

"And today," Lambe said, "people who made bad decisions will pay with their lives."

Reed wanted to know who. "Which people?"

Lambe gazed at the ants as though Reed hadn't spoken.

"What bad decisions?" Reed asked.

More silence.

"What did these people do *wrong?*" Reed persisted.

Lambe tapped his finger along one tunnel. A large ant paused, then continued crawling ahead. "They were disloyal. Their decisions caused many people pain."

"Caused *you* pain?" Hallie asked.

Lambe's lips bent in an indulgent smile. "People can't cause me pain."

Give me thirty seconds to try, Reed thought. "How were sixty thousand people disloyal?"

"*Many more* were disloyal," he said, tapping the glass. "But sixty thousand deaths will teach the others a lesson."

"What lesson?"

"One they need," Lambe said with the tinge of impatience.

"*Why* do they need it?"

Slowly, Lambe faced him, his eyes dark pools of evil. "You're just like your brother. Too many questions."

"Which is why you killed him!" Reed glared at Lambe, wanting to ram the bastard's head into the ant farm.

Another indulgent smile. "Kyle's blind persistence killed him. Like yours will kill you and beautiful young Dr. Hallie." He pointed at the dead ants. "Like them, you two took the wrong path. You got nosy, asked too many questions."

Reed forced himself to remain calm. "This lesson they need ... will *we* be around to learn it?"

Lambe checked his watch, then leaned against the window and looked out at the lake. "Unfortunately, no."

A ray of sunlight crawled onto Lambe's scarred, purple fingers. He noticed it and quickly tucked the withered hand into his pocket. He signaled Luca over, whispered something, then walked over to the steel door and looked back at Reed.

"But there's good news in all this, Kincaid," Lambe said.

"What?" Reed asked.

"You'll see your brother soon," Lambe said, smiling as he walked through the steel door and bolted it.

"Stand over there!" Luca demanded, pointing near the desk.

Hallie and Reed moved over beside the desk.

Luca dialed a number, began speaking in hushed tones, then turned and stared out at the lake.

Manny walked over to the lab bench. From his pocket he took two tiny dog magnets, one black and one white, and placed them on his gun barrel. He moved the black dog so that it chased the white one around the barrel. Manny chuckled at his little dogs.

If only his bullets were as slow as his brain, Reed thought. Looking around, he realized that the only known escape route was the hall they'd walked down. He saw no potential weapons. The roll-top desk held only a book, *Toxic Fish, Tetrodotoxic Poisoning*, and a leather folder. As he turned, his eyes locked on the folder, specifically on a page sticking out. Its heading read, *Shikei*.

Reed's heart slammed into overdrive. He had to get the paper.

As Luca whispered in the phone and Manny played with his doggies, Reed inched closer to the desk. No one seemed to be paying particular attention to him. He moved to within six inches.

Suddenly Luca spun around and stared at him.

Does he know what I'm going for? Reed wondered.

Luca turned back and continued whispering into the phone. Reed leaned against the desk and slowly slid his fingers toward the *Shikei* page. As he started to grab it, an ice-cold gun barrel touched the back of his neck.

"Expectin' mail?" Nick asked, grabbing a chrome letter opener from beneath the leather folder.

Reed hadn't even seen the letter opener.

"He been bad?" Luca asked, covering the phone with his hand.

"Real fuckin' bad," Nick said.

Reed turned toward Nick.

Suddenly Manny's powerful karate chop slammed into Reed's neck from behind, spiking pain down his shoulder and back. Before he could react, another heavy blow struck the other side of his neck. His arms felt paralyzed.

Luca arrived with long pieces of rope and bound Reed's wrists and Hallie's, then shoved them into the small side room and locked the door.

Hallie took Reed's head in her hands and studied his eyes. "Reed, are you okay?"

"Sort of." Slowly, he rotated his head, wondering if his collarbone was fractured. Looking around the small fourteen-foot-square room, he saw nothing he could use as a weapon. Along one wall was a black sofa and chair. Above it, a narrow six-inch window ran just below the ceiling. A corner bookshelf was stuffed with books on Middle East politics, a thick Japanese-English dictionary, computer company annual reports, and chemical industry journals. The scent of gooey-sweet potpourri hung in the air.

"I saw a paper marked *Shikei*," Reed said.

"Where?"

"On the desk. I was trying to get it when Nick caught me."

"We have to get it," Hallie said.

"And Lambe."

Forty

So far, no ambulance sirens, Hallie thought, praying it meant the *Shikei* had not started, or at least not in Detroit. Either way, they might still have time to stop Lambe.

But first Reed had to cut the rope binding his wrists. He'd been scraping it against the abrasive metal frame of the sofa bed. Slowly, the metal frayed the rope's fibers—but the fibers were fraying Reed's wrists, which were beginning to resemble raw hamburger. Hallie had seen him wince in pain and was worried about infection.

She sat a few feet away, listening at the door, growing more tense with each minute.

"What's with Luca and Manny?" Reed asked.

"Still snoring."

"What's their total?"

"Fifteen cans."

"Then it's true."

"What?" she asked.

"Twenty percent of beer drinkers drink eighty percent of the beer."

She forced a tight smile. "Not if these two guys drink it first."

"Correct."

Hallie knew Reed was trying to relax her, and she appreciated the effort. But it wasn't working. Cold, hard logic suggested the men in the outer room were going to kill them soon.

She stared out the narrow window at the gray sky. "Maybe the FBI's tracking Lambe here?"

"They'd be here by now if this house was in his name."

She nodded and looked at his bloodied ropes. "How are your wrists?"

"Okay. The ropes should be severed in minutes."

She decided to go over their escape plan again. They'd reviewed it several times, looked for flaws, found some, fixed them. Reed said it could work.

She wasn't so sure.

A car honked out on Jefferson Avenue. For the last few hours, the only sounds they'd heard were cars honking, beer cans fizzing, lake freighter horns groaning, and gulls squealing past the long, skinny window.

Hallie turned and stared at Reed for several moments.

"What?" he asked.

"Our chances of escaping…. They're not good."

"They're better than if we did nothing."

But still lousy, she knew. "Take me through the plan again."

"Okay. First you knock on the door. You say something's seriously wrong with me. Manny's blow to the side of my head caused a concussion. Maybe a coma. You feel sick, too. Maybe it was the sandwiches."

"Food poisoning. The mayonnaise tasted funny."

"That works," he said. "One of them will check me out. I'll be lying face down on the sofa, hands beneath me. He won't be worried since he knows my hands are tied."

She envisioned the scene and nodded.

"If," Reed said, "he's holding his gun in his hand?"

"I say your hands are covered with a terrible rash."

"If his gun is in his shoulder holster?"

"Your shoulders have the rash."

"And if the gun's in his belt?"

"Your stomach has the rash."

He nodded. "Then he walks over to me, sees me face down on the bed. Again, he's not worried. My hands are tied. He says, 'Get up.' I don't respond. So he shakes me. Nothing. He shakes me harder. Still nothing. Then you say…."

"My *breasts* are covered with the rash."

"He'll turn to look. I nail him hard. Grab his weapon."

"You make this sound like a workout."

"It'll work if we do it right."

"Then what?"

"Then Lambe."

"What if he's left?"

"We grab his *Shikei* paper and escape in one of the cars."

"They'll chase us in another car."

"*Only* after they break out of this locked room, and change the tires I shoot out."

Hallie nodded, toying with her silver bracelet, trying to persuade herself it could work. "We really have no other choice."

"We have theirs." He gestured toward the lake.

An icy shiver ran down her spine. "Hypothermia would kill us in minutes."

Reed nodded, then turned to his rope and scraped furiously for a couple of minutes. Finally, the last fibers split and his arms swung out. She could almost see the blood rushing to his aching shoulders. She walked over, and he quickly untied her ropes. "I'll retie these loosely just before they come in," he said.

She looked at his bloody wrists, then wrapped them with fresh Kleenexes from a box on the shelf, then forced him to lie back on the sofa. "You need to rest a moment."

Hallie lay beside him and gently massaged his warm, taut shoulder muscles. She heard his breathing slowly return to normal. They remained in each other's arms without speaking, resting, preparing their minds and bodies for their escape.

Wind rattled the narrow window. She looked through it at the white clouds, realizing she might not see tonight's sunset, or tomorrow's dawn, or walk along a shore, or make love to Reed again. She was embracing him for what could be the last time. Despite killers in the outer room, she wanted him now. She wanted her final memory to be of love, not a failed escape. She looked over at him and whispered, "I love you, Reed, and…."

He turned toward her. "And what?"

She stared into his eyes.

He smiled. "Now…?"

She winked and smiled.

"I thought you'd never ask," he said, looking toward the door. "But we may have spectators?"

"Luca whispered about coming for us in an hour."

"And they're still snoring," he said, smiling and kissing her lips softly, then with more passion.

Their clothes fell away, and in the soft daylight they made love with a quiet desperation that can only come from knowing they might never make love again. She'd never felt such depth of passion before.

Later, they rested in each other's arms, silent, knowing that this moment was theirs alone, an indelible memory, cherished for as long as they had, even if it was only minutes.

Reed turned toward her and whispered, "When we escape, I'd like to take a walk."

"Where?"

"Down the aisle."

She smiled. "Might this be a proposal?"

"Yes. Might it be accepted?"

"It is," she said, her eyes filling with tears of joy.

They kissed and held each other in silence for several moments until a loud snore erupted in the other room.

Reed leaned over and said, "It's time."

"Now?"

"They're beer-sleepy. Their reflexes will be slower."

She knew he was right. She stared into his eyes for several moments, then kissed him.

He embraced her, whispering, "*Shinu-hodo aishiteru*, Hallie."

She smiled at his awkward 'I love you' in Japanese.

Suddenly wind rattled the window hard. *A warning?* she wondered. *Maybe we should wait. Rethink this? Maybe the FBI have seized Lambe's bank records, maybe they've traced Lambe to this house and are minutes from rescuing us.*

Maybe-thinking, she realized. *The kind that may get us killed.*

Hallie stood up and steeled her muscles for action. "In the words of a great 9/11 American hero–*Let's roll!*"

Reed retied her ropes loosely. She walked toward the door and took several deep breaths, working herself into a frenzy. She patted her cheeks and she felt her face flush. Unbuttoning the top of her blouse, she rubbed her upper chest hard until it was red. She nodded at him, then knocked on the door.

Reed turned face down on the sofa, hands beneath him as though still bound.

"Help!" she shouted. "He's very sick. Help me, please!"

She heard nothing.

She knocked harder. "Please help! I think he's in a coma!"

Still, no sound from the outer room.

She pounded the door. "Help me! He's *very* sick! Please!"

She heard cursing, mumbling, shuffling, someone rattling keys and sliding one into the slot.

Luca banged the door open and lumbered into the room. "Fuck's wrong with him?"

"He's in a coma," Hallie said. "Manny hit him too hard. And he has a red rash all over his *stomach*!"

"We never touched his gut."

"It's those sandwiches. I feel sick. The mayonnaise tasted bad. I think we all have salmonella."

Luca belched and walked past her, his vile body odor nearly gagging her.

Luca shook Reed's shoulder. "Wake up!"

Reed lay stone still.

"Wake the fuck up!"

"What's wrong in there?" Manny croaked in a sleepy voice from the other room.

"You whacked him too hard," Luca shouted as he shook Reed's shoulder again.

"My God," Hallie said, "now *I* have the rash all over my breasts."

Luca froze, then spun toward her.

Suddenly, Reed slammed his elbow solidly into Luca's thick neck, stunning the huge man. Reed grabbed for his gun, but Luca was falling sideways, struggling to maintain balance.

Reed tried to pull the gun from his waist, but Luca twisted away, making it impossible. Reed head-butted him and Luca's hands shot up. Reed yanked the gun out and jammed it in his ear.

"Freeze, asshole!" Reed said.

Luca froze.

"What the...?" Manny mumbled from the doorway, rubbing his eyes, his gun tucked in his waist. Seeing what'd happened, he snapped to attention.

"Jesus, Luca, you fucked up bad. The boss is gonna—"

"The boss is holding the gun," Reed said. "Put yours down."

Manny hesitated.

"Gun down or Luca dies. Choose quick."

Manny paused as though weighing several more options.

"Put the gun down, you fuckin' moron!" Luca yelled.

Slowly, Manny placed his gun on the floor.

"Hands on head!" Reed said.

Both men did as told.

"Now, slowly walk into the other room," Reed said, directing them into the outer room. As they walked, he reached down and slid Manny's gun into his pocket.

It's working, Hallie thought, excited.

"Sit in those chairs." Reed gestured to two chairs facing the lake.

The two men sat down. Manny began to hiccup wildly.

"Where's Lambe?" Reed said.

They did not answer.

Hallie glanced at the desk and saw the *Shikei* file was still there. Reed saw it too. Hallie started to go get it.

Behind her, she heard movement.

Suddenly, someone grabbed her around the waist and stuck a sharp steel blade against her neck. One quick move, she realized, would sever her carotid artery.

"Drop the gun, Kincaid!" Nick said, jabbing a handgun into Reed's back. "And take the one outta your pocket real slow, or Martin'll bleed your bitch."

Hallie saw their options were zero.

Reed paused, then slowly placed both guns on the floor. From the corner of her eye, Hallie saw Luca walk slowly toward Reed, then suddenly karate-kick him in the back, knocking him to the floor.

"Nobody cheap-shots me, you bastard!" Luca screamed. His shoe dug into Reed's ribs, again and again, like he was driving spikes into him.

"Stop!" Hallie screamed, trying to pull Luca away.

Luca's shoe speared Reed's neck. With each kick, Reed jackknifed further into a defensive curl.

Luca's kicked his head.

Reed fell unconscious.

Forty-One

Phillip Lambe sipped hot spice tea and felt its warmth comfort him. He was excited and eager, feelings he rarely experienced. Feelings from very long ago. It reminded him of early one Christmas morning, when he was seven, sitting on the stairs looking down at the cheap tabletop Christmas tree with its three white bulbs and scrawny aluminum branches drooping down over his one and only present. A chemistry set. He'd wanted it more than anything and within days had performed each experiment in the booklet flawlessly.

His father, of course, had ridiculed his experiments, called them infantile, elementary, said blind monkeys could do them. And three weeks later, during his nightly drunken rage, he'd grabbed a crowbar and smashed the chemistry set to pieces.

Today, certain people will receive my chemistry present. And their deaths will teach all people a lesson: that committing a traitorous act against America could cost you your life.

Traitors *should* be put to death. After all, life's best teacher is death. The more deaths, the better the lesson is learned. Like World War II, Vietnam, the World Trade Center deaths, the Iraq War, the ongoing war on terrorists....

Today's *Shikei* would teach Americans that today they were in an even more insidious war, a war they had slowly been losing.

Lambe picked up a large envelope and removed three color photographs. He smiled down at the top photo, which he referred to as "Sven—Lambe the Nordic." A computer had morphed his face into longer cheeks, thinner nose, blue eyes, light blond hair. Norwegian, maybe. Most acceptable.

He looked at the next photo, "Marcello—Lambe the Neapolitan." Nut-brown eyes behind tinted horn-rims, pronounced nose, dark wavy hair with a trace of distinguished gray. Mediterranean, Latin-American maybe. Also acceptable.

Flipping to the third photo, "Shimazu—Lambe the Nip," he looked at the jet-black hair parted and combed to the side, rounder cheekbones, tawny skin, dark eyes slanted slightly. Perfect.

This is my new face. A part-Asian face while the police of five continents search for a Caucasian face. His fluent Japanese and genuine passport would ensure his authenticity.

He sipped more tea and dialed a phone number. After several international clicks, Dr. João Machado, his plastic surgeon in Rio de Janeiro, answered.

"Shimazu," Lambe said.

Dr. Machado cleared his throat. "When?"

"Next Friday."

"But I've scheduled—"

"Perhaps an extra fifty thousand dollars...?"

Dr. Machado paused. "Well, yes, I suppose I could reschedule things."

Lambe hung up. He took a cigarette lighter, lit the Japanese photo and watched it curl to ashes. Then he placed the other two photos between some books, where the police would easily find them. A little misdirection. Let the fools waste time looking for the Scandinavian and the Mediterranean.

Lambe walked to the window and looked out at the blue-gray water sliding south toward Lake Erie. The water always calmed him. He followed the gentle, rippling reflections over to the Canadian shore and found his mind drifting back to another foreign country, Japan. The painful years. The years of his abusive father, their cramped Tokyo apartment, the taunting neighborhood children. Lambe had been thin, awkward and unable to speak Japanese well. One day, older bullies had beaten him and forced him to eat dog feces. Weeping, he'd run home and told his father. For crying, his father had broken Lambe's jaw with a wine bottle.

That day, Lambe vowed to repay his father and anyone else who ever hurt or victimized him. He'd kept his vow. Transgressors had paid. Some, like his father, had paid with their lives.

Lambe strolled into the bathroom, turned the hot water on and lathered his beard with lime-scented foam. The soft foam smelled nice and felt good against his skin. He'd forgotten what shaving felt like and what he looked like without a beard.

He began shaving in short, careful strokes. He smiled as he realized the authorities were looking for a bearded man and he'd be clean-faced. And in seven days he'd be *new*-faced, as Shimazu. Clumps of foam plopped gently into the water.

Suddenly, a police siren screamed toward him. He flinched, nicking his chin, but the siren quickly faded away down Jefferson Avenue. He watched a drop of blood spill into the water, turning it pink.

Lambe gripped the sink hard, remembering the blood-red water in the

Kansas City Holiday Inn where at age nine, he and his mother had stayed after his father abandoned them in Japan. He remembered drawing her the big house and garden she'd wanted so desperately, and pushing open the bathroom door to show her. He remembered proudly walking in, then seeing her in the dark red bath of blood, hcr wrists flayed open, the razor blade on the floor, her face gray as old porcelain, her empty scotch bottle floating on her breast, her eyes at long last peaceful. Just below the surface of the bloody water, her watch read November 14, burned into him forever.

He'd shaken her cold hand, crying, begging her, "Momma, wake up! Please, Momma, please!"

"Suicide," the medical examiner said an hour later.

Murder, Lambe knew, even as a young boy. Murdered by his father's cruelty. For which Lambe had repaid his father one night years later. Lambe thought back to that night and felt warmed by the memory of handing his father an aperitif and watching the sea wasp toxin slowly and painfully twist life from the evil man's body. His father had begged for help.

Begged and wept and died.

What a blessed night....

Forty-Two

"Look at my red-orangy one," said six-year-old Jennifer, pointing to the clown's face she'd made on the laptop computer.

"What a beautiful clown," Sister Megan O'Malley said, watching Jennifer's chubby face crinkle in a beautiful smile.

O'Malley was warmed by her smile and the smiles of the other preschoolers sitting around the gleaming conference table in the chairman's office at NBL Components Corporation. Smile, giggle, and squirm. It's all they'd done since yesterday when she'd told them that NBL's chairman, Nate Lieberman, Sister O'Malley's close friend, had Shrine Circus tickets for them. It was their first circus and, she hoped, the first of many escapes from their impoverished, abusive homes.

Today, you'll laugh like little monkeys, she knew.

They deserved to laugh. They also deserved homes without fear, and rats, and black holes in dry wall, and icy radiators in winter, and loud screams in the night, and bullet holes in their windows. They deserved warm, loving homes, like the one Megan O'Malley had been so privileged to grow up in.

She thought back to the night she first realized just how fortunate her life had been. As part of her sociology class, she was required to do real-world social work. She'd chosen a shelter for abused women. One night she'd driven one of the women home to get some clothes, then watched in horror as the woman's husband started beating her with his fists, and came after Megan. They'd barely escaped. Megan had reported the incident to the police, who could only issue a three-week restraining order.

Four weeks later, the woman left Megan a frantic voice mail begging Megan to come get her *quickly!* By the time Megan picked up the message, the woman and her young daughter were dead, stabbed by her husband, who'd disappeared.

Their deaths changed Megan O'Malley's life. She'd vowed that day to help as many victims of abuse as she could. She'd managed to aid several dozen battered women and children over the last few years, and later tonight she'd thank her uncle, Bob Magill, a vice-president at General Motors, for GM's generous contribution toward another new shelter for abused women and children.

She glanced over at Shoshanna, the six-year-old, across the table, creating a blue clown on another computer. Megan's heart went out to her. The young girl lived with her mother and an alcoholic pimp in a filthy trailer-brothel. Some nights, when her mother was out, she hid from the pimp because he 'touches me.' Social services had promised to check things out but hadn't yet gotten around to it. Tomorrow, O'Malley would stay in their office until they got around to it.

Megan suddenly felt a wave of exhaustion pass through her. Finally, my sixteen-hour days are catching up with me. *But why am I so hot?* She pushed the laptop computer to the side and took a small mirror from her satchel. Her cheeks were flushed pink, like her eyes, which sort of matched her red hair. But hey, she thought, not bad for a thirty-one-year-old nun who chases ankle-biters around a day-care center.

"Look at Shoshanna's funny clown," O'Malley said, pointing to the little girl's green-haired, orange-faced clown.

"Oooohs" wafted from the other kids, but not quite as enthusiastically as earlier. One "ooooh" developed into a harsh cough.

"Where's Nate?" Sister María Rodríguez asked from the end of the conference table.

"In a meeting. His secretary said he'll be here in about ten minutes."

Megan O'Malley was delighted that sixty-six-year-old Sister Rodríguez had come. The perky nun had last been to a circus fifty-four years ago and was as excited as the kids.

"I still can't believe Nate Lieberman gave you such a large donation," Sister Rodríguez said.

"He gave the donation to our *shelter*, Sister."

"Yes, of course." Rodriguez grinned like a mischievous cherub.

"Did you happen to tell Nate our shelter fundraising was a little short?" O'Malley said.

Sister Rodríguez fiddled with her hands. "Oh, no. But maybe one of his friends told him."

"Did you happen to tell his friend?"

Sister Rodríguez's cheeks flushed a bit. "Well, I chat with so many people...."

So that's how Nate found out. Megan O'Malley smiled and thought of Nate Lieberman, a good friend since seventh grade and now owner of NBL

Components, a highly successful components supplier to the computer industry.

"Thank God you dated him in high school," Sister Rodríguez said, grinning.

Megan O'Malley felt herself blush and smiled. "We were totally infatuated with each other. The quiet Jewish boy and the mouthy Irish girl. We called ourselves Star-of-David-crossed lovers."

"So what happened?"

"In our junior year, Nate and his family transferred to Paris. Nate and I had a very tearful farewell. Then came college. He went to the Sorbonne. I heard he was serious about someone. Later, I discovered that he wasn't. In fact, he'd been asking a lot of people where I was."

"Where were you?"

"Taking my final vows."

Sister Rodríguez cleared her throat. "Well, God bless him."

God will, Megan O'Malley thought, remembering all the times Nate had quietly helped people in need.

She glanced over at Shoshanna. The little girl was rubbing pink eyes and seemed to be coming down with something.

O'Malley's eyes also felt hot. She blinked and felt a wave of nausea suddenly wash through her. *Maybe I'm catching Shoshanna's bug.*

Moments later, Megan blew her nose, igniting sharp pain in her nostrils. Her eyes burned and flooded with tears. Nearby, Jessica started crying, then rubbed her neck.

"What's the matter, Jessica?"

"Hurts," she said, rubbing her throat.

"Me too," Shoshanna said, her brown face damp with sweat. A small blond boy, Jason, moaned and lay his forehead on his computer keyboard. His lips trembled.

What's going on? she wondered. *Food poisoning? No—Jason and Shoshonna have eaten nothing.*

More coughing....

Suddenly, piercing pain gripped Megan O'Malley's chest so hard she had to lean back to keep from passing out. *What's happening?* Her throat burned like she'd swallowed acid. Perspiration drenched her body. She tried, but she couldn't get enough air into her lungs.

She tried to stand but fell back in her seat. Squinting, she saw two—no, three tables, tilting, twisting like angry serpents in front of her.

God help us!

She heard cries, forced herself to stand, then stumbled. Her vision

215

tunneled to a circle, then the circle grew smaller. Her lungs were being squeezed in a vice.

"Sister ... get kids out," she gasped.

Sister Rodríguez did not respond.

She looked down the table and saw the elderly nun slumped over, blood spilling from her lips onto her white habit. Next to her, Sean bolted forward, vomiting.

Shoshonna moaned and clutched her stomach. Beside her, two children, still as stones, had collapsed in their chairs.

Must get out!

Please, God, save my babies....

Forcing herself forward, she managed to grab Shoshanna, open the door and push her into the hallway. Shoshanna fell on the carpet, gulping air.

Swallowing hard, O'Malley stumbled over and grabbed Jason by the shirt and pulled him out into the hall. She rested a moment, crawled back in and dragged Jessica into the hall.

Megan O'Malley tasted something warm and coppery. Blood. Her lungs were being crushed.

Seeing Sean, she crept back in and reached toward the young boy as pain cut through her like a machete. She fell forward onto the floor.

Save my babies ... please, God ....

Forty-Three

Hallie's head felt warm on Reed's shoulder as they rested on the sofa, waiting. She watched his breath gently lift strands of her hair and set them down again. Things were quiet, peaceful, calm.

The calm before the storm....

She wanted to remain in Reed's arms like this forever, even though forever might be minutes. She flicked lint from his sleeve, knowing their lives could soon be flicked away as easily. Luca and Manny were whispering in the outer room.

Gently, she checked the one-inch gash on the back of his head. It was dry. She'd cleaned it with a handy-wipe she'd found in a drawer, then made him rest.

She smiled at Reed, silently thanking him. He had awakened her to an important lesson in life. Don't let past negative relationships prevent you from developing new ones fully. She'd let her David Harrington experience greatly restrict her relationships with men. In recent years, she'd pulled away from men when she felt the relationship becoming too close. Too close meant pain was near.

Then Reed Kincaid walked into her life and changed everything. Her fears and concerns simply melted away. And she *knew* now that she could give her love fully, unconditionally, probably already had, to the man whose arms were around her.

In the outer room, Luca whispered, "Hatteras ... northeast corner."

Manny mumbled something back, belched and laughed himself into a hacking cough.

"They'll be coming back soon," she said.

Reed nodded. "I'll look for the right moment, grab a weapon. I'll either *succeed*, or divert them long enough for you to run out onto Jefferson and flag down a car."

She nodded as a door slammed somewhere.

They waited in silence, conserving their strength. Moments later, a key clicked into the lock and she felt Reed's muscles harden. The door opened and Luca and Manny stood there, guns drawn.

"You lovebirds need a little fresh air," Luca said.

"Maybe a boat ride," Manny said, winking to Luca, subtle as a train wreck.

Luca and Manny pushed them into the outer room and over near the roll-top desk. Glancing down, Hallie couldn't believe her eyes—the *Shikei* paper was still there. Reed was also looking at it.

"Wait here," Luca commanded, then pushed a wall buzzer.

Seconds later, Nick strolled into the room and whispered something to Luca and Manny.

Reed inched closer to the desk. Hallie nodded that she knew he was going for the *Shikei* paper. She stepped forward a bit to partly block their view of him. Then, unclasping her silver bracelet, she signaled to Reed that she was going to drop it—create a diversion—while he took the paper. He nodded agreement.

She undid the clasp and flipped her bracelet several feet away. It *thwacked* onto the oak wood floor.

The three men spun around, their eyes locked on the bracelet.

"Sorry," she said. "The clasp is broken. May I get it?"

Luca's thick brow knotted as though he thought she might be up to something. Grunting, he motioned with his gun to pick it up. She walked over and bent down, hiking her skirt halfway up her thigh. She sensed Luca and Manny gaping at her long, tan legs. *Look all you want....*

She picked up the bracelet, purposely fumbled with it on her leg, then dropped it again as Reed reached the desk.

"It's slippery," she said, draping the bracelet over her bare thigh, fiddling with the clasp, nearly dropping it again. Pretending to lose her balance, she tugged her skirt even higher, revealing more bare thigh. Their eyes riveted on her legs. Manny's tongue actually slid out.

Out of the corner of her eye, she sensed Reed hesitate, then slip something —not the paper—into his pocket.

He still had to get the *Shikei* paper into his pocket. She had to create some *covering* noise. Finally, she clasped the bracelet. Then, coughing loudly and standing, she grabbed a nearby chair for balance and scraped it loudly along the floor as Reed slipped the paper into his pocket.

"There!" she said, brushing her skirt down. The men blinked themselves back from their dreams.

"We're outta here," Luca shouted.

At gunpoint, Luca and the others led them out a rear door into a landscaped garden which sloped toward the lake. They walked down a fieldstone path, past flower beds, to a narrow dock which jutted one hundred feet into the water. Hallie looked around. No one on the beach, no one in the yard next door, no faces in windows, no boats on the horizon.

Luca gun-nudged them out onto the dock. Cold, damp lake wind hit her face. She heard gulls squeal redundant warnings, then the soft gurgle of a yacht engine.

Turning, she saw the large white *Hatteras* creep around the boathouse and head toward them. Diesel fumes filled her nose. Martin, at the helm, guided the gleaming fifty-foot yacht alongside the dock.

Nick jumped onto the deck and lifted a green tarp.

Hallie's knees weakened when she saw what was beneath: Two scuba jackets with thick objects sewn into the large pockets.

Grinning at her, Nick picked up a jacket and dropped it purposely on the deck. It *thudded* like a barbell weight.

The jackets would drag Reed and her straight to the bottom.

* * *

Reed stared at the weighted jackets and knew any hope of treading water had just vanished. Near the jackets were a pair of oil-stained Adidas, a fishing tackle box, a red gasoline can and two sun-faded buoys. No potential weapons.

Hallie looked terrified as she stared at the weighted scuba jackets.

"Get on the boat!" Luca said, jabbing his gun into Reed's back.

Reed helped Hallie onto the deck. As he stepped on the toe-rail, something glinted behind the tackle box. Pretending to lose his balance, he fell beside the box and slid the small object inside his shirt.

"Get up!" Manny demanded.

"The deck rail's wet," Reed said, wiping his hands on his shirt, praying no one saw what he took.

"Get up *now!*"

Reed stood slowly.

Luca shoved them into the cabin, where Reed found himself surrounded by rich dark woods, polished brass, leather sofas and chairs. His feet sunk into an expensive Persian carpet. A Miró graced the back wall. On a chrome table he saw a photo of Philip Lambe on the yacht with three dark-haired men with mustaches and Middle-Eastern worry beads laced through their fingers. They wore white linen suits and serious expressions and held gleaming, leather briefcases. These guys weren't walleye fishing. Beyond the photo was a wall map of Lake St. Clair, with a red dot indicating the mansion they'd just left.

In his pocket, Reed felt the small cell phone he'd taken from the roll-top desk. He couldn't believe they'd left it there. But they had. Now, it warmed his leg, begging him to dial 911. But Luca hovered nearby, checking him every few seconds.

Reed considered trying to dial 911 *in* his pocket, but he couldn't determine the buttons and feared they'd beep too loud.

And what if this phone rings? he wondered.

Manny lugged the heavy scuba jackets into the cabin and dropped them beside Hallie. As Luca aimed his gun at Reed, Manny hoisted a jacket onto her shoulders, then padlocked the straps together in front. He lifted the other jacket onto Reed's shoulders and padlocked the straps together.

Reed estimated the jackets weighed at least twenty-five pounds. More than enough to take them straight down.

He noticed Hallie shivering and wanted to let her know about the cell phone and what he'd grabbed behind the tackle box. But he feared the goons would read his signal.

"Sit!" Luca grunted.

Hallie and Reed sat facing each other six feet apart. Cold November wind blasted through the window onto his face.

At the helm, Martin gunned the engine. The yacht lifted and surged forward, smacking hard against the whitecaps and soon reaching what Reed estimated was about twenty knots.

When Manny and Luca planted themselves in nearby chairs, Reed's hope sank.

The phone has to remain in my pocket for now.

Scanning the horizon, he saw no other vessels, except a dark speck, a fishing boat, heading the opposite direction.

Luca and Manny strolled over to a refrigerator and pulled out two six-packs of Budweiser. Each man speed-chugged a can within ten seconds. Laughing, they yanked off two more cans and walked to a map of the lake on the wall. Luca fingered a spot about three miles off the Canadian shore. Reed calculated the spot was fifteen to twenty miles away. The two men whispered something, walked back, sat down and chugged more beer. Every few seconds, Luca looked back at him.

How can I use this phone? Reed wondered. Then he knew—the bathroom. He could run water and flush as he dialed 911.

"I need to use the bathroom," Reed said.

Luca and Manny turned and stared at him.

"In a few minutes you can piss all you want," Luca said.

Manny chuckled.

"Come on! I can't hold it!"

"Then you'll get kinda wet," Luca said, grinning.

Laughing, Manny flipped on the television.

Reed was down to his last chance, what he'd slipped into his shirt when he fell. Slowly, he moved his hand inside his shirt and touched the handle of the rusty, three-inch fishing knife. He scooted the knife up his sleeve.

Luca glanced back at him and Reed pretended to scratch his stomach. Luca turned back. He and Manny sucked down their third beers, opened two more, then zapped through the channels and began arguing over whether to watch cartoons or *Jerry Springer*. Luca won, insisting that watching *Springer* would improve Manny's I.Q.

Leaning forward so they couldn't see, Reed eased the knife into his hand. With slow, short movements he began cutting the padlocked strap. Even Hallie hadn't yet noticed what he was doing.

Seeing the fear in her eyes overwhelmed him with guilt. *He* got her into this. *He* would be responsible if she died in this icy water.

When he met her just eight weeks ago, he'd known she would change him. And she had. So had the last few days. He now knew life was about balance, specifically balancing family and career and everything else.

The balancing, he sensed, was life's great big little secret, the secret that made each part work better. Balance was maturity. Imbalance was immaturity.

Ironic, he thought, *to finally understand all this, minutes before my execution.*

Whether they had minutes or decades, he wanted to spend them with her. As he sawed the thick strap, he visualized the slim possibility of their future, the happiness that might somehow still be theirs. He could see her wedding dress with a full-length white lace train. He saw sunlight streaming through the church window, highlighting her face, her beauty transcending description. He saw their wedding ceremony, the raucous Irish-Japanese reception with families and friends, their children, a son and daughter, squealing with delight as they ripped open Christmas presents and sped down Disney World's Space Mountain; he saw Hallie and him growing old together, traveling, spoiling their grandkids.

A gust of arctic wind jolted him back to the present. He looked outside and saw the mist had mostly disappeared, revealing thick whitecaps rolling toward the shore. To the northeast, a sliver of horizon curved like a dirty fingernail.

Luca continued to check him every few seconds but was clearly riveted to the *Springer* show, featuring transsexuals suing over their breast implants. The subject, fortunately, confused Manny and required him to barrage Luca with a lot of questions.

Minutes later, the dark horizon grew into an evergreen forest hugging the Canadian shore. Reed cut faster and finally felt the vest strap split. He slid the knife back inside his shirt.

Martin slowed the engine, then cut it to idle. The large yacht sputtered in place, waves slapping against its hull. Reed studied the map, trying to fix their location with the shore.

"Outside!" Luca said, waving his gun.

Covering the severed strap with his arm, Reed stood and ushered Hallie outside to the deck. If one of the men got close, he would attack with the small knife and grab his gun. But they remained several feet away, their guns constantly pointed at him.

Manny opened a large storage bin and pulled out an olive-green raft. He jerked the cord, and the raft inflated in thirty seconds. Holding its tether, he lowered the raft into the water beside the yacht's ladder.

"Get in the raft!" Luca commanded.

A raft makes no sense, Reed thought, *unless someone is getting in with us. But why would they?*

Still, if someone boarded the raft, Reed realized he could possibly attack him with the knife. If no one boarded, he'd use the phone once they were out of sight. But why the weighted jackets? And why leave the oars in the raft? Things weren't adding up.

Reed took Hallie's elbow and walked her over to the ladder. She hesitated, her eyes wide with fear.

"It's real fuckin' simple," Luca said, "get in the raft *now*, or I shoot!"

Reed nodded for her to board, then stepped down the ladder into the raft. He guided her into a raft seat opposite him. No one appeared to be getting into the raft with them. Reed was afraid to hope.

"I think we're forgetting somethin'," Luca said, sipping some beer.

Reed didn't want to hear.

"Yeah?" Manny asked, grinning.

"Uh-huh," Luca climbed down the ladder, his knees touching the water. "What?"

"This," Luca said, pulling out a shiny ten-inch fishing knife. He ripped the knife up into the raft's underbelly twice. Air bubbles hissed onto the water's surface.

"Damn—another raft nicked by an outboard motor," Luca said, smiling. "Ain't it a shame?"

Manny nodded and laughed.

His mind racing, Reed watched bubbles explode on the water's surface. On the bridge, Martin waved goodbye, threw the yacht into gear and sped off. Reed saw no other boats on the horizon.

His fingers gripped the raft, already as soft as Jell-O.

Forty-Four

Reed watched air bubbles stream onto the lake's surface. He felt the raft quickly deflating, crumpling inch by inch, sinking slowly into the icy blue water. A thick wave washed over the side, soaking his shoes. They had only minutes....

Crouching, so the men in the departing Hatteras couldn't see, Reed slid his weighted vest into the lake.

Hallie stared at the vest. "How'd you–?"

"With this," he said, showing her the small rusty knife. "It was next to the tackle box. And this," he said, yanking out the cell phone, "was on the desk."

She blinked in amazement as he punched in 911.

"Quick, move over here," Reed said.

She moved over and he began slicing her strap. The raft dipped and a wave drenched the phone.

"9-1-1 Emergency," a woman said.

"We're in a raft in Lake St. Clair," Reed said, "sinking *very* fast!"

"Where in the lake?"

"About two miles off Walpole Island."

"Which point?"

"I can't tell."

"How long will the raft float?"

The phone crackled and hissed.

"Maybe two minutes."

The phone sputtered.

"'peat, sir. Phone breakin'...."

"Two minutes!"

"... *few* minutes?"

More crackling.

"*TWO!*" he shouted as a large wave drenched the phone again. The connection went dead. He tried to re-dial. No dial tone. He tried again. Nothing. She thought he'd said a *few* minutes.

He continued slicing Hallie's strap like a madman. Another wave

224

slammed the raft's side, knocking an oar from its lock. The raft sank lower, just three inches above water. Air bubbles exploded onto the water's surface.

Reed hacked away at her strap. Just a quarter-inch to go. Another wave soaked her scuba jacket, making the strap harder to slice. He checked the horizon. No boats.

Then he saw it....

A monster whitecap, six feet high, racing straight toward them. Seconds later, it crashed into the raft, slamming the heavy oar against Hallie's head and knocking her backwards out of the raft.

He lunged for her, but his foot got tangled in the flimsy fold of the raft. Working free, he dove under but couldn't see her. The weighted vest had pulled her straight down. How far down? The yacht's map had indicated a depth of thirteen feet in this area.

Swimming down into dark water, he soon felt something begin to pull him left, a current. Had it also pulled her? No, the weights would have dragged her straight down. He swam deeper, fighting the current, scooping the frigid water.

Seconds later, his fingers clawed muck, stirring up sand. He could only see about three feet ahead. He swung his arms, trying to touch her, but felt only water.

She was gone. Panic gripped him.

As he turned, something flashed, then disappeared. He moved toward the flash in the swirling sand, his lungs begging for air.

Another flash. Silver. A fish?

Swimming toward it, his head bumped something – her silver bracelet. She was suspended, bubbles streaming from her mouth. He fingered down to her scuba jacket strap and sliced fast. His lungs felt like someone was driving spikes into them.

Finally, the strap split and he ripped off her jacket.

Clutching her, he sprang off the sandy bottom, pulling water with one arm, kicking wildly, lungs screaming for air. Daylight looked miles above. He choked, swallowed water.

Bursting onto the surface, he coughed water from his mouth, gasping for air. Hallie lay unconscious, limp in his arms, water streaming from her mouth. He squeezed her hard and more water exploded from deep within her. But she remained unresponsive. He squeezed again and more water gushed out, but she did not move.

Panicking, he crushed her harder. Nothing.

"No! Breathe, Hallie, breathe!" He squeezed. "Please...."

Limp. Not breathing.

A second later, he thought he felt her body flinch. Then, it *did* flinch. She jerked and water trickled from her mouth. Her eyelids flickered.

"You're okay," he whispered, his tears mixing with lake water.

She coughed again, opening her eyes. She gasped for air and tried to speak. "Ree...."

"I'm here." His heart slammed into his throat.

She nodded, clutching him now, gulping in air.

"Are you with me?"

"Uh-huh."

"Can you float?"

She nodded as her breathing gained some rhythm.

"Lie back. I'll pull."

Another nod. He saw a one-inch gash on her temple where the oar cut her. Her purple lips trembled as he eased her onto her back and began pulling her through the water.

Suddenly reality hit him. They were in freezing water, about 45 degrees, he estimated.

"Hypo ... therm...." she whispered. "Got to ... get out."

He nodded and looked at the shore, at least forty minutes away. His muscles were already numb with cold.

Reed watched Hallie's gray fingers pull the water as her legs dragged behind like giant icicles. Each stroke drained more energy. His arm movements and thought processes were slowing. The icy water clawed through him inch by inch, leeching his strength, numbing his ability to think, to even remember how quickly hypothermia killed.

Minutes later, the shore seemed no closer

"S-s-stop!" she said.

"What?"

She tried to speak, but her jaw seemed frozen shut. Finally, she blurted, "D-d-don't swim."

"Have t-t-to!"

"S-s-wim b-b-bad ... b-blood to surface. Lowers t-temp fast."

"But—"

"Have to s-s-stop! How f-far?"

Reed looked toward shore. "Forty m-minutes."

"Don't have f-forty."

"How m-much?"

"T-twenty ... if float. Watch for b-boat."

Will one come in time? he wondered. To stop swimming for shore went against every instinct in him. But she was the doctor and her knowledge of hypothermia ruled.

"Okay," he said, rolling onto his back.

Scanning the shoreline again, he suddenly recognized a building and panicked. The building, the Island Yacht Club, was on *Harson's* Island, not Walpole Island as he'd told 911. If there were 911 rescuers, they were six miles to the east.

Any hope of rescue had just vanished.

He glanced back where they'd begun swimming minutes ago. On the southwest horizon, a white yacht, a half-mile away, cruised directly toward them. Squinting, he realized it was the yacht that dumped them here.

They were coming back. Making sure.

Forty-Five

Philip Lambe eased back into the warm black leather of his Eames chair and sipped a twenty-five-year-old scotch, feeling its mellow heat and smokey flavor soothe him. He drew deeply on his Cuban cigar as its obscenely pleasant aroma wrapped around him like a velvet blanket. From his Bose speakers flowed the hypnotic drums of Kitaro's *Ancient of Wind*.

Looking outside, he saw shafts of sunlight break through clouds and dapple the blue water with gold. A perfect day. Which he would soon make indescribably perfect when he pushed Enter and exacted his *Shikei*.

Just minutes away....

The sense of power surged through him, an adrenalin rush more delicious and tactile than anything he'd ever known. But then, he'd never harvested sixty thousand people before. People who richly deserved to die for betraying America.

Like certain business associates betrayed me, and for that reason, died earlier today.

Pulling out a thin, leather directory, he flipped to the R's and dialed a number.

Quite predictably, a secretary, weepy and sniffling, answered. She explained that earlier that day her boss had suffered a sudden, horrific attack at his computer and died within minutes.

"My sincere condolences to his family," Lambe said, trying to keep delight from creeping into his voice.

"Of course."

He hung up, then phoned and spoke with two more sniveling secretaries who blabbed out somewhat similar sob stories. Again, he offered his deep, heartfelt sympathies, but he wanted to shout that their bosses deserved every excruciating twist of pain they'd suffered.

Savoring the good news, Lambe decided to reward himself with one more pathetic sob story. He dialed the number.

"Nate Lieberman's office," a shaky-voiced secretary said.

"This is Philip Lambe. Is Nate there?"

228

"Yes...."

Lambe bolted upright in his seat. *Nate Lieberman should be dead.*

"But," the secretary continued, "Mr. Lieberman's not available now. There's an emergency."

"A medical emergency?"

"Yes."

Lambe smiled, realizing the delivery mechanism must have exposed Lieberman to the lethal agent later than programmed. "I hope Nate will be fine."

"Nate *is* fine. But his good friend, Sister O'Malley, and some children who were visiting him are critical. They were rushed to the hospital. Nate's on his way there now."

Lambe stood and stared out at the water. "Which hospital?"

"St. Joseph's on Woodward."

Lambe hung up. This shouldn't have happened. *Lieberman* was supposed to die, not nuns and kids. Lambe phoned St. Joseph's Hospital and was put through to ER.

"Emergency," a woman said. A child shrieked in the background.

"You've admitted some nuns and children?"

"Yes, just a while ago...."

"Use atropine!"

A long pause. "They were dead on arrival, except for a young nun and three children. We think they might make it."

Lambe did not respond.

"Who is this?"

Lambe said nothing.

"Who's calling?"

Lambe hung up, walked over and stared out the window at the water. He sipped some scotch, drew hard on his cigar and unleashed a long stream of smoke toward the lake.

Nuns and kids, he thought. *Dreamers. The cruel world would have eventually disappointed them, crushed their naïve illusions.*

I've done them a favor....

Forty-Six

Hallie's body jackhammered in the icy water as she watched the white speck on the horizon grow into her worst nightmare. The Hatteras was coming back.

They're making sure we're dead, collecting the deflated raft and hiding it. No raft, no missing bodies, no crime.

Her mind felt sluggish, as though she'd awakened from a drugged sleep and knew what to do, but couldn't react. She paddled with arms she barely felt, breathed with lungs she could barely fill, saw with eyes that barely focused.

"L-l-look," Hallie said, pointing toward a white yacht.

"Uh-huh."

"Is it t-t-them?"

"Yes."

Her last ray of hope faded.

"Can't let them s-s-see us," Reed said. "When it g-gets close, go under."

She nodded or trembled, she wasn't sure which. Biting wind whistled past her ears.

The big yacht chugged closer. Squinting, she saw Luca and Manny, on the bridge, staring in their direction. *Have they already spotted us?* she wondered.

The yacht crept within one hundred yards.

Reed took Hallie's hand in his. "When you need air, squeeze."

She nodded.

They ducked under and floated inches beneath the surface. Her head felt like it was in a block of ice. She opened her eyes and saw Reed watching her. Thirty seconds later, her lungs bursting, she tightened her fingers on his. They surfaced, gasping, sucking in the freezing wind.

The yacht was only seventy yards away, cruising directly at them. She tried to regain her breath.

"Now!" Reed said.

Filling their lungs again, they ducked back into the icy water. Twenty-five seconds later, the pain was so excruciating, Hallie squeezed his hand. Breaking through the surface, she saw the yacht had steered hard right.

They did not see us.

But something was wrong. She blinked and couldn't believe her eyes. Along the yacht's side, in red letters, was the word *DEALERSHIP*. She blinked again, but the word remained.

"*Help!*" Reed screamed, waving his arms.

Neither man moved. They faced the opposite direction, one sipping coffee, the other gazing toward Canada.

"Over *HERE*! Reed screamed, nearly ripping out his vocal cords.

Still, the men didn't budge.

Hallie realized his screams were being drowned out by the gusting wind and engine noise. The yacht was past them now, cruising away, the men facing the wrong way.

It's too late....

The wind whistled past her—suddenly reminding her of something, a panic signal her father taught her. Placing two fingers in her mouth, she let loose with an ear-piercing whistle that spun Reed's head toward her. She unleashed another whistle that rocketed over the water like a howitzer.

Both men spun around.

Reed waved and the men waved back.

Overwhelmed, she swam into Reed's arms as the yacht sped back toward them. Seconds later, the men lifted them aboard. Hallie saw her face in the cabin window. She looked like blue ice. Lightheaded and shaky, she had to steady herself against the railing.

"Body t-temp up," she mumbled. "Warm w-w-water?"

"Shower's downstairs," said an elderly gray-haired man with kind blue eyes the color of water.

Shaking uncontrollably, Reed said, "We n-n-need police fast."

The old man's bushy gray eyebrows raised. "I'll get 'em on VHF now. We've been searching for you."

Suddenly, Hallie's mind dimmed like a blown fuse and she leaned against the railing, fighting to remain conscious.

"You two need heat!" the old man said. He turned to his colleague, another silver-haired senior with thick tortoise-shell-rimmed glasses. "Harold, turn this thing around and get her over to the St. Clair police station fast! And tell 'em we're coming in!"

"Right, LaMar Don."

LaMar helped them down the stairs, turned on the shower, put out fresh towels and a stack of fresh cotton sweatsuits and sweaters. "There's heaps of hot water," he said, then headed back up to the bridge.

Reed turned the shower water to Hot.

"W-w-warm," Hallie said, trembling. "Hot is d-dangerous." She dialed to Warm.

"You first," he said, helping her into the narrow stall, then steadying himself.

Hallie pulled him into the shower with her. Too weak to remove their clothes, they clung to each other under the blissfully warm water. Minutes later, piece by piece, they shed their clothes like thick, dead skin. Their frozen bodies melted together as warm water washed over them, slowly raising their core temperature, thawing them inch by inch.

Water, which had nearly killed them, was now saving them.

Several minutes later, she began to *feel.* Her skin, fingers, arms, legs, her breasts against his.

"Warm is a good thing," he said.

"Mummmm," she purred, half asleep on his shoulder.

They clung to each other like Siamese twins as the yacht pounded over the waves at breakneck speed, jostling them about the cramped shower stall. But the warm, delicious water gushed on and on. Several minutes later, their core body temperatures nearing normal, they toweled off and put on the thick cotton sweat suits, over which they pulled sweaters, over which they pulled more sweaters.

Huddling near the heat vent, they gulped in the delicious warm air wrapping around them like an electric blanket.

Carefully, Reed took the soggy *Shikei* paper from his dripping pants and started to unfold it. A tiny fleck of paper peeled off on his finger.

"Too wet to unfold," he said.

"Place it near that heat vent."

He leaned over and laid it next to the vent.

"You warmin' up down there?" LaMar shouted down the stairs.

"Thanks to you," Reed said. "Please come down."

LaMar climbed down and placed two large mugs of steaming coffee in front of them. Hallie stood and embraced him. The old man blushed and picked at a yellow mustard stain on his sweater. Palsy jiggled the red and silver fishing lures on his hat.

"LaMar Don McCue," he said, shaking hands with her and Reed. "And you two are looking heaps pinker now."

Sipping coffee, Hallie vaguely recalled the name. "We owe you our lives, LaMar. Thank you."

McCue shrugged. "My big chance to be on *Emergency 911*, and no TV crew around!"

"Speaking of 911," Reed said, "we need to phone the police immediately."

"You can *talk* to 'em. We're docking now."

Hallie and Reed gulped their coffee down and followed him up to the bridge. McCue pointed to the dock, where she saw a tall young police officer waiting for them.

Hallie said, "Tomorrow, we'll return your clothes."

"No rush." LaMar handed her his card. Hallie read, "McCue Cars & Trucks," and remembered that LaMar Don McCue was a legend, a mega car dealer who at seventeen had walked out of the Kentucky foothills, found work as a car washer in a dealership. Today, he owned the dealership and thirty-six more nationwide.

Hallie and Reed thanked him again and hurried toward the young policeman. As they got closer, she noticed the policeman's terror-stricken face.

Had the *Shikei* already started?

Forty-Seven

4:33 p.m.

"Have any deaths been reported yet?" Hallie asked the thin, freckle-faced officer, who'd introduced himself as Officer Cook.

"What deaths?" Officer Cook asked as he hurried her and Reed inside the St. Clair police station.

Hallie exhaled with relief. Obviously, the *Shikei* had not started in the metro area.

"Some deaths that the FBI is trying to prevent," she said.

"Special Agent Manning's on our phone for you two. He's got every cop in the state looking for you and a guy named Philip Lambe. Are you involved with this *SEVERE* alert?"

She nodded.

Cook's Adam's apple bobbed like a cork. He rushed them down a hall past a skinny teenager protesting his reckless Sea-dooing ticket to an officer, then bulletin boards with photos of stolen boats and missing persons. Hallie saw desks covered with computers, folders and photos of families, pets and Red Wing banners. One desk was a shrine to Elvis, another to glistening female bodybuilders.

Officer Cook led them into a small gray cubicle and pushed the phone's speaker button.

"Drew? It's Hallie and Reed," Reed said

"My God, how are you?" Manning said.

"Alive. We saw Lambe."

"Where?"

"At 328 Lodgemont," Reed said, "a mansion on Lake St. Clair."

Hallie heard Manning direct FBI agents to the address.

"I took a paper from the house," Reed said. "It has *Shikei* information."

"What information?"

Reed looked at the still damp, partly unfolded paper, "Lambe's *Shikei* starts at eleven minutes past five."

234

"That gives us only … thirty-eight minutes," Manning said.

"It also lists the ten cities."

"What are they?"

"New York, Boston, Detroit, Philadelphia, Atlanta, Washington, Cleveland, Louisville, Baltimore and Pittsburgh."

Manning was silent a moment. "All in the Eastern Standard Time zone. That suggests his 5:11 launch is simultaneous in all cities.

"There's also an engineering drawing," Hallie said.

"Of what?"

"Sort of looks like a ventilation duct."

"For an office building?"

"Can't tell," she said. "There's no scale. Inside the duct is a long, black thing, a container maybe."

"Can you fax the paper here?"

"It's too wet," Reed said. "I can't even unfold it all the way."

"Xerox the unfolded part and fax that. How fast can you get the original here?"

Hallie asked Officer Cook, who pointed outside at a police helicopter, its rotors whirling, then held up six fingers.

"Six minutes," she said. "We're boarding a chopper now."

* * *

Hallie and Reed hurried into the Ren Cen conference room and found themselves surrounded by the smiling crisis team. She realized it was the first time they'd all smiled since she'd met them.

"Here," Reed said, unfolding the *Shikei* paper, except for the soggiest flap. He placed the paper on the table. Hallie watched everyone crowd around and stare down at it. The blue ink had bled, but the city names, the five-eleven p.m. launch time, and the remaining words were still legible.

Manning, McKay and Livingstone hovered over the paper like surgeons, searching for any bit of information that might help clarify the situation.

"What are these?" Manning asked, pointing to a series of numbers.

"*Korusu* sarin's toxicity," Janet McKay said.

"Death within two to four minutes," Dr. Livingstone whispered.

Hallie heard the room go silent, except for the hum of fluorescent lights overhead.

"This," Manning said, pointing to the sketch of the long, hollow tube, "seems to be a ventilation shaft. Looks like a forced-air system."

Heads nodded.

"This black container is attached inside the shaft," McKay said, "and appears to release the sarin."

More nods.

"And these directional arrows," Manning said, "suggest the sarin moves *upward* in the duct."

"That black container," Reed said to McKay, "is shaped like the long, thin object you found in Lambe's lab."

"You're right," Dr. McKay said, nodding.

"How big was it?" Manning asked.

"Ruler length, inch thick, hollow," McKay said.

Hallie raised her hand. "But doesn't that size suggest a *small* ventilation system?"

"It does," McKay said. "For a very small building or home."

"Too impractical," Doctor Livingstone said, shaking his head. "To kill sixty thousand people, say at fifty people per building, with ruler-size containers, would require, let's see ... nearly twelve hundred buildings. Too many containers to install."

"Maybe the black container is scaled-down for test purposes," Hallie said.

"That's possible," Livingstone said.

"Or maybe he puts several containers in a large building," Manning suggested.

"Also possible, but why several?" Livingstone said. "Why not make *large* containers? Again, large sarin containers in big buildings or enclosed stadiums, thousands of people together. That makes the most sense."

The conference room door banged open. Conversation froze.

All eyes locked on Agent Dan LaCage. He stood there, ashen-faced, paper trembling in his hand, staring at Manning with death-camp eyes.

Hallie knew before he spoke.

"It's started...." LaCage whispered.

Silence.

Hallie felt like a bullet had pierced her chest. She couldn't move. Beside her, Reed slumped back in his chair and stared at the floor.

Manning swallowed. "How many?"

"Thirteen reported deaths in the Detroit area so far."

Hallie felt nauseated. Lambe *had* started earlier than his 5:11 launch plan. The maniac was slaughtering sixty thousand innocent people and there wasn't a damn thing they could do about it.

"Who?" Manning whispered, his face dark.

"Three people at Crittendon Hospital. Five businessmen at Henry Ford Hospital, one at Flint Memorial. Also, three small children and an elderly nun at St. Joseph's Memorial."

Manning frowned. "Businessmen. Children. A nun. What's the connection?"

"None we see."

"All Catholics?"

"Seven were not."

"Any Japanese?"

"No," LaCage said.

"What were their symptoms?" Janet McKay asked.

LaCage steadied the trembling paper with his other hand. "Blurry vision, runny nose, breathing difficulties, followed by gasping, choking, convulsions."

"Consistent with sarin," Livingstone whispered.

The room remained graveyard quiet. No one wanted to confirm the crushing reality that they'd failed to save thousands of people now dying from sarin nerve gas poisoning. No one wanted to give voice to the collective guilt gnawing away at them, a guilt they would feel the rest of their lives.

Angry, Manning stood and gestured to nearby agents. "Find out everything these thirteen people did in the last forty-eight hours. There's got to be a connection. Find out where they came into contact with sarin. And find out *fast!* Maybe we can still save some lives."

Several agents repeated the message into their cell phones.

"One more thing," Agent LaCage said, "Hospital staffs are whispering about the mysterious deaths."

"Whispering what?" Manning asked.

"Outbreak. Some untreatable new disease or bio-weapon."

"The media will be on this like flies on honey," McKay said.

"They already are," LaCage added. "And the mayor wants you to call him immediately."

"I'll phone him in three minutes," Manning said.

"How many deaths in the other nine cities?" Hallie asked.

"None," LaCage said.

Hallie wasn't sure she heard correctly. She looked at LaCage, afraid to hope.

"But Lambe targeted ten cities," Manning said.

"As of one minute ago," LaCage said, "our bureaus in those cities reported no deaths with similar symptoms."

"But it doesn't make sense for Lambe to stagger his launch time, city by city," Hallie said.

"Agreed. Too risky," Manning said. "If we learn his Detroit delivery system, he knows we'd warn people away from it in the other cities."

Hallie decided to voice a terrifying possibility. "What if he has a different delivery system for each city?"

Manning looked at her and shrugged. "Then we lose." He punched the speaker button on the open line phone.

"Get me Hatcher."

Seconds later, Hallie heard the director come on the line.

"Hatcher."

"Manning."

"Has your team reached Lambe's Lake St. Clair home?" the director asked hopefully.

"They're two minutes away." Manning swallowed hard. "Sir...."

"Yes?"

"It's begun."

Hatcher sighed deep and long, like a death rattle.

"But only in Detroit, sir," Manning said. "Thirteen cases in the last hour or so. Symptoms consistent with sarin death."

A long silence. "You're absolutely certain?"

"Yes, sir."

"Only in Detroit?"

"Yes, as of one minute ago."

"How's he delivering the sarin?"

"Don't know yet."

"The victims?"

"Businessmen, small kids, a nun."

"Kids and a nun?"

"We're working on the connection, sir."

"Find it fast."

"Yes, sir."

Hatcher breathed out slowly. "Probably just minutes before other cities start to report similar deaths."

"Probably, sir."

"Anything else?"

"No."

"I'll inform the President." Hatcher sounded like he was walking in front of a firing squad. "We'll have military units secure Detroit hospitals immediately. Establish control. Let me know the instant other cities report deaths."

"I will." Manning rubbed his eyes. "Sir?"

"Yes?"

"I'm sorry, sir...."

Hallie felt Drew Manning's pain. The man never had a chance. The odds had been stacked against him from the moment he got the assignment.

"We had no time, Drew," Director Hatcher said. "Congress did. But they spent most of it playing politics. Today, both parties will get blood on their hands."

They hung up.

Hallie watched a nearby FBI agent, obviously worried about something, snap his cell phone closed and rush over to Manning.

"Reporters, sir," the agent said. "They're demanding a briefing now. Networks, cable, local TV, press."

"What do they know?" Manning asked.

"That military medical units moved into Detroit early this morning. They demand to know why."

Manning stared ahead, apparently considering his options.

"If we don't talk with them," the agent persisted, "they're going with what they have on the five-o'clock news."

"Which is?" Manning asked.

"An NBC reporter saw three soldiers carrying HazMat suits near Henry Ford Hospital. She linked that to the *SEVERE* Advisory Alert. She plans to run with everything unless we brief her."

"Does she know about the thirteen deaths?" Hallie asked.

"No. But it's only a matter of time until she does."

Manning nodded. "Tell her and the others I'll brief them at five till five, in time for their five o'clock newscasts."

The tall agent hurried from the room.

Hallie glanced at her watch. No more deaths had been reported in several minutes. Why only thirteen deaths? Did police scrutiny force Lambe to postpone full implementation? She doubted it.

She looked at the people seated around the conference room table. Their initial departmental posturing had faded quickly and they'd forged themselves into a solid team.

But a losing team.

"Thirteen deaths. Why not more?" Janet McKay asked the group.

The room fell silent for several moments.

"Maybe it's another test," Reed suggested.

"Or his delivery system failed," Livingstone said.

"I doubt that," Manning said. "Lambe's a perfectionist. It works, believe me."

"Agreed," said Agent Merle Whitlock, nervously tidying several gum wrappers in front of him. "He'll succeed or die trying. Man's crazier than a shithouse rat, and he's *driven*."

Hallie looked down at the ventilation drawing again and knew the game was over. Even if they determined the drawing was for office buildings, they still had to find the right ventilation systems in thousands of buildings in the ten cities—and get people away from them in *minutes*.

There was a word for what they were trying to do.

Impossible....

Forty-Eight

4:48 p.m.

Manning's phone rang.

All conversation froze in place. All eyes locked on the large black multi-line telephone.

Hallie got black-cord fever just looking at it. The caller was going to shatter their prayers with more cities reporting deaths, children dying in mothers' arms, corpses cramming hospital corridors, cars clogging expressways.

Manning leaned over and punched the speaker button.

"Woody Beachum...."

Sighs of relief swept through the room.

"We're at Lambe's lake mansion," Beachum said. "The SWAT team's just outside the den. Four guys are in there watching wrestling."

"What about Lambe?"

"Not among them. These guys are big, mean-looking. Hang on, I'll patch you into our listening bug."

Hallie heard two clicks, then a television announcer. "And now, tonight's Slam-Bam-A-Rama Main Event: The Dump Truck takes on the challenger, Battleship Billy Miele...."

"Gimme a fuckin' beer," a man yelled.

"That's Luca," Hallie said.

The beer can fizzed open, a man belched.

"We're going in now!" Beachum whispered, sounding restless.

"Check the steel door *behind* the mini-lab," Hallie said.

"Right," Beachum said.

Silence. Then a loud crash and a door banged against something.

"FBI! Freeze with your hands up!"

Hallie heard an empty beer can clang onto the floor as the television announcer shouted, "Battleship Billy has entered the ring!"

"Where's Lambe?" Beachum shouted.

241

Silence.

"I want an answer—*now!*"

No one spoke.

"Talk, or plan on life in a federal slammer."

Nervous coughs, then silence.

Hallie heard doors opening and banging shut, SWAT team members calling out "Clear!" Moments later, someone walked up to Beachum. "We checked all rooms, including the one behind the steel door, everywhere. Lambe's nowhere around."

Hallie felt a sinking sensation in her stomach.

"Where's Lambe?" Woody Beachum shouted. "You've got five seconds!" Beachum sounded like he was about to lose it.

"Never heard of the guy," Luca said.

A shot rang out. Glass crashed onto the floor, then the television announcer's voice groaned into silence. Someone had shot the television.

Hallie heard shuffling, table legs scraping, something hitting the floor hard, men scuffling, running.

"Get him!" Beachum shouted.

A door slammed.

"What's happening?" Manning asked.

"Luca ran outside!" Beachum said. "We're in pursuit."

Hallie heard SWAT team members shouting orders to surround Luca.

"Stop him!" Beachum yelled, sucking air like a wounded bull. Hallie knew the detective's heart was pounding, his face probably scarlet. She prayed he didn't have a heart attack.

"Luca's down," Beachum huffed.

"Who shot him?" Manning asked.

"No one."

"What...?

"He tripped over a lawn sprinkler," Beachum said, gulping air. "Fell on the driveway. Rubbing his leg. Says a bottle broke in his pocket. Cut him. Big deal."

Hallie heard Luca moaning. "Stuff's gettin' in my blood. Do something!"

"You cut your leg, you wuss!" Beachum said, still puffing.

"I need a doctor!" Luca screamed.

"And I need Lambe!" Beachum demanded. "Where is he?"

"Shit's gettin' in me! Gonna kill me like that Indian doctor."

Dr. Shah, Hallie realized. She closed her eyes and again felt his loss.

"Hey, this guy's sweatin' like a Delta faucet," Beachum said. "Looks like shit."

"Can't breathe...."

Neither could Dr. Shah, Hallie thought, *or Kyle.*

Luca gasped violently, then everything went silent for several seconds.

"Jesus...." Beachum whispered. "I think this guy just cashed in."

"Woody!" Hallie said.

"Yeah?"

"Don't let anyone touch him. Especially the substance in his pocket. It kills on contact."

Beachum paused, then barked out the order.

Drew Manning asked, "Are the other men still in the house?"

"Yeah...."

"Get Lambe's location from them."

Back inside, Beachum caught his breath, then shouted, "You saw what just happened. Luca is history. Tell me where Lambe is, or plan on joining Luca." Beachum sounded like he was about to go ballistic.

"Police brutality!" Manny screamed.

A shot rang out.

Manny yelped.

"My gun kinda misfired," Beachum said. "And this headphone's acting kinda—" ·

The connection went dead.

Hallie sensed Beachum had probably wounded Manny, then turned off his phone to get some answers. Drew Manning shook his head at the legal implications.

Manning turned to Rob Bradleigh, the computer expert. "What's the status on the test victims' computers?"

"We've inspected most," Bradleigh said, "and didn't find any clear evidence of sarin or other toxins. But the scientists need to use special equipment to be absolutely certain. We'll know later."

"But even if he didn't use computers in his test," Hallie said, "he might use them for his *Shikei* delivery system."

Heads nodded.

Suddenly, the conference room door swung open. All eyes turned and focused on a young red-haired agent holding her cell phone. She was very excited.

Please, no.... Hallie prayed.

The agent scanned the room, then hurried over and handed her phone to Reed. "This man says he's Philip Lambe. He'll only talk to you."

Reed froze as everyone faced him.

How does Lambe know Reed's here? Hallie wondered. Did someone watching the conference room entrance tell him? Or worse, did someone *in* the room tell him?

A technician hurried over and attached two headsets to the phone. Manning took one and signaled for Hallie to take the other, since she could also confirm Lambe's voice. Manning gestured for a trace, then signaled for Reed to take the call.

Reed picked up the phone. "Reed Kincaid."

"Congratulations," Philip Lambe said. "You're more resilient than your brother."

Reed and Hallie nodded to each other, then to Manning that it was Lambe.

"Of course," Lambe continued, "Luca and the boys will pay for their ineptness."

They just did, Hallie wanted to shout in Lambe's ear.

"Also, I'd like to congratulate your esteemed colleagues who are undoubtedly listening in. You've done well considering how little time you've had. But your efforts are wasted. My *Shikei* is unstoppable."

"So why phone us?" Reed asked.

"To make our game more interesting," Lambe said. "Level the playing field a bit. You'd like a clue, wouldn't you?"

Hallie was suspicious. *Why would Lambe help us?*

"What kind of clue?"

"*Where* my *Korusu* will be released."

"You've already released it in Detroit," Reed said. "Thirteen people died."

Lambe was silent. "A little test. Business associates. Bad people. They deserved to die."

"Kids and a nun?"

Another long pause. "Collateral damage. Casualties of war."

Hallie watched Reed's hand curl into a fist.

"What war?" Reed asked.

"You'll understand soon," Lambe taunted. "It would help to know *where* in the ten cities I'll release my *Korusu* sarin, wouldn't it?"

Manning was nodding. The agent tracing the call made a stretch-it-out gesture.

"Yes. But I'll tell you what would really help, Lambe."

"What might that be?"

"Don't release it."

Lambe chuckled softly. "My, my, as naïve as your brother. Interesting family trait, isn't it?"

"So is our persistence. The police of five continents will track you down,

Lambe. So will I. You'll live on the run, hunted like Eichmann and Mengele and Saddam Hussein. We'll find you."

"Another pathetic waste of resources. You'll never find me."

Hallie heard the confidence of someone who had a new passport, a plastic surgeon, unlimited funds and bribed officials in a Third World country waiting for him. Lambe could vanish.

"What did these people do to you?" Reed said.

Lambe did not respond.

"Your *Shikei* solves nothing," Reed said.

"Oh, but it does," Lambe said with obvious pleasure. "Remember my ant farm?"

"Yes."

"The ant that made the bad decision?"

"Yes."

"These people did too. They will die for their decision."

"Are these people Japanese?" Reed asked.

Lambe paused as though caught off guard by the question. "What an odd question. Why would I target Japanese? I grew up in Tokyo, speak the language."

Something in his answer doesn't ring true, Hallie thought.

"So whoever these people are," Reed said, "why are they dying for their decision?"

"So others don't make the same bad decision. Get it?"

"No," Reed said.

Lambe was silent. Hallie sensed the man was deciding whether to reveal more.

"Like I said, you'll know very soon," Lambe said.

"But—"

"You want your clue or not?" Lambe's voice suddenly cut like a hot knife through butter.

"Yes," Reed said.

Lambe paused. "Office buildings."

"You're saying office buildings are where your *Korusu* sarin will be released?"

"That's what I'm saying."

Hallie saw Manning whisper to an agent what Lambe said.

"But there are thousands of office buildings," Reed said. "There's no time to check them all."

"Really?" Lambe said with a smile in his voice. "But you already know which ten cities, thanks to the *Shikei* paper you stole from my desk."

"The paper," Lambe continued, "also gives you a sketch of a building ventilation shaft. If you had time, you could find the right buildings and shafts and remove the sarin containers easily. By the way, they're held on by Velcro strips."

As much as she wanted to believe Lambe, Hallie still had her suspicions.

"And one more thing," Lambe said. "If you're thinking of simply shutting off the building ventilation fans, go right ahead. My system has its own mechanism for circulating the sarin."

Everything Lambe said made sense, but Hallie's instincts told her Lambe might be manipulating them.

"One more question, Lambe," Reed asked, apparently drawing the conversation out more.

"What's that?"

"Why?"

"Why what?"

"Why help us?"

Lambe sighed with impatience. "I told you. To give you a sporting chance. Makes my victory even sweeter."

Hallie noticed the agent tracing the call frantically pushing buttons on a console.

"Look, the game is simple," Lambe said, his voice ice cold. "Can you morons evacuate the *right* buildings before I push Enter at 5:11? That gives you … let's see, about nine minutes and twelve seconds. Not much time to clear all major buildings in the ten cities. But you'll clear some. So I only kill forty thousand or so. Still enough to teach a lesson, don't you think?"

"Give us until 5:30."

"It's 5:11. The more you talk, Kincaid, the more time you waste, the more people *YOU* kill."

Lambe's words seemed to cut through Reed like a machete.

Hallie heard the line go dead.

All eyes riveted on the agent tracing the call. The man tossed his headset on the table. "No luck. He's cloned a San Diego cell phone. Without the phone's ESN, we couldn't triangulate him."

Manning shrugged as though he hadn't expected a trace.

"So it's office buildings," Livingstone said.

"Says the psycho…." Manning said. "Can anyone give me one reason Lambe would suddenly help us?"

"Like he said," Livingstone said, "to give us a sporting chance. He knows we can't empty all the buildings in time. He still kills thousands, makes his point, teaches us his lesson, whatever."

"At least we might save thousands," Janet McKay said.

"If we accept his newfound humanitarianism," Manning shot back. "On the other hand, if the bastard is somehow telling the truth and we don't act now, we'll have more blood on our hands."

Hallie felt Manning's dilemma. To believe Lambe was dangerous. To not believe him was dangerous.

"Maybe he's using us to lead his lambs to slaughter," Hallie said.

"How?" Manning asked.

"By evacuating people out of the buildings—out in the streets—where his trucks or whatever disperse the sarin."

"But," Manning said, looking at the *Shikei* paper, "this sketch is some kind of ventilation shaft. The victims' homes are too impractical. Office buildings shafts make more sense."

Though Hallie's brain agreed, her intuition didn't.

Manning glanced at his watch and stood, his jaw muscles tightened into hard knots.

"It's decision time. We've got eight minutes. Tell the media to issue warnings instantly in the ten cities. I want all buildings with more than three hundred people emptied in the next six minutes. Make especially sure that all Japanesee affiliate offices, buildings and plants are vacated. And despite what Lambe says, I want the ventilation systems turned off. We're not going to help circulate sarin. The media should tell people their buildings may contain nerve gas which can kill them in minutes. Use fire alarms, whatever it takes. But get people out of the damn buildings—and *off* the streets—in their cars heading home *now*!"

A group of agents repeated Manning's orders into cell phones.

The phone beside Manning rang. He punched the speaker button.

"Manning."

"Beachum. The boys here talked. Lambe's at 937 Cromwell. Southeast corner office, second floor."

Hallie's hope soared again.

Manning leapt to his feet. "That's just blocks from us. Good work, Woody."

Manning turned to an agent. "Have a SWAT team meet us outside the Cromwell building in two minutes."

Manning hurried toward the door, then stopped and looked at Reed. "You've seen Lambe a few times. You can point him out."

"Yes," Reed said, standing.

Hallie's heart began to pound. She reached over and placed her hand on Reed's. "Be careful...."

"The SWAT team will handle everything," he said. "I'll be out of harm's way."

"Like at Lambe's lab?"

He shrugged. "I have to identify Lambe."

Nodding, she touched his cheek.

"Let's go nail this son-of-a-bitch!" Manning said as he and Reed hurried toward the door.

Hallie glanced at her watch. Only seven minutes.

If Lambe told the truth.

Forty-Nine

"That cinder-block building on the corner," Reed said, as Manning braked his Monte Carlo to a silent stop beside an alley, two hundred feet from the building.

Reed studied the five-story building. Its large glass entrance was guarded by two marble lions and tall, cone-shaped evergreens. The ground floor was occupied by Auntie Ada's Italian Ristorante and several boutiques, the top three floors by Wellbourne Casualty Insurance. The second floor, Lambe's, had the blinds closed.

Reed and Manning ran over to the FBI-SWAT team, a group of seven well-armed FBI and Detroit cops, near the entrance. The team leader, a sinewy man with a brown buzzcut, quickly diagramed how they'd enter Lambe's area.

"How much time?" Manning asked.

Reed checked his watch. "Five minutes, fifty-three seconds."

"If he sticks to 5:11," Manning said, hoisting a heavy ballistic Kevlar vest onto Reed's shoulders and fastening it. Another officer slapped a Smith & Wesson .38 into his hand and gave him a ten-second demo. Reed remembered this model .38, thanks to his Ann Arbor cop days.

"Just point Lambe out," Manning said to Reed. "Then disappear."

Reed nodded, but realized that Lambe could have dyed his hair, donned a wig, shaved his beard, puffed his cheeks with collagen, whatever. By now, he could be a ninety-year-old man with a walker. But his disfigured hand would be difficult to hide. And so would the cruel insanity in the bastard's eyes.

"Let's move," the team leader said.

Manning and Reed followed the SWAT team through the lobby, past a startled receptionist, then up the gray marble stairwell to the second floor. The leader squinted through the tiny window in the door, then turned and whispered, "Two guards outside Lambe's door playing cards. Move quietly.

249

Surprise them."

"No shooting," Manning whispered. "We can't tip off Lambe."

What if he's already been tipped off and escaped? Reed wondered.

The leader eased the door open, creating a soft, sucking sound, like opening a can of coffee. Reed and Manning followed the SWAT team as they moved silently down the hall, weapons drawn, and stepped quickly in front of the two guards.

"Hands up!" the team leader said.

A startled, bug-eyed guard with curly black hair quickly threw his hands up, scattering cards onto the floor. The other guard, a red-faced man, hesitated, booze-bravado welling up in his eyes. His hand inched toward something under the table.

Reed's finger tightened on the .38.

"Hands *up now!*" the team leader repeated.

The drunk yanked out a gun—and was riddled with bullets, knocking him back against the wall, polkadotting his shirt with blood as he hit the floor.

"Open the door!" the team leader said to Bug Eyes, who gawked at his colleague's bleeding body.

Bug Eyes was catatonic.

"Open it!"

Bug Eyes didn't move.

A muscular SWAT team member jammed his gun hard into Bug Eyes' ear. "*Now,* asshole!"

Bug Eyes quickly tapped in the wall panel code. The door clicked open and the team rushed inside. Reed scanned the enormous room but saw only empty cubicles, floor-to-ceiling cabinets, computer terminals. The lights were off, but dusky light filtered through the cloth window blinds.

Has Lambe escaped? Reed wondered.

The team leader signaled that the SWAT team would search the larger side of the room, while Manning and Reed checked out the small side. Manning and Reed stepped ahead, passing dark cubicles and large computer mainframes. The office seemed empty.

Seconds later, Reed heard faint tapping. The tapping came from the far end of the room. Manning nodded that he heard it and they moved toward the sound.

A few feet further, Reed saw a man's shadow on the wall. They inched toward the shadow. The man was tapping on a laptop. Leaning forward, Reed saw the man's back, but couldn't tell if it was Lambe. The man turned partly. No beard. Hair combed differently, straight back.

Is it Lambe? Reed wondered.

Manning was looking at Reed to confirm it was Lambe. Reed wasn't sure.

The man turned a bit and continued tapping on the laptop—*tapping with a scarred, purple hand.*

"It's Lambe!"

"Freeze, Hands up!" Manning shouted at him.

Lambe paused.

"Hands up now!"

Lambe, his back to them, nodded. "Okay … okay."

Slowly, Lambe started raising his hands, then spun around and fired three shots, splitting off chunks of a bookshelf just inches from Reed's head. Glancing up, Reed saw Lambe take his laptop and disappear behind a row of large blue cabinets in the center of the room.

The laptop launches the Shikei! Reed realized.

Lambe leaned out, fired two shots. Manning fired back, but missed. Three members of the SWAT team crawled up beside Manning and Reed.

"He's behind that row of blue cabinets," Manning whispered.

Seconds later the other three SWAT team members arrived. Reed kept his eyes on the cabinets as Manning explained that Lambe was armed and still holding the laptop.

Reed pointed to a nearby fire escape door beyond the cabinets. The leader nodded, and directed a team member to crawl over and guard the door.

"Come out, hands up!" the team leader said.

No response.

"Come out now, or we're coming around!"

Again, nothing.

"Last chance, Lambe—come out *now!*"

They waited a few moments, but Lambe still refused to come out.

On the leader's nod, the SWAT team fanned out to both ends of the row of cabinets. On a silent count of three, they rushed around to the other side.

Reed listened for, but didn't hear, some sign they'd apprehended Lambe. Then he heard them opening cabinet doors.

"He's not here!" the team leader shouted.

Reed felt his blood stop. *That's not possible. I haven't taken my eyes off the cabinets since Lambe hid behind them.* The fire escape door had not opened. Beyond the cabinets was a solid brick wall.

He has to be there!

Amazed, Manning and Reed ran over and looked in the four floor-to-ceiling cabinets. Three cabinets contained shelves stacked with folders, a fourth held paper supplies and an old desktop printer.

Philip Lambe had vanished before their eyes.

Fifty

Dumbfounded, Reed stared at the four empty cabinets, the tile floor, the brick wall.

Where the hell is Lambe?

SWAT team men pounded the brick wall for a concealed opening but found none. They checked the floor but found no lift-up doors, then tried the fire escape door and discovered it had not been opened.

Lambe had seemingly vanished into thin air.

The team leader walked over and started reopening the cabinet doors. Reed watched him stop at the third cabinet, stare at the old desktop printer on the floor, then bend down and lift the printer.

The *floor* lifted up with it.

Reed stared down into Lambe's escape stairwell.

Silently, the SWAT team squeezed down the dark, shadowy stairs, Manning and Reed behind them. The stairs took them down past Auntie Ada's Ristorante on the first floor to an empty storage room in the basement. The dark, damp storage room led to a hallway that ended eighty feet further at an open space with an elevated passageway. They crawled up through the passageway to the end and splashed down into three inches of water.

They were standing in a city sewer.

Lambe was still nowhere in sight.

About one hundred feet ahead, Reed saw sunlight pouring through a street level sewer opening. The group ran to the opening and saw the cast iron lid had been shoved aside. They climbed up the ladder and found themselves in an alley.

Lambe was gone.

Reed saw Manning's Monte Carlo at the far end of the alley, and as he turned back, he glimpsed a blue Sebring driving out of a garage—a scarred, purple hand on the steering wheel.

"That's him!" Reed said.

The Sebring sped out of the far end of the alley and disappeared into the city traffic.

"Come on!" Manning said as he and Reed sprinted to his car and jumped in.

"He was tapping on the laptop," Reed said.

"He's launching *Shikei* with it," Manning said, flooring the accelerator.

Reed's head snapped back against the headrest. Within seconds, he saw Lambe's blue Sebring weaving through cars and vans, then ducking behind a yellow Ryder truck. Rush hour traffic was so thick, Lambe could easily disappear down a side street and unleash the *Shikei.*

I've got to keep him in sight!

"Stick this on top," Manning said, handing him a red police flasher.

Reed lowered the window and stuck the magnet-based light on the roof. Ahead, Lambe's Sebring ducked behind a large furniture truck.

Manning punched a button on the dash. "Doris, we're pursuing Philip Lambe. Put out an APB. He's in a new light blue Sebring heading west on Fort. He has a laptop computer which must be destroyed before he uses it, and he'll use it in less than two and a half minutes. Repeat, do not let Lambe use his laptop. Shoot to kill."

"Affirmative."

"Shoot the laptop, too."

"Shoot the laptop?"

"Yes!" Manning swerved around a rusty Honda as Lambe's Sebring disappeared behind a city bus.

"Doris?"

"Yes?"

"What's the status on office buildings?"

"We're evacuating them now."

"In all ten target cities?"

"Yes. We estimate nearly seventy percent of the major buildings are now being evacuated."

"How empty are they?"

"Maybe ... twenty, thirty percent."

Not fast enough, Reed thought. Ahead he saw workers hurrying out of the towering Buhl building and felt somewhat relieved. But he couldn't shake the unsettling feeling that Lambe might *want* people out of the buildings, *on the streets*.

Do you want people on the streets, Lambe?

"You're getting people *off* the streets?" Manning asked.

"Yes. Most are driving home."

"Good. Start evacuating smaller buildings. One hundred to three hundred people."

"Yes, sir."

They passed near the massive Joe Louis Arena and Reed saw conventioneers rushing outside, heading toward their hotels and vehicles. The fact that they were not clustering on streets and many were heading home was good.

Unless, of course, home is where he'll attack.

Manning skidded to a stop behind a large red truck. Reed's view ahead was blocked.

"Where is he?" Manning asked.

Reed leaned out the window. "There, two blocks up. Turning left."

Manning screeched around the red truck, honking like a madman, then spun onto St. Anne Street and accelerated to sixty, barely missing a gold-grilled Mercedes, whose driver gave them the finger.

Overhead, a police helicopter streaked toward Lambe's car. Reed was relieved that other eyes were tracking Lambe.

"Watch out!" Reed shouted as a Coke truck backed out of an alley and blocked them.

"Shit!" Manning shouted, screeching to a stop. Lambe sped ahead. Manning honked, but the driver couldn't see the flashing light and wouldn't budge.

"We're losing him!" Reed shouted.

* * *

Hallie watched the lab technician turn off the hair dryer, then delicately touch the damp flap of the *Shikei* paper.

"Should be almost dry enough," he said, moving aside for her to look closer.

Carefully, she lifted the corner of the flap and peeled it back, revealing blurry, smudged *Kangi* symbols.

"What is it?" Dr. McKay said.

"Japanese," Hallie said.

Using a magnifying glass, Hallie leaned closer and studied the words. The beginning symbols were blotchy and ink-smeared, barely legible. Those in the middle were clearer. She deciphered the clear phrases first. Then, slowly, she translated the smudged words, one at a time, fitting them into the overall message. A couple of words puzzled her, but she quickly found them in the Japanese dictionary and wrote down their English equivalents.

As the full message began to come together, her heart started pounding. Perspiration dotted her face. When she realized what the full message said, she couldn't speak.

This is not possible!

"Get Reed and Manning!" she finally shouted to an agent.

* * *

Manning pulled around the parked Coke truck and sped onto the sidewalk, causing a purple-clothed pimp to fall backward into a puddle of rainwater.

"Right, two blocks up," Reed said.

Manning accelerated and skidded around the corner. "Time?"

"Two minutes, ten seconds."

"I can't see him!"

Reed leaned out the window and glimpsed Lambe's blue Sebring. "There—passing the OfficeMax truck!

The cell phone rang and Reed punched the speaker button.

"It's Hallie...."

"What's up?" Reed said.

"The *Shikei* paper...." Her voice was trembling, terrified. Something was wrong, terribly wrong.

"What about it?"

"The wet flap. I opened it, found Japanese words and translated them."

Reed knew it was bad. He didn't want to hear the translation.

She cleared her throat. "It says....

> *The signal releases sarin. The sarin floats up the ventilation shaft and out through vent openings ... into the passenger compartment of those traitors who brought death to American workers, traitors who will now breathe death into themselves. Those who chose to drive with the rising sun, will never see the sun rise again."*

"Those who drive...." Reed whispered, "with the 'rising sun'.... Oh Jesus, it's...."

"What?" Manning shouted.

"It's Japanese cars!" Reed said.

"We agree," Hallie said.

Reed felt blood drain from his face.

Manning shouted, "But that's not poss—"

"He's *done* it!" Reed said. "It's Japanese cars. Somehow the bastard has managed to get sarin into their ventilation systems and can trigger it.

Everything fits. His family was destroyed in Japan. He believes he was fired twice because of Japanese imports. He believes people who bought Japanese imports contributed to his firing and are traitors. They had a choice. They chose non-American brands, they betrayed American workers and destroyed their jobs, and now he's killing them as punishment, teaching a lesson."

Manning stared ahead, frozen. "And I've helped the crazy bastard, *by making people drive home now in their Japanese cars!*" He slammed the steering wheel so hard it looked bent.

"He set us up," Reed said. "He gets even more people in their cars now; maybe kills more than sixty thousand."

"And I'll kill *him!*" Manning's jaws locked shut. "Doris?"

"Yes."

"New media directive."

"Yes sir."

"All media—especially all radio stations—must break into programming *immediately.* They must tell drivers of Japanese vehicles to get out of their vehicles *immediately!* They must get far away from their vehicles. I repeat, everyone must get out of Japanese vehicles *now!* Is that clear?"

"Yes," Doris said, obviously puzzled.

Manning squealed around a corner on two wheels.

"Tell drivers why," Manning said. "Sarin gas may be in their vehicle's ventilation system. If they breathe it, they'll die."

"I drive a new Honda."

"Not tonight."

Reed leaned over. "Doris, the media should tell people to *phone* friends with Japanese vehicles and tell them to get out immediately."

"Right."

Reed pointed to Lambe driving around a construction barricade and disappearing down a side street.

"Hallie…?" Reed said.

"Yes?"

"Did the message say *how* the signal was sent?"

"No. It just said, 'signal releases sarin.'"

"What kind of signal?"

"The Japanese word suggests some kind of electronic signal. Maybe a radio signal, or microwave, or maybe a beeper-pager signal. Wait—didn't you see a folder for a beeper company on Lambe's desk?"

"Yes." Reed tried to recall the company name. "It was NorthStar Signal Communications, a local beeper-pager company we've used. Maybe he's using a beeper signal."

"Hey, Rob Bradleigh," Manning said. "Can local beepers relay the signal to ten cities?"

"Bradleigh's not in the room," Hallie said.

"Shit!" Manning's face went beet red. "Find Bradleigh! Get me an answer! Nobody leaves the room until this is over."

"Left!" Reed shouted and pointed ahead as Lambe careened around a corner.

Moments later, Manning squealed around the curve, machine-gunning his horn. Women yanked children back inside stores. Pedestrians gawked as the cars sped past.

Then finally, a break.

A Budweiser beer truck blocked the narrow street ahead of Lambe. His Sebring could not get around it. He skidded to a stop, honked at the driverless truck to no avail, then glanced back at Reed.

He's trapped, Reed thought, taking out his .38.

Suddenly, Lambe darted from the Sebring, clutching the laptop, and ran around the Stroh's truck.

Reed heard a gunshot, then a car door slam. A black fender raced backward from the scene. "He's in a black car."

"What model?"

"I couldn't see enough of it."

The truck driver ran from the store, saw Manning's police flasher, and quickly pulled his truck onto the sidewalk.

As Manning drove ahead, Reed saw a terrified young woman sitting on the curb, clutching her screaming infant. Blood seeped onto the shoulder of the woman's white dress. *She'll live,* Reed realized with relief.

"There," Reed said, "He's in a black Olds Alero."

Manning raced down the street and squealed on two tires into the intersection, narrowly missing a moving van. Reed looked for the black Alero but didn't see it. He noticed two Toyota drivers making no effort to leave their cars.

Where are the damn radio warnings? he wondered.

"Where's Lambe?" Manning asked, leaning out the window to see ahead.

"There—the Ambassador Bridge!" Reed said. "Second toll booth. He's heading to *Canada*!"

Lambe swerved in front of a van and headed onto the bridge.

"Jesus!" Manning said, whipping around an old truck. "How much time?"

"Forty-four seconds."

Manning sped onto the bridge entrance, drove around the line of toll booth trucks and cars. He flashed his badge at a group of open-mouthed toll booth officers, then careened up onto the bridge.

"Doris," Manning said, "tell Canadian Customs to stop the man in the black Olds Alero from using his laptop. He's armed. Shoot to kill if necessary!"

"Yes, sir."

Ahead, Lambe passed a slow-moving truck. Manning caught up and swerved in behind him. He tried to pull even, but Lambe blocked him.

"Time?" Manning asked.

"Thirty-one seconds!"

Amazingly, Lambe leaned out and fired two shots back at them.

"Nail the bastard!" Manning said.

Manning and Reed began firing. Bullets slammed into Lambe's Alero and spider-webbed the rear window, but he sped ahead.

Reed fired again. Lambe's car swerved but still kept going.

"Shoot his tires!" Manning said.

Reed pumped off four bullets, blowing out the right rear tire. The Alero fishtailed, swerved and slammed into the bridge side railing, inflating the airbag. Lambe jumped out and ran with the laptop.

Manning and Reed screeched to a stop, blocking all traffic. They leapt out, aimed their weapons, but held their fire as Lambe hid behind a school bus loaded with kids. Drivers stared at the bedlam, then ducked to the floor of their vehicles.

Lambe ran toward the bridge's thick iron girders.

Manning fired, hitting Lambe's leg.

But Lambe limped on, got off two shots, then crouched partly beside a girder. He fired again, hitting a fender beside Reed. When Reed looked up, Lambe was punching keys on the computer.

Manning and Reed fired off a barrage. One bullet nicked Lambe's shoulder, but he hid behind a mini-bus filled with seniors and continued working on the laptop.

Reed and Manning ran along the rail, to avoid hitting the senior citizens. Reed fired, missed him.

Then, Lambe, his eyes maniacal, locked on Reed and the entire scene seemed to fade into slow motion.

Lambe jammed his finger down on Enter.

Then he smiled, *knowing* what he'd just unleashed. *Knowing* they could not stop it now.

The Shikei is launched....

Reed's heart stopped. Everything stopped.

Except Lambe. Incredibly, he fired off two shots, nearly hitting Manning, then limped away along the railing. The man was not human.

Manning and Reed fired off another salvo of bullets that slammed Lambe back against the girder. A second barrage spun him around. The third blew off a chunk of his skull and flipped him backward over the railing, plummeting him toward the river.

Reed checked his watch. Fourteen minutes past five. Too late.

Lambe had launched the *Shikei.*

Reed felt like razor blades were carving up his insides. His heart pounded in his ears. Defeated, he slumped against a girder and stared at the laptop screen. *Transmission successful* blinked cruelly up at him, fading in and out of focus, like his mind.

Manning, crazed, fired several shots into the laptop. The bullets splintered the plastic casing and the screen slowly faded. But Reed knew it was useless. The signal had been sent and received instantaneously.

Thousands were dying. Lambe's smile was proof.

Reed and Manning walked to the railing and looked down. Lambe was impaled face down on the masthead antennas of an ore freighter on the river. His back was jackknifed into a grotesque hump. Sailors hurried toward his hideous, misshapen body pooling blood on their deck. Coast Guard boats raced toward the freighter. Police sirens blared onto the bridge from both the Canadian and US sides.

Reed stared down at the corpse. Lambe was dead, but so were sixty thousand innocent people he took with him. Sickened, Reed imagined their bodies floating in the river ... imagined the water red with blood ... *blood spilled by my failure to act sooner.* A gust of icy wind hit his moist eyes.

Reed and Manning walked toward their car in silence, stopping only to persuade a family with three crying children to get out of their Nissan van. The family said they'd heard no radio warnings. Reed tried to calm the children.

Back in the Monte Carlo, Reed and Manning sat in silence, unable to speak, unable to move, staring at the river. Moments later they drove off toward the Ren Cen, listening for radio warnings.

A minute later they heard, "We interrupt this program...."

259

Fifty-One

Reed's mind was vacant, his body numb, the last drop of emotion wrung from the deepest recesses of his being. He felt like he'd been hollowed out, and scarred forever. He'd been powerless to prevent the slaughter of thousands of innocent people. Their deaths would weigh down on him every day of his life.

He pushed the Ren Cen elevator button and Manning and he swept upward, away from the ambulance sirens mocking their failure. The ambulances were *hearses*. *Korusu* killed within two minutes.

It was time to count bodies.

He looked out at the Ambassador Bridge and saw police car lights flashing across Lambe's stolen Alero. Trucks and cars were backed up into both Windsor and Detroit. News choppers circled the bridge like vultures.

Rush hour. Lambe's plan all along. More people in more cars. More deaths. 5:11 was just enough time for people to leave the office and get in their cars. We should have realized it when Lambe insisted on 5:11. We should have realized it when he told us to empty the office buildings.

Reed's mind flashed back to Lambe's eyes. Demonic. Dead. Eyes that felt nothing for people, yet ignited with pleasure when he knew he'd just killed thousands.

Reed tried to swallow, but his throat felt raw and dry, as though *he'd* inhaled sarin. His chest felt like steel bands were slowly tightening around it. He'd failed. He should have found a way to enter Kyle's laptop sooner, should have taken the *Korusu* file, opened the wet flap sooner. And because he didn't, sixty thousand....

Manning was whispering

"Sorry, what?" Reed asked.

"Radio stations were confused by our changed directives. They must have spent time verifying it. At best, drivers heard the radio warnings two to three minutes *after* they started breathing sarin."

"*If* their radios were on," Reed said. "Many were listening to tapes and CDs."

"Or talking on cell phones."

As they trudged into the crisis center room, Reed looked around for Hallie but didn't see her. The team was huddled over the open phone to the Washington crisis team, talking in hushed tones, obviously tabulating the deaths. Agent LaCage turned and stared at them with anxious eyes.

"You're okay?" LaCage whispered.

"Fine," Manning said.

"Your phone is off."

Manning shrugged. "Must of nudged it."

"We were afraid Lambe had shot you."

Manning shrugged. "No such luck." He dropped hard into a chair, hissing air from the cushion. "What's the body count so far?"

LaCage looked at the paper trembling in his hand and ran his finger down to the bottom. "At this point, our estimate is approaching seventeen—"

"Seventeen thousand people ... Jesus!" Manning whispered, placing his head in his hands.

Reed couldn't breathe.

"No," LaCage said, "*People.*"

Silence.

"What?" Manning whispered, still holding his head in his hands.

"Seventeen *people,*" LaCage said. "And that's probably the final tabulation."

Reed's eyes locked on LaCage.

Slowly, Manning looked up, confused.

"But I saw Lambe start the program," Reed said.

"And we stopped it. Thanks to Hallie and you," said Rob Bradleigh, a gummy grin filling his pizza-dough face.

Reed stared at the smiling man, wanting to believe him, but couldn't.

"Stopped it?" Manning whispered.

Bradleigh picked up a roughly drawn diagram on the table. "When Hallie remembered that you saw a beeper file on Lambe's desk, and then you gave us the NorthStar Signal name, we called NorthStar. Nine months ago, Lambe had NorthStar set up a special network which linked NorthStar here to affiliate beeper companies in the ten target cities. Claimed he had to reach lots of sales people simultaneously. He created a coded signal which reached thousands of mini-beepers he'd cloned. Somehow he must have had the mini-beeper receptors built into the ventilation shafts that eventually were installed into the Japanese cars at the assembly plants. His signal released the sarin in *all* of them simultaneously. We explained who we were to NorthStar and what Lambe was really up to. NorthStar had already heard our broadcast

261

warning. They cooperated."

Manning stared back in disbelief. "But his signal—it had already gone out! I saw his laptop screen flashing *Transmission successful.*"

"NorthStar stopped it."

"How?"

"The towers."

"What?" Manning said.

"They shut off the transmitter towers!"

Reed stared at Bradleigh. "When?"

"About forty-three seconds *before* Lambe sent his signal."

Reed swallowed, looked at LaCage and Bradleigh. He looked at their smiling, relaxed faces. "His signal never got there?"

"Nope," LaCage said, smiling. "Not in Detroit. Nor in the other nine cities."

"Sank like a golf ball in sand," Bradleigh said, his blue marble eyes gleaming with delight. "When the towers were turned off, NorthStar then went in and deleted his signal."

Manning closed moist eyes, slumped back in his chair and shook his head. Reed reached over and placed his hand on the big man's shoulder.

Reed felt lightheaded as the tentacles of guilt began to detach from his soul. Emotion and feeling were pouring back into him like manna from heaven. He felt reborn, alive....

Hallie rushed into the room and ran over to him, smiling the most beautiful, trusted smile he'd ever seen in his life.

He believed in miracles.

Epilogue

St. Martin's Island, two months later

The young gull was magnificent, a mystery of grace, hang-gliding like a still photo, white feathers framed by azure sky, gold beak spearing the gentle wind. Hallie silently warned her feathery friend, hovering over her, that their friendship would be sorely tested, if as she suspected, the angelic creature planned to deposit major doo-doo on her warm, tan skin. The wise bird eased to the right, paused to admire Reed's considerable manliness, then swooped off to a chunk of sun-bleached driftwood.

Hallie turned to admire Reed's considerable manliness herself. He lay beside her on a pristine beach on the island of St. Martin. The sun had tanned his muscles, streaked his hair with blond and turned him into *Le Hunk*, as evidenced by the flirtatious smiles of two French women strolling the beach. Nearby, palm fonds did their graceful hula in the silky breezes sweeping off the turquoise Caribbean.

Reed turned off his cell phone and stuffed it back in his Nike Air Max.

Good, she thought. *No more calls. No more world. Just the two of us here, melting into this paradise:* soft waves hissing ashore, morning sun warming her skin, spice-scented air filling her lungs, unseen birds chanting in the bushes, island kids diving for shells up the beach, the man she loved lying beside her. *A woman can only handle so much stress,* she thought.

"Who called?" Hallie yawned, closing the latest Tess Gerritsen paperback.

"Woody Beachum."

"How's Woody?"

"Terrific. Visiting his daughter and grandkids in North Carolina."

"Why'd he call?"

"To warn us."

"About what?"

"About spending our entire honeymoon in bed."

Laughing, she reached over and snapped his swimming trunks. "He's a smidgeon late.”

“Yep. He also said Drew Manning accepted a new FBI directorship near DC.”

“Good for Drew,” she said, wondering why Drew was moving back where memories of his deceased wife would haunt him.

“Drew thinks Congress is finally serious about protecting *all* Americans against biological and chemical weapons.”

“Did you just use ‘Congress’ and ‘serious’ in the same sentence?”

“Whoops. Must be this hot sun.”

She fingered a small circle in the sand. “But I thought Drew didn’t like desk jobs in DC?”

“This desk’s actually in nearby Aberdeen.”

Why Aberdeen? she wondered, deepening her circle in the sand. Suddenly, she knew and couldn’t keep the smile from her face. “Near Janet McKay?”

“Give the little lady a ceegar!”

“Janet will love the idea, too,” she said excitedly. “You saw them at our wedding reception.”

“Shameless!”

“They were like prom dates.” Hallie recalled how they’d danced every dance, smiled into each other’s eyes, a marriage within a wedding. “Drew deserved the promotion.”

“No more than you, Doctor.”

“Why, Mr. Kincaid, how kind of you.”

“Hey, Gretchen Nordstrom had T. Rex figured out all the time.”

“I wasn’t so sure when she called me into her office,” Hallie said, smoothing suntan lotion on her arm. “T. Rex was already sitting there, licking his chops. I thought they were going to hand me my head. When she fired *him* and asked me to assume his responsibilities, I nearly went into shock.”

“Bet old T. Rex did.”

“A major hissy fit. He turned as red as last night’s sunset. His eyelids fluttered like window shades. When he started to protest, Gretchen pulled out a thick file.”

“What was in it?”

“Hard evidence that T. Rex had been selling Genetique’s research to a Palo Alto firm for two years.”

“What a sleaze….”

“Ten minutes later, security escorted him from the building.”

“Serves the jerk right,” Reed said, rescuing a gnat stuck on her lotioned arm and placing it on the sand. The gnat wobbled a bit and flew away. Reed rolled on his side facing her, increasing the muscle definition of his perfect body, which, being the lusty lady she was, made her think of last night's wonderful lovemaking.

"T. Rex got what he deserved," Reed said. "Like his clone."

"Who's that?"

"Huey Hastings the Third."

"How's young Baby Huey?"

"Also gone as in fired."

"What? Big Daddy didn't protect him?"

"Big Daddy *asked* us to fire him."

She stared back, confused.

"Turns out, Baby Huey was using daddy's name to strong-arm our agency people and his people as well. Daddy found out. Daddy was not pleased."

"Poor Baby Huey."

"Maybe not poor. He's going to work for one of dad's new subsidiaries." Reed started to smile....

"What's so funny?"

"It's in Kabul."

She smiled. "Yikes, no Brooks Brothers there."

"Not even Ralph Lauren."

"What's he doing there?"

"Opening a Japanese car dealership."

She stared back, having trouble picturing the pompous, Armani-clad Hastings hawking Hondas on the dusty, camel-clogged streets of Kabul.

"Actually," Reed said, "it could eventually become a good market." He thumped the *Wall Street Journal* beside him.

"Why's that?"

"According to this article, Japanese vehicle manufacturers are diverting hundreds of thousands of their imports away from the US to newly developed markets."

"Because Lambe put sarin in Japanese vehicles?"

Reed nodded. "Nearly three-million Americans have traded in their Japanese vehicles for US-made brands. Japanese vehicle sales in the US are down eighty-three percent."

"That's incredible," she said, shaking her head. "Did the authorities ever determine how Lambe got the sarin containers in the ventilation shafts of the Japanese cars?"

"He lied to the shaft suppliers. Told them the containers were testing a new, more durable, lightweight plastic that would cut their shaft costs in half.

He also promised them a share of the profits. They checked the early prototypes, which were okay. The later containers held sarin. The vehicle makers had no idea."

"But how could he release the sarin in Japanese vehicles in just *those* ten cities?"

"He programmed the beeper signal to only activate in those cities."

"And if it hadn't worked?"

"He had his backup plan. Sixty thousand deaths in Los Angeles, San Francisco, and Portland."

Hallie shook her head from side to side, amazed at the insanity and genius and planning that went into Lambe's *Shikei.*

"There's one good result," Reed said.

"What's that?"

"The new proposed addendum to the US-Japan automotive trade agreement. When severe economic factors, or wild currency fluctuations, or anything else displaces a significant percentage of auto workers in either the US or in Japan, both countries will work with arbitrators to resolve and compensate the economic impact to those workers. If they fail to resolve it within sixty-one days, the World Court can impose an equitable solution."

"And if you fail to impose *this* solution on your nose, it will burn off," Hallie said, coating his peeling nose with a gob of number-32 goo. The stuff smelled like someone dumped Chanel n° 5 into a pina colada.

She turned and gazed out at the serene, blue water. She had never felt more at peace in her life. She was filled with love for the man beside her and with gratitude that they'd been given a chance to share their lives together.

"The world seems safe from here," she said as the breeze tousled Reed's hair.

"It sure does."

But it's still not safe enough, she knew. No matter how hard she tried, she couldn't shake the feeling that some day in some city, al Qaeda or another terrorist group would deliver another September 11, or worse.

Beyond the peaceful blue horizon, other Philip Lambes were developing new weapons, new ways to circumvent defensive measures, new ways to slaughter innocent men, women and children. She would never understand *why* terrorists killed innocent people.

But she *did* understand that *governments* had to protect citizens. All their citizens. Which meant governments had to fund the technology that detects the deadly biological and chemical weapons quickly, and give citizens the protective equipment they need.

And governments had to do it *fast!*

Once done, they should spend as much time and money resolving the issues that drive people to kill innocent citizens around the world.

She watched the aquamarine waves seep into the soft, sandy shore. A small, white cloud swept in front of the sun and her skin cooled.

"So what would you like to do today?" she asked.

He turned to her with his lusty blue eyes, then raised his eyebrows à la Groucho. "How about what we did a lot of last night?"

"Sleep?"

Laughing, he hoisted her into his arms, ran toward the ocean, and they splashed into the warm, foamy water.

*

Printed in the United States
34237LVS00008B/82-111

9 781413 747003